The Promise

Mary Ryan

HEADLINE

First published in 1997
by HEADLINE BOOK PUBLISHING

First published in paperback in 1998
by HEADLINE BOOK PUBLISHING

10 9 8 7 6 5 4 3 2 1

ISBN 0 7472 5823 6

Typeset by CBS, Felixstowe, Suffolk

Printed and bound in Great Britain by
Mackays of Chatham plc, Chatham, Kent

HEADLINE BOOK PUBLISHING
A division of Hodder Headline PLC
338 Euston Road
London NW1 3BH

For Breda

ACKNOWLEDGMENTS

My thanks to the following who were so helpful and generous:

My sister Anne who made the journey to Florence with me and who provided her professional help and insight into the more difficult and painful subject matter in this book.
My son, Pierce, for writing Colm's poem at page 96 and giving permission to reproduce it.
My brother-in-law Barry Greene for sharing his memories of New York.
Professor Risteárd Mulcahy for information on coronaries.
Ken Beaton for information on the procedures of the Irish Stock Exchange, and the requirements for becoming a stockbroker in the 1960s.
My family, as ever, for being there.

Some of the boarding school events depicted in this book really happened. They took place at a time when clerical power in Ireland was at its height. The perpetrator is now dead and all of the characters in the novel are fictitious.

Mary Ryan
Dublin, May 1997

In the middle of my life's journey
I found myself in a dark wood
Where the straight way was lost

Dante Alighieri
L'Inferno

Part One

Chapter One

In the dream she said, 'Hi, Colm . . . remember me?' Her young face was clear to him, down to the freckles. He started and woke, calling, 'Robin.' No one there; only her voice in his head like an echo. Funny the way some people got a hold on you.

The light from the porthole confused him. Realisation dawned quickly: he was on board the *St Killian*, somewhere off the Irish coast, already en route for France. He had boarded early, gone to his cabin immediately, lain on his bunk and slept. Despite his recent illness he was going to Italy the long way, the tiring way, for reasons that had more to do with whimsy and nostalgia than with sense. He had embarked on this journey in search of something he had left behind him when he was twenty-one. That was before life had taken him over, before success had flattered him, before marriage had benumbed him with its monotony.

There had been a time when his wife Sherry had tried to jolly him, to make him fit her desired mould: dinner parties, gardening at weekends, plenty of socialising. She loved his success for what it brought – endless shopping, a lovely house, lovely clothes. But she had sensed his restlessness, his lack of fulfilment, feared it because she could do nothing about it. In Irish, she had once reminded him, as though by way of appeasement, Colm meant 'dove'.

'I know, Sherry. I went to school once too!' In the early days she had even called him her pigeon. She was merely uncertain of him then; the fear of him, the awful bloody hesitancy, as though she walked on eggshells, had not come until later. It was as though she had realised too late that there was a side to him which would always be inaccessible, a dark watcher at the heart of his life.

He got up to look through his porthole, saw the Irish coast recede into the evening mist. He heard voices in the adjoining cabin; but mostly he was aware of the powerful background throb of the ferry's engines, beating like a great heart. Sherry would have smiled at this fancy and then agreed. Over the years she had become good at agreement; he had controlled her to an extent he found astonishing, and done it by sarcasm and glacial exasperation, until she had come to doubt the parameters of her own understanding. This manipulation was incredibly easy; all it required was the occasional endearment and she would think he was the soppy kind after all, that he was really concealing passion. He did not know why he manipulated her; he only knew that he did it because he could; she gave him a certain kind of power and he punished her by using it.

But now she was gone. It was a *fait accompli*; she had confronted him with the shallow front that was their life, walked out of the door, obtained an English divorce and remarried. Everything, Colm mused, even certainties graven in stone, contain within themselves the seeds of change.

Typically and maddeningly, she had held her colour chart up to catch the sunlight at the window on the day she left him. 'Yes . . . That will be perfect . . . I just love burnt sienna.' This more to herself than to him, adding as a careful *non sequitur*, without looking at him, 'I'm leaving you, Colm. I've met someone else. Michael in fact!'

Colm experienced this announcement as a punch in the stomach, but did not overtly react. In fact, he already knew about their affair. But why mention it; why bring it to this? Such things flared and should then be allowed to die.

He caught her nervous glance, but she looked quickly away. He knew Michael well. They had attended the same school. A widower, Michael had been made redundant a few years earlier and was now an interior decorator, a total nonentity.

'Am I permitted to know why?'

'I just can't stay with you.' Voice very low, nervous. 'You're too . . . cold.'

'Have I failed you in some way? Deprived you of a decent standard of living, been unfaithful, ever offered you violence?'

He said all this mildly. As long as he projected indulgent scorn, she must doubt herself. He certainly did not want her to leave. He was used to her; her departure would redound to his discredit and he liked his image the way it was. For a moment he wished that things had been different; that he'd been able to give her what she craved; that the courage to love had been his.

She watched him carefully for a moment, but the new Sherry was not to be side-tracked into self-distrust or drawn into any foolish conformity with his perspectives.

'. . . Look, I must be off. I've a meeting with Rosalind Lefeu. She's just bought the most beautiful house on Killiney Hill and Michael is trying to land the contract for the interior.' When he didn't answer she added, 'You remember Rosalind Lefeu. She was in "Dangerous Times".'

'I'm not interested in Rosalind Whatever-her-name-is, or any other celluloid nit-wit. You've just dropped a serious bombshell, Sherry! And I've just asked you some serious questions!'

'Very well . . . I'll answer them!' She turned to face him and her eyes flashed. She raised her voice. 'You haven't deprived me of a good standard of living; you haven't offered me violence . . . at least not the physical variety, but your brutality in emotional terms has been nothing short of cruelty. Even after Alan died you couldn't . . .' Her voice faltered, then resumed. 'You haven't been unfaithful for precisely one year three months and five days. I'm not dense, you know! I

5

knew the signs – the smug self-satisfaction, the bedroom brush-off. And I also remember that whore, Catherine Whatever-her-name-was, that I wasn't supposed to know about! Oh, you have surrounded me with every luxury all right . . .' She was breathing heavily, angry, but at this point she dropped her voice suddenly, as though aware she was falling into a trap. 'The cage was nicely gilded. But it is also true that you have starved me of everything I long for!'

'What you long for, my poor Sherry, does not exist.'

'It does!'

The colour chart was now rolled tightly in her hand. Colm smiled. 'Do you subject the bold Michael to these meanderings? Or does he think, perhaps, that you will receive a hefty settlement?' He shook his head. 'Unhappily, there are no settlements for unfaithful wives who desert their husbands . . .'

But Sherry, instead of hitting the roof, as he had expected, looked at him with something close to pity.

'My solicitor will write to you, Colm . . .'

Colm wondered who the hell was Rosalind Lefeu. He did not recognise celebrities, had sometimes never even heard of them. He used to go with Sherry to parties where he failed to recognise the recent additions to the halls of fame, American and European VIPs who bought homes in Ireland. Sherry was into interior décor for the rich and infamous. It was how she had met the bold Michael.

'I don't care who he is,' he told his wife afterwards on more than one occasion, 'the guy's a self-centred, presumptuous oaf!'

'The trouble with you, Colm, is that you dislike everyone.' This was a post-Michael comment. Once she would not have dared to say it.

Sherry had some notion that life should be other than ordered and rational. He hated this mental messiness; logic and reason had been his mentors for as long as he cared to

6

remember. If you lived by them you could control life. If not, life controlled you. He suppressed the occasional prompt that this assessment was mistaken; that ultimately life could not be controlled; that it already dogged him, demanding recognition from him of something he dared not turn and face.

His house, 'Glendale', a Georgian manse near Greystones, was decorated with flair and imagination. Once it had been House of the Month in a glossy magazine (this was Sherry's doing; he had looked on indulgently). People exclaimed when they came through the door, suddenly conscious of light and space and elegance. 'How lovely!' She waited for this exclamation, smiled each time with delight. He was aware of Glendale's attractions too, the view, the twisting avenue, the small copse near the road, the interior on which his wife had spent so much money, time and trouble. She had looked longingly around the house on the day she had left; even as Paddy the gardener was humping her cases to her car, even as she crossed the threshold for the last time she had looked wistfully back, not at him but at the gracious hallway and front door, the Georgian elevation with the Virginia creeper, the drawing-room windows and their draped Sanderson curtains. This house was her image, her standing before the world, and she was walking away from it!

He refused to feel dismayed. He had not believed she would bring it this far; he had put it down to women's mid-life lunacy. But the sudden unexpected draught of loneliness caught him somewhere around the heart.

'Goodbye, Colm.'

That was it! Twenty-one years!

'Goodbye, my dear . . .'

When all else fails you can fall back on a sneer. She hesitated, looked back once more and then she was gone, the Audi disappearing down the rhododendron avenue for the last time. There was grim satisfaction in the knowledge that she had forfeited the house. He had made that quite clear; it was in his name. Not a penny was she getting; nothing except her clothes, her jewellery, her car and a few odds and ends from the house, pictures and furnishings. She could fend for herself with her decorator nonentity.

And yet, when he woke that first night in the empty house her absence was more than comment or condemnation. It was something he could not abide – failure. And with this knowledge the hopes of yesterday rose to taunt him, touched something deep. Do we ever really escape from ourselves? he wondered angrily, throwing his arm across the empty bed and listening to the bluster in the chimney. For a moment he felt disembodied, an elemental creature who inhabited the moan of the wind.

Colm's office was a plush suite in the city centre, where he worked from eight until seven. It represented years of graft and effort, his successful partnership in the firm of Harrisons Stockbrokers. Before the break-up with Sherry their evenings had frequently been spent in entertaining and being entertained. There had been only themselves to think of. Once there had also been Alan. Colm did not like to think of him, to remember his small fat limbs secured in the car baby seat, to recall his thirteenth birthday and the bicycle, to relive the accident which had deprived him of his only child. 'Look, Daddy . . .' and the new mountain bicycle hurling itself at the makeshift ramp, his child suddenly in the air, his head hitting the kerb of the driveway. They didn't even have a name for it. Children who lost parents were called orphans. Parents who lost children were the greatest orphans of all, but no one had yet coined a name for their unique, bone-crushing sorrow.

The Irish coast became a thin line against the horizon and vanished. There was only sea stretching into sky. He looked around the spartan cabin, felt suddenly claustrophobic, as though alone with infinity. His mouth was dry. In a sudden burst of longing, the sort of thing he had long ago suppressed, he needed to be away from his own company. He left the cabin and found the cafeteria, bought a small pot of tea and a bun, chose a table. His fellow travellers were mostly families, holidaying French returning for *La Rentrée*, Irish tourists, young people setting off to jobs in France. The long evening at sea was ahead. They would not arrive at Cherbourg until ten the next morning. But the passengers could read or talk and play cards and have a few drinks or patronise the on-board cinema. His longing to travel like this was recent, to make a deliberate odyssey. He wanted to come upon it, Italy, as he had long ago, through France by train; then he would take the route through the Alps, hurtling down to the lakes and the Lombardy Plain. It was another life and yet it was yesterday. Sometimes he thought that the years in between were like smoke; in some ways he might as well never have had them. They were moribund with the weight of something important that had not happened.

Certainly he had had good moments: success, spousal approval as provider, and wifely acceptance of the standard of living he made possible, as though it came, like photosynthesis, with the sunlight. But it had not been enough for Sherry. She had wanted more, a spiritual intimacy.

'You're so damned independent of everything!' she had flung at him one day before the break-up. 'I used to think a man as intensely focused as you are had to have passion. But I'm tired of looking for it, and waiting for it. You're so self-sustained you might as well be a robot!'

He felt this was a compliment. Independence was something he insisted on. But he had to admit that he was dependent on his work, not economically any more, for his investments were many and secure, but intellectually and emotionally, for he knew nothing else.

In an unformed way he had expected Sherry to provide the missing elements, the things he had had no time to pursue – culture, the challenge of new thought, books, music, and perhaps even some ferocity of spirit. But Sherry did not possess ferocity of spirit. If she had, things might have been different. They might have been different if she had turned on him occasionally, ruffled his certainties; if she had dismantled some of his agendas. If she had forced him to talk about Alan, to talk about the past. If she had really loved him.

But she had enjoyed his success, reaped the fruits of it, become something of a socialite. Because of her they were invited to wonderful parties without spontaneity, carefully orchestrated buffet lunches, where the talk was of hunts and shoots and new diets, and everyone was thoroughly vetted for their standing, their social desirability.

It was fine by him. Except that he was becoming allergic to social approval. He thought it was fine by her too, until she confessed to unbearable loneliness. 'I was supposed to find all this stuff fulfilling, but it doesn't mean a thing.' This, after so many years of dedicated social climbing, he found amusing.

But, privately, he was himself tired of the subtle assessment of one's worth and stature. Like most things in life, it bored him stiff. At the last party he and Sherry had attended together someone had asked him what he did, and he had replied in a surge of weariness that he kept four cows in County Roscommon.

'Oooh . . .'

How easy it was to disconcert the fatuous!

Fear na ceithre mbó is ea me. It sounded better in Irish, like a title. In Irish even cows had gentility.

'What's wrong with you?' Sherry had demanded in a dangerous tone afterwards. 'Anyone would think you were going off the deep end . . .' But then the thing had struck her as funny. 'I mean, you never know who might actually have believed you. The woman you were talking to was English. They're not attuned to our wisecracks. They believe what you say!'

'Maybe it wasn't a wisecrack. How do you know that I haven't got four cows in County Roscommon?'

10

'Have you?'

Sherry, his emotionally hungry wife, would most definitely cavil at being married to a man with four cows. Still a tawny beauty, still zestful, striking, dressing perfectly in designer clothes for which he paid a fortune, worn with just the right touch of careless insouciance. She had left not long afterwards, cows or no cows. Women!

Was it the following week that he felt the sickening flutter and then the pain, a chest cramp which squeezed the air out of him and flattened him across the desk? It went on and on, this pain, lasted for ever, but in reality about half an hour. Certain that he was going to die, he saw, in a state of heightened interior awareness, his life, the secret part, the professional part, the files, the spread sheets, the profit and loss accounts, the highs when his forecasts were fulfilled, the frenetic drive for success, into which he had poured not just his will and energy, but his life force. The secretaries he had seduced along the way, the casual one night stands when he was away from home, hardly featured. Kattie, whom he had plundered, floated into focus, bringing guilt. But he also saw Robin. Her face was clear, young and laughing, gilded by the evening sun on the Ponte Vecchio. And he was twenty again.

I was real then, he thought. For a while I was a person. But the memory touched something deep. It was as though part of him had not aged at all; part of him, the best part, still stood there on the old bridge in the Florentine evening, camera raised.

'A mild coronary, Colm! It's a warning of sorts . . . a reminder that you cannot live a sedentary life, starve your heart by smoking, fill your blood vessels with saturated fats, and expect to go on for ever. You and Sherry should go off on a holiday for a month or so. Not one of those beach holidays, mind, but somewhere you would walk a lot . . . view the sights . . . You

11

should walk about twenty miles per week. No more smoking, and a very low-fat diet. Come back in six weeks for another cholesterol check. If you do what you're told you'll be as right as rain . . .'

Colm regarded the old GP's face. His hooded eyes had seen them through it all, early miscarriage, successful pregnancy, Alan's tonsillitis, measles, mumps, the time the boy had gashed his face in a fall, Sherry's bout of pleurisy, Alan's cooling body on the gravel.

'We've split up. She's got an English divorce, remarried . . .'

'I'm sorry! I didn't know . . .'

'That's what comes of having healthy patients!' Colm quipped. 'But I think I will take off, have a break, go to Italy perhaps . . .'

'On your own?'

'Why not? Are you afraid it might happen again?'

'No . . . not if you follow instructions. If you do you'll feel better than you have for a long time.'

'Oh, I'll follow instructions! I've already given up smoking . . . and I've lost weight.'

'That's the ticket!'

When Colm got home he found his old photo album, the one pre-dating family serfdom. It was dusty, the cover discoloured. He leafed through the pages, the black and white snaps of the early years in Ballykelly, parents, siblings, but he stopped to study one picture. In this photograph the girl's face caught the evening light on the bridge above the Arno. She stood there, laughing, frozen in time, young enough now to be his daughter. 'Robin!' he said, smiling into her eyes, remembering with an instant's private embarrassment that twenty-three years ago, five years after this girl had disappeared from his life, he had tried to find her by placing an advertisement in the *New York Times*. All that was long ago, pathetic youthful folly. But it didn't mean that Italy, its sun and *joie de vivre*, might not still work some alchemy.

Through the drawing-room window he saw the rhododendrons dripping in the rain, and his black Mercedes waiting like a hearse at the foot of the granite steps. The house was silent around him.

It would be a change anyway, he thought, aware of the silence. It would introduce a bit of variety to this enforced convalescence of mine. If I stay here I'll be bored to death.

He recalled his sickly childhood, the four walls of his room, the National School and the Master with his daily visits, and directed a hasty dismissive grunt at this intrusion of the past. Above all else he must not think of what had happened next; he must not think of Clonarty.

Seán and Sue Donnelly lived in a bungalow nearby. Colm phoned to ask them to keep an eye on the house.

'Florence in September!' Sue exclaimed. 'How nice! Are you going alone?'

'I suppose you wouldn't like to come and hold my hand, Sue?' he replied with what he thought the right amount of wickedness.

'Tempt me some other time! Right now I don't think Seán would buy it.' She was referring to her husband. 'But seriously, Colm, is it wise to go alone . . . After your . . . illness and everything? Wouldn't it be better if you waited . . .'

Colm ignored this. 'Sue, will you contact Sherry and tell her you have the keys: she'll be coming around to collect some odds and ends . . .'

'OK.' Then she added, her voice curious, 'But what made you decide to do a language course?'

'A notion . . . I had a smattering of it once; I spent some time in Florence when I was a student, had a yen to go back. So I've bought some Linguaphone tapes, and I'm practising.'

'Who's running the course? Is it in the university?'

'No. An outfit called Scuola Linguistica . . . "Linguistic School" in English. They come well recommended . . .'

'Where will you be staying?'

'With a family.' He sensed her surprise and added, 'It's all arranged for you. You get maximum conversation exposure that way. And besides . . .'

He left the rest unsaid. He was not going to revert to the topic of his illness. It could not be helped that she already knew about it. And Sherry knew about it. In fact, the reason she was coming around to collect some things she didn't need – a few silk cushions and an ugly modern painting – was probably a pretext to see how near he was to croaking.

'But why this sudden yen for Italy?' Sue pressed on. 'It seems out of character . . . you having a yen. Forgive me,' she added hastily, 'I didn't mean to be rude; it's just that you always seem to be so self-sufficient.'

Colm could not tell her because he hardly understood it himself. However he might look for a pretext, he was being pulled back to Florence. He had rationalised it as a birthday present to himself, a piece of sentimentality for his half-century, but privately he had wondered why, in his recent crisis, the strongest image in his mind should have been of a girl to whom he had said a silent goodbye one wet evening at the end of a long-ago September.

'We'll meet here . . . in the Piazza della Signoria,' Robin had once said, laughing, gesturing around her at the Florentine square, and then at the Rivoire restaurant, where people were eating in the shade. 'When you hit fifty! On your birthday. Is it a deal?'

'Sure . . . I'll be an old geezer and you'll be . . .'

'I'll never grow old,' she replied hastily. 'I'll still be Robin . . . still me!'

That evening, while the *St Killian* made her way to Cherbourg, Sue Donnelly discussed Colm with her husband.

'Colm is usually so straight-laced, but I got the feeling it's a sentimental thing . . . A return to his youth!'

Seán went back to his newspaper. 'Like many another poor eejit looking for his life,' he muttered, 'wondering where it went and why it never happened.'

Sue started. She rose, crossed the room and kissed the poll of her husband's head. 'I know where my life is!' she said, laying her cheek against the remains of his hair.

In Florence Paola Nosterini reviewed the list of her guests for September, sent to her by Scuola Linguistica. She would have as paying guests three women and one man. She re-examined their ages and occupations. Two of the women were students in their early twenties, which meant they could share a room. The third was a young widow, English, a publishing editor.

Paola looked at the man's name, wondered how he would fit in: Colm Nugent, aged forty-nine, occupation stockbroker, nationality Irish. The organisers had originally put him down for a different family, but a change in arrangements had resulted in his appearing on her list.

It was the name which stirred something in the depths of memory: Colm. She frowned, looked through her dining-room window on to the darkening roofs of Florence and the blood-red sunset. She heard her front door open. It was Pasquale, her son, home from his friend Tommaso's, suddenly in the doorway, a book in his hand.

'*Ciao, Mamma!*'

Paola registered relief that he was home. She crossed the room to him, kissed his cheek, ruffled his hair, asked him, as she always did, how he was. '*Ciao*, Pasquale; did you have a nice time?'

'*Abbastanza bene!*'

'Speak English!'

'Well enough, Mamma . . .'

He smiled. Paola tried to make it a rule that they spoke English when they were alone.

He put the book – an English anthology – on the table, leafed through it, commented on the year's work ahead of him. As Paola saw his fingers turn the pages, the earlier frisson of memory stirred again, causing her to start. Pasquale looked up, raised his eyebrows.

'What is it? You look as though you've seen a ghost!'

'It's nothing!' Paola said, shaking her head with a small dismissive laugh. 'It would be far too much of a coincidence . . .'

'What would?'

'. . . to be suddenly confronted by a fragment of the past.'

Chapter Two

The piers of Cherbourg stretched out into the bay, embraced the *St Killian*, brought her safely to dock. A thin rain was misting the ferry's windows. Passengers queued for disembarkation, endured the drizzle as they walked down the gang plank.

Colm took a taxi to the station. The streets were wet and shining. The French shop fronts – *Charcuterie, Boulangerie, Chevaline, Brasserie, Tabac*, reminded him pleasantly that he was indeed abroad. The taxi driver attempted conversation, but gave it up after a few hesitant responses. In fact Colm's French was reasonably good, but as he hated making mistakes he preferred silence to error.

The next train to Paris was at noon. Colm had a coffee in the station cafeteria, sat beside his suitcase clutching yesterday's copy of the *Irish Times*, which he had not yet got around to reading. He glanced at the front page, but didn't open the paper. He was filled with a vague sense of unease: the morning advanced, no work done. It was always like this when he was away from his office: he felt divorced from his element, disempowered. The cut and thrust of the international stock market was his life blood, his sense of his own worth. He knew its labyrinths so thoroughly that without it the world was not entirely comprehensible. He distracted himself by watching the passers-by – the travellers pulling bags on castors, the goodbyes; a young woman bidding farewell to her husband and hanging, weeping, on his neck. Their son stood beside them. Colm watched the boy for a moment, was shocked by the sudden yearning. Twelve years old or thereabouts, he thought. Do they know how rich they are?

He turned back to his paper, opened it, scanned the pages. A paragraph caught his eye, then riveted his whole attention.

FORMER HEADMASTER HAS LUCKY ESCAPE!
Father Seamus Madden (70), former headmaster of Clonarty College, Roscommon, had a lucky escape yesterday when his car went out of control near Haffners Bridge, a notorious accident black-spot near Tuam, County Galway. The car narrowly missed an on-coming vehicle and ploughed through a ditch before it came to rest in a nearby field.

Father Madden, once tipped to replace Dr Noonan as Bishop of Clonerris, is a well-known author of books on early Irish history and an expert on early Christianity. Although shaken after his ordeal, he said God must still have work for him.

Colm stared at the paper, re-read the article, screwed the *Irish Times* into a tight wad and put it down.

He felt suddenly hot, as though the humid day had overpowered him. 'So you're still going strong . . .' he said to himself, half aloud. A woman who was about to sit near him, gave him a strange look and moved away.

Colm went to the men's toilet, ran a comb through his thinning hair, regarded himself in the mirror, saw the grave face, the grey eyes, the frown lines etched into his forehead, the gold-rimmed spectacles, the expensive suit and tie. He saw how the person reflected in the mirror held himself with assurance, how he gave off an aura of professional aloofness, how his body was still reasonably taut, well muscled.

A young man came in, dressed in jeans and sweatshirt, a grubby canvas rucksack hanging from his arm. Colm watched him in the mirror.

Memories crowded. How does that, he wondered,

regarding the youth and then glancing at his own reflection, become this? How does the jaunty ownership of the moment turn into pomposity?

But I wouldn't be his age again, he thought, even if I could. If he knew what was ahead, the recalcitrance of life, that it will never be satisfied!

The priests at school used to say that our hearts were restless until they rested in the Lord. This thought conjured briefly the smell of chalk dust, the incense in the chapel, the black soutanes moving like shadows along eighteenth-century corridors.

Twenty-one, he estimated, watching the young man from the corner of his eye; lush with youth. What was I at twenty-one? A backpacking student . . . living the freedom of that extraordinary summer in Italy.

In Florence, Paola Nosterini, home for lunch, took her guest list from the desk, went to the balustraded balcony overlooking the courtyard, and read it for the tenth time. Then she stared into the sunny courtyard. It had returned to her in the course of the morning, the memory of the Roman amphitheatre in Fiesole and the young Irishman with whom she had spent most of the day. She allowed herself to feel amused at the frisson of curiosity as she re-examined his name and occupation. Colm Nugent, stockbroker. But could it really be the same Colm? She was almost sure he had the same surname. 'Colombo' she had called him on that far-off day.

She remembered him well, not his face, but his gravity, as though he was already weighted with responsibility, and the long, thorough, English lesson in the shade. There was a photograph somewhere that Maria had taken. She glanced at her bookcase wondering where the old album was, scanned the shelves. The more recent photograph albums were stacked together, but the old one, with all her photographs from her young days, was nowhere to be seen.

'What do you think, Bellina *mia*?' she asked her cat who

came mincing from the balcony. Bellina made an interrogative mewling sound and padded to the kitchen. I know what you mean, Paola said to herself; the odds against such a coincidence have to be enormous. It can't be him. It has to be someone else.

She knew by the music coming from his room that Pasquale was already home. She switched on her computer, deciding, before making lunch, to give a few minutes to her article about the abuse of young refugees from Bosnia who were being forced into prostitution to keep body and soul together. The phone bleeped beside her, causing her to jump.

'*Ciao, carissima,*' a male voice said. It was Silvestro, her second cousin and fellow journalist. He had looked after her since Giovanni's death, bringing her presents from his family's farm at Vallambrosa, showing a fatherly interest in Pasquale. She and Silvestro had been close as children. She knew he was ready to look after her in more intimate ways, that he was, in fact, ready to warm the bed Giovanni had left. The unrequited hunger of several decades still burned in him. It was an adolescent love, rooted in a kiss, a first for each of them, one torpid afternoon under the pines.

She kept his ardour at bay with laughter. If you did not treat something seriously you were safe from it.

'How are you, Silvestro?' she said in English. 'Did you have a good weekend?'

Like her, Silvestro was also fluent in English. Unlike her he had no English blood, but he had often stayed in Cambridgeshire with her great-aunts, Augusta and Theodora Rachet. Those two maiden ladies, horrified that anyone could embrace English vowels with passionate abandon, had schooled both Italian children in syntax and accent. ('Dear child, dear child, English is all about restraint!')

'A lazy weekend!' Silvestro said. 'Are you and Pasquale free this evening? Erica and I would love to have you for dinner.'

'You'd fare better with one of your fat chickens from Vallambrosa!' Paola retorted. 'We'd really love to, Silvestro, but three of my new guests will be arriving tonight . . .'

'I'll call around afterwards then.'

'Do. And bring Erica. I haven't seen her for ages.'

Paola was half English. Her mother, Mabel Huntley, 'Mamie', blonde and English, had been a war orphan. Her father had died at Dunkirk, and her mother courtesy of an unexploded bomb which detonated as she searched through the rubble of her London home after the worst night of the blitz in May 1941.

Young Mamie had never fully recovered from the double loss. Taken in by her aunts, she proved fragile and impulsive. She had met Paola's father, Guido Anguillante, on a holiday in Italy, when she had lunched in his family's restaurant on a stifling July day in 1951. They had married within a matter of months, but she had died the following year giving birth to a daughter, Paola Anna Maria.

Paola grew up a Florentine; she went to school in the city, lived with her father in Fiesole, the hillside town overlooking Florence. Here she helped her step-mother, Maria, in the restaurant, was dreamy and ambitious, had a pet cat called Miranda, and liked to read in the Roman amphitheatre beside her home. She became a journalist. At twenty-six she had married Giovanni Nosterini, formidable lover, witty, volatile teacher, and had lost him just eighteen months ago in a casual accident in a Roman street, leaving her with Pasquale, their delicate only child.

Paola prepared the *risotto con funghi*, knocked on her son's door, was assailed as she opened it by the powerful rhythms of U2.

'Lunch is ready . . . Silvestro and Erica will be coming around this evening after dinner.'

Pasquale was lying on his bed. She was taken aback, as she frequently was, by his beauty; he had the bearing and features of a fifteenth-century aristocrat. His colour is all right, she thought, covertly looking for the deterioration she had been warned about. Every time she thought of this her heart felt as though her stomach had swallowed it. He was due to see the doctor again the next day. If he needed an operation Paola was determined that he would have it done by the famous cardiologist Professor Santini, and as quickly as possible. There was a plot of land in Sicily, Giovanni's investment, that was due to be re-zoned. She would sell it, lose the pending bonanza gladly, if it would fund the private operation. She would do anything gladly for her son. Pasquale smiled. 'Good,' he said, punching the air in time to the music. Then he added, 'What about our new guests?'

'There's just the three ladies tonight. Our fourth guest will arrive tomorrow.'

Pasquale said with a sigh: 'Another nice lady with four words of Italian and a terrible accent! I wish we didn't have to have these people . . .'

'No! I told you already. Our fourth guest is a man.'

Pasquale raised his head. 'That will make a change!'

Paola nodded. 'He's Irish.' Then she gave a half-laugh. 'I wonder . . .' she said, 'if . . . ?'

'If what?' her son demanded.

'Oh . . . nothing . . . You'd better have your rest now.'

When Colm came out of the men's toilet the train was at the platform. He found his reserved first-class seat, stowed his luggage, sat down. Then he took out his Filofax, settled his spectacles, checked his itinerary. He saw the name Signora Paola Nosterini and the address in the Via de' Tornabuoni in Florence. He remembered that street; he had walked it long ago with Robin, recalled its centrality, its upmarket shops. Ideal! He brushed away his reservations about staying *en famille*. He would try it for a few days anyway; it might be interesting. It would certainly be something out of the ordinary.

He put his Filofax away, leant back and closed his eyes, imagined himself as twenty-one again en route to Florence.

His small inheritance had made his journey possible. His ailing mother had given the money to Father Doran, the parish priest, on the strict understanding that he would let Colm have it when he was twenty-one. It was her money, the profits from the dairy produce she sold in Kilgarret, her savings over several years. She had made no Will, had no other estate except a few bits of jewellery – her wedding ring and a cameo brooch set in gold, which she had given to Alice. The relentless industry of her life had otherwise sunk without trace.

Had she been happy, he wondered, in her life of selflessness, living in the rambling farmhouse which had been in her husband's family for generations and into which she had married? Bits had been built on to it, such as a second storey with non-aligned windows, and this gave it a strange, irregular and rather pleasing appearance with a sense of movement. Ivy had mantled its walls, blending it completely with the countryside around. The kitchen had flagged floors, the hall was tiled, the stairs made of pitch pine. The sitting room was called the parlour and there was no dining room. Had it pleased her aesthetically, this house, where everyone – family, hired help, visitors – ate off the scrubbed oak table in the kitchen? She ensured that the kitchen was always warm; the old range was in use winter and summer. It was run on their own turf; all the meals were cooked on it. But what had she really felt and thought behind all the domestic effort, behind the love and care? Did she have needs for her own emotional survival that could not be met by family life? Even now he could not see her as anything other than mother. Even after he had been expelled from Clonarty College she had gentled him, stifling her own bitter disappointment, loving him first.

'I've left some money for you, Colm!' she had said towards the end when they were alone together. Voice low, breath coming in small gasps, mouth white, effort patent and terrifying – his mother as he had never seen her. 'You'll get it when you're twenty-one . . . Use it to travel . . . broaden your

23

horizons, learn to forget . . . And you must forget . . . everything that has happened . . . What you hate will possess you for ever! You must forgive, Colm . . . so that you can be free!'

Colm experienced astonishment, even embarrassment. He had never known his mother to indulge in drama. But he was fourteen, observing death, drowning in mucus and tears. Grief displaced everything except the suffocation of loss. But even then he thought of Clonarty College, of his expulsion, wondered if his mother knew more than he had told her, if she had divined the truth. I will never forgive, he told himself. But he nodded to please her, and held her blue-veined hand.

She had died a few days later; her last breath came and went. In the cold light of dawn they waited around her bed for her to take another hoarse gulp of air, to give another flutter of her eyelids. But all was still now, the vigil over. She looked the same. Only her eyes were different, open and blank, pupils dilated at eternity. His father leaned over and closed them, kissed her forehead, touched her hand with a gesture of old hopes defeated, and abruptly left the room.

Colm's siblings, Liam and Alice, looked accusingly at him through their tears.

He was fourteen and left to the not so tender mercies of his father and his siblings. Later, he wondered that his mother had not bequeathed her savings to his father. Colm wanted to tell him he could have the money anyway, however much or little it was; but he became angry at his parent's taciturnity, at the way he addressed Colm with the same abrupt command with which he addressed the dog.

Around this time Colm had a strange dream. He dreamt he was walking through a forest. It was a fine summer's evening – birds in the branches, dappled patterns of light and shadow on the forest floor. A stream, its banks swathed in bluebells, tinkled nearby. The sense of evil, incongruous in this sylvan place, came without reason or warning. It was suddenly a presence, filling the forest and dimming the day. The ground opened before him and he was falling, precipitated into a deep hole from which he looked up at the canopy of trees and the light. He knew, in the manner of dreams, that at precisely six o'clock – three minutes' time – he would be buried alive. Horror engulfed him; he threw himself at the surrounding wall of earth. The sides were slippery, and every time he was just on the point of gaining the surface he slid back again. He knew he was about to lose the light, be swallowed into the darkness. Then he heard a girl's voice calling him from somewhere above. It was an accent he had never heard.

'Colm,' the voice said. 'Use your will, not your fear! Your will, Colm, your *will*!'

He made a last, deliberate attempt at the wall of mud before it engulfed him. He found pockets of hard earth for footholds, handholds, hauled himself out just as the ground closed under his feet.

He lay on the firm earth, in the dim forest light, and looked around for her, but there was only a small movement among the trees, a sudden flutter of wings. 'Wait!' he called, realising that his saviour had been a bird and not a girl at all. 'I want to meet you!'

'You will!' her voice came to him, almost indistinct from the birdsong.

Colm gradually forgot about his inheritance, ascribing it to the rambling of the terminally ill. In the succeeding years of being a farm boy by day and a student by night, the thought of it would sometimes surface, only to be dismissed. The only things you can rely on, he told himself fiercely, looking at his hands and putting them to his forehead, are these and this. There is nothing else except illusion, nothing else to trust!

When his siblings smiled at his efforts, he hardened his determination. Father Doran never alluded to an inheritance, although Colm saw him from time to time, and he never had the courage to mention it himself. After the debacle at Clonarty the parish priest had first tried enquiry, even remonstrance, but on his protégé's proving unforthcoming he had distanced himself, acting in apparent concert with the rest of the world. It was clear that he believed, as they all did, the version of events which the college had given them. And Colm, damned with a small, blank memory space, which no amount of thought and effort could fill, struggling with shame and pride, was unable even to articulate anything in his own defence.

Six years went by. During this time Colm marshalled his energy and determination. Reaching for control of his life he made a decision – someday he would be rich and invulnerable. He focused on this, slogged for a university scholarship and obtained one, went to University College Dublin to study Commerce.

For three years he was a model student. He lived in a small bed-sitting room in the South Circular Road, saw little of student life, topped the exam list consistently, sat his degree finals with adrenaline flowing. He had forgotten the whole business of his 'inheritance', thinking only of his forthcoming articles with Harrisons Stockbrokers. Three years of this lay ahead of him, three years on the Stock Exchange floor, three years at the coal face of financial analysis, of dealing on behalf of the firm. He would be talking to clients, assisting partners, becoming involved at every level, concerning himself with how the market was going at any particular time. He envisaged his commission earnings with a great deal of pleasure. After his articles he would become a broker and then a partner. He knew he would have to buy his partnership and was already dreaming of the day.

And after that . . .

From now on, he told himself, it is merely a matter of stamina.

In July 1968, when Colm's finals were over, he went home to Ballykelly. He tidied his room on his first day back, bundling together all the redundant paperwork of the years, including the college notes he no longer had use for, putting them into a big cardboard box. He wanted a clean slate, now that he expected to graduate; a fresh new life.

He made a pile of his childhood toys; they could go on the bonfire: an old teddy bear with one eye, various jigsaws with pieces missing; a musty assortment of comics. At the bottom of his wardrobe drawer he found a tired cardboard box with a faded red and yellow legend: THE MAGIC WIZARD. When he opened it the past smote him. There, in this quiz game which had beguiled many an hour, were the seeds of his early interests; there were the sheets of Knowledge, questions to the right, answers to the left. The History sheet was still uppermost, waiting for the touch of his child's hand. 'Who was Savonarola?'

He took the game board out, set it up. He was back again in his sick bed, and his mother's tired footsteps were coming up the stairs. The wizard, who did not know that ten years had elapsed, whizzed around and pointed with his wand to the answer. 'Savonarola was a monk who lived in fifteenth-century Florence and was said to be mad!'

'Mam, what's a monk? Is it a monkey?'

'No, *a stór*!' Laughter. 'It's a priest!'

'Why was this Sav-on-ar-ola monk mad?'

His mother looked at the game. 'I don't know, *a cushla*. Ask the Master!'

'Mam, where's Florence?'

'It's in Italy . . . You know, the hot country down south!'

'Yes. I know . . . Italy has lots of ruins. I saw them in a book. It's where the volcano went up long ago, at a place called Pompeii. I'm going to see it when I grow up!' Then he added, as his mother put a loving hand on his forehead, 'I'll take you with me, Mam! We'll go together.'

His mother smiled. 'We will, *a stór*!'

When Mr Roche, the Master, had called, Colm asked him why a priest would go mad and his teacher looked at him in perplexity.

'It's that new game of his!' his mother said.

Mr Roche inspected the game. On his next visit he brought Colm a book about medieval Italy. There was a section on Florence, a plate showing Savonarola in black and white. 'Girolamo Savonarola,' the legend said, 'born 1452; died 1498'. All that could be seen, in this portrait, was a powerful face in profile emerging from a black cowl. The rest of the picture was completely dark.

Colm stared at it, fascinated at the combination of the sinister and the powerful, read the brief story of the monk's life, his crusade against ecclesiastical corruption and moral laxity, his huge following in Florence, his defiance of excommunication, his capture, his torture and death by hanging, the burning of his body.

The strange face in the portrait haunted Colm's nights. How could a priest go mad? Why did they torture him, kill him? Why was what he said so terrible? Why was it wrong to say what you believed?

He was feverish. His mother listened, read the book, took it away from him, returned it to Mr Roche.

Colm could still hear her voice: 'That fellow,' she said reproachfully, referring to Savonarola, 'was only fit for the lunatic asylum . . . Just imagine, a monk defying the Pope!' Then she had lowered her voice, looked at his teacher meaningfully: 'It's not suitable reading for a gentle boy like Colm!'

Standing there now, holding the game in his hand, listening to the echo of her long-lost voice, Colm thought, with the cynical perspective of his twenty-one years, what a poor bloody eejit the monk had been. He rubbed his hand over the plastic wizard who had once opened so many doors. Then he chucked the box on to the heap for burning, went downstairs, donned his wellingtons and headed for the meadow.

They were making the hay, raking the rich sun-dried grass into small cocks; these would soon be moved on the hay float to form a great rick in the haggart. It was a glorious day; the air filled with the dry, sweet smell he loved, meadow dust and grass seeds. The priest's car, a Ford Consul, came slowly down the narrow, untarmacadamed road, turned in the open gate of the Nugent farm and stopped in the yard.

Colm, looking up, saw the parish priest walking down the boreen to the meadow.

'Hello, Father,' Alice called, holding the rake in one hand and pushing back her old cotton sun-hat with the other. Liam called a greeting. His father waved from the tractor. Packy Flynn, the workman, tipped his sweaty cap. Colm hung back, raised his hand perfunctorily and redirected his attention to his work.

The priest came into the field, walked towards them, exchanged banter. 'How are you, Alice? No rest for the wicked!'

'Well, we must be damn' wicked, Father!' Laughter.

'Well, you've the weather for it anyway.' And in the midst of this Father Doran said almost as an aside, 'Can I have a word with you, Colm . . .' And drew him out of earshot of his siblings.

'There's some money your mother gave me for you,' the priest said gruffly. 'She wanted you to have it this summer . . . Did you know about it?'

'She said something when she was dying,' Colm said, 'but I thought she might have been . . .'

Father Doran looked across the meadow to where the thatched roof of Johnny Munroe's house rose above the hedgerow and the stone wall. He didn't approve of old Johnny Munroe who read the cards and scared the daylights out of the gullible.

'Oh, she was fully *compos mentis*, if that's what you mean. She gave me the money in trust for you . . . She specified that you use it for travel.'

The parish priest's thick hair had once been dark brown, but now it was silver; his tangled eyebrows were like briars in hoar frost. The winter of his life was fast setting in; fatigue was patent, as was disappointment. For years he had been drawn to a woman in his parish, a Mrs Annie Kennedy, a farmer's wife and the mother of four children. She was a perfectly ordinary woman, but she had a wistful way of talking, a gentle nature, and a smile that would have moved a statue. He acknowledged eventually, as he found himself searching for her face at Mass, that he loved her. He set out to avoid her, living out his days in the lonely presbytery, refusing the golden lure of the Jameson bottle. The bottle offered surcease, but with it a problem greater than the one he possessed. Ultimately he had triumphed over the flesh, resisted his temptations, but now, in the chill realisation of approaching age, he did not feel sanctified or elevated because of his success. He felt empty, a man who had put the substance of his will into defeating his life.

He pursed his mouth, pinched it in at the corners. He did not approve of the deceased Maura Nugent's trust; he had a respect for money. And he did not want to give it to a boy who was capable of inexplicable and violent behaviour. But to stand on too much nicety would be to betray a promise. He could not break his word.

'There's nearly two hundred pounds . . . do you want to go abroad? It was a pre-condition.'

Colm gasped.

'The money could be put to better purpose, but your mother was adamant. She said it was to be spent by you on travel, that you were to see those places you were so interested in . . .' He paused. 'Strange woman – worked all her life, never wasted anything before . . .'

But all Colm felt was the surge of euphoria. Into his mind's eye came vistas of foreign places, beaches, different languages, different faces. He remembered his early dreams of travelling; he remembered the books on classical history, the Greek and Roman myths read so avidly during the long days, and sometimes nights, of childhood illness; he remembered what he had read of Florence. He knew immediately what he would do with his windfall.

'Where will you go?'

'Italy. I want to see Rome and Herculaneum and Pompeii . . . Maybe even Florence! Is there enough for that?'

'Yes. More if you are economical, stay in hostels . . . But if you go by plane . . .'

'I'll get the boat to France, hitch-hike.'

'When will you go?'

'After the hay . . . maybe the end of next month . . .'

'Well, come with me so to Kilgarret. We'll pay the bank a visit. Can you come now?'

Colm glanced around him. 'Yes, Father!'

He sat in the passenger seat of the Ford Consul and accompanied Father Doran. He did not initiate conversation, but Father Doran warned him in grave tones to be careful of the company he kept abroad.

'Don't be led into sin by any fast young people you meet when you're on the Continent. Many of them don't have the values you were reared with here . . .' He lowered his voice. 'Even if you forgot them once, Colm, don't do so again . . .'

Colm felt the resentment, the stab of pain, but he was silent. He thinks I'm a lost cause, he thought, as he stood beside the priest at the cashier's counter in the Munster and Leinster Bank in the main street of Kilgarret. The teller counted the money slowly; the priest gathered it up, led his young parishioner outside. Once in the car he thrust a wad of notes into Colm's hands.

'Put it into your pocket, Colm,' Father Doran ordered. 'Put it away where it can't be seen!'

Colm obeyed. The priest then produced a receipt. Colm signed it. In it he acknowledged that the secret trust established by Maura Nugent had been satisfied, and that Colm Nugent had received one hundred and ninety pounds. Father Doran put the receipt into his breast pocket.

Colm allowed himself to be driven down Main Street, past

31

Clohessy's general outfitters where the wellingtons were hanging outside in rows, past the chemist and the doctor's surgery, past the small row of county council cottages where the village merged into the open country. He felt dazed, a master of riches.

When they got home Father Doran declined the invitation to come in. Colm thanked him, watched as the car turned at the gate and went away down the dusty road. Then he went to his room, counted the money and secreted it away, hiding it in the lining of an old overcoat at the back of his wardrobe.

'What did Father Doran want with you?' his father asked later.

'He wanted me to go with him to Kilgarret . . .' His father, always taciturn, nodded, asked no further questions.

When the haymaking was over, and the cocks safely transmogrified into a great rick in the haggart, and the smell of the new-mown hay was fading from his nostrils, Colm cycled into Kilgarret and went to Clohessy's shop. This shop was an important feature in the town. It bore a legend over the door which said: Clohessy and Company, Drapery and Footwear. Outside, wellingtons hung on pegs alongside men's trousers, waterproof jackets, stacked boxes of boots. A sign near the awning with the Singer Sewing Machine logo said: Sewing orders taken here.

Once he had loved this emporium, with its smells of newness – its bolts of men's suiting, women's dresses, household goods, shining galvanised buckets – loved it because of Catherine Clohessy, Kattie to her friends, eldest of Dan Clohessy's three daughters, and his sister's friend. Today she came out to serve him. Her father, who was busy with another customer, said a brief 'Hello, Colm' but without warmth. Kattie was home on holiday from her Dublin job in the bank. She blushed and smiled. He didn't see her much now; she didn't visit the farm as often as formerly. Colm ignored the small frisson at his heart, asked for what he wanted: 'You wouldn't have an ol' rucksack . . . and a sleeping bag, Kattie?'

'Are you going somewhere?'

'Italy!'

'Cripes! Are you serious?'

He nodded.

Kattie glanced at her father who indicated where she should look. She extracted a couple of canvas knapsacks and three rolled-up sleeping bags from some cavern at the back of the shop.

'Are these what you're looking for?'

'Yes . . .'

'God, you're the lucky one, Colm Nugent!' she exclaimed. 'Off to Italy!' Her tone was light badinage, but he thought he detected curiosity and envy.

He chose a black rucksack with metal supports, and a light sleeping bag, paid for them with his new wealth. Yes, Catherine, he thought, I'm off to Italy! He damped down the old flutter of his heart when their eyes met, and let cynicism replace it. She was only a little provincial girl, after all. The world was full of them.

'Thank you, Kat,' he said a little stiffly, as he took his leave.

'Will you send me a card?' she said lightly, smiling at him with sudden diffidence, displaying her winsomely askew front teeth.

'Sure!'

He left Clohessy's and walked down the main street of Kilgarret with a smug sense of escaping it all, the pointing of fingers, and the sudden whispers: 'There's the Nugent boy who was expelled from Clonarty College.'

For years he had longed to show them all. This was the burn which had driven him to study, poring over the books night after night, propped in bed, or at the table in his room, his overcoat on against the winter cold, blowing on his fingers to warm them, secretly, patiently, plotting his future, plotting his revenge.

Sometimes he even wished he could remember the full

details of his disgrace. But the dark spot in his memory persisted, becoming, because he could not penetrate it, a place he feared, a ghost in the shadows he dared not turn and face.

'I'm going to Italy,' he told the family a week before his departure. 'I'm spending next month there!'

They were at supper. Moll Flannery, the 'girl', was serving out the bacon and eggs. Packy Flynn, who hailed originally from Donegal, had joined them in the kitchen, eating at the back table. He had been ogling Moll in the covert way he always did, but now he sat up to attention, struck dumb like the rest of them, recovering first.

'A wee laddie like yourself to be off to forrin places! Well, be the hokey . . .'

Colm's father ignored Packy and said abruptly: 'Where are you getting the money for this expedition?'

Colm made a non-committal gesture, looked from his father to Packy and back. Packy's ears were straining. Alice made a signal with her eyes, a warning: anything Packy knew the parish knew. Colm shrugged. Silence resumed until the meal was over and Packy had gone.

'Well, sir?'

'It was Mama's money, Dad. She left it to Father Doran for me. She said I was to travel with it! She wanted me to use it this summer . . .'

His father started; his mouth dropped open for a moment. He had not known of this lunatic bequest; after her death he had searched for his wife's savings in the tin box she used to keep in her wardrobe, had finally conceded that either she'd spent them or they had been stolen. He did not suspect his children of crime; he did not even suspect Moll or Packey. He knew the kitchen door was unlocked during the day; if Moll was out any ambient tinker could have taken the money.

His face displayed no emotion; but inside, the fierce resentment he felt against this prodigal son of his gathered greater and more bitter force.

34

'You could use it to pay for your keep here!' he said. Colm felt suddenly sick. A sharp retort was on the tip of his tongue, but he kept his voice even. He had learnt the first lesson years before at Clonarty: you never showed your feelings.

'I do pay my way here. When I'm at home I work from morning till night! I haven't cost you a penny for years. I get scholarships, I work in Dublin at night for extra money; I do without when I have to. I know how to live on porridge. In Dublin, when I'm hungry I improvise . . . once I boiled an egg box into mush and ate it, rather than ask you or anyone else for money . . .' He stared his father in the eye. 'I'm going to Italy!'

His father stood up and left the room.

When Colm went out into the summer evening he met Packy coming from the cowhouse.

'There does be statues of naked wimmin in them forrin places!' Packy advised in a fervent whisper. 'Pictures and statues and them all bare as the day they was born!'

Colm thought of the soft porn magazines he had found in school. He was suddenly washed by a wave of anger and lust. Packy looked at him slyly. 'Don't be doin' the bold thing with any forrin wimmin now . . .' He grinned, showing blackened stumps of teeth.

Colm said nothing further about his proposed journey, got on with his chores on the farm. A fortnight later a letter arrived from University College Dublin with his degree results: first-class honours grade two. He showed it to his father, who grunted, glancing at him with a sudden arrested expression, before rearranging his features into their customary severity.

'I'll be conferred in November,' Colm said. 'Will you be coming, Dad . . . for the ceremony?'

'Ah, sure I'd be out of place in anything like that,' his father said.

Stung, Colm retorted, 'Mam would have come!'

Tom Nugent did not reply. But that evening he sat alone in

35

his room with a bottle of whiskey. He did not emerge until the following midday; he said nothing to his children, but his eyes were bloodshot and his face the colour of putty.

Colm's siblings looked at their brother askance. He felt the void, the tacit blame, the responsibility for all this domestic devastation. He walked away across the meadow, trying to stifle the demons of frustrated love, and anger, the surge of powerful emotions with which he felt he had been damned and for which there was never an outlet. He found the small stretch of woodland at the farm's perimeter, walked away from the path among the trees, sat at the base of an old beech and put his arms around the bole. He sensed its timeless serenity and gradually his turmoil lessened. He leant his face against the bark. Is it better, he asked himself, to live or to die? If life is pain what is the point of it?

Then he thought wearily: I won't go to Italy. Dad can have the money. What happens to me doesn't matter anyway!

Johnny Munroe, the local eccentric, said by some to have second sight, was coming through the woods and saw the youth at the tree before the youth saw him. He was a few yards away before Colm was aware of his presence. Colm started up, embarrassed, but his chagrin was immediately replaced by a sense that Johnny Munroe saw nothing incongruous, that in fact he was looking at something other than what was in front of him. He was a man of about sixty years at this point, with the thin, drawn face of someone who has spent his life at the edge of privation.

'I'm looking for a bit of tabaccy I lost hereabouts last year,' he informed Colm with a twinkle. When Colm bestirred himself to search the dry woodland floor for a piece of yesteryear's tobacco, the old seer said softly, 'Go on your journey, boy! There is something you will find on it . . .' he lowered his voice '. . . which will matter very much to you in the end!'

Colm stashed away the sum of twenty pounds among the pages of a text book and converted most of the rest into lire in the Kilgarret branch of the Bank of Ireland. 'Oh, and I'll need a few francs as well,' he told the teller expansively, 'for a short stay in Paris!'

The teller's eyes widened.

That evening Colm sat alone in his room, surveying his possessions; the homemade shelves with his text books, the cardboard boxes filled with old stuff for the bonfire, the table where he had worked like a demon night after night. He looked at the bed which he made every day with military precision, and in which he had tossed in the grip of many a nightmare, the bed where he had, when the sense of his impotence had overpowered him, lain awake in the dark concocting fantasies of revenge. He told himself that he was closing a chapter, that a part of his life was over and done with. But there was one more thing he needed to do, something which should be said and should be heard. He took a sheet of paper and wrote a letter to the Most Reverend James Noonan, DD, Bishop of Clonerris.

Your Grace,
This letter is to advise you that Father Seamus Madden of Clonarty College is not what he seems. He committed crimes with at least one boy in his care. He may have done so with others and may do so in the future unless he is prevented.

I regret that I cannot give my name. But I assure you that I know from first-hand experience what I am talking about!

He sealed the letter, and cycled to Martin's shop near the Cross where there was a post box, slipped it into the custody of the Department of Posts and Telegraphs. Something will be done now! he thought with grim satisfaction. He returned to the farm, took down his cardboard boxes, and burned them behind the barn. Next day he hitch-hiked to Rosslare and the ferry.

When he arrived in Le Havre, he found his way to the highway and hitched to Paris, stayed in a youth hostel in Rueil-Malmaison, and next day took the train to Turin. From there he hiked southwards along the Riviera. Alone with a rucksack and happy as he had not been for years, away from silent censure, he learnt the burning blue of Mediterranean sea and sky, the sense of Arcadia. It was a revelation, this anonymity, this preparedness of the world to accept you at face value; to be where no one knew your secrets or used them to confound you. When he thought of his father and siblings he felt they inhabited another dimension. When he thought of Johnny Munroe and the day they'd met in the wood, he permitted himself a smile. Old Johnny had been right.

He thought he was learning peace. He thought he was learning to confound and bury the past. But his serenity was shortlived. Into his Italian idyll Fate sent him Robin. He could see her still, the small girl from New York, with a dilapidated old rucksack and a canvas shoulder bag.

The train pulled out of Cherbourg, gathered speed. Colm, in his first-class seat, allowed himself a quick, satisfying comparison between his travelling arrangements now and then. The rain touched the window, separated instantly into tiny beads, slid along the glass. Nothing to do except think.

Chapter Three

What was the world doing in 1968? How could he have lived through it, Colm wondered, as he watched the flying countryside, and remember so little? The Information Age had yet to dawn; man had not yet set foot on the moon; President Johnson had initiated the first Vietnam peace talks; students had spent much of the summer rioting in Paris; the Soviets had invaded Czechoslovakia. In Ireland Jack Lynch was Taoiseach; the economy was burgeoning, the slow ascent from centuries of depression.

But at twenty-one what did he care for anything except sea and sky and the delirium of freedom?

The beach at Civitavecchia had been almost deserted. It was off the tourist track and Colm had come on it by accident. He was heading for Rome, but his lift, an articulated lorry, had almost reached its destination. The driver, Ferdinando, friendly, garrulous, with black, wavy hair and a day's beard, indicated that all his passenger had to do was wait at the side of the road for the next lift. He had given Colm the name of a cheap restaurant in Rome which was owned by a cousin, in the working-class district of Trastevere, written it down.

'. . . *"La Rivetta". Molto buono, ma non troppo caro! Capisce?*'

Colm thanked him, said he understood. A cheap restaurant was welcome information. '*Grazie!*'

He jumped from the passenger seat to the hot verge. Ferdinando handed him down his rucksack. '*Arrivederci . . .*' Friendly wave of the hand and with a roar the giant vehicle drew away, leaving behind the acrid smell of exhaust and a small eddy of warm dust.

Colm waited. Traffic whizzed by. The sun drove needles of fire into his face. He heard the staccato song of the cicada, crickety-chirp . . . crickety-chirp. The land pulsated with sound.

He kept his thumb up. Fiat after white Fiat at substantial speeds, but no takers. When he looked behind him he could see the sea. It sparkled, blue and almost still. He caught a glimpse of a tiny beach, some rocks, pale sand, shade. Was there a path? He could have a swim, eat his packed lunch in the shadow of the cliff, and resume his journey then. Or perhaps it was a private beach. He walked a little way to where the verge widened and saw a path going down. He hesitated; he did not want to stumble on private property, find himself renegotiating the cliff with a mastiff at his heels. Italy was not Ireland. Here, as he had already discovered during the course of a small misunderstanding on the Riviera, territoriality knew nothing of sociability.

But as he progressed down the steep path he saw little to bother him. There was no sign of life; the tiny beach seemed to be cut off from the remainder of the coast; there was no building impinging on it, no house or summer villa. The sand was coarse; the rocks plentiful; the water was turquoise and amethyst. Under the rippling wavelets he could see the sand shimmer in small, vivid patterns of light and shadow. When he was a child he had thought the slippery patterns of light were eels, that the water boiled with life.

He took off his clothes, left them with his rucksack in a small rock gully and ran naked into the sea. It was when he was coming out that he saw the girl picking her way down the same path from the road. She was wearing jeans and a white halter top and carried a rucksack. A canvas shoulder bag was slung over one shoulder. She was wearing sunglasses, had short fair hair. She paused and looked about from time to time and only saw him when she had almost finished negotiating the steep path to the shore. When she saw him her back straightened and her demeanour altered, like a doe sniffing the wind for danger. She stood still. She did not look at him directly, but he knew that she was considering him. Although she was young, her strange immobility reminded him of an old tinker woman he had once seen studying tea leaves, watching Fate. She was not Italian; either English or American judging by her colouring and bearing, probably the latter.

'Hello,' he shouted. 'The water is lovely!'

'Hi,' she shouted back, but she did not move. The 'Hi' was American, a tell-tale cadence in the middle.

'I'm hitch-hiking to Rome,' Colm continued, calling across the water with the freemasonry of shared youth and shared language in a foreign land.

But she was silent and immobile. Colm swam and was soon back at the rocks by the shore. He knelt in the shallows. He could see her more clearly now, small ruffle of hair in the soft breeze.

'Look the other way,' he called. 'I'm coming out! I haven't got anything on!'

Colm stood up and came out from the sea. He walked to his clothes. He did not look at her and when he regained the relative privacy of the cliff quickly he threw on his shorts and shirt.

When he was dressed he came on to the beach. It was empty as was the cliff path. He thought she had gone. But then he saw her, hidden by the rocks to the right of the path, sitting on the sand, her bare feet in the sea, her rubber flip-flops on top of a rock, her jeans rolled up. She was eating an apple and resting her back against her rucksack. The canvas shoulder bag was wedged to one side; he saw that it bore the Stars and Stripes.

She barely glanced at him as he came towards her. But she spoke. 'You a Mick?'

'I'm Irish if that's what you mean!'

She took another bite of her apple. 'So am I,' she said. 'At least sort-of. My dad's folk were Irish . . . place called Listowel. Ever hear of it?'

'It's in Kerry,' Colm said, perching on a rock and looking down at her. 'South-western corner of Ireland. Have you been there?'

'Nope! My dad thought it was a good place to steer clear of.'

'Is that so?'

'Yeah . . .' Then she added, 'I've got some Italian blood in me too . . .'

'So you're quite cosmopolitan!'

She shrugged, looked out to sea. A speedboat was crossing the bay about a half-mile away, towing a skier who described an arc of consummate grace.

'It's a relief to talk English,' Colm said. 'My Italian consists of "*Buon giorno*" and "*Vado a Roma*".'

'Mine stinks, although I did it at school for two years.'

'When did your folks leave Listowel?'

'My dad left thirty years ago.'

He studied her. She was long-limbed, although small. Her cropped hair was sun-bleached. The sun played on it, on blonde lights among the coppery tones. There was a defiant cast to her face. He could not see her eyes behind the sunglasses. Her skin was dark honey, except at the back of her neck where pink patches indicated recent sunburn.

'Where are you headed?'

'Florence,' she said. 'What about you?'

'Rome. Are you on your own?'

She regarded him for a moment. 'Maybe.' Her eyes returned to the sea. She finished the apple and threw the core out into the water.

'Which part of the States are you from?'

'New York.'

'Are you a student?'

She hesitated for split second. 'Yeah! I'm studying art.'

He took out his lunch, offered her a roll. 'Just salad, I'm afraid . . .'

'You needn't be.' She laughed. 'Afraid, I mean . . .' She accepted a roll. He opened the bottle of beer, handed it to her. She took a swig, handed it back.

'What's your name?'

'Colm. Colm Nugent.'

'Mine's Robin. Well, really Roberta . . . but that was my mom's idea!'

'Do you have a surname?'

'McKay.'

Small waves caressed her feet, slapped on the sand. After a moment's silence she asked, 'What do you do?'

'I'm a student. I'm going to be a stockbroker.'

'No kidding? You should get my daddy to give you an account.'

'Is he a stockbroker?'

'Nope . . . But he's rich,' she added, regarding him out of the corner of her eye. 'Made himself a fortune!' she added, glancing at him as though to assess his reaction.

'What are you doing all on your own in Italy, Robin?' Colm asked after a moment.

'I've run away! My daddy wanted to send me to a snotty college, but I prefer to be free.' She sent him another swift measuring glance. 'But he'd get his goons on anyone who laid a finger on me.'

Colm straightened, but she smiled. 'Where did you say you were headed?' she asked.

'I told you, Rome. Then I'll probably go south. I want to see Herculaneum and Pompeii.'

'Why don't you come with me to Florence first? It's more important – artistically, I mean – than Rome.'

He turned, surprised.

She laughed. 'Never mind, Irish, I'm taking the piss!'

Colm could hardly believe his ears. Here was a pretty young woman inviting him to be her travelling companion; it was not the time to stand on ceremony. In a way it was a fantasy come true. It represented new horizons: the opportunity to be normal, to engage in sexual conquest, to swagger a little in his own esteem.

'If you come to Rome with me, I'll go with you to Florence,' he said as lightly as he could.

'I've just come from Rome,' she said. 'But you've got a deal!'

For a moment Colm felt almost light-headed with anticipation. This was the stuff of dreams. Many of his peers had already made it with women, or boasted that they had. And she was American, with luck even on the pill.

Colm and Robin hitch-hiked to Rome, found a cheap lodging in Via Palestra near the station; there was one room left, with a double bed.

'Which side do you want?'

'Which side do *I* want? I'm taking the middle! You'll have to sleep on the floor!'

Colm felt the disappointment, then the grudging respect. He was dog tired anyway. Maybe tomorrow.

He unrolled his sleeping bag. 'All right.'

The floor was mosaic. She looked at it doubtfully, as though relenting of her harshness. 'OK. But tomorrow night you can have the bed and I'll take the floor. Fair is fair!'

'Yes, ma'am.'

She took out her sleeping bag and handed it to him, passed him a pillow. 'Put that under you as well!'

She turned out the light, undressed in the dark. He heard the small rustle of her clothes.

He lay awake; dim light came through the slats of the shutters. He thought of Ballykelly and Kilgarret, as though they were figments of the imagination. He listened for the girl's breathing, wondered if she were asleep. The drone of a mosquito impinged on his drifting consciousness. Her sudden spasmodic movement startled him awake. She turned on the light.

'Got the bastard!' she said, leaning over and displaying a squashed and bloody insect slapped flat against her forearm.

'How did you do that?' Colm said sleepily. 'They're so fast!'

'When they cut their motors you know they're coming in for the kill. They think they're on a winner, so you surprise them with their pants down.'

'I never feel them,' Colm said, keeping his eyes half shut against the light, laughing silently at the absurdity of being stretched on the floor, while a pretty girl squashed mosquitoes in a nearby bed.

'You're not trying!' She turned the light off.

But sleep did not return easily. The floor was hard. Through the window came the nighttime sounds of Rome. He thought of his father, sitting grim-faced by the fire, drinking alone in his room, turning in to his lonely bed, and a rush of sorrow enveloped him. He thought of Alice and Liam who were a clique unto themselves. He thought of Kattie Clohessy whom he loved and hated.

'Are you asleep?' he murmured at one point.

'No.' Her voice was very soft. 'I'm a light sleeper. I'd make a good watchdog!' After a moment she added in a fragile voice, 'Do you ever get scared?'

'Why should I be scared?'

'No reason.'

'You needn't be scared of me.'

She laughed softly. 'I'm not . . .'

'You're a funny girl. Are all Americans like you?'

'I can't be the first one you've met.'

'You're the first young American woman I've met at close quarters.'

'Is this "close quarters"?' He heard the smile in her voice.

'Well, it's the same room and it's the middle of the night.'

'Think of us as soldiers,' she said after a moment. 'After all, I've just killed the enemy!'

She's a child, Colm thought, as he tried to decipher her reply. I've landed myself with a child!

45

He slept. It came with bone-softening sweetness. His last conscious thought had to do with wondering if she would be there in the morning, or if he would wake to find his wallet gone. And if she was there in the morning . . .

He woke just before dawn. Something had disturbed him; in his dream Alice had been crying. He realised as he surfaced that the crying was real. It was the girl. He listened in silence to her bitter sobbing, half muffled as though she had shoved the sheet into her mouth. He wanted to speak, to ask her what was wrong, but his instinct told him to do nothing and after a while the sobs petered away.

He got up at first light, full of desire. He was in a bedroom, alone with a girl; she had slept in the same room as him. What that meant should be obvious. He thought of her utterances in the middle of the night, childlike, brittle in some way. Well, she wasn't a child, or a soldier either for that matter, thank God!

He bent over her, saw that she was asleep, that she was wearing a thin, white cotton shift. The sheet was down at her knees. He could see the contours of her small breasts, the thrust of her nipples, the darker shadow of the aureoles, the mystery of the space she inhabited, strange girl who had been blown to him by the wind. He wondered if she might be slightly unhinged. She had run away from home by all appearances. But her people were rich and would be searching for her.

Her eyelashes were long, gold brown. He wanted to get into bed beside her. All the strictures came crowding in, the sense of honour, the purely practical, the covert fear, the inhibitions which were his personal cross. He didn't know her; it would be taking advantage. She might wake up and raise the roof. He mightn't be able to do it; he had never done it.

He went out to the bathroom on the landing, shaved and had a shower. You're lily-livered, he told himself. You had to move in on women quickly, before they knew what was happening, before their defences were up. That's what Eamon

46

Keaveney had told him and Eamon, if his boasting was anything to go by, should know.

When he returned from the bathroom she was still asleep. He made a noise in closing the door but she slept on. Light sleeper my foot! This one would sleep through the Last Trumpet. He watched her sleeping face. Yesterday she had looked twenty. Now she looked about fourteen, childlike. The scattering of freckles reminded him of his sister. The wish to intrude on her, take her, evaporated. He dressed quickly and sat by the window, watching the old city come alive in the cool air, the shutters opening, the bed linen aired on the windowsills, the escalating noise of traffic and horns and scooters, and the warm haze in the sky as it prepared for another scorching day. Church bells sounded nearby. He glanced at the bed to see if they had woken her, but apparently not. He knew he had behaved decently and was enveloped in an unexpected sense of peace.

When he looked around again her eyes were open, watching him.

'I didn't know you were awake.'

'I've just surfaced. I'll meet you downstairs,' she added hurriedly as he stood up, as though to pre-empt any other suggestion. Her voice had a pragmatic ring to it. 'Why don't you have your breakfast and I'll join you in a minute. Give me time to get dressed.'

Sleepy eyes, tousled hair, thin cotton shift. It was her vulnerability which was on-turning. Helpless, knicker-less, warm from sleep.

Desire. A surge of ruthlessness; why be a wimp? Why shouldn't he try his luck? It was now or never. Every other fellow in his year had managed it. She was probably dying for it anyway.

He came to the bed, leaned down and kissed her, tried to force his tongue into her mouth. She froze, pushed him away with surprising strength, sat on the edge of the bed with the sheet around her, stared at him with accusing eyes.

47

'Forget it, Irish. I hate sex and I'm good at screaming!' She spoke through her teeth. 'And I don't believe in love or any of that crap, so don't waste your breath telling me how much you adore me and how you fell in love with me the instant you clapped your horny Irish eyes on me!'

'It was your idea that we travel together,' Colm said. '*You* talked me into it! You're the one who took the room. Now you're behaving like a nun in the Middle Ages!'

'Sure it was my idea! And a double room was cheaper and it was all they had left. But did I mention anything about sexual services?'

'Did I?'

'No. But I don't need them! And I don't want to be used by a big hungry Paddy with an even bigger, hungrier, cock!'

Colm turned and walked out of the door, struggling with rejection. For a moment, as he walked down the stone stairs, he wanted, absurdly, to cry.

She came down ten minutes later in jeans and white sleeveless shirt. She had a map in her hand bearing the legend '*Pianta di Roma*'. He was sitting in the small breakfast area, by the balcony. The window and shutters were open; a pigeon with crimson feet landed like an aircraft on the balcony rail, looked at him interrogatively, head cocked. 'Shoo . . .' he said, flapping his hand. It left with a clatter of wings.

'Look,' she said in a mollifying voice, as she opened the map. 'We're here. Near the station. Let's walk to the river and see the sights. I suppose you want to see St Peter's, like a good Catholic!'

Colm was trying to think of something suitably vitriolic. He had spent ten angry minutes concocting rejoinders to the gibe about his hungry cock. She studied him for a careful few seconds.

'Irish,' she added, as though she had divined his thought, 'you'll have to make allowances. Sorry if I've hurt your feelings. It's my spoilt-rotten childhood coming out. I'll tell you all about it sometime . . .'

He looked at her face, now open and smiling, eyebrows raised, eyes dark blue, almost violet. The fingers with which she had pointed out their position on the map were brown and strangely worn, nails chewed. In the jeans and sleeveless shirt she looked less like a girl than ever, thin, hammered bronze by the sun, almost an urchin. She ordered *caffè latte*, and drank it greedily, wolfing down a roll and apricot jam. She gathered the crumbs into a little pile, and picked them up, scattered them on to the balcony. The house sparrows came for them instantly, like creatures who had been watching this particular balcony since the dawn of time.

'I think we're better off on our own,' he said sulkily. 'You go your way and I'll go mine. That way you needn't waste so much energy playing hard to get.'

She stared at him stonily. Then, to his astonishment, her eyes filled with tears. She blinked them away.

'All right. You're mad with me because I was mad with you. You shouldn't have made a pass at me. It makes me want to throw up. I can't help it!'

'I was only trying to kiss you,' Colm said. 'Anyone would think I was trying to rape you!'

Her cup clattered on the table.

'Why are you so nervous, Roberta?' Colm demanded after a moment.

'Name's Robin. And I'm not nervous!'

'I think you are scared.' He said this unkindly.

'Maybe someone is chasing me. Maybe I committed a crime and Interpol are looking for me!'

When Colm looked at her in startled interrogation she gave a dismissive laugh, stood up, slung her canvas bag over her shoulder. 'Well, seeing as you want to say goodbye – nice knowing you. I'll just pick up my stuff, pay my half and be on my way.'

Colm watched her leave the small breakfast area. He experienced her loneliness and fragility as though they were his own. He felt he had wronged her in some way; he knew what it was like to be wronged. He swallowed his coffee-dregs and followed her.

He met her coming out of the lift, struggling with her rucksack, and knew immediately that he did not want to see her go.

'Wait. Robin . . . as we're here let's see the city. We'll be friends . . . brother and sister! We could stay here another night . . . and then see about tomorrow?'

She considered him gravely. 'Fine by me . . . now that we know where we stand . . .'

He took hold of the rucksack. 'I'll bring this back upstairs!'

A cheeky grin; her face lit up. 'I'll wait for you at the door, Superman!'

When he came down she was standing on the cobbles just inside the great black door into the Via Palestra.

A vivid city: hot, burning blue sky, the Tiber winding its way. Bliss to walk without a rucksack. She had spent a few days here, knew her way around, brought him to the Forum, the Colosseum, a long walk by the river, crossing it opposite the fortress of Castel Sant'Angelo, where stone angels guarded the approach to the Vatican. Now footsore, they walked down the Via della Conciliazione to the square of St Peter. Guards at the door of the great Basilica refused them entrance because her arms were bare. Colm was incensed. 'The arrogance!' he said.

'You go ahead,' she said. 'I'll wait outside. You go right in and see the magnificence, the display of wealth, the boys in the blue and yellow stripes, the rows of empty pews they won't let you sit on, no matter how sore your feet or how long your Catholic lineage, or how much of the money they couldn't afford was contributed by your ancestors to build this pile; see the bronze statue of what's-his-name whose toe is worn away with kissing, and Michelangelo's *Pietà*, real private passion, small and intense in the corner!'

Colm looked at her doubtfully. 'You're a funny girl,' he said.

'Go on,' she repeated. 'I'll be here when you come out.'

The interior was vast and cool. It reeked of power. He moved around quickly, absorbing atmosphere rather than detail, saw the queue to kiss St Peter's foot, stood for a few moments before the *Pietà*.

When he emerged he tried to find her and failed. She was not by the portal, where he had expected her. A sense of let-down, of anti-climax, filled him. Her vivacity, her mystery, were such that without her there was a comparative void. Maybe she had gone back to the hotel, taken her rucksack and vanished!

But there was also a seasoning of relief in the thought that she might be gone. Relief because he could relax again, return to the self he knew; resentment also because he felt he had been taken for a patsy, and because, despite everything, she had kept him on the edge, interested, alive; foolish because he thought she had accepted him, when patently she had not.

He saw her sitting on the base of one of the columns at the square's perimeter, out of the sun. She was perusing the map, which she had open on the ground in front of her. Around her a group of youths circled like vultures, but she did not raise her head or look at them. He had already seen this in Italy – lone female foreigners automatically attracting the persistent attentions of young males. But she must know they're there, he thought, as he walked across the burning square towards her. She can't be so immersed in the map that she's oblivious. She sat with almost defiant poise, flexed her shoulders a little as though from weariness, and then, still without glancing at the small mob around her, got up suddenly, moved about fifty yards away and sat down again. The youths followed her, took up positions once more. 'Signorina . . . you are Engleesh? *Vous êtes française? Sprechen Sie Deutsch?*'

She made no response. She might as well have been deaf.

When he was a few feet from them he said loudly and clearly, 'Is Éireannach í.'

This stumped them. They vetted the language and found it incomprehensible. Irish came into its own sometimes, he thought with a queer sense of triumph.

She looked up, gave him a smile, appeared relieved. Her admirers, seeing that she was claimed, dispersed.

'What did you say?' she asked suspiciously. 'What language was that?'

'I said you were Irish. In Irish.'

'I didn't know you spoke Gaelic!'

'It's your ancient ancestral tongue, the oldest language north of the Alps. You had quite a string of admirers there!' he added, looking after the stragglers.

'It's always like that! The trick is never to make eye-contact, play deaf!' She moved to close the map, and he saw to his surprise that her hands were shaking.

'Are you all right?'

'Of course I'm all right! You don't think a few little guys like that would bother me! I'm just hungry!'

He stared at her, decided she was joking. 'Must be something wrong with your blood sugar so . . . We could have lunch in a place I've heard of . . .' He fumbled in his pocket for the address of the restaurant in Trastevere which Ferdinando, the lorry driver, had given him. 'They do a tourist menu, three courses for something quite small . . .'

'Are you paying?' She laughed. 'I'm kidding! We'll go dutch. Or I could get some bread and stuff and make some rolls and we could eat them in the Pincio gardens. Wash them down with a bottle of *aqua minerale*? Cheaper!'

'Where are the Pincio gardens?'

'Not too far . . . a good walk There's a great view from the terrace over the city! I'll show you the Spanish Steps nearby. It's where Keats used to live. Ever hear of him?'

'Everyone has heard of Keats. We had to study him in school.'

'Did you like his stuff?'

'It was all right. Something about a nightingale and a Grecian urn. Poetry is really a bummer – poofs waffling!'

'Yeah,' she said. 'You'll make a great stockbroker.'

They crossed the river by the Ponte Cavour, found themselves in Via Ripetta, walked to the Piazza del Popolo. They passed several shops bearing the legend '*Drogheria*', multi-coloured plastic strips hanging in the doorway, various fruits and vegetables on display in the shade of the awnings. The midday sun sent fire; heat swarmed from faded ochre walls, from the pale stone of the piazza.

'Hang on . . . I'll be with you in a minute.'

She was gone before he could reply; he turned to see her disappear back the way they had come. He stood, looking at the obelisk in the middle of the square, feeling foolish and irritated, conscious of the sun beating on the back of his neck.

She returned, walking quickly. She patted her shoulder bag, opened it. Inside he saw some tomatoes, a loaf of thick white bread and a bottle of mineral water. 'Lunch!'

'You're a fast mover. You disappear and reappear like you had cornered a fifth dimension.'

'I'm a trick of the light,' she said. 'Come on, the way to the Pincio terrace is just over there. I'll show you Keats's pad later!'

She moved ahead of him and, when she reached the balustraded terrace, raced into the shade of the trees. He turned, leaned on the balustrade to survey the square below.

At the top of Via Ripetta he saw a woman in an apron gesticulating to passers-by, and turning her head to gaze angrily around. Colm shaded his eyes with his hand to get a better view. The woman raised her head and swept the piazza and the terrace with her eyes.

When he rejoined Robin she was seated on a bench by a

shaded walk and had already split the loaf and was cutting the tomatoes into rough slices with a penknife. She waved. 'Grub's up!'

'How much was all this?' he asked, putting his hand in his pocket. He was so acutely aware of his own budget, that he wanted no mounting debts.

'All this?' She giggled. 'This stupendous feast?' She glanced at him with exasperation. 'Not much . . . Stop fussing. You can buy the dessert!'

She handed him his 'roll', sank small white teeth into her own, chewed with pleasure.

'God, food has a lot going for it!'

'Yeah . . .'

They swigged the water, leaned back, looked up through the bottle-green pines at the sky.

'I feel as though I know you, Irish!' she said suddenly and softly. 'I guess I knew you in a previous incarnation, but I can't remember which one.'

Colm, borne on a surge of levity, said: 'Last time around I was a worm!'

She gave a small shriek of laughter.

'What are you laughing at?'

'I've just remembered: last time around I was a bird!'

He glanced down at her face. 'So I'm in a lot of trouble . . . is that what you're trying to tell me?'

Colm fell silent, touched by some gossamer memory, whether of dream or reality he hardly knew. She grinned. He watched the way she saved the crumbs, gathering them in a scarf she took from her bag. 'For the birds,' she said.

On impulse he reached out and touched her hand. 'Robin,' he said. 'You wanted to see Florence, so how come we met on the road to Civitavecchia? It's the wrong direction!'

'I took the wrong road. Guy who gave me a lift wasn't going to Florence at all! He took my money – I had to get out of the car in a hurry – so I've very little left.'

Colm felt dismayed. He was lumbered with a penniless

girl. 'If you wanted to see Florence so much why didn't you go there direct?'

She thought for a moment. 'I took the plane to Rome. They told me it's easy to get to Florence from here, but I mucked it up.' She glanced at him. 'OK? Happy with the explanation or is there a lie detector test?'

He laughed, shrugged.

A police uniform could be seen through the pines, moving along the sandy path not far away. Robin saw it, started, whipped the ethnic scarf which had been minding the crumbs, and tied it quickly over her head. Colm instinctively blocked the speculative gaze of the policeman, by leaning over her. When he looked up the uniform had gone.

'Why were you afraid of the policeman?'

'What policeman?'

'You put on your scarf . . .'

'Look,' she said patiently, 'girls put on scarves to save themselves from the sun. Ever hear of heat stroke?'

He regarded the sunburn at the nape of her neck. 'Pity you weren't more aware of it when you got that!'

She looked at him sideways, but her eyes reverted to the uniform until it was out of sight. She had the look of a naughty child, expecting Nemesis.

I don't care what you have done, Roberta Robin McKay, Colm thought, beset by a certainty that this girl had not told him her full story. I don't care if you've murdered the President; I don't care why you have really run away.

The rain had stopped. Probably heading for Ireland, Colm thought from his comfortable train seat. Every cloud in the world headed, sooner or later, for Ireland. But here the sky was clearing fast. The flat fields of France sped by, sun-kissed fields of rape and wheat, long acres of vegetables blessed by sprinklers, old villages in huddles, sandstone towers of local churches, cattle and goats, small stations rushing towards him and as quickly left behind. He saw famous names on stations

– Bayeux, Caen, Lisieux. Here and there he saw a château, fairytale turrets, long avenues of poplars, tall and straight as masts. Beautiful France! He felt that at last his journey was really begun. Paris awaited him. He would stay there overnight and take the TGV in the morning. He would change at Lausanne, cut through Switzerland to Milan. After that it would only be a short hop down to Florence. Robin wouldn't be there, of course; that was not to be expected. But he would tread the same streets, stand outside their pensione, savour again for a moment the taste of being young.

Chapter Four

The train from Cherbourg got into Paris St Lazare in the mid afternoon. Colm took a taxi to the Hôtel Regina in the Place des Pyramides. He'd once stayed in this four-star hotel with Sherry, had booked a room there out of a half-hearted nostalgia, telling himself he liked the district.

'You have a choice,' the young receptionist told him as she perused his booking, 'a single room with a bathroom or a double room with a shower. Which would you prefer?'

He chose the double. He was used to a big bed. The porter took his case, escorted him in the lift to the first floor. The room was high ceilinged, the furniture elegant mahogany. The hotel whispered of *la belle époque*, the age of innocence when people assumed a future of enlightenment and never dreamt two cataclysmic wars would swallow up their children.

He looked around, thought of Sherry; the room was similar to the one they had shared on their last trip to Paris some two years before. Then he had taken her for granted, as much an unquestioned fixture as his house, his career, his stocks and shares. He missed her now, not the anguish of having lost someone deeply loved, but the absence of the known, the strange unease of being unfamiliar with his own life. It was as though he had left her in possession of the maps.

He wondered how she and Michael were as a couple; clandestine passion was one thing; indefinite close quarters was another, requiring either enduring love or skills and diplomacy. For a moment he imagined them together in bed, shied away from it. It conjured the realisation that he had never known what was nearest him, brought a swell of betrayal and rage. And rage, like every other emotion, he had striven to put behind him.

He had known Michael at school, one of the seniors when he was in first year, aloof, one of the gods. Later Michael had held a managerial position with a manufacturing company, been made redundant, and had opened an interior design business. Sherry had met him at a school reunion to which wives were invited. How long their affair had been going on before he rumbled it, Colm did not know. A year, perhaps more. Michael's own wife had died some four years earlier of cancer; he had two sons, one a solicitor and the other a newly qualified doctor. But he was financially straitened, had invested heavily in his struggling business, lived in a small apartment in Monkstown with a view of the sea. It was Michael who had spoken to him of their school days with nostalgia. 'They made men of us,' he said, nodding his head in anticipation of agreement. But when there had been no agreement, a recollection, which Colm recognised and hated, dawned in Michael's eyes. 'Oh,' he said suddenly, 'I forgot . . . of course in your case . . .'

But all of this was before Colm had returned unexpectedly early from a business trip and found Sherry and Michael asleep together in the matrimonial bed. He had looked at them for a while, saw how his wife's head was cushioned on Michael's breast, saw the satisfied sensuality, the tenderness. He had never seen that expression on her face, the relaxed trust of the child. He had left the house quietly, parked the car in a lay-by with a view of the entrance to his home and phoned on his mobile.

'I'm on my way home, darling!' he had said to a sleepy Sherry. 'Did you miss me?'

He had enjoyed her confusion, waited for the sight of Michael's car emerging from his gateway. It had appeared a few minutes later, speeding off in the opposite direction. He was surprised how little outrage he felt. There was no point in confrontation. He was not in a position to throw stones and, quite simply, he didn't care. Why am I so cold? he wondered. Once I saw the world with passionate interest; everything that impinged on my life mattered desperately. At what precise moment did all that involvement die? It's almost as though I ceased to be me!

Now he stood by the heavily curtained window and looked out at the Louvre and the traffic. What concerned him now was not Sherry and Michael, but this journey he was already regretting, this recent obsession with an interlude in his life which had returned to haunt him, unfinished business demanding resolution.

'Where were you at school?' the American girl had asked their first full evening in Rome. They were at a tourist restaurant, not the one recommended by Ferdinando the lorry driver, but one near the Stazione Termini, the city's mainline station. The tables, covered in white paper cloths, stood on the warm pavement. Colm, who had exercised frugality since his arrival in Italy, decided he could afford to stand her a meal. She looked as though she needed one, thin enough to have survived on bread and tomatoes since time began.

'I was at boarding school – a Diocesan college.'

'What's that?'

'The college for the diocese! It was just an old Georgian mansion converted into a school.'

'Did you like it?'

'Does anyone like school?'

'Good point!' She took a swig of beer. Blue eyes regarded him gravely above the glass.

'How long have you been here, Robin?' He did not want to talk about himself. He particularly did not want to talk about school.

'Four days.'

'How long are you staying?'

'Till I get tired of it.'

'Isn't it dangerous for a young girl to be wandering around alone?'

'Sure!' She shot him an arch look. 'But maybe not as dangerous as not wandering around alone!'

'I'm not dangerous!'

'Aren't you?'

'Of course I'm not . . . But do your parents approve of what you're doing?'

'More questions!' she exclaimed. 'I've got some as well . . . like where in Ireland do you come from, and what kind of a family do you have, and where are you at university?'

'That's quite a list!'

'I've got all night. I'm listening.' She grinned at him as she ate her minestrone. 'Go on!'

He watched the careful method with which she ate, every noodle cornered and demolished. Evidently she did not take food for granted.

'I come from County Roscommon, Ireland,' he said. Then he changed the subject. 'Why don't you tell me first about New York?'

Robin threw back her head, smiled. Her eyes lost their wistfulness and became merry. When she smiled, she seemed absurdly young.

'New York has five boroughs . . . but most of the action is in Manhattan. It's laid out precisely, not like European cities. But it has everything, shops, art galleries, museums, bars, banks. There's Greenwich Village and Chinatown and Little Italy. There's wonderful skyscrapers, the Chrysler Building, the Empire State . . .'

'It must take loads of money to live there.'

'Money sure helps! I can only speak in relative terms of course, as this is the first time I've done any serious slumming. But it lets me see how the other half lives.'

'Other half?'

'Well, the other ninety-five per cent . . .' she said.

Colm felt suddenly irritated. He took another swig of beer.

'Why are you so fixated on going to Florence?'

She shrugged. 'My Florentine blood, of course!'

'Be serious for once.'

'I am serious! I told you I was half Italian. I have Florentine blood. I got interested in the city when my art teacher told me about its history, gave me stuff to read. Did you know that in the Middle Ages the city was a democracy, in the days when nearly everywhere else was ruled by dukes and princes?'

'I don't know that it could be called a real democracy,' Colm said. 'There was too much power knocking around. What about the Medici; what about that mad berk Savonarola?'

'The monk who frightened them all to death with promises of hell fire . . . Who told you about him?'

'The Magic Wizard!' Colm said.

Robin gave him a careful look. 'The what?'

'A quiz game. When I was ten I got double pneumonia and was in bed for several weeks. My mother bought me a quiz game called "The Magic Wizard". One of the questions was "Who was Savonarola?" I asked my teacher, and on his next visit he brought me a book about medieval Italy. It had a picture of Savonarola.'

'What was he like?'

Colm remembered the plate in the heavy library book, the intense saturnine face. 'Queer . . . he fascinated me for a while . . .'

'Were you sick much when you were a kid?'

'Yes. I think everyone in the family, except my poor mother, was praying I would die and be done with it! The doctor had almost given me up. My mother might have done the same if Johnny Munroe hadn't called. He lived locally and was a bit weird. He came to see me, looked into the fire, turned to my mother and said: "He will live, missus . . . there are years ahead of him, and many troubles!"' Colm grinned. He remembered suddenly his last meeting with Johnny Munroe. 'In fact the last time I met him he encouraged me to come on

61

this journey . . . He seemed to know I was going away, without being told!'

'Someone probably had told him,' Robin said tartly. 'None of these weirdos are as weird as you think!'

Colm conceded that this might be true.

They wandered back to their hotel in the Via Palestra. He felt mellow. A bottle of beer had been included in the tourist menu, but they had ordered another one each. The night was warm. They decided to take a walk, around by the Colosseum and the Forum. Floodlit, they showed a startling face, antiquity in brilliant focus against the night. He held her hand. It felt small and dry, the skin surprisingly rough.

A group of youths came suddenly out of the shadow of a doorway, demanding money in broken English. Colm shrugged, raised his hands to indicate they had none.

'*Siamo poveri*,' Robin said, '*poveri studenti.*' Her voice was calm but her hand in Colm's became so tight that she hurt his fingers.

They looked at her, then back at Colm. '*E molto bella!*' the apparent leader of the pack said admiringly.

'*Si.*' Colm realised that she was beautiful with sudden proprietoriness, as though he had been personally complimented. But however calm he tried to remain, he knew his interrogators were predators of the night, hunting in packs, and he felt the rush of adrenaline. There was no possibility he and Robin could fight their way out of this. The youths outnumbered them three to one.

There was silence among these pirates of the darkness, as though the weight of some decision had to fall. The leader of the gang, face scarred, wary and calculating, gave some unspoken signal, and suddenly the pack was gone. Colm felt Robin's hand relax its grip.

'Did they scare you?' he asked.

'Scare me? Don't be silly . . . I don't scare!'

He flexed his hand to restore circulation. 'Well, at least

they didn't produce knives! And they seemed to accept that we had no money. You were very good, Robin, very cool, even if you did almost break my hand!'

She did not reply, but walked as though on eggs, turning her head abruptly with a sudden intake of breath when a cat moved behind them by the wall. She glanced up at him when he put a hand on her shoulder.

'It's all right! Why are you so jumpy?'

She had a shower in the bathroom, returned to the room already dressed for bed.

'There's only one dry towel left out there.'

He went to the bathroom, stood under the shower, soaped himself and watched the water whirl and, with a sucking sound, disappear through the plughole. He found the dry handtowel and rubbed himself, put on the clean pair of shorts. In the mirror he examined his body; it looked lean, wholesome, tanned. He wondered what she really thought of him; he wished he were taller, wished that his eyes did not look so earnest. How to be irresistible to women? It made him think of his attempt to seduce her that morning, and her reaction. He felt ashamed of his clumsiness. She hadn't taken to the master technique, and now they had an agreement. Not only that, but he did not want to jump her any more; he just felt she was a friend.

When he returned to the room he found her lying on the floor in a sheet bag, on top of both sleeping bags.

'Your turn for the bed,' she said crisply. 'I don't want special concessions.'

'Nobody said you were going to get them!'

She giggled. 'And I was so afraid you might be a gentleman . . .'

'You can have the bed if you want,' Colm said, repenting, but she said she didn't and he got into it, turned out the light. He heard her soft breathing, felt it as fragile and strangely companionable. Accustomed to solitude, he found her presence bizarre but oddly comforting. But he was still on edge from his encounter with the gang of youths, and found he could not sleep. The threat they had represented prompted memories he would do anything to evade.

'Well, Robin, tell me about yourself. I'd like to know a bit more about you.'

'You must have kissed the Blarney Stone!' Her voice was tired, childlike. 'I live mostly in New York, although my daddy has a house in New England. I am almost twenty-one. I would like to study Art . . .'

'You don't look twenty. When will you be twenty-one?'

'In a week's time, fifteenth September . . .'

'You have the same birthday as me! But I'll be twenty-two.'

'No kidding?' She laughed in the darkness. 'We should have a celebration!'

'But why won't you be at home for your twenty-first? Wouldn't they throw a party for you?'

'Sure . . .' she said after a moment's hesitation. 'All my friends, all my daddy's friends, you name it . . .'

'Tell me about your family?'

'My folks? . . . Corporate Daddy. House in New England; swimming pool; awful, boring, self-important friends, country club, slim gorgeous step-mommy, aged twenty-eight, who loves diamonds and hates my guts! Our apartment in Park Avenue overlooks Central Park. There's a roof garden. You can see the lake in Central Park . . .'

Colm felt a sharp stab of envy. He had heard of Park Avenue; he had heard of the super rich, of their jets and yachts and partying.

'Which part of New York is Central Park?'

'Manhattan! You've probably seen pictures of the skyscrapers. They're best seen from the air or from the Staten Island Ferry. And you must have seen pictures of the Statue of Liberty, holding up her torch . . .'

'Yes . . .' Colm said softly. 'Hope triumphant!'

Robin's voice was small in the darkness. She added after a

moment's silence: 'That's a nice way of putting it. I believe in hope!'

Colm was more touched than he wanted to acknowledge by the sad cadence of her voice, by the sudden sense of her loneliness, by all the things about her that didn't fit.

'But what happened to your own mother?' he asked after a moment.

'She died when I was nine.'

'I'm sorry.'

'So am I. Daddy would have traded her in by now anyway.'

'Would he?'

'Sure! Even the present model had better watch it. She has a Caesarian scar.'

'So you have a sibling?'

'I have a baby brother . . . which makes me surplus to requirements.'

'What's your step-mother's name?'

Robin hesitated. Then she said, 'Elizabeth Jane. I call her Lizzie sometimes . . . drives her nuts!'

'What does your father actually do?'

Robin was silent, as though she was drifting to sleep. Then she said, 'He owns a shipping company . . . thinks he's God . . . probably is! He has a yacht and all the paraphernalia . . . Course I can't stand all that stuff myself. He also has a private jet . . . bit of an extravagance, but Lizzie likes it. She made him paint it shocking pink to go with her favourite nail polish!' Then she added musingly, 'My daddy came up from nothing, you know, poor as a rat when he arrived back in the thirties.'

'From where in Ireland did you say he came?'

'From Listowel,' Robin said in a voice full of nostalgia. 'In what he called "the Kingdom of Kerry".'

'You're sensitive to lyrical turns of phrase . . .'

'At school they said I had the makings of a bad poet.'

'You wrote poetry?'

'Sure! Didn't you?'

'Real men don't write poetry,' he said gruffly. 'But right

now, my interrogator, I need to sleep!'

Robin was silent for a moment. Then she whispered, "Night . . .'

How everything came back when he really tried to find it, instead of escaping it! Colm thought. How everything was encapsulated in memory, tied into the neurons, held for ever. You might think you had forgotten, but it was there, buried, waiting its moment.

He looked through the window. The colour of the Paris sky had altered subtly with the approach of evening, deepened into hazy cobalt. Colm got up, ran a comb through his hair, put on his jacket, ventured out into the busy Place des Pyramides, crossed the Rue de Rivoli and found himself in a courtyard of the Louvre. A queue still lingered before the glass pyramid; he turned instead to the Tuileries gardens, walked with the evening sunshine on his face as far as the Place de la Concorde, where he could view the splendour of Paris. Fountains played on the very spot where Madame la Guillotine had once decapitated the French nobility; beyond them stretched the Champs Élysées; to his left was the gilded dome of Les Invalides, and to his right the Hôtel Crillon. He noted the magnificence around him coldly. He approved of splendour.

Retracing his steps in the gardens he lingered for a moment outside the Jeu de Paume, wondering if it was too late to see the exhibition. A young girl with long hair was sitting on the grass nearby, playing with a Siamese cat, teasing it with a ping-pong ball. The cat arched over the small, white sphere, patted it, jumped on it. Something somersaulted into recollection, something to do with Italy, heat and nausea, a girl and a black cat, a rooted feeling almost of *déjà vu*. It had nothing to do with Robin, he knew that, and yet for the moment it was powerfully evocative of that summer long ago. But it slipped from him before he could place it.

He went back to the hotel, changed his clothes, came

downstairs and dined at seven-thirty in the hotel restaurant. He had a window table and looked out directly at the back wall of the Louvre.

When he had dined he returned to his room and tried to watch television; but there was nothing interesting and the French was at the speed of light, so he turned it off. He lay on the double bed in his pyjamas, trying to fix the source of the fleeting memory that had returned to him outside the Jeu de Paume. Such a rag-bag of memories, jumble waiting to be sorted! It was central to whatever had drawn him on this pilgrimage.

He considered his reflection in the wardrobe mirror. This was Colm Nugent, this middle-aged man who looked younger than his forty-nine years, greying at the temples in what Sherry had assured him was a distinguished pattern. The youth who lived in him was invisible, but he was there, like an artefact buried under the rubble of the centuries. It was the youth Colm who had forced on him this journey.

'Robin,' he thought in a sudden fit of whimsicality. 'Do you remember how we wandered around Rome, how you were so curious . . . ? Do you remember that first evening in Florence? Will you be there, Robin, on Sunday the fifteenth, in the Piazza della Signoria as you promised? Will you come to meet me again?'

Silly sentiment, his mind assured him. The time is over.

Somehow he had imagined the future as a static place, where you reaped the rewards of work and nailed down security. He did not know that life was organic, ever-changing despite every determination of the will. He had had no clue then that he could not simply shelve the past; that he would marry someone called Sherry, the artistic girl who would eye him carefully every morning to divine his mood. He did not know that marriage would not exorcise old attachments, or that he would have a son called Alan. He did not dream that he would love Alan with all his soul, and never be able to show it. He could not foresee how his son would shine at school and never receive the praise he craved, trying desperately to please an implacable father.

'Seventy per cent! OK I suppose for the average boy, but I expect better things from you, Alan!'

Oh, the uncomprehending past, that could not know the bitter Nemesis when an only child, presented with a new bicycle on his thirteenth birthday, would build a ramp with a few planks he found in the garage and try to emulate Evel Knievel. And he had heard the cry, the last sound from his fearless child.

The blood, a thick blob from the nose, the eyes half open, the pulse erratic and then still. Roaring at the gardener to get an ambulance. Sherry had come screaming, incautious for once, her eyes wild, her face like chalk. Paddy, the young gardener, had run to do his bidding, sprinting across the lawn, leaping the flowerbeds and through the French windows to the phone. Colm did not remember who else had come: there were some visitors; but he had hunched there, stiff and silent over Alan's body, gathering him up, his lovely child, when the doctor said he was already dead. But even then he had not been able to weep.

Well, he thought, the world is cold and Alan is with God. Tomorrow is the second leg of this foolish journey, tomorrow I hit Milan and then Florence. The TGV will leave the Gare de Lyon at seven.

Why am I doing this? For a moment he wondered if he should abandon this journey, return home. But there was nothing at home now. He set the alarm on his small digital clock, and tried to sleep.

Chapter Five

Paola left the doctor's surgery in the Via Guelfa and dropped Pasquale home. He had been advised by the doctor to stay in bed for the day. He would study to the strains of pop music no doubt, an ability which always amazed her. The doctor had gently confirmed the outlook. An operation was definitely needed to replace the damaged heart valve. Why did this have to happen to us? Paola wondered, as she parked the car and rushed to her office. We were just recovering from Giovanni's death. Why can't life ever stay the same? But my boy will have his operation as quickly as possible, and by the best surgeon. As she waited for the lift she thought of the piece of land in Sicily with its view of the bay and Mount Etna, wondered how much it would bring her, shrugged away the disappointment that she would have to sell it before the pending re-zoning. Giovanni had been so sure that they would make a fortune from it. She composed herself, entered the office with a smile for the receptionist.

'*Buon giorno, Serena!*' she said, and Serena responded with the news that Signor Banderi, her editor, wanted to see her. Paola went straight to his office.

Antonio Banderi had a moustache. He growled in mock menace at Paola for being late, and then expressed concern for Pasquale. He congratulated her on her article on prostitution. It would be printed the following week, he said, when better photographs were available. Then he suggested a new assignment, an article on police corruption. Certain sources had come forward with information, would have to be interviewed.

'How would you like to review these?' he demanded as Paola was leaving, indicating a couple of books on his desk. One of them was entitled *Firenze del Cinquecento*, a work on Florence of the fifteenth century, something straight into her barrow. She loved this period of her city's greatness, when art and commerce flourished and the name de' Medici had become synonymous with political acumen and artistic patronage.

Paola took the books to her office, sat at her desk and phoned an estate agent and then her friend and lawyer, Cinzia. She told the latter that the plot of land in Sicily was now on the market.

'Pasquale?' Cinzia asked. 'How is he?'

'All right for the moment. The drugs are still working. But there's no room for complacency. The sooner he has the operation the better!'

The Gare de Lyon was uncrowded at seven in the morning. Colm perused the clicking *Départs* board, saw that the TGV left from *Voie A*, had a quick coffee at the snack bar, then found his carriage and reserved seat. Embarking alone on a journey which contained no element of duty, he was surprised at the sense of adventure.

As he walked down *Voie A* he examined the sleek train which shrieked of efficiency and modernity: and air conditioned to boot. Not like the train he had taken all those years ago from Paris to Turin, a sweaty affair with corridors, compartments, and its own ineffable brand of mystery. In fact there were two TGVs at the platform; one proclaimed its destination as Besançon and the other announced its terminus as Lausanne.

The TGV slid out of the station at seven-twelve precisely. Paris was seen momentarily as endless blocks of apartments, but soon the city was left behind and the train was knifing through the countryside. There was little sensation of high speed or sound. It was cool and comfortable. Colm hung his jacket from the hook by the window, looked out at the flat fields, the industries, the forest on his left, more fields and poplars, water towers, villages, pylons marching with great strides across the land. He glanced around at his fellow passengers, mostly business-suited men who opened their briefcases and began perusing papers. Some had lap-top computers. The man across the aisle from him was evidently an accountant. Colm began surreptitiously to examine his reading matter, a thick profit and loss account, deciphered it upside down, saw umpteen millions of francs and a deficit. The man suddenly focused polite, enquiring eyes on him, and Colm redirected his gaze to the scenery, the farmhouses in mellow brick, felt the train slow and stop in the middle of nowhere as it waited for another to pass. The land became hilly and wooded as they approached Dijon; he saw an old château surrounded by poplars, golden in the morning sun. His eardrums hurt as they entered the tunnel before Dijon; but, emerging, he saw with pleasure the town below and the lake with four white swans. The train pulled into Dijon-Ville.

Silvestro came into Paola's office at midday, kissed her hand in his courtly way.

'*Cugina mia!*' he said. 'May I be permitted to take you out for lunch?'

Paola hesitated. She regarded the handsome, smiling face of her cousin with a great deal of affection.

'I'll phone home, see if Pasquale . . .'

He nodded. She picked up the receiver, pressed out the number, heard Pasquale's voice.

'How are you?'

'Fine! I'm doing French at the moment. Tommaso is coming from the Liceo with tonight's homework.'

Tommaso was one of Pasquale's friends who also attended the Liceo, the classical school.

'I won't be home for lunch. There's pizza in the fridge. Tell Tommaso to help himself. Is that all right?'

'I'm not a baby,' Pasquale said. 'Of course it's all right.'

71

Are you tired, my son? Paola wanted to say. Will you eat properly and rest? But she knew from the timbre of Pasquale's voice that she would be courting rejection. She thought of her new guests, three of whom had arrived the night before. But they were out all day and unlikely to trouble Pasquale. She turned to Silvestro, smiled and said, 'I'm ready.'

Silvestro drove to Fiesole. He turned into the driveway of the Hotel Villa San Michele, the splendid five-star hotel with a terrace overlooking the valley and the city.

'Oh,' Paola exclaimed, 'this is unexpected!'

'Nothing is too good for my cousin . . .'

They had a drink on the terrace, wandered into the garden, inspected the fountain, plucked a lemon from a small tree, went to table. Paola chose from the menu, brill, green salad. Salvatore ordered *vitello tonnato*, chose the wine. He was a wonderful host, charming, attentive. Paola mused how good manners made life a delight, just as their absence made it a purgatory. But she was uneasy in his company. The chemistry he exuded was powerful. He was ready to commandeer her space, offer her love, glory in her body and then . . . What then? After she had been seduced by the promise and the promises, after she had allowed herself to play with the prospect of a full life, what then?

I am flesh and blood, she told herself. I can distance myself from the inevitable. I can enjoy the moment. She felt the pressure of his hand as it reached for hers across the table. '*Ti amo*,' he said softly.

Oh God, Paola thought, why do you tempt me!

Colm, comfortable in his train seat, distanced himself from the sensation that he had become a ghost on the fringes of the real world. All around him were business people, working on lap-tops, speaking quietly into cellular phones. The carriage was more a subdued office than a vehicle, he mused; such are the wonders of technology. He laid his head against the headrest, drew the curtain beside him a little to ease the light.

What had they done, day by day, he and Robin, until that final denouement in Florence? He closed his eyes, and searched into the labyrinths of the past.

When Colm had woken that next morning in Rome he found Robin already up, dressed and sitting by the window. She had a sketch pad on her knee, a pencil in her hand. She closed it, turned to him.

'Have a good sleep, Irish? Sweet dreams?'

'Can't remember my dreams.'

'You sure were grunting!'

Colm saw that her hair was newly washed, and that her eyes were smiling.

'Was I?' he said mildly. But a shadow darkened his face. He pulled himself out of bed.

'They were really very small grunts,' Robin said hastily, having divined sensitivity. 'Really!'

'It's OK. You just reminded me of school . . .'

'Why?'

'We slept in a dormitory . . . if you snored they let you know about it. Once they tied me up while I was asleep and drenched me.'

'Who's they?'

'The other boys . . .'

'Did they get into trouble?'

'No.' He laughed. 'Anyway, who'd blame them? You can't live with people who snore!'

'I'm sure glad I don't snore. Tell me about your school.'

'It was nothing special. A place called Clonarty . . . the former home of the Lords Montgomery and Moyne . . .'

'Sounds cool!'

'Well, I don't know about cool. But it was one thing . . .'

'What?'

'A toughening experience. Made a man of me.'

'That's great!'

He smiled at her again and went to find the bathroom.

73

Later, in Trastevere, the pigeons strutted across the piazza on crimson feet. Colm and Robin had found Ferdinando's eating place, 'La Rivetta', and were sat at a table in the noonday sun. Colm took his map out of his rucksack, spread it out on the table as they waited for their orders.

'Where would you like to go to next?' she asked.

'There's so much to see! I don't want to hold you up if you're in a hurry to see Florence.'

'You're not holding me up. I'm holding myself up!' She straightened, laughed, made a face.

He smiled at her antics. 'It must be nice to be rich! It'll be years before I can afford to come back to Italy. The only reason I got here at all was because my mother left me some money. Not a lot,' he added hastily, 'just enough.'

Robin chewed on a toothpick. 'But even though my folks are loaded I haven't got a bean.'

'I know. And the Mafia are after you! And your rich daddy.'

Her eyes flickered, but she smiled. 'So what!'

'Don't worry. Lunch is on me.'

Robin's eyes became very soft, as though she were on the verge of tears. But Colm's head was bent, his eyes examining the map. 'You see . . .' he said, pointing. 'There's the *autostrada del sole*. We could hitch to Naples . . . see Pompeii and Herculaneum!' When she did not respond he raised his eyes and regarded her for a moment. 'Or are you mad keen to go to Florence first?'

'It's just that I promised myself I'd go there . . . a couple of years ago – when I was a kid.'

'And I suppose you're not a kid any more.'

'No! I told you, I'll be twenty-one soon!'

Colm studied the soft angle of her chin and decided it had never seen nineteen, much less twenty.

'Stop lying. More likely you'll be twelve soon!' he exclaimed with sudden irritation.

'Eighteen actually,' she replied after a moment with a wide grin, looking at him from the corner of her eye. 'If you gotta have the truth!' For a moment she reminded him of Kattie, the impish eyes, the small, irregular teeth.

'I want to see Florence too. But Pompeii and Herculaneum are fascinating – they were covered by volcanic dust and lava about two thousand years ago . . .'

Robin said: 'Yeah, but other things are more interesting! There's this bridge . . .'

Colm waited. When she didn't continue he demanded, 'What bridge?'

'When I was thirteen,' Robin said in the tone of one who wished she had kept her mouth shut, 'I found a page torn from a travel brochure lying on the sidewalk. It had a photograph of the weirdest bridge . . . the Ponte Vecchio in Florence.' She glanced at him defiantly. 'It's a bridge with shops. It fascinated me – I'd never seen anything like it. I want to walk on it, stand on it! But you go to Pompeii and I'll go to Florence!'

He regarded her indulgently. 'Aren't you the intrepid one!'

'What does that mean?'

'Courageous.'

'Am I really?'

'You sure are . . . seventeen years old and wandering off to Italy on your own . . . just because you saw a photograph of some old bridge. Your father must be worried sick!'

'Not his style!'

Colm heard something in her voice he thought he recognised; a timbre which had rubbed shoulders with rejection, or something worse. In Robin there was an episodic nervousness which was very close to fear, like someone picking her way through an earthquake zone. He was subsumed in a sudden surge of protectiveness. 'OK,' he said. 'I'll go with you to Florence. Pompeii and Herculaneum can wait!'

Spaghetti carbonara arrived with side salad, two beers and a basket of bread. They ate; conversation ceased. They were in the shade of a sun umbrella, but beside them the hot light played on walls with crumbling plaster, old brick, and on the

75

fountain in the centre of the piazza which gushed water upwards and caught it in a great stone basin. Old buildings looked down on them, peeling shutters protected the interiors from the noonday fire. The scene was timeless serenity, baroque peace.

Robin finished her meal and leant back, adjusting her sunglasses, observing the scene around them in silence. The piazza was torpid; at another small restaurant a few yards away people ate leisurely lunches in the shade. She gathered the breadcrumbs towards her and made them into small mounds. Then she flicked them gently at the pigeons and a number of house sparrows which arrived as though waiting their cue.

Robin watched them peck and bob for the food.

'God, it's so wonderful here!' She whispered this. Colm heard the emotion in her voice. He sat in silence, inscrutable behind his sunglasses.

'Thanks for the meal,' she said gravely after a moment, turning to him. 'You are kind and generous. When I come into my millions I'll remember you!'

He laughed, said she was welcome, but that she could hold on to the millions when she got them. 'I'll make my own!'

'Yes, I think you will. You've got what it takes. It must be the toughening experience you had in that school of yours.'

'Oh, that,' Colm said, 'was just a bit of hyperbole! You wouldn't want to take everything I say seriously.'

Robin waited for him to continue, but when he did not she said, 'Ah, talk to me, for Chrissake, and don't be so bloody pompous!' Then she added archly, as though she would provoke in him some kind of self-disclosure, 'Tell me about the first time you fell in love.'

Colm glanced at her in surprise. She was so good at projecting a hard-bitten exterior that the word love on her lips seemed incongruous. But its articulation contained an element of vulnerability, as though she were a child seeking verification that love existed.

'Or maybe you never fell in love . . . ?' she added with a shrug. 'I don't care either way!'

'Did you?' Colm demanded. 'Ever fall in love yourself? You don't seem the type!'

Robin was silent. Colm felt he had hit a nerve, without knowing why.

'Why don't I seem the type?'

'Ah, you're too strong for any of that crap!'

'As a matter of fact,' Robin said, 'I fell in love with my cute art teacher. He told me about Italy, about Botticelli, and the other great artists, and he knew all about the Ponte Vecchio . . .'

Colm made an interested noise. 'And what else did this paragon teach you?'

'If you tell me about your love affair,' Robin said primly, 'I'll tell you about mine!'

Colm had a decision to make. He could tell her some of the story, or he could shut up. He thought of Kattie Clohessy. Part of him longed to talk, to unburden at least some of it. Robin was a stranger; she represented an open ear that would soon pass out of his life.

'When I was twelve,' Colm said shortly, 'I fell for a girl called Catherine Clohessy.' He glanced at his companion who looked at him encouragingly. 'It was the year before I was sent away to school. Catherine was my sister's friend. I even wrote her love poems!'

He expected a snort of derision but she just said wistfully: 'That was lovely . . .'

'Those particular poems,' Colm said drily, 'acquired a history!'

Christ, he thought angrily, what am I talking about this for? I don't want to bloody remember. I just want to forget.

Once Colm's life had been a very simple place. His home a country farmhouse, his mother, Maura, busy in her wrap-around apron, loving the child for whom she had fought with

Death: 'How are you, *a cushla*? Sit down and tell me how you got on today!'

The flat countryside around had only enough intermittent rise in the land to save it from being a plain. The fields were separated by stone walls; the land on the farm was reasonably good, carefully tended over several generations, generously fertilised. The grazing was abundant on most of the hundred acres, although the low-lying fields bordering the Sureen were flooded in winter. The daffodils came in spring to the strip of woodland at the edge of the farm, known in Irish as the Seomra Mór. On summer days the sunlight would move from one side of the barnyard to the other and flit across the fields; at harvest the breeze would carry the warm scent of new-mown hay. A tribe of wild cats lived in the woods and came to the house for food in winter. Once a cat shoot was embarked on to cull them

'Poor cats!' Colm had said. He hadn't been on the shoot. His father and Liam and Alice had gone. He wasn't very well. His father hated him not being well, could hardly contain his irritation, his disappointment that his wife's love should be almost exclusively channelled to the sickly first fruit of her womb.

'They all have cat flu, *a ghrá*,' his mother told him, bringing him his lunch on a tray. 'Sure 'tis only a kindness to put the creatures down!'

There was bickering, jealousy, each of his siblings casting an eye on the land. Liam, hardy and hardworking, would get it, not Alice, who suffered from the irredeemable complaint of being female.

'Don't be annoying me about all that,' Mrs Nugent said to Alice. 'Sure you'll be getting married and then you'll live in your husband's place!'

'I mightn't get married. I mightn't want to live in my husband's place.'

The storms between mother and daughter had whorls and patterns. Alice was challenging her mother's perspectives. Her mother wanted them left the way they were. But Alice loved her fiercely and her challenges were cries for attention and respect, a yearning for visibility.

At her mother's deathbed, a year after his expulsion from Clonarty, Alice stared at Colm, white-faced and accusing, blaming him because otherwise she might have blamed herself.

Liam and his father blamed Colm too. Their bitter silence said: When your mother was alive you monopolised her with your endless bloody illnesses. Now she's gone and we'll never have her. There'll never be a time when she'll turn to us . . .

And the unwitting precipitant of all of this sorrow had been little Catherine Clohessy, Alice's friend.

In later years Colm would wonder what colour had her hair been as a child? In later years she put a copper rinse in it, but in those early days it was actually nondescript, a mouse brown without pretensions.

Eleven years old, arriving for the weekend from Kilgarret, Kattie would smile at Colm out of merry blue eyes.

'Howa'ya, Colm!' Later she might whisper, 'Let's go to your castle.'

Colm's 'castle' was a collection of huge rocks in the pasture, one above the other, ice-age detritus, shaped like a small fortress. They were covered with lichen, had mossy crannies. The place was his keep and his refuge. Kattie Clohessy had tracked him down at an early age, sat beside him, listened to him tell her stories of Finn McCumhaill and other great heroes from Irish mythology, her small face still, eyes wise, hands gravely folded in her lap. They had hidden from the grown-ups when it was time for her to leave, had skulked among the rocks until Alice had come to find them. 'Ah, come on, Kattie; what do you want to play with a boy for!'

Sometimes, if he was quick, Colm was able to hide there when Father Doran called. Father Doran often came to the house. Mrs Nugent greeted him like royalty, offered him sherry and cake, made tea. If evasive tactics were unsuccessful, Colm would be left alone with him in the parlour. The priest would question him about spiritual matters, warn him about the impending trials of adolescence. Colm didn't want to talk about his bad thoughts, or whatever they were supposed to be, but his tongue always seemed to twist in his mouth, and he stifled the words before he could utter them. Clerical power was a given, like the seasons and the certainty of death. Father Doran, the ascetic priest for whom Colm often served Mass, had marked him out as a potential candidate for the seminary, and consequently treated him as a neophyte in the arcane world of ecclesiastical politics. 'We'll make a bishop of you yet, Colm!' There was a conspiratorial air to all of this, priest to potential priest.

'Where's Colm gone . . . skiving off again . . .' Alice might say, quickly hushed by her mother.

'Whist now, can't you . . . he's inside in the parlour with Father Doran . . .'

Having saved him from the grim reaper on successive occasions, Maura Nugent could not help her pride in her clever son; she was certainly blind to his siblings' jealousy, blind to her own partiality, blind to her husband's need to be more than provider and barely tolerated sexual partner.

Maura's hope, never articulated in so many words, coloured the air around her. Colm would become a priest, and then she would have achieved the ultimate, have given a son to God. Did she dream of kneeling before her child for his blessing on the day of his ordination? She often examined the photographs in the paper, the tired parents, grey heads bowed, on their knees before their son.

But Colm did not want to be a priest. His mind was elsewhere; when he was twelve it was with Kattie sleeping and waking. But he could not say this to his mother. She had shielded him from his father's ire when he proved too sickly to help on the farm. 'That boy will be a priest someday . . . So leave him alone! God has a special place for him!'

Sundays saw her dressed in good coat and hat. Her husband Tom would get out the old Ford Prefect and they would all

80

drive off to Mass. The car had a distinctive sound: the silencer was gone. Tom saw no reason why he should put his hand in his pocket for another one. Occasionally the car backfired, frightening the horses pulling traps, causing them to buck in the traces.

But, for Colm, the highlight of Sunday afternoons was when Kattie Clohessy came with her parents, driving down the avenue in the Clohessy Austin which did not stutter or backfire, and which had a rotund boot like a great bottom. It was on one such Sunday afternoon that she had gone with him fishing for pinkeens and had, during the silence, while the home-made rod slanted into the river, and the sun spun patterns over the fields behind them, and the beeches whispered, leaned over and kissed him.

The Master, Mr Roche, announced to Tom and Maura Nugent that Colm was a definite scholarship prospect. 'That boy will go far. Mark my words! He works things out and he remembers everything.'

At the age of ten, confined to bed for months by rheumatic fever, which had followed pneumonia in a matter of months, Colm read from morning to night, devoured everything given to him, puzzled out maths problems in his head, astonished his teacher when he called. Mr Roche had taken to calling almost daily to oversee his star pupil's progress, bringing him library books because he quickly outstripped everything on the curriculum. Propped up, nothing expected of him except that he recover, Colm honed his intellect, and did it in large part to impress his wiry, hardworking father who hated sickly children.

In the end he had won a grudging respect. His father recognised that there was more than one kind of effort. He also knew the way to fortune and worldly preferment was through education.

When Colm won his scholarship to secondary school there was a celebration. His mother boiled a ham, invited the Master,

81

Father Doran, and the neighbours. They discussed which school he should attend.

'Boarding school is good for boys,' Father Doran said. 'Gets them to jump to the bell!' The company laughed. The men had been drinking whiskey, the women sherry. Their faces shone.

Colm felt proud. He also felt despair. He would be miles from his beloved and would only see her during the holidays.

'Clonarty College is the place for him,' Father Doran said. 'One of the best schools in the country. You should make an appointment at once to see the Rector. I'll make it for you if you like?'

When the meal was over Colm walked into the road. He did not go to his 'castle' where they might look for him, but took a walk along the nearby boreen as far as the ruined Norman keep which was on Johnny Munroe's five acres, near the stone wall which divided Johnny's plot from the farm. He sat with his back against the ancient stones of the keep, his mind in too much turmoil even to think. He heard the whisper of motor cars from the main road, and the sudden staccato braying of the old man's donkey which nearly frightened the life out of him. He did not know how long he had been sitting there, watching the play of light and shade across the fields, before he became aware of another presence. It was Johnny Munroe himself. He was seated on the truncated remains of a fallen tree and was staring into the distance.

Colm started. 'Hello, Johnny . . . I didn't see you.'

'Grand day,' Johnny said, adding after a moment in which he turned and scrutinised the boy with his strange eyes, 'So they're for sendin' you off?'

'Yes.'

Colm waited for the old man to congratulate him, but while Johnny moved his lips as though in private conversation with himself, he said nothing.

'Clonarty College!' Colm said, rising. He was uneasy in this company.

'Be careful, child . . .' the old man said. 'Give your trust to no one. Do not hurry to pull grief upon you!'

When Colm got home he told his mother about this encounter.

'That Johnny Munroe is three sheets in the wind! Don't take a bit of heed of him!'

Clonarty College, diocesan boys' secondary school, occupied one hundred and fifty acres of parkland. A limestone Georgian mansion, the former seat of the Earls of Montgomery and Moyne, it was reached by a long and winding driveway from the main road. The back of the great house, which faced south, was bordered by a balustraded terrace, where stone urns were inscribed in memory of two dogs, a former owner's whimsy. This terrace, in turn, overlooked a sunken garden. The house had a beautiful entrance hall with black and white tiles, and a magnificent staircase sweeping up to a circular landing.

When Colm arrived with his parents for the initial interview, they came through the pillared portico into the wide hall, were shown into the library, a room covered from ceiling to floor in books with old dark leather bindings. There was a fine marble fireplace with an overmantel; tall windows looked on to the terrace. Colm felt his mother's intake of breath, his father's dour approval as he surveyed his surroundings, his tweed cap in his hand. He loved this sense of his father's impressed astonishment; it came on a small surge of triumph and vindication.

The Rector put his hand on Colm's shoulder. 'We hear great things of you, Colm!'

He was glad his father was listening. For a moment he felt visible to this dour parent, knew he would never let him down, felt the surge of his own power. He had managed all this, he thought as he looked around him, alone. Something as easy as studying was the golden key.

Study was second nature to Colm; it had sustained him during the long months of illness, when he had lost his isolation in the minds of others, in poetry with its mystical cadences, in the problems of mathematics. Denied a normal childhood, he had found life, movement, challenge and creativity between the covers of a myriad books. But because of it, he had also, without being aware of it, absorbed Victorian perspectives, unyielding precepts to do with duty and honour.

'He won't let us down,' Colm's mother said to the Rector, looking at her son in worship. 'He is an exceptional boy . . . and I don't say this just because he is my son!' Tom Nugent shifted uneasily, but the Rector merely nodded.

They were shown the school. The dormitories and classrooms, the spartan gym, were housed in what had once been the old stables. The infirmary, the chapel and the study halls were in the big house itself, where the priests lived. As they were conducted down a shining first-floor corridor to the chapel, they passed an open door. They glanced in; the room was large, comfortably appointed with a circular table and armchairs.

'The Community Room,' the Rector said, 'where we have our communal life . . . Each of the community has his own study, of course, where he can pursue his work.' He gestured to a succession of mahogany doors, some adorned with small, printed names.

The Stations of the Cross were hung along the corridor. Jesus, persecuted and burdened, dripped blood and sweat. The chapel was small, silent, smelt faintly of incense. A few priests knelt in prie-dieux, reading the Holy Office. A pair of marble angels knelt, one on either side of the altar. The altar itself was white marble with a gold and white cloth. The golden tabernacle door shone. The Rector invited his guests to kneel and say a short prayer. They complied, first genuflecting before the altar.

'Thank you very much, Father,' Maura Nugent said as they were leaving. 'We can see that Colm will be in excellent hands!'

'Good,' the Rector said, nodding urbanely. 'I promise you

we'll take good care of him. We'll see you on the second of September then, Colm.'

A well-fleshed priest in a soutane came through the front door of the mansion and passed them in the hallway. He glanced at Colm and then at the Rector.

'Father Madden . . .' the Rector said. 'Meet one of your new pupils . . . Colm Nugent.'

Colm shook the extended hand, felt the aura of pleasant condescension and robust physicality, found himself looking into a pair of slightly bloodshot grey eyes. Father Madden shook hands with his parents: 'I'll be Colm's housemaster,' he said. 'We have a house system . . . provokes an atmosphere of healthy competition . . . keeps the boys on their toes.'

'Father Madden is an author,' the Rector went on. 'He is an expert on early Irish history.'

Colm knew his parents were impressed. 'How wonderful to write books,' his mother said.

'Keeps *me* on my toes!' Father Madden said with an expansive laugh, and moved away, with a brief parting pat to Colm's head.

Colm felt the touch. He saw his parents smile and nod, smile and be charmed, smile and be proud. But for a moment something like a shadow touched his own soul, something which swooped and enveloped him, a foreknowledge, a small taste of death.

When they got home Colm's father put the car away. He was humming. Maura Nugent bustled into her kitchen, doffed her coat, donned her apron, and started preparing the evening meal. Liam and Alice sat at the table, all agog to hear about the day. Packy Flynn, who had just finished the milking, came into the kitchen to wash his hands and listened too, avid for news of the wider world.

'Well, be the hokey!' Packy exclaimed, taking off his dirty cap and putting it in its appointed place on the windowsill, before seating himself at the back table for his tea. 'Isn't it grand entirely to be off to a school the like o' that! But what I do wonder is this: what do thim priests do with thimsels of an evenin'? All those grown men sittin' around lookin' at each other. There's somethin' terrible queer about it!'

'Ah, don't be going on like that, Packy!' Maura Nugent said sharply. 'They're not like everyone else; they're holy men.'

'If you say so, ma'am,' Packy said, muttering *sotto voce*: 'But they're men all the same!'

The uniform was bought in Dublin, grey pullover, grey shirt and striped tie. For the first time Colm wore long trousers, the mark of manhood; he felt his heart lift with pride when he saw his reflected self.

A new trunk and a list of other necessaries were bought in Clohessy's. Dan Clohessy served them in person, gave a good discount.

'Good luck, Colm,' Kattie whispered to him as the purchases were brought out and placed in the boot of the car. 'Don't work too hard . . . Write to me.'

He smiled at her. He thought she looked lovely. She had grown and was nearly as tall as he was. Her chest had small contours, where it had once been flat.

'I will . . .'

She stood outside the shop and watched them drive away down the main street of Kilgarret. Colm looked back until Clohessy's and the waving Kattie were out of sight. He waved himself. He wanted to put his hand out of the window, but his mother said he would be in a draught. But he looked back at her, the smiling girl, standing there beside the hanging wellingtons and the boxes of boots, until the car turned the bend in the main street.

The farmhouse at Ballykelly buzzed with activity. The parlour was made over to the business of packing. Colm's trunk lay in the middle of the floor. It was carefully packed with his new blankets, sheets, table napkins, cutlery, pyjamas, dressing-gown, slippers, towels, toilet things, indoor shoes, rugby boots, spare grey pullover and long pants, shirts. The scholarship did not extend to all the incidentals, but Colm's father had not complained as he laid out money for all the extras.

Maura Nugent sang snatches of songs – '*Che sera sera*', a hit from many years before – was gay, like a young girl. Thomas Nugent seemed relaxed. He looked around him at the visible signs of his son's thrust towards excellence. He said gruffly on the evening before Colm was due to leave, with the demeanour of one who had to acknowledge effort and success: 'Fair dos to you, son!' nodding his head as was his wont when any grave matter required his judgement.

Thomas Nugent's expansiveness continued on the drive to his son's new school. 'You've earned a chance that will set you up for life, Colm. Remember that!'

Maura stayed at home on this occasion. There was the dinner to get for some workmen who had been drafted in to help with the potato picking and she could not justify her absence, even though Moll Flannery from a nearby farm had come in to help. But Colm saw tears in his mother's eyes as she kissed him goodbye. He stood in the yard by the laden car and looked back at her in the kitchen doorway. Each wanted to embrace the other. But the family was looking on; Packy was looking on.

'Goodbye, my son. God bless you!' Maura said in a firm voice.

An hour later the old Ford Prefect turned in the massive gates of Clonarty College.

Clonarty had an air of fête. Fleets of cars were parked in what had been the stable yard where boys and parents were milling. Luggage was piled on the cobbles and was being carried upstairs to the dormitories. Boys' voices were loud with greetings for old classmates. Into the midst of this Colm's father drove his noisy car, stopped, removed the trunk from the boot. Some boys stared. Colm got out, looked around and met curious eyes. He had the sensation of being silently vetted, his father and the car inspected. His father looked around awkwardly, took his son by the shoulders in a gruff paternal farewell.

'We'll drop over to see you in a few weeks. Work hard, use your time well. Remember, time is like money . . . once it's spent it's gone.'

So it began, the quasi military discipline of boarding school life: up at seven, to bed at nine-thirty; classes, games, recreation; all the minutes in every day accounted for, taught by priests in white collars and long soutanes. Colm found himself in a class of twenty-eight, many of whom had known each other in the junior school. His house was St Finbar's. There were four houses in all, named for different saints; their league tables were posted in the school hall.

He quickly realised that in the new pecking order he was fair game. He did not shine on the rugby or soccer pitch; he was uncertain in his new milieu among confident peers. No longer did his academic prowess make him the automatic star of the class. No longer did whispered praises, such as those the Master had often confided to his mother, come to his ears.

Boarding school was not as he had imagined it would be. It was a colder and lonelier place than he had envisaged. But he set out to show his mettle. He shone at English, particularly essays and poetry; he enjoyed maths, loved history and geography. He was well in advance of the class. The time spent with books in his sick bed had given him an unbeatable edge.

In geography class Father Canning introduced the study of Italy, asked if anyone could tell him anything about it. He unrolled a big map, hung it from the board.

'Where do you think the wealth of Italy is concentrated, boys? Hands up!'

Colm put up his hand. It was the only one raised.

'The Lombardy plain is the source of Italian agricultural wealth,' he said. 'They don't have a lot of good land; the Apennines, the backbone of Italy, runs down almost the length of the country. But there's manufacturing mostly concentrated in the north, and of course they have a big tourist industry . . .'

'Have you ever been there, Colm?' Father Canning said, taken aback at the quality of the answer from a first-year boy.

'No, Father. I just read a lot about it. I wanted to see where Pompeii and Herculaneum were after I read about them . . . you know, the places that were destroyed by Vesuvius . . .'

'Can you show them to us on the map?'

Colm stood up, went to the map, pointed to Naples and said Pompeii and Herculaneum were just south of it, reached up to put his finger on their approximate location.

'Now show us the backbone of Italy.'

Colm drew his finger along the line of the Apennines.

'What are the most important cities in Italy?'

'Rome is the capital; Milan is the manufacturing capital, and then there's Turin. But Florence is very important too. It's got lots of art galleries and old churches.' He pointed. 'There it is!'

'And what do you know about Florence?' Father Canning asked, sounding a bit astonished.

'It was a Republic at one time. Then a rich family called the Medici became rulers, and they helped artists and sculptors. Oh . . . there was a monk who used to terrify everyone with his sermons during the Middle Ages, until they all came out and burnt their luxuries. Eventually he annoyed them so much that they burned him too!'

'Savonarola?'

'Yes.'

'Well done!'

Colm sat down triumphantly. But there was no accolade from the class, only a subterranean murmuring, a kind of hiss. He was about to learn something about the law of the jungle – the survival of the fiercest. You kept your mouth shut in the jungle and kept your head down. The only knowledge required of you in the jungle was that you knew your place. Colm did not know it, but was about to learn it.

* * *

'Are you asleep, Colm?' Robin's tentative voice said beside him. The sun had moved and the umbrella no longer protected her shoulders. He saw the sunlight on the healing sunburn.

'No.'

'You were going to tell me about your poems . . . you said they had a history, and then you stopped. Are you all right?'

'Of course I'm all right!' Colm muttered, aware of the light on the cobbles and the serenity of this place. 'Why wouldn't I be?'

'I dunno. There's no need to take the head off me.'

'I was just trying to think,' Colm said. This was not true. He was just trying to stem the internal panic which was threatening to close his throat.

In the first year at Clonarty, Willy O'Dwyer, the biggest boy in the class, ruled the roost. He had a proud, sensual mouth, an acid tongue and deep-set eyes. A demon on the rugby pitch, he was feared because his need to dominate made him invincible; what his strength did not accomplish for him, his tongue did.

'What are you gazing at, you little twerp?' he asked loudly when he caught Colm studying him.

Colm fell back automatically on the put-down used with his siblings. 'The cat can look at the queen!'

He had often said this to Alice; the last time she had retorted, 'I'm glad you appreciate the relative importance of our positions.'

This should have taught him to reconsider his wisecracks, but the retort was out again before he could think. He gritted his teeth inwardly, watching the burly boy before him with uncertain dread.

There was subdued laughter. Willy glowered; his lip curled. But his response was pre-empted by the clattering of seat hinges and the chorus of 'Good morning, Father!' as the class rose for Father Madden. Colm missed the venomous look O'Dwyer shot him from narrowed eyes.

He worked hard; it was second nature. As the days went by his academic prowess became increasingly startling. Father Madden, nicknamed 'the Goat', whom Colm had first met on his introductory visit, took the class for English. He smiled thinly when Colm recited *Morte d'Arthur* by heart, the only boy in the class to be word perfect.

'Pray for my soul, more things are wrought by prayer

'Than this world dreams of . . .'

When he came to the last line:

'. . . And on the mere the wailing died away,' Colm felt the cadence of the words, the pleasure they gave him, prick their way along his backbone.

'Good!' the priest said. 'You've certainly shown up this shower of layabouts.'

Father Madden regarded him with curious eyes. When Colm met them, he found in them a private speculation which he could not read.

Later, when he heard the boys refer to him as 'Swotty Nugent', he knew he had made a cardinal error, that he was branded, categorised, set apart. He would have done better to have aped stupidity.

His comfort was his passion for Kattie. He could not write it to her; his letters were handed up open, were read by his housemaster. It would be silly anyway, as her parents might read his missives. But in his loneliness his love grew into something all encompassing. He vented it in verses of poetry, writing them into his diary when he had finished prep. Someday, he thought, I may show them to her. Someday I may even be a poet, get my poems published in the paper! He dwelt on this with pleasure, the thought of getting his picture in the paper alongside his poems, imagining her face!

In Clonarty College the strap was not spared; it was applied to hands or buttocks, mostly the latter, a thick leather weapon inspiring terror and known as 'the Biff'. Colm escaped the attentions of the Biff for several weeks, became presumptuous enough to think he would escape it for ever.

One evening he found some magazines in his dormitory locker the like of which he had never dreamed existed. He did not know who had put them there. The magazines were filled with photographs of beautiful naked women. An explanatory sentence accompanying each photograph referred to the women in tones of triumphal glee, implicitly as fools from whom something precious was being stolen. The pages were filled with the thrill of plunder, with the illicit ecstasy of having disempowered and demeaned the naturally powerful, a perspective that oscillated between hatred and revenge.

One young woman had a rope around her neck. Another, with enormous breasts, referred to as a law student, was mocked with having aspirations to the Bench.

But Colm enjoyed the pictures with guilt and disbelief; he saw the bare breasts swelling, the coy smiles, the pouting lips. He looked at these wonders under the bedclothes with the aid of a torch. They fuelled his fantasies through many a night: did Kattie look like that under her clothes? He tried to remember the burgeoning contours of her chest. He dreamed of opening the buttons on her blouse, unhooking her brassiere, touching the flesh of her breasts. Were breasts soft or were they hard? Did they have smooth round bones inside them to give them that shape? He wasn't sure, longed to find out, drowned repeatedly in nocturnal sensual possibilities, until he was hardly able to stir when the bell rang in the morning.

The naked women intruded on his study time, swirled in his brain even at Mass, turned his life upside down. His work deteriorated. But caution intruded eventually. He knew the magazines were perilous and promised himself he would get rid of them. He would have preferred to keep them for ever, so that he could return to them again and again, a cornucopia overflowing with sensual stimulus. This made him hesitate, as did his inability to decide where he could dump them that would be safe from discovery. But his hesitation proved fatal.

After breakfast one morning his classmate John Hegarty

whispered to him, 'There's been a locker bust!'

Colm felt his heart stop. A 'bust' was a locker raid carried out by the prefects, designed to find any illicit belongings, such as cigarettes, beer, or improper books. He knew he was in serious trouble, waited all morning for the dreaded summons. It came at midday while he was in maths class.

'Father Madden wants to see Nugent in his study, Father!'

They were doing geometry. He had been brought to the blackboard to work out Pythagoras's theorem for the class. 'The square of the hypotenuse is equal to the sum of the squares on the other two sides . . .' Colm had drawn the configuration on the board. Now his teacher grunted with irritation, but he nodded to Colm who put down the chalk obediently and left the room.

Father Seamus Madden had his room in the 'priests' corridor', the long polished landing on the first floor of the mansion, which led to the chapel, where Colm had first walked in the company of his parents.

The study door had a small printed cardboard slip bearing the priest's name. When Colm knocked and entered he saw that his housemaster had the pornographic magazines in a pile on his desk, and he blushed to the roots of his hair. The priest gestured with his hand, but did not look up, ostensibly busy with an essay he was marking. Colm waited, glanced around the study at the bookcase, the marble fireplace with the turf fire, the worn leather armchair, the tall window with eight panes against which the rain was spitting.

Father Madden ignored Colm for a few more moments, before leaning back in his chair and regarding his pupil. He had a short neck and the white dog collar bit into the ample flesh of his chin. His face was red.

'Nice reading material, Nugent,' he said dangerously, indicating the magazines. Then he gathered them up and threw them into a drawer, a small heap of lovely breasts and bottoms and winsome pouting faces thrown in beside the breviary and the Rules of the Order.

'They'll be burnt. How dare you bring dirt like this . . . dirty women . . . into this school!' He was breathing heavily, emanating contempt for these women, for all women. 'You come here, to one of the best schools in the country, like some kind of rodent-carrying plague. Where did you get them, you filthy brat?'

'I found them in my locker.'

The priest got out of his chair, drew himself up. He seemed very tall in his black soutane, God's wrath personified. Although Colm dared not look in his face he realised at once that the priest felt the response as flippant, a challenge. But Colm seldom lied, was used to being believed.

He saw Father Madden take a thick leather strap from his desk. 'Take down your trousers, boy, and bend over that chair . . .'

Colm was aghast, but he obeyed, lowered the long grey trousers he was so proud of and presented his bare buttocks. The Biff was applied with such virulence that Colm bit through his lower lip to stop himself from screaming. He felt the blood trickle back into his mouth, salty and thick, felt the tears start in his eyes, tasted the humiliation.

'Let that be a lesson to you!' Father Madden said. Colm wanted to say that he was not responsible for the magazines, that they had been planted, but he could not trust himself to speak.

When he returned to class Father Andrew looked at the boy's white face and bleeding lip, at how he stood uncertainly beside his desk, and for a moment something like compassion crossed his face.

'Sit down.'

'I'd rather stand, Father,' Colm said with foolish integrity. He was trembling. The class, knowing the reason for his trouble, sniggered. Or most of them sniggered. Tim O'Loughlin, who slept in the next bed in the dormitory, and who until now had ignored him, did not laugh, nor did another new boy, John O'Neill, who looked on, ashen-faced.

94

'If you want to stand you'll have to go to the back of the room . . . I don't need any storks up here.'

Laughter. The class convulsed at the legitimate chance to take this swot down a whole row of pegs. Colm learnt another rule that day. You never show vulnerability.

Later Tim said to him sympathetically, 'Everyone gets their arses biffed by the Goat. It's his favourite pastime! But it was O'Dwyer who planted those magazines . . . He was joking about it to his pals after lunch . . .'

Colm seethed all that evening. In prep he saw his enemy's head bent over his work, felt his triumphant eyes on him when he wasn't looking. He hardly slept; hate kept him alert; he heard the sounds of the dormitory, the creaking of bedsprings, the sighs, the deep rhythmic breathing of his peers, the snores. Next day his eyes felt dusty and hot, as though sand had been thrown in them. He waited until morning break, when he was behind O'Dwyer in the corridor. He put a hand on his shoulder. When Willy turned Colm hit him with all his force in the face.

'Keep your wank-rags out of my locker!'

Willy fell back against the wall, hissed, 'I'll see you in the arena, Nugent, at half four.'

The boys around them drew bated breath. There was nothing they liked better than a fight.

The arena was the hand-ball alley, out of sight of the school windows. Here Colm, at half-past four, loosened his tie, rolled up his sleeves, and fought his foe with the whole of his strength and will. He did not defeat Willy O'Dwyer – he was too small for that – but the fight was broken up by the spectators when it became apparent that the new boy would not yield. 'That's enough, O'Dwyer,' someone said. 'Come on . . . leave it . . .'

Colm's tormentor went away with a torn lip and bloodied knuckles. His own nose was bleeding; his body ached, but he knew what he had achieved when the small group made way for him, and someone came forward with a clean handkerchief and mopped the blood.

'Good for you.' It was Tim O'Loughlin. 'But watch your back, Nugent,' he added *sotto voce*. 'He isn't finished with you.'

Later, one of the priests stopped him. 'What happened to you, boy? Were you in a fight?'

Fights were forbidden. 'No, Father,' Colm lied. 'I fell.'

Two days later Colm found that his diary was missing. He knew he had left it in his desk and searched for it frantically, painfully aware of the love poems it contained. He knew with sudden blinding insight that he had courted disaster by leaving it out of his hands.

The following day the diary reappeared on Father Madden's desk. He was introducing the class to the Romantic poets, Keats and Shelley.

'But we have our own romantic poet in our midst, boys, did you know that?' he said with a thin smile. He held up the small brown diary. 'Within these pages, boys, we have stern stuff . . .' And to Colm's horror he cleared his throat and began to read in a mincing falsetto the words which Colm had squeezed from his lonely heart:

'My eyes cringe, my tears sting,
Hopeless love tears at my heart,
It rends my soul and smashes my might,
It breaks me down till there's nothing right.

Vapours of confusion strangle my mind,
With searching fingers that are far from kind,
Clouded uncertainty corrupts my brain,
Violent passion courses through my veins.'

The mincing voice stopped. '"Vapours of confusion" is right, Nugent! You've shown plenty of those! But we can do without the violent passion! Haven't you found out already where that leads you?'

The class tittered, then released the morning's tensions in loud guffaws. The priest looked at his small victim with a thin smile.

Colm remembered the beating this man had given him; he listened now to the jeer. He saw the red haze before his eyes as he lurched to his feet, and to a roar from the class launched himself at the rostrum. But he tripped over some books he had left on the floor, and fell.

'Get up, you stupid boy,' the priest said contemptuously, 'and control yourself!' There was a gleam in the priest's eyes as though this challenge had touched some nerve in him, as though he foresaw subtle pleasures in breaking a spirit that had dared him to his face.

'I can see we'll have to do some work on that temper; but I'll overlook your histrionics this time – seeing as you're suffering from glandular fever!'

As the class laughed he stared into Colm's face, established eye contact. Then, with a smile full of scorn and power, he flipped the diary on to Colm's desk. 'We'll make a man of you yet!'

Colm looked at Robin. 'Look, I wrote a love poem and it was found and I got into trouble. That's all.'

'Did they beat you?'

'Yeah.'

'Did you ever tell Catherine What's-her-name about it?'

'No.'

Into his mind came Kattie's nervous question the next time he saw her – on St Stephen's Day some three months later: 'Colm, have I done something . . . why won't you speak to me any more?'

'Because I have better things to do!'

He saw her recoil, saw her hurt and bewilderment. But by then there was far more to it than she could have dreamed, or than he could cope with.

She seemed far away now, in this sun-baked piazza, far

from the meadows where they used to walk together, the banks of the Sureen where he taught her to fish, where he held her hand and where, gravely, at the age of twelve, she had kissed his cheek, looking at him in sudden alarm, the blush staining her from hairline to throat.

Everything that happened could never have happened here. There was too much light. He looked at Robin pinching crumbs and throwing them to the birds.

'What did you do with the diary?' Robin asked.

'I tore it up.'

'Did you write more poetry?' She seemed unimpressed by the incident; mildly compassionate, but otherwise unimpressed.

'Don't be ridiculous!' Colm said. 'Poetry is for wimps.'

He did not want to continue talking, to be the subject of her compassion, to feel the nausea of recollection and the fear of what he could not recollect, the missing piece. He knew other people's version of it – he had assaulted his housemaster – but he could not remember it. Better not to remember it, perhaps; better to dismiss it. But if he could not remember it he did not know who he was.

'It was my coming of age,' he said firmly. 'My initiation. They made a man of me.'

'Good!' Robin said tartly. 'Nothing like a man if you can find one.'

Colm dragged himself back to the present, resumed his watching of the countryside as the train left Dijon. He regarded the canal running beside the railway, remembering that the nearest he had ever been to Dijon was the time he had taken the train to Lyon, hired a car, driven to Peruges, explored the region over a weekend. The memory was bitter-sweet. Perhaps now he understood things better; perhaps now he would have done things differently. But the time was gone!

The TGV slinked through flat, cultivated land. Colm began to doze, surfacing to hear the sound of passing trains: like nylon cable, he thought sleepily, being pulled at speed through a steel loop; then he dozed again. The beep of a lap-top computer woke him; the train was slowing into the station of Dole where it stopped.

This journey is going on for ever! Maybe I should just get off and be done with it, Colm thought. But the train pulled out quickly, through forest and then the flat land was back again with isolated houses. Then there was Mouchard and after that the track was on higher ground with wonderful views; the TGV flew in and out of tunnels, and, between them, Colm had a view of wooded and gently rolling countryside, farmhouses with stacks of logs in their sheds, pine trees, logging works, a gradual change to Swiss-type scenery.

At Frasne the ticket inspector came through advising passengers to have their passports ready for inspection, and as the train moved away from this station a leather-coated official, wearing a badge saying '*Police Nationale, Contrôle Frontière*' inspected Colm's passport.

The TGV raced to Vallorbe and the Swiss border. Colm saw the gorge, the chalets in the valley below. At Vallorbe – the first enclosed station so far on the route – Swiss customs officials and border gendarmerie boarded the train.

'*Vous avez une déclaration, Monsieur?*' Colm was asked by a blue-jacketed customs official and he shook his head. He looked out at Switzerland, its pines, its ribbon roads, its peaks and valleys. He gave his passport up for inspection to a grey leather jacket with a holster at its hip, and turned back to admire the sweep of woods and towns and snowy peaks, landscapes ringed around with mountains. But he hated the officialdom, the tacit menace. Their job was normal, of course, merely routine; but he hated the uniforms and the firearms and the whole implied readiness for coercion.

At last came Lausanne. He realised with relief that he had completed the first leg of his journey. He collected his luggage, alighted to the chill Alpine air, and waited on the other side of the platform for the Cisalpino, the express which would bring him across Switzerland and into Italy. He felt like a homing pigeon, or a salmon returning to its natal river. I am a foolish middle-aged man, he thought, in search of his youth. But even that assessment seemed somehow short of the truth.

Chapter Six

The Cisalpino left Lausanne and snaked by Lake Geneva, swaying in high-tech fashion to the camber of the track. Colm had a window seat beside an elderly woman who moved sideways to allow him access. She hardly glanced at the scenery, was immersed in a book. Colm put his baggage on the overhead rack and settled down to watch the panorama – the lake with its pleasure boats and behind it the snow-capped peaks reaching into wispy clouds. The mountainsides rose on either side of the track; Colm saw the succession of farmed terraces, and above them the white summits touching the sky.

Aigle, then St Maurice came and went. He saw the castle, perched on a crag, overlooking Sion. The train raced along the valley floor, flying towards the looming bulk of the mountains. They plunged into a tunnel, then another and another. They arrived at Brig; he saw the torrent gushing down a precipice and a picturesque urban sprawl enclosed by mountains.

Armed Italian border police came on board, with Alsatian dogs on leashes. The '*Polizia Passaporto*' began inspecting passports and enquiring about baggage. They held the dogs on a tight rein. Colm identified his baggage overhead. Further down the carriage the police became exercised about a bag which no one claimed. Someone said the owner was in the dining car, but they opened it, nonetheless, searched it; the dogs sniffed. Shades of the Third Reich, Colm thought sourly, aware that in the era of terrorism and drug smuggling, his thought process was unjust.

The elderly woman beside him muttered: '*Plus ça change, plus c'est la même chose!*'

She glanced at Colm, laughed suddenly. 'Sorry!' she said in English. 'It just reminds me of the war.'

'I don't remember it,' Colm said with a smile.

'You're too young. It was a bad time. Uniforms everywhere justifying everything.' She spoke English with a French accent.

'Are you French?' Colm asked.

'Yes. I'm going to visit my son and his family. They live in Milan.'

'And I'm going to Florence.'

'Is this your first time?'

'No. I was there long ago . . . In fact I'm going to meet a friend I knew when I was a student. I haven't seen her since!'

The woman smiled. 'That is quite exciting! But you are wondering how much she will have changed?'

Colm gave a non-committal laugh. 'She will have changed physically, of course . . .'

'But the biggest change will be in you,' she said. 'You will not see her with the same eyes. You will bring the wisdom of your own life to your meeting. And so will she.'

She glanced at him, smiled. 'But it will be so interesting for you!'

Colm nodded politely. After a while he decided to have some lunch and excused himself to visit the dining car. There was a complete menu on offer, with an excellent wine list. He had a half-bottle of Chianti and a salad, sat by the window and continued to watch what he could of the scenery. In straining to see, between tunnels, everything he could of the landscape he became pleasurably subsumed in the moment. But this was temporary. He was assailed by a feeling that the past was perilous, that it had caught up with him. It was like a bloodhound on his trail, sniffing him down, straining to seize him, finally impossible to elude or circumvent.

Robin had known how to deal with the hounds of one's

personal history. She understood defiance. She had the trick of not identifying with circumstances. What if she were to come back into his life, what if she were to be there in the Piazza della Signoria in two weeks' time? A middle-aged Robin who had once said she would never grow old?

Memory was notoriously self-serving, notoriously false. Or at least some memories were false! Others were branded into you, like a coulter's furrow.

'So we hit Florence today?' Colm said. They were at breakfast in the small breakfast area of the Pensione Gallina. The night was behind them, another night which they had shared in talk, she in the bed this time, he on the floor, another night when he had heard her cry in her sleep. But now, the morning had come and the window of the small breakfast room was open to the Via Palestra. Robin tore a piece of bread into small pieces, arranged the pieces in a little pile, swept up the crumbs, pinched a few between thumb and index finger and threw them on to the balcony of the breakfast area for the house sparrows.

'You always do that,' Colm observed, 'feed the birds.'

'Why waste food? The birds are hungry!' He saw her half-profile, the curve of her cheek and the chin, the sunburn healing at the nape of her neck, the way her short fair hair curled, the gentleness of her hands, the contrast of her present body language to her usual air of urchin defiance. She was bronze as a statue, sun-bleached lights in her hair. She would be stunningly beautiful, he realised, given a little time and a little more flesh. He visualised her at home in her father's house in New England, saw it as a huge mansion with black and white tiles in the hall, a curving staircase, with Robin in evening dress descending. It didn't seem to accord completely with the girl before him.

'Have you ever been hungry, Robin?' She raised her eyebrows as she glanced at him. Her face was suddenly uncommunicative. 'Silly question!' he said.

She smiled. 'Where I come from, Irish, they keep the fridge well stocked. Sometimes I ask the cook to make me something special and he does whatever I want.'

'And what would that be?'

'Oh . . . just things like caviar on toast.'

'I've never eaten caviar. What's it like?'

'Overrated!' Robin said after a moment.

'So I should expect,' Colm said drily. 'Do you know where it comes from?'

'Course I do!'

Colm let the matter drop. It reminded him of the trick question in a school quiz as to where they grew spaghetti. He reached for safe ground. 'It must be nice to have a cook. My mother used to do all the cooking; now Moll Flannery does it.'

'Who's she?'

Colm thought of sturdy Moll, who had been with them since his mother died.

'Our housekeeper!' he said rather grandly.

'Is she very fussy?' Robin asked. 'Our housekeeper is Hispanic . . . she goes into a sulk if I leave a mess around . . .'

Colm said their own housekeeper was a real stickler too, remembering her frequent muttering: 'In the name of God, isn't one of thim able to pick up for thimselves?'

'Do you get on well with your family?' Robin asked him suddenly.

'Of course. We're a close-knit family. "One for all, all for each" is our motto!'

Robin was suspicious. 'I thought that kind of stuff only happened in books. Where do you live?'

'We live in an old house in the country.'

'Is it very big?'

'Big enough,' Colm said.

'And your farm . . . fields with lots of grass and cows and stuff?'

'Of course . . .' He laughed a little indulgently.

'My daddy has a ranch in Texas,' Robin confided. 'Not that we go there very much . . . Lizzie can't stand the heat. It's thirty thousand acres . . . How big is yours?'

Colm felt the humiliation of not being able to see her acre for acre.

'In Ireland no one has a farm that big. The land is good, so farms are much smaller. In our case it's about . . . well, it's not more than a thousand acres.'

How he despised himself even as he spoke! He thought of the one hundred ancestral acres which were the subject of his siblings' covert strife. Alice demanding all those years ago: 'It's not fair! Why should the boys get everything? It's as though girls didn't matter!'

'Will you leave me in peace!' his mother had intoned angrily. 'I've the dinner to get.'

Robin was avid for more information. 'Tell me about your home.'

Colm began to describe the ivy-covered house. He improved it, broadened its elevation, populated the barn with owls, invented horses in loose-boxes, invented a winding driveway and a gracious hall and a huge drawing room overlooking the river. He borrowed from Clonarty, the only great house he had ever been in.

'The river is called the Sureen; it overflows in winter, but in summer it has grand places to sit or fish or have a picnic . . . You can swim there too. There are a few nice spots, safe, underneath beeches which are almost two hundred years old. And in spring there are the daffodils – all along the bank . . .'

This, at least, was true, although the Sureen was not in reality so noble a flood as he depicted it, and it did burst its banks in winter with monotonous regularity.

'Could I visit you sometime . . . meet your family, see the place where you live . . . ? If I ever go to Ireland.'

Colm felt first the delight, then the sinking of the heart.

'Sure.'

'Give me your address.'

She wrote it down with a pencil she took from her pocket.

'Is that all!' she exclaimed. 'Ballykelly, Rathhanny, County Roscommon? The mail gets to you with just that?'

He smiled, nodded. 'God,' she said, 'you must be very important!'

Colm did not make any disclaimer.

'Next year, perhaps,' she said with a teasing smile. 'Maybe next year I'll get to Ireland.'

Colm avoided her eyes, but he nodded, trying to still the panic at the thought of this rich American finding him in his ramshackle home, in his hornet's nest of a family, in his funny added-to house which would not answer the description given, where there was no winding driveway or barn owls or a drawing room overlooking the river.

Why did I tell her a heap of lies? he asked himself. What kind of a half-eejit am I?

But, watching her, like a drawing in which only the outline appears, leaving the eye of the beholder to supply nuances of character, of light and shadow, watching her in her freshness and newness, he already knew the answer. She was Hope and he was already enchanted.

'Give me your address now,' he said.

She wrote on a piece of paper and he put it in his pocket.

'Robin,' he said suddenly. 'If it's not a rude question . . . is there some particular reason why you cry so much in your sleep?'

She started. 'Maybe I get scary dreams,' she said shortly, smoothing the last of the crumbs into a last small collection, and not meeting his eyes. 'Maybe it's got something to do with my lousy upbringing. Anyway, as it's in my sleep, Irish, I don't remember. As far as I'm concerned I sleep like a baby.'

She met his eyes briefly and looked away. 'I'll talk to my daddy's shrink about it when I get home. OK?'

She smiled brightly, said they'd better be going or they'd never get to Florence. They collected their rucksacks, paid their bill, walked out into the street, their heads full of their itinerary. They would get to the city's outskirts and then thumb their way.

'Did I tell you I'm part Florentine?' Robin demanded later as they waited on the verge of the highway.

'You made some such noise. But are you really?'

'Sure. I get it from my maternal grandmother.'

'So do you have relatives in Florence?'

'Yeah . . . maybe! If they're still there.'

'Are you going to look them up?'

'If I can find them.'

They got into Florence in the evening.

'There's just one place I want to see before we find somewhere to stay,' Robin said, a little breathlessly.

'I know . . . that bridge!'

She glanced at him to see if he understood how important this was, if her excitement was shared.

Their lift dropped them off in the Piazza Vittorio Veneto. They had to ask directions, finding their way first to the station and from there, through the screaming rush-hour traffic and down the Via de' Tornabuoni to the river.

The old bridge, with its rows of jewellery shops, was gilded by the evening. Robin paced it, joyous, impatient, laughing in sudden small bursts of disbelief. They stood at the open mid-section of the bridge, beside the bronze bust of Benvenuto Cellini, and looked along the length of the river at the city, its red-tiled roofs, its domes and towers against the sky. The setting sun shone directly down the Arno and into their eyes. For the first time since their nighttime adventure in Rome he took her hand. It lay in his, strangely rough and small.

'I'll take a picture,' he said, reaching for the camera. 'Stand back a bit!'

She did, smiling. Her skin shone, as though she had been touched by Midas.

'The sun is behind you!' she cried. 'You look as if you are on fire! Let me take a picture of you.'

He handed her the camera. 'If you take it with the sun behind all you will get of me is a silhouette.'

'I know,' she said, laughing. 'I'm not dumb! So move your butt and go and stand over there!'

He obeyed, laughing back at her.

That night they both had beds for a change, a twin room in a pensione called the Zellini in the Via Nazionale. The usual protocol was observed; she went to the bathroom and came back in cotton nightie, put her newly washed underwear over the seat of a plastic chair on the balcony, got into bed and turned off her light. Colm enjoyed all her little rituals; he liked the creak of her bedsprings, the small sound of her slipping down under her sheet, her sigh of pleasure, the sense he had every night of her fragility. He turned off his own light, and as his eyes adjusted to the darkness and the small rods of street light through the shutters he made out her form in the adjoining bed.

'Colm?' she whispered.

It was the first time she had used his Christian name.

'Yes?'

'You can tell me some more about your life if you're not too tired. The kind of things you were taught . . . your teachers . . .'

'I've already told you too much of that stuff. It would only bore you.'

'No,' Robin said. 'No, it wouldn't bore me.'

Colm sighed. 'We had lessons in what used to be the stables, the place where the Earls of Montgomery and Moyne once quartered their horses and grooms. It was a horseshoe-shaped building, with a coach entrance, and was just behind the big house.'

'So who used the house?'

'The priests lived there and the infirmary was there.'

'Do you feel angry that you were beaten with that strap?'

'No. Everyone was. It was probably good for me!'

'You don't sound convinced.'
'Of course I'm convinced. Go to sleep, Robin.'
He heard her turn in the bed.
''Night.'

What had returned to him suddenly was O'Keefe, the day pupil. He was in the fourth year, one of the big boys. It was rumoured that a priest had seen him with a girl in the town around eleven o'clock at night. The priest had been driving past and had seen them, arms around each other, standing in the darkened doorway of Linehan's drapery shop. O'Keefe had not seen the priest. He had been much too interested in perfecting his kissing to notice anything else.

Colm saw the Goat coming down the corridor at midmorning break, saw him take O'Keefe by the ear, propel him towards the gym.

'O'Keefe is in for it!' Tim O'Loughlin said as they were queuing at the tuck shop. Colm and Tim left the queue, followed Father Madden and his prey, spied on the proceedings through a chink in the gym door. They fully expected that O'Keefe would be flogged, but they had not anticipated the sight of a burly soutaned priest beating a boy with his fists up and down the gym, up and down, until the soutaned man was exhausted and the boy lay against the wall as though he had been broken.

The voyeurs crept away, whispering, disappearing like rodents.

'He should tell his parents,' Colm confided to Tim later in the boot room. 'He should tell them it was Father Madden who did that to him!'

'They wouldn't believe him. They think the sun shines out of the Goat's backside!'

'He has no jurisdiction over day pupils outside of school hours,' Colm said hotly.

He heard a footstep behind him, saw Nemesis reflected in

the eyes of his friend and turned to find Father Madden regarding him.

'Hmnn,' the priest said. 'If it isn't our poet laureate, the fairy lady of first year, the reader of dirty magazines, giving the benefit of his wisdom!'

His eyes bulged a little. Colm stood petrified. 'The fairy lady of first year . . .' he repeated, before turning away.

'Close call,' Tim opined under his breath as they went back to class. But Colm felt the premonition, the terror in his bones.

He shook himself free of his reverie, became aware of Robin's heavy breathing. She was evidently sound asleep. There was no way he was going to tell her everything about what had happened, however she might badger him. He wondered what her life back in the States was really like. If she had a wealthy father she was presumably used to plenty; and yet she treated food with the utmost care, never wasting a crumb. If she had a wealthy father she had presumably been cosseted growing up, and yet her hands were rough, like someone who was no stranger to domestic work. Her story definitely did not add up. Robin had some kind of secret. He was sure of it.

Are you really who you say you are? he asked her silently. And if you're not, then *who* are you?

She slept on obliviously, her presence strangely comforting. He felt a rush of tenderness towards her, even protectiveness, as though she were a child.

Colm left his reverie when his eardrums stabbed at him momentarily. He felt the painful pressure, swallowed, was aware that he was tired, saw his reflected face in the darkness of the tunnel.

Say what you like, he told himself, but there is a reality about travelling overland. You suffer the real inconveniences, the fatigue, that have been the lot of travellers since time immemorial, understand geography in ways you could not do otherwise. You are touched by a reality which air travel and the technologies of super-convenience have made redundant. You are reminded of your humanity and your kinship with the earth.

This thought-process suddenly seemed self-indulgent. His mind returned to Robin. Is it unhealthy, he wondered, to fixate on something that happened long ago? What can I do to exorcise it, all of it? Why has it come back to haunt me recently, hounded me until I decided to make this journey? When I fell across the desk, in that fog of suffocation, why did so much surface that has been buried for years?

The train emerged from the Simplon tunnel to a view of the Italian Alps and valley below, and moved slowly into Domodossola. He was finally in Italy!

In Florence Silvestro sat in Paola's office. He leaned back in the chair and regarded her whimsically, as though wondering at what point she would finally melt.

'That was a wonderful lunch!' she said.

He reached across the desk and took her hand, gazed into her eyes.

'Erica has gone to Vallambrosa,' he said. 'She will be away until the weekend . . . She said she will bring you back some things – cheese, mushrooms. Perhaps I could cook you supper this evening . . . After you have fed your students, of course!'

Paola looked back at him, smiled. 'I think I should be at home this evening. The last guest is arriving. All the way from Ireland!'

'I see. They are like children, these guests of yours.'

Paola thought of her new batch of students. In a way they *were* like her children. Darina the American, Renate the German, both studying Italian, and pretty Jill Sinclair, the publishing editor, who had registered for a course on the history of art.

'Erica is very kind to bring me so much from the farm,' Paola said. She wanted to remind him about Erica.

'She feels for you, *carissima*! And for Pasquale, of course.'

He lowered his voice. 'What does the doctor say about him now?'

'I saw him this morning. Pasquale will definitely need the operation to put in a new valve. Professor Santini is the top man and I want him to do it. I'll have enough money soon. I'm going to sell the land in Sicily . . .'

'Giovanni's investment? But you will miss out on a fortune!'

Paola shrugged. 'I know, but I need the money now.'

'I would gladly give it to you, Paola, if I had it.'

'I know, Silvestro. Thank you for being so kind to us . . .'

He moved around the desk, put his arms around her and drew her head against his breast. Paola left it there for a moment, closed her eyes. Then she detached herself.

'It's late, my dear cousin . . . I must get back to work!'

Silvestro released her, kissed her hand. 'I wish . . .' he said with a sigh, but he did not complete the sentence. Instead he asked, 'The student who is due to arrive this evening . . . are they male or female?'

'Male. His name is Colm Nugent . . .'

Silvestro said: 'What miserable little names these foreigners have!'

'I am half-foreign myself, Silvestro.'

'I know. That is why you are so delicious!'

He left the office, turned in the corridor as he always did to wave at her through the glass.

Chapter Seven

Lago Maggiore seemed to go on for ever. Fairytale against the backdrop of the Alps, warm blue serenity with islands and pleasure boats, it looked like Paradise. It stretched on and on, seducing the eye, until eventually it was left behind and the Cisalpino sped through the sunny landscape to Milan. Colm felt the impatience, the sense of excitement, the prospect of nearing his journey's end.

Like a child! he thought. Like the times when we would go to Galway. Or like the time we all went to Lough Key when I was nine, and Kattie, a tomboy of eight, came with us. Like me, she was small for her age. He could see her even now trying to build sandcastles on the lake shore.

'You can't make castles with that sand. It's too coarse.'

She had leaned back on her hunkers to look up at him, her limbs and pink swim suit dusted with sand, the small white grains in their thousands on her forearms, the cotton sun-hat shading her eyes. He saw her innocence through the prism of forty years. He saw his nine-year-old self.

She considered the ruins of her castle, said, 'Stupid, isn't it?' and rushed off after a few moments to find some reeds.

'Come on, let's build a moat instead. We can prop it with these.'

Colm took charge, setting Liam and the two girls to plait the rushes to create a support lining. The sand bucket was inverted and firmly shoved into the shore, a moat constructed around it. This was duly flooded, its banks lined with plaited reeds, a sluice gate constructed from a piece of wood found in the boot of the car.

Laughter, accord. Liam excavating a new channel behind the 'castle', Alice bringing stones to cover the bucket, 'To make it look real!' Maura Nugent knitting in the shade, smiling as she raised her eyes to look at the children; Tom Nugent visible in the distance as he walked by the lake shore.

Where had Robin been then? Six years old and living in New England? Or New York? Or had anything she said been the truth? So many of her utterances were clearly outlandish, the imaginings of a child. Even obscenely rich men did not paint their private jets pink to go with their trophy wife's nails. Who was this filthy rich father who had allowed his seventeen-year-old daughter just to disappear? Colm had covertly examined the foreign and national press; there had been no pictures of a missing schoolgirl, no cries from a billionaire for the return of his child.

Sometimes Robin had been withdrawn, as though she had retired to a space known only to herself. She was a strange little ship that passed beside him, contacted him with a shining Aldiss lamp, established the miracle of communication. And then she was gone!

Is life, he wondered, a series of interlocking patterns? He'd had a glimmer of hers, the puzzle of her life. The strange thing was that, as he got older, he'd discovered the value of communication, knew at last that it was gold; but he was condemned to be inarticulate in its service, mute.

On their first morning in Florence Colm had woken to a small rasping sound, reminiscent of a hay knife being sharpened; but it was only Robin, a sketch pad on her knee, scraping with a piece of charcoal. He watched her surreptitiously for a while. She sat on the bed by the open window, brow knitted, lips compressed. She seemed far away, despite her vigorous attention to the task in hand. She was sitting cross-legged, fully dressed in jeans and T-shirt, on her bed. The morning light filled the room, touched the mosaic floor and the faded yellow walls. The ceiling was high, and in its centre hung a huge tarnished candelabrum. This was almost a Renaissance room, but run down, ceiling plaster chipped, paint peeling, wash basin in the corner loose from the wall. Occasionally Robin would lift her head to look through the window and the balcony rails to the street.

'What are you drawing?' Colm asked suddenly, and Robin started, shutting her pad and turning to look at him with accusing eyes.

'You gave me a fright! I was just drawing the street. I love the crazy rooftops.'

'Can I see it?'

Robin opened her pad, brought the sketch to him and he held it at arm's length. The street was alive; the tiled roofs spoke to each other. It was as though they were not composed of tiles and mortar, but were living entities with their own agendas, endlessly discussing together the goings-on in Florence.

'I've never seen roofs at that angle . . . but don't let that bother you!'

He ducked as Robin made a mock swipe at him, compressing her lips, her eyes laughing.

'But it's good, Robin. I mean it!'

'Bullshit!'

They breakfasted in a small café on the corner, *caffè latte* hot and milky, crisp rolls with apricot jam. The place had a counter with high stools, and a few round tables by a plate-glass window. The smell of espresso wafted from a hissing Gaggia. Long multi-coloured plastic strips separated the interior from the bright morning.

Robin suddenly began to talk about medieval Florence and the Medici. 'They were some bunch,' she said, 'those Medici! Incredibly rich, politically crafty, yet they threw up someone like Lorenzo the Magnificent who loved art above all things. They should have been Americans!'

115

Colm laughed.

'Yeah,' Robin continued. 'Think of how the American electorate would love Lorenzo . . . *Il Magnifico!*' She rolled the name on her tongue. 'They'd have made him President. The Kennedys could have eaten their hearts out!'

Colm dredged his memory of the book Mr Roche had brought him all those years before. 'Lorenzo de' Medici,' he said, 'was the president of a city state in everything but name. And he knew how to consolidate power; his son became a pope and his nephew became a pope!'

'Sure . . .' Robin agreed, 'have as many popes in the family as you can. That was always my motto!'

She looked at his expression and laughed.

'You're a cynic, Robin McKay,' he said. 'And a mystery girl to boot! Why don't you tell me your real story? I'm having problems with jets painted shocking pink!'

'That's because you have no imagination. My daddy used to say that imagination is the key to happiness and success.'

'Did he indeed! Well, I say that I'm also having problems with a billionaire's daughter scrimping her way around a foreign country with only the clothes on her back.'

'Tough!' Robin said. 'But that's the way it is!'

When Colm had finished his breakfast he said: 'Don't you think you should look up the phone book to see if you can locate your Florentine relatives? You know . . . the ones you told me about on the way here?'

He said this casually, suppressing a smile. If it were not for the fact that she actually spoke a little Italian he would have lumped her Italian blood into the same category as the pink jet. He suspected that Robin liked to create her universe, but he was not sure of the extent to which she did this. Part of him half believed what she said; she was strange enough, he told himself, for anything! Was she not here with him, wandering Italy with him, sleeping in the same room? Given that bizarre circumstance alone anything else was possible.

She shot him a swift assessing look, radiated uncertainty.

'Yeah, OK,' she muttered, 'when I feel like it. There's no hurry,' she added grandly when she looked up and caught his eyes, 'I'll phone them when I'm ready . . .'

Colm looked around. In the corner of the café, just inside the door, was a phone. Underneath the phone was a small wooden shelf on which lay a telephone directory, secured to the wall by a piece of string.

He took her hand and pulled her to the phone. A customer seated at the counter stared at them. Colm opened the phone book.

'Come on . . . there's no point in pussyfooting around. If you have relations in Florence look them up! Think of the window that would give you on the world. They'd be interested in meeting you . . . why wouldn't they? Unless of course everything you've been saying is pure bullshit!' He glanced at her: 'So what name do we look for?'

Robin seemed to have lost something of her assurance. She shrank a little into her shoulders.

'No hurry,' she said suddenly. 'We can do it anytime!' Colm narrowed his eyes. His doubts were vindicated and he wanted to laugh.

'I thought you were just spoofing, Robin. Now I'm sure of it!' he said in a righteous, pedagogic voice. 'You'll have to stop telling whoppers!'

She shot him a dangerous look. But when she didn't reply immediately he repeated: 'Why don't you admit you're just gabbing? You've no more Florentine blood in you than I have!'

Robin scowled. 'I was just trying to remember . . . Their name was Gabbi . . . you just reminded me!'

Colm laughed out loud. 'Gabbi . . . ! What kind of a name is that? I never heard such a load of old codswallop! How do you spell it?'

'I'm not sure of the spelling,' she said modestly. 'It was my grandmother's maiden name, but I never saw it written down. My mother died young too, so I have nothing much to go on

117

except my memory.' She added, 'And my memory is usually pretty damn good!'

'Really? So you saw no birth or marriage certificates, no family records? And you come from a rich family. What a strange girl you are!'

She shrugged. 'The Italian side was not regarded as important,' she said primly. 'My grandmother was more or less cut off because she didn't marry the man they wanted her to!'

'Well, what was your grandmother's Christian name? I presume she had one?'

Robin compressed her lips. 'Very funny. Her name was . . . let me think . . . Carmina. That was it! And she came from an excellent family but ran away with her sweetheart to America.'

Colm sighed. He looked Robin in the eye. She met his gaze with candour. 'Why don't you tell the truth?' he muttered.

'Oh, for Chrissake . . . I am telling you the truth. But you're so suspicious you wouldn't know honesty if it bit you on the ass!'

Colm experienced renewed uncertainty. The small girl beside him folded her arms and pursed her lips. 'You're like a wasp in winter,' he said. 'All sting and nowhere to go!'

He opened the directory at G, searched it, went down through the Gs, found not a single Gabbi.

Robin seemed oddly devoid of disappointment. 'They've probably moved. Or died out. Sad to think of it . . . my granny may have been the last of the line, the long and illustrious line of the Gabbis!'

'The only one of the line, more likely,' Colm muttered to himself. Then he added, 'Could it have one B? The name?'

Robin thought. 'I suppose so.'

They checked it again.

'It's not there,' Colm said, adding suddenly, 'Hey, wait, look at this!'

The directory entry said, 'Di Gabiere Dott. F., Via Ghiberti 12, Fiesole.'

Colm turned to her. His incredulity was undented.

'That's them!' Robin said triumphantly. 'I told you I had relatives in Florence!'

'Di Gabiere is not the same as Gabbi,' Colm said severely. 'In fact the resemblance is more or less non-existent!'

'I told you I couldn't remember exactly!' she said in a tone of exasperation. 'The "Di" is only a goddamn prefix. It's to show they're of aristocratic lineage!'

Colm clapped his hands together. 'Good. I'm sure they'll be delighted to see you – their long-lost cousin, all the way from New York!'

Robin leaned back against the wall. 'I can't just arrive on someone's doorstep, now can I?'

'Where's Fiesole?' Colm asked as he noted down the address. 'The place where this Gabiere fellow is supposed to live?'

'Dunno.'

Colm approached the counter. The assistant was serving espresso in a small white cup.

'Scusi . . .' Colm said. 'Fiesole . . . ?'

Brows were wrinkled. Incomprehension was patent in both assistant and customer. 'Fiesole?' Colm repeated, realising that the problem lay entirely with his pronunciation.

But when understanding dawned both assistant and customer vied with each other in explanation. Arms and hands indicated direction. Colm gathered that you had to get the bus. The bus was from the station.

'Grazie . . .'

He returned to the table, where Robin had re-seated herself, her arms folded. 'You don't learn, Irish!' she hissed. 'In two more minutes the whole of Florence would have been in here with directions!'

'Never mind the smartass commentary. Let's check the map. It's back in the room.'

They returned to the pensione, got out the map. Fiesole, they discovered, was in the hills overlooking the city. And the bus left from outside the station.

'What do you expect me to do?' she said in answer to Colm's expectant stare. 'You needn't think I'm going to present myself on the doorstep . . . "Hey, chums, I'm your long-lost kin!"'

'What you really mean, Robin, is that you've just made up a heap of lies and don't know how to extricate yourself!'

Robin shook her head. 'I only lie sometimes. You don't have to believe me if you don't want.'

'Well, you can always enquire,' Colm persisted, wondering what he had to do to get her to acknowledge her rampant invention. 'It would be something to do. And they can't eat you!'

She thought about it. 'Not now,' she said nervously, when she realised that Colm was serious. 'The proper way to do it is to write to them. So I'll send a note to my cousin Signor Di Gabiere and tell him I'm here. OK? I'd rather see the city today.'

Colm sighed. The farce had gone on long enough.

'All right! We'll relax, see the sights today.' They went out, bought a cheap guide book and commenced exploration.

They crossed the Piazza della Signoria, stood on the spot where Savonarolo's body had been burned. It was commemorated by a circular inset in the stone of the square, just beside the old palace.

'Poor old Savvy,' Robin said sadly, reading the snippet in the guide to Florence. 'That's what you get for ranting and raving!'

'He trod on too many toes. Remember the Church was sitting there, all powerful, and along comes this bloke unreasonably disapproving of debauched popes, and the lads with ecclesiastical power doing anything they wanted and calling it anything that they liked.'

'Move up to the top of the class,' Robin said. 'You could take over where old Savvy left off!'

Colm laughed. He paid the entrance to the Palazzo Vecchio. Together they wandered through the great Hall of the Two Hundred and the other rooms of this ducal palace once trodden by *Il Magnifico*.

'Can you imagine him looking out of this very window on the city of Florence?' Robin said, stopping at a window recess and putting her hand on the mullioned glass. 'Lorenzo the Magnificent! Go on, strain your imagination. *Il Magnifico*, one of the great figures of history, standing right here, where your feet are . . . on this very spot!'

Colm felt a small shiver climb his spine. 'How come you've got such a good imagination?'

Robin shrugged. 'I had a good teacher . . .' she announced sententiously. 'He was wonderful!'

The bloody art teacher, Colm thought to himself. There was definitely more there than met the eye. He wanted to question her about this fellow, but she was pacing ahead of him, examining paintings and ceilings, gazing out of windows to the square below.

They came to the map room and Colm nearly laughed out loud when he saw the lop-sided map of Ireland. But other maps, of Italy, of places nearer home, were brilliant in their accuracy.

The Uffizi Gallery was next; they had to queue, but once inside they climbed the seemingly endless staircase to the long gallery with its statuary, and entered the first room. Robin seemed to be in a hurry. She scanned the work and moved swiftly to the next room.

'I particularly want to see Botticelli's stuff. My art teacher taught me all about him.'

Colm was by now in a lather of resentment. He had paid good money to get in here and she simply tore ahead of him to see some daub or other. And what was so wonderful about that teacher bloke? he asked himself. Some little wimp teaching girls! But Robin was in a hurry and could not be questioned, however obliquely.

'Do you ever stand still for two minutes?' he demanded irritably.

'Ah, piss off . . .' and she was gone ahead of him. He found her at last, standing before Botticelli's huge canvas, *The Birth of Venus*.

Colm came softly behind her, but she did not move. She seemed rapt in contemplation of the painting before her, the nude goddess of love blown shorewards in a shell, her gold hair flowing. It's all right, I suppose, Colm thought sourly, studying the picture, but I don't see why she's so taken with it. Your woman's feet are too big anyway! For a moment he thought of Packy Flynn's likely perspective . . . *There do be pictures of naked wimmin and them all bare as the day they was born!* . . . and for a moment he saw Packy standing here, round-eyed, his mouth open. He almost laughed out loud; poor Packy would have a heart attack.

He moved away, leaving Robin to her trance-like study, passing into an adjoining room where he was himself riveted by Leonardo Da Vinci's *Annunciation*, with its exquisitely deferential angel and intelligent, inquiring, young madonna. Here was no celestial rape, with macho seraphim dictating terms; in this picture a girl was the subject of an angel's reverence and was being offered an informed choice.

I never had a choice, Colm thought.

When he went looking for Robin he found her still before *The Birth of Venus*, listening with a rapt expression to a guide, who was conducting a party of English tourists through the gallery.

'The model for this picture was said to be *La Bella Simonetta*, the mistress of Lorenzo's brother Giuliano. She was so beautiful that when she died they carried her body through the streets so that the people could look on her lovely face for one last time. She died at the age of twenty-two.'

'Did you hear that?' Robin said, turning to Colm, as though oblivious of his erstwhile absence.

'So what? You're talking about the fifteenth century. In those

122

days beauty was a serious business. Without photography or television, people wanted to feast their eyes on the real thing.'

Robin looked at him with scorn.

'It still is a serious business . . . Beauty goes hand in hand with power. Which is why,' Robin continued after a moment, 'they do what they can to humble it.'

Colm was irritated. 'Sometimes I wonder why you are such a scold.'

'Sometimes I wonder why you are such a clam.'

'How do you mean?'

She snorted. 'You have this trick of saying just so much and then shutting up . . . snapping shut your little shell in case anyone gobbles you up!'

This made Colm pause. When he glanced at her her mouth was pursed aggressively, ready for further combat. He wanted suddenly to kiss her, to make her laugh. 'My birthday is coming up!' he said with a grin. 'So you have to be nice to me.'

She smiled. 'It's my birthday too, remember.'

'Yeah, the great twenty-first! Do you ever tell the truth?'

'My dad used to say it's the ruination of a good story,' she said with a twinkle. 'But of course I do. Sometimes!'

'Your dad? It doesn't sound in character! It sounds as though he actually has a sense of humour. Why doesn't he look for you, Robin? A man with his resources would find you in a jiffy. Why has he forgotten you?'

He took her hand, but she pulled back from him. 'You think you know everything, don't you? Well, there are things you don't know, could not even imagine . . .'

He reached for her hand again, knew there was no point in questioning her. 'Come on, little one,' he said gently, suddenly noticing how pale she looked. 'I know nothing. Call a truce! Let's go to the Bargello.'

The Bargello, a fortress dating from the thirteenth century, was not far from the Uffizi Gallery. A prison at one time, it was now a museum. Its massive stone staircase led from the courtyard to floor after floor of treasures, sculptures by

Michelangelo, Cellini, Donatello.

'What are you going to do with yourself?' he asked when they were back in the courtyard and standing in the shade. 'I mean when you're grown up.'

Robin gave a toss of her head. 'I am grown up!'

'I mean what are you going to do with your life? Are you going to be a painter or a teacher or something? Even with heaps of money life must be pretty boring unless you are doing something with yourself. Freedom has to have a point.'

Robin was silent for a moment. 'I dunno,' she said, sounding uncharacteristically grave and uncertain. 'I suppose I'm scared of the future.'

'Why?'

She shrugged, and to Colm's consternation her eyes filled with tears. She blinked them angrily away.

The sun was broiling the Via del Proconsolo when they emerged from the Bargello and turned towards the river. Two policemen approached on the opposite side of the street. Robin turned into the Via dell'Anguillara. Colm followed her.

'Why did you do that?' he demanded.

'Do what?'

'Turn away when you saw the police?'

She stared at him. 'Are you crazy? I just wanted to go down this street. We haven't been on it before. Anyway, I was afraid my daddy might have sent them to look for me!'

'Your daddy could afford a team of private detectives. He doesn't need to rely on the police.'

She was silent. They came to the river, crossed it by the Ponte Vecchio.

Robin stood on this bridge for a while, leaning against the first shop window she came to, as though riveted by the jewellery within, the pearls and gold chains, the cameos set in gold.

'Robin, are you all right?'

'Sure . . .'

They moved to the centre of the bridge and stood side by side, looking into the Arno, raising their faces in unison towards the hills where the cypresses could be seen through the haze. 'This Fiesole place must be up there somewhere,' Colm said.

An urchin approached and tried to sell them postcards. Colm bought two. The boy looked from him to Robin, wished him happiness with a small, knowing smile.

Happiness! Colm thought, suddenly tired. Where do you find it? Was it here, in a hand-to-mouth existence with an enigmatic semi-stranger, with whom, for the first time in years, he felt like a real person? It wasn't in Ballykelly at any rate. They would be harvesting the barley now, or whatever of it had not been lodged by the downpour just before he had left. They would bring plenty of hot sweet tea into the fields at midmorning; at lunchtime the hired hands would gather in the kitchen, hands freshly washed, sweaty caps left on the windowsill, gaucheness relaxing into laughter.

If he brought Robin home what would they say? Once, before his disgrace, there would have been covert pleasure and pride in having her there. Her foreignness would have made her interesting; her accent irresistible. But perhaps, if she did actually come, her presence would redeem him to some extent, change their perception.

In Robin he had an ally. Her defiance, her vulnerability, the silent sense of recognition as though they had shared experience, was terra cognita, familiar, almost necessary.

They walked to the Piazza di Santo Spirito where the fifteenth-century church of the same name dominated the square. At a corner shop they bought some fresh *panini* – crusty rolls, cheese, and *aqua minerale*. Robin sat on a bench near the fountain, under some trees which favoured the east side of the square. There was a small open-air market at one end of the piazza – a few stalls set up in the shade, selling fruit, vegetables, household goods and items of clothing. Colm bought some apples and joined Robin, sitting beside her, biting into a crusty roll with pleasure. The pigeons, grey-green and subtle turquoise, swaggered and bobbed over the cobbles. Robin was quiet. She drank some water, but declined food. 'I've still got a yucky stomach,' she said when he asked why she wasn't eating.

'Look . . . I'll nip back and get you something from that *Farmacia* we passed.'

'It's closed. They're all closed this time of day.' She collected the crumbs from Colm's repast in a paper bag, and distributed them to the birds with evident pleasure. A few small, brown house sparrows joined in the foraging.

'You are so kind to the birds,' Colm said. 'You never forget them.'

'We don't need the crumbs.'

'How are you feeling now?' he asked after a few minutes.

'Much better!' she said. 'I think I was just tired.'

At one end of the square the shadows were already gathering. Noon was past; the heat was intensifying; the vendors began to pack up shop; the small narrow streets off the square, the houses with centuries of shuttered vigilance, evoked an inscrutable power, something secret and puissant, deeper and older than dogma.

Some young people sat around the fountain; one couple held hands and stared into each other's eyes, oblivious of the world.

'Do they remind you of being in love?' Robin asked, indicating the young pair with an inclination of her head. Colm did not want to return to this particular topic. He reached for the macho mantle which kept him safe, because despite her new importance in his life, he felt himself exposed in the face of her relentless questioning. She was fixated on this love business.

'I was cured of all that crap.'

'You never told me the rest of the story,' she said, 'of what happened . . . with Catherine . . .'

'What happened is that I know that I will never fall for that particular trap again.'

He wasn't going to be drawn into any more self-revelation; it was presumptuous of her to harp on it. He gave her a supercilious male smile, the sort of smirk favoured by James Bond, in which superiority sported with triumphalism. But, privately, he was thinking of a winter's evening, a sudden, spontaneous hooley in the kitchen, the flagged floor cleared, his father playing the fiddle; it was the first moment of gaiety since his mother's death, albeit unplanned. Liam and Alice began to dance, as did two other friends who had dropped in. Kattie, now fourteen, had come for the weekend: she was sitting in the rocking chair by the fire.

Colm came in from hosing down the milking parlour; his face and hands were raw with cold, but his heart turned in his chest when he saw her. She looked at him shyly. He generally avoided her now when she came to stay, too burdened, after the debacle at Clonarty, with anger and shame, but now, in a rare expansive moment, when he changed from his wellingtons and washed his hands at the sink, he approached her, asked her to dance, extending his hand to help her to her feet. But Catherine refused, huddling into the rocker and blushing scarlet. 'Ah, no, Colm . . . thanks. Sure I can't do the reel!'

The music had stopped; the others had looked at him in silence and then looked away. She knows! he thought in sudden horror. She knows the whole story. She has guessed it or someone has told her. And she despises me! In that moment he hated her; in that moment he hated them all. He felt he could take no more, that somehow or other he would have to assert his identity. It was a need, like the need for revenge.

He felt the heat of the Italian noonday, looked at Robin. 'No,' Colm repeated, 'I will never fall for all that stuff again!'

Robin was frowning. She had been watching his face. 'Me neither,' she said equably. 'Don't believe in it any more!'

But she continued to examine him covertly, with a long sidelong glance.

'How do you feel about Catherine now?' she asked suddenly as she leaned towards a fat pigeon with a piece of crust.

Colm felt as though he were being crowded, squeezed into a dark space, but he shrugged. 'I don't.'

'Yes you do. You're blaming her for something . . . every time her name is mentioned I can feel you blaming her.'

'I told you, I was cured of her.'

'So how were you cured of her? Why did you want to be *cured* of her?' Robin persisted.

It was like a needle thrust into the quick. What gave her the right to such persistent curiosity?

He gave an exasperated sigh, and then explained in a patient, superior tone: 'Because I'm a man and I have masculine agendas.'

Robin smiled. 'What kind of agendas are they?'

'Look, men and women are different! Men like to make money, have power, possess women. Women go for soppy stuff. Men pretend to believe in it too, so they can get the women.' He glanced at her. 'As far as most men are concerned, most women – present company excepted of course – are for the three Fs!' He sat back; he had resumed invulnerability.

'What are the three Fs?'

Colm already regretted that he had regurgitated this piece of received wisdom. But it had come from an overflow of something he could hardly control, the need to protect his quick.

'What are the three Fs?' Robin repeated.

'Feeling, fucking and forgetting!' He glanced at her again, sorry at the way she started, but triumphant in the sudden rush of masculine superiority. Parameters, hierarchy, had now been re-established. 'Or so it is said,' he added to soften the remark's bald effrontery. 'I didn't invent it.'

Robin's face had closed, clouded with sudden sadness. Colm, feeling like a heel, suddenly wished himself dead. After a moment she said softly, 'I'll say this for you, Irish . . . you're a real polite guy.'

'You're not "women",' Colm said in gruff apology, to bring her within the pale of male approval. 'You're a friend.'

128

But Robin did not smile. Her mouth tightened and she said without raising her voice: 'It must be kinda nice to get to make all the decisions. But will you tell me one thing, Irish . . . what the hell are you, and the guys who make up such schlock, so afraid of?'

'What makes you think we're afraid?'

Robin threw him a contemptuous, measuring glance. 'People who behave like dogs are afraid!'

He bridled.

'Present company excepted of course,' she added sweetly.

That afternoon they visited the Duomo, the cathedral in pale green and white marble, and then the Baptistery, with its famous bronze doors. They had hardly spoken since the lunchtime exchange of insults, and now listened in silence to yet another English-speaking guide. The Baptistery was built outside the medieval churches, the guide explained, because only baptised persons could set foot within the portals of a church, so you couldn't go in unless you were baptised.

'Like a club,' Robin murmured. 'Get the exclusivity bit working . . . And I used to believe in all this crap. I really believed!'

Colm glanced at her. 'What made you stop?' but she silenced him with a look: she was listening to the guide.

The guide was saying that Dante had been baptised here, but Colm hardly heard; he was too busy being puzzled by Robin and relieved that she had lifted her silence. He wanted to apologise, but could not find the words.

'Can you just imagine it?' he said a little later, trying to jostle her out of her introspection. 'Life then, I mean; no global concept as we understand it, the western world consisting of this city and a few other cities and above all the power of the Papacy. France an important power on the doorstep, but nothing else, except almost as myth: Cathay, and rumours of lands beyond the setting sun. What was happening in England or Ireland might as well have been happening on the moon.'

She shrugged. 'I always thought they were on the moon!'

He laughed. 'Did anyone ever tell you you are a very exasperating girl?'

'No, but other deficiencies were occasionally mentioned.'

'Like what?'

'Turning fantasy into reality.'

'Hah?'

'There's no "hah" about it. It was stuff my dad told me.'

'What did he tell you?'

'That he was descended from the last High King of Ireland.'

Colm laughed in good earnest. So the billionaire ogre actually laid claim to a lineage.

'Let me see . . .' he said, stroking his chin. 'Ruadhri O'Connor? High King in 1170 or thereabouts? Half of Ireland claims to be descended from him! Your daddy is in good company. I'm probably related to him myself. Which makes us cousins!' He turned to her, clicked his heels: 'Top o' the mornin' to yeh, coz?'

Robin sniffed, but laughter played around her mouth. She examined the guide book in an attempt to stifle it. She wasn't ready for full-scale reconciliation yet.

'I want to see the *David*!' she announced when he suggested that they go back to the pensione.

'What David?'

'Oh God . . . Michelangelo's *David*!' She consulted the map. 'He's not far.'

'Nothing is far in this town,' Colm said with bad grace. 'But there's so much of what is "not far" that you end up with flat feet and varicose veins!'

Robin laughed. 'Don't be such a Philistine!'

Michelangelo's *David* was in the Galleria dell'Accademia, which was, as Robin had said, but a walk of some minutes. David stood, in all his marble majesty, commanding the long hall of the gallery.

Robin gazed up at this masterpiece and, to Colm's consternation, her eyes filled with tears.

130

'Isn't he wonderful!' she whispered.

'His hands and head are too big,' Colm said, exasperated. 'And he could do with a pair of underpants!'

Robin clicked her tongue, but she said in tones of awe: 'Look . . . to sculpt something like this, out of a single block! How do you think Michelangelo did it?'

Colm stared up at the statue for a long time. The young David had his sling in one hand, a stone in the other, was looking sideways to judge distance and opportunity, poised to take down the giant Goliath. Colm found himself thinking of the sculptor working away, releasing musculature from the stone, the face and limbs from marble durance, knowing where to put the next chisel stroke to find the veins. He thought of the millennia before Michelangelo, when every atom of this work before him had been lost in the living rock. And looking at this marble David with his youth and beauty, he thought of the mind that conceived him and the fever that worked on him. And then he thought of himself, Colm, the youth, who had met a reverse kind of sculptor who had turned him into stone.

'Maybe he was real once,' Colm said. 'Maybe he was turned to marble by an evil spell. Maybe he didn't kill Goliath; maybe the giant destroyed him, not with strength but with cunning.'

Robin touched his hand. 'You only have to look at him,' she said softly, 'to see how he won! He *knew* that nothing could hurt him.'

Colm wanted to sit down, looked around for a seat and found none. 'Well, madam,' he said, 'what do you want to drag me to next? I can see I need expect no quarter.'

'What about San Marco, the church of your old pal, Savonarola?' She got out the map. 'It's just down the street from here and across the square . . .'

Colm sighed and followed her outside, down the street with the screaming mopeds, across the sunny piazza to the church.

* * *

San Marco had a baroque interior, ornate ceiling and altar, flickering candles. It was empty. They stood for a moment in the silence, glad to be out of the heat and the noise of the square, then walked quietly around the perimeter.

Midway on the left-hand side they found a seated bronze statue. It was a monk, cowled, his shoe just visible below the hem of his garment. He was alone; no admirers were grouped around him; no halo indicated his destination; no pious pose proclaimed his allegiance.

'Who's this?' Colm demanded, searching for a name plaque. But he knew already. There was only one person this could be, and Colm looked at him with a start of recognition, like a long-lost friend.

Sinister in his cowled habit, Savonarola sat, leaning forward, a book in his hand. The statue was lifelike, but larger than life, and the monk's intense face was fierce with vision and principle.

It was completely different from anything else they had seen so far in Florence, completely different from anything Colm had seen in his life. Here was no hedonistic piece of art, with torso of perfect muscle tone; here was no pious saint with eyes fixed on God. Instead the whole form possessed a metaphysical tension that transferred itself to the hands, the foot, the chair. It was rage, Colm thought. Rage, rage, *rage*.

The two young people studied the sculpture in silence. Colm, having been taken unawares, felt a lump in his throat. This monk, who had provoked so much interest in his ten-year-old self, sat before him as though he would speak. He touched the shoe which protruded beneath the robe, tentatively, as though afraid Savonarola would spring to life.

'Some guy,' Robin whispered after a moment. 'Although I wouldn't have expected them to put him in a church after him being excommunicated.'

'He was Prior of this gaff,' Colm whispered, looking around at the ornate splendour of the church, and then back to the ascetic before him. 'Before they tarted it up. They flocked to hear him. And they must be proud of him. After all, the noise he made reverberated throughout Europe!'

'He's quiet enough at the moment,' Robin whispered, slowly tracing the veined, bronze hand with her fingers. 'He cannot open his mouth.'

Colm said unkindly, 'He would probably have had you burned!'

'For what?'

'For interfering with his person and having a sharp tongue. He doesn't look like the kind of bird who would need much of an excuse . . .'

Robin, undaunted, laid her palm over Savonarola's hand, looked into his terrible bronze eyes.

'When I think of his life,' Colm said, his voice very low, 'I wonder did he dream of his terrible end? Tortured, hanged, burned in the principal square of his own city . . .'

Robin's eyes filled with tears. 'That's what scares me about life!' she confided. 'You just can't tell what's going to happen . . .'

'But *you* have everything, Robin . . . You don't have to worry.'

'No . . . When I try to get a fix on the future . . . I can't really see it. It's as though the future doesn't know me . . . or hasn't made up its mind about me.' She paused, looked around the quiet church. 'I keep getting this feeling . . . I just know something weird is going to happen!'

Colm felt a shiver climb his backbone. He turned her around to face him. She smiled shakily, shook her head.

'It was OK for old Savvy here . . .' she faltered. 'He had belief. He knew God was up there on that cloud. I used to believe that crap too, but when I needed God He wasn't there.'

Colm stopped what he was about to say and looked into her eyes.

'Robin, what happened to you?'

She turned her face away. '. . . I tried very hard to do things right . . . But if nothing works when you try . . . If you can trust nothing . . . then you don't know who you are any more. That's why I'm so scared of the future . . .'

Colm put his arm around her shoulders. 'Your future will be wonderful!' he said fiercely in her ear, as though his will would direct the course of Fate. 'I know it will.'

He turned to the statue of Savonarola and said, *sotto voce*, gazing into the powerful, obsessive face: 'I ask of you, who once preached in this very place, who loved justice and hated hypocrisy, to kelp make this girl's life a fulfilment, a reward!'

His voice, which had started on a jocose note, ended on a perfectly serious one, made strange by involuntary intensity.

'Reward for what?' Robin whispered, sounding stunned and intimidated.

'For being you. Isn't that reason enough?'

Subdued, they stood up to leave. Colm put some lire into the box and lit a candle. 'This is for Robin,' he said to Savonarola.

Robin searched in her pocket, found some change and did likewise, glancing up at the fierce bronze face of the one-time Prior of San Marco. 'This is for Colm!

'He gives me the creeps!' she said, making a sudden nauseous gesture, putting her hand on her stomach.

'You shouldn't be so nervous,' Colm said. 'That's what's making you feel sick. You're so nervous sometimes you make *me* feel nervous. Sit down and just relax for a while.'

They sat together in a pew until Robin said she was feeling better.

'Oh, the stories I could tell you!' Robin said that evening when they were having supper in the Piazzale Michelangelo, the huge terrace overlooking the city. She seemed completely recovered from her earlier indisposition, and ate a plate of pasta with evident relish. Below them they could see the tower of the Palazzo Vecchio, the dome of the Duomo, the Ponte Vecchio and its sister bridges, the river winding through the night-time sparkle. She had had three glasses of wine and her voice had assumed the giddy register of one who is tipsy and enjoying it.

Colm was enjoying her profile as she stared from the balustraded parapet at the view, the small evening breeze ruffling her hair. Robin, he felt, had begun really to relax around him. He loved their friendship; it redeemed him, restored him to a self he thought he had lost, diluted his self-hatred to the point where it evaporated.

'What stories?' Colm demanded, avid for them whatever they were, half aware that she wanted to tell him something, that she had been angling around it for some time. 'Why don't you tell me about this art teacher of yours.'

'What art teacher? Oh, you mean poor Mario . . . Are you jealous?'

When Colm gave an exasperated grunt she went on, 'OK, OK, I'll tell you. I was fifteen. He was twenty-four and divinely handsome. His name was Count Mario Vespucci. He was an Italian Count – you needn't look at me like that! – his family had lost their money and he had to work for a living, so he taught art and Italian. They had a castle in the Romagna – that's further south. It was falling down: he showed me photographs. I showed him the picture of the Ponte Vecchio, and he told me about Florence. He told me about the painters, about Botticelli . . .'

'So that's why you were so fascinated by his stuff. Some little poof got you all wound up.' He glanced at her. 'Well, don't stop! What happened?'

'I started seeing him . . . after school. We used to go to Central Park and walk and talk about everything. Then I began to meet him at weekends. Sometimes we hired bicycles from the Seventy-second Street boathouse . . . We were madly in love of course . . .'

She shivered suddenly, rubbing her bare upper arms with the palms of her hands. 'He said that when I got older we would be married: then I would be Contessa Vespucci . . .'

'Bullshit, Robin!'

'You needn't believe me if you don't want.'

'Quite a romance, between a teacher and a pupil. How long did this go on?'

'Not long. The nuns found out . . . someone saw us. He was fired . . .'

'And you were in big trouble?'

She didn't answer for a moment, then glanced at Colm, shrugged. 'It's gettin' kinda chilly . . .'

Although he was almost certain that Mario Vespucci did not exist, Colm was jealous of him. He took her sweater from the back of his chair, stood up and draped it across her slim shoulders. He did this very slowly, letting his hand linger, longing to touch her, even the back of her head where the hair curled, wondering if this non-existent Mario fellow, or someone, had done this . . . or more. She sat still during this ministration, her face inscrutable. Encouraged by her passivity he allowed his fingers to touch the curve of her neck where it met her shoulder, let his palm move down inside her cotton blouse until he was cupping one small breast. It was done in a moment.

Her breast was soft and firm; the nipple stiffened; there was a sudden sharp intake of her breath. Suddenly, desire was a tidal wave, so powerful it took his breath away; it seemed to tower over him, urgent and intractable. He wanted to put his mouth to her nipple, to suck, to hold her and penetrate her, to lose himself in her. His hand moved to the other breast; it was silken and warm and vulnerable. The excitement was suffocating.

But, instead of yielding, Robin started like someone awakened from a trance.

'Get the fuck off me,' she hissed, abruptly pulling away from him. 'I guess this is all part of that wonderful "feeling, fucking and forgetting" routine . . . If you had the smallest idea of what it's like . . . when someone is just fucking using you . . .'

'Robin, I'm not . . .'

136

But she was on her feet, walking away by the stone balustrade, no longer looking down at Florence but losing herself almost immediately in the crowd.

Colm ran after her. 'Robin,' he called. 'Robin!'

But she was gone.

He returned to the pensione in the Via Nazionale in bleak mood. 'Women,' he kept saying to himself. 'A bunch of bloody prick-teasers! And they can't even take a joke . . .' He was deadly tired. Something she had said – 'If you had the smallest idea of what it's like when someone is just using you!' – reverberated. He took a shower and got into bed, telling himself he didn't give a tinker's cuss if she never showed up again. He'd had enough of her prima donna stunts. He thought briefly of his day, and for a moment the time spent at Savonarola's statue in San Marco returned to him vividly. Why did I act the bloody eejit? he asked himself, conjuring the future like some sort of second-rate fortune teller!

He turned off the light, drifted into sleep.

But sleep brought no surcease. It was not Savonarola who troubled his dreams, but Father Madden. The Goat's hands . . . the Goat's breath . . . his small smile.

'Father Madden wants to see you in his study!'

Dragging unwilling limbs down the corridor. Heart hammering, stomach lurching, bowels on the point of loosening.

The mahogany door, beautifully panelled, the brass doorknob, the small plate which read 'Father Madden'.

He knocked. The calm, authoritarian voice said, 'Come in.'

He turned the knob and found himself inside. Except for the desk-lamp the room was almost in darkness. A fire burned in the grate; the wind blustered in occasional bursts in the chimney. A breviary, bound in black, sat on the mantelpiece. Above it was a steel engraving, framed in black, Jesus teaching the old men in the temple, a twelve-year-old Jesus with a halo and a pointing finger. The glass door of the bookcase reflected the firelight. The striped curtains, brown and beige, were drawn across the eighteenth-century windows.

Father Madden was sitting behind his desk, reading some papers. Behind him on the cream distempered wall hung a crucifix.

He barely glanced at his pupil, returned his eyes to his work. The lamp shed a greenish light and gave a macabre cast to his face. He seemed a giant, huge and godlike, emanating the charisma of power. Then Colm saw his former tormentor: at the far end of the long desk lay the Biff.

The boy stood uncertainly. He was spellbound, aware of his impotence, desperately trying to read the situation. How much trouble was he in; what kind of beating would he get this time? As he stood there came the longing to please. He wanted suddenly to be approved of, by this man who was so much larger than life, who knew everything, who wielded omnipotence in the world to which Colm now belonged. He wanted to ingratiate himself, but he did not dare to smile.

'Well?' Father Madden asked in a stern voice. 'What are you here for then?'

'I don't know, Father!'

'No idea at all, I suppose? You think I call you out of study just so you can stroll the corridors?'

Colm looked at the crucifix on the wall. 'No, Father.' He felt the firelight on the backs of his trouser legs.

'What then?'

Colm shifted his feet, harkening back to his comment to O'Loughlin earlier that day, that the priests had no jurisdiction over day pupils outside of school hours.

'I said something I shouldn't have, Father . . .'

'Treason, sir!' the priest shouted. 'Is that the way you would treat your teachers, the people who work so hard for you, who are so concerned with your moral welfare, with all your moral welfares? Who have given their lives,' and here his voice rose, 'their *lives*, to your education!' The ferocity of this address pushed Colm to the verge of tears. He felt the weight of this man's sacrifice, his own wrongdoing, wondered why he had not realised its gravity. He saw the priests' perspective. They were only thinking of the moral good of their pupils; he had undermined that in questioning their authority. He knew their sacrifice was real. He wanted to be elsewhere, glanced towards the door, but it was firmly closed as he had left it. He felt the sweat break out; he anticipated the Biff which Father Madden now caressed. A sob escaped him; it was a bodily terror which had side-stepped conscious control.

The priest was on his feet. He towered dramatically over the boy; long black soutane, white dog collar, Biff in hand.

'Lock the door!'

Colm obeyed. He went to the door and turned the key.

'Take down your trousers and bend over that chair!'

Again Colm obeyed even while he vetted all the possibilities, flight, fight, outright refusal, but he was cowed by what would accrue from that and, he told himself, it would be over quickly. He endured the blows without murmur. He stood up then, tried to pull up his trousers. There was a momentary silence.

'It's time we had a chat, Colm . . .'

Father Madden's voice was suddenly of a different register, a little husky. He took Colm by the elbow, guided him to the armchair by the fire, sat down.

'Do you know how much it hurts me to have to biff you?' Colm did not reply. He did not understand this change of tone, this new persona who looked at him with kindness. He was holding on to the waist of his trousers to haul them up.

'It hurts me more than it hurts you . . . Do you believe that, Colm?'

Colm nodded. He was beyond veracity. He studied the floor, saw the geometric precision of the parquet with a strange objectivity in which Pythagoras's theorem suddenly surfaced, informing him about the square of the hypotenuse.

He tried to distance himself from the pain and the

humiliation, tried to prevent his eyes filling with tears. This kindness, so unexpected, was intolerable. He continued to hold on to his trousers with one hand as the priest held his other arm by the elbow. Then suddenly he was aware of something in the air, cloying, ominous, something which demanded a certain kind of surrender, which promised rewards.

He turned to look in Father Madden's face and saw how his pupils had dilated and how his mouth was slightly open and his lips heavy. There was the thrill of insight, of the priest's instinctively felt need, as though he had opened a secret door and found himself suddenly in possession of a profane power. The priest reached out and took Colm's other hand. As the boy's trousers fell about his ankles the priest placed him on his knees.

Colm was small for his age. His everyday alert self watched in repelled curiosity while the priest stroked his thighs. Even his repulsion had a sexual component – the confused but intuitive sense of evil, the tacit bargain, the astonishment that God, the boss, the great one, should sit there stroking his legs, right up to his groin, should slip his hand between his legs, should press with his palm, should stroke and explore, should breathe heavily, should elicit in him an involuntary response, should divide him, now and for ever, against himself. Presumption of this order had a hypnotic component, invited capitulation of something he hardly knew he possessed.

He pulled away, but the arms of the priest pinned him. He was breathing heavily.

'Just checking to see how you're growing . . . Good boy . . . Good boy . . . No need to tell anyone about this . . . It's a thing between men . . .' He winked, breathing faster. Invasion. He opened his own trousers, took Colm's hand, and positioned it, worked it with his. Total power, complicity exacted.

'We'll keep it between us!' he said afterwards. And then he took the Bible and placed Colm's hand on it. 'Repeat after me – I will never divulge this secret. I swear by God!'

Colm swore. Father Madden took a chocolate bar from a drawer and handed it to him. 'I know how young lads are always hungry!' he said with a wink.

He heard someone calling his name. 'Colm, Colm . . . it's a dream! Wake up, for Chrissake!'

Robin was bending over him. He was wet with sweat. The sheet was sticking to him.

'Jesus!' he said. 'I thought you were the Goat.'

Robin gave a short laugh. 'Many things I may be, but I'm pretty sure I ain't no goat.' She sat on the edge of his bed and regarded him quizzically.

'Sorry about earlier . . .' Colm said after a moment, when his heart had resumed its normal rhythm. 'I shouldn't have pawed you.'

She looked back at him gravely. 'No,' she replied. 'You sure shouldn't.' She would have gone on, but Colm turned on his side away from her. He did not want her to see that he was trembling. He closed his eyes.

Robin did not disturb him further. Through half-closed eyes he watched her pull a fresh nightdress from her rucksack. Something was caught in it and clattered on the mosaic floor. It was a small crucifix.

He shuddered. She put it back in her rucksack. He heard her go out to the bathroom, heard her return, heard her getting into bed, knew when she turned out the light. As his eyes became accustomed to the dark he saw the dim rods of light coming through the shutters.

I should have killed that bastard, he thought. I should have gutted him there and then.

Colm arrived in Milan.

Twenty-eight years, he thought, since I first set foot in Milan, on the way home from Florence at the end of that September. Does anybody dream how life will accelerate, until the years have gone? Once Robin had said, 'Our time is already

141

over . . . Don't you see – the future is already looking back at us with nostalgia.'

He alighted, dragged his case along on its castors, listened to the chant of the public address system as it announced departures: '. . . *partendo da binario dodici, fermando a Piacenza, Parma e Bologna* . . .' Italian male voice with a mechanical lilt, like a poetic machine gun. He glanced at his watch, saw that he had thirty minutes to make his connection to Florence.

He walked to the main hallway, gazed down the long flights of steps to the station loggia below. Crowds scurrying, the scrape of suitcases over mosaic, the hubbub of feet and voices, the overlying intonation of departure information, the billboards, the shops, the smell of coffee, all as before. But there was no Robin now, no small sun-bleached head and bronzed face, screwed up with defiance. He watched a young woman in jeans with cropped fair hair, imagining that the years had reversed themselves and that she would turn and smile and say, 'Hey, Irish, you looking at something?'

Robin was more than an enigma. In retrospect she had been a very insecure and frightened young woman, who had tried to hide her fear with her pride. But in her he'd had a friend such as he would never see again.

You left her behind and in danger, a small self-accusatory voice informed. You failed her just as you have failed everyone.

Show me one perfect thing that I have done, he thought in panic, one thing to redeem me. But even as he searched his mind he could think of none.

The Inter City to Rome was leaving from platform nine, stopping at Bologna and Florence. He found his first-class carriage and reserved seat, stashed his case, sat back and watched the scurrying on the platform.

I have changed, he thought wearily; there is no point in remembering too much. I am no longer the same person. I have acquired the scarred baggage of the years.

He wondered how they were getting on without him at the office. He searched for his mobile phone, fished it out and placed a call. In half a minute he was talking to Jane, his secretary. Everything was fine, was running like clockwork. Jack was working on all his current files; there were no problems. Yes, they had his phone number in Florence if they needed him. He was to enjoy his holiday.

Colm put away the mobile phone, sat back and wondered at the increasing complexity of life. There were many things that had been thrust on him: Sherry's defection for that nobody Michael, for instance. Well, she was living in relative penury, and had only herself to blame. Kattie, that secret torrent of passion, had defected too. He should not have sought her out again; he should have left her alone, kept her only as a childhood memory. But it would have been impossible to have ignored his adult chance with her; too much had hinged on her acceptance of him. His self-image, even his identity, had hinged on it. He shrugged off the niggle of guilt. Perhaps the truth was that when he was twenty-one a waif from another world had stolen what was left of his soul. When something in the back of his mind whispered that his life was too complex for such ready analysis, he dismissed the intrusion and tried to sleep. He was beginning, in good earnest, to regret this journey.

In Florence Paola sat at her office desk working over her latest article. Her contact had informed her about bribes taken by certain members of the police. Paola was cautious, but sketched the story, finishing a first draft, suppressing judgement, as always, until later. She would hone the article, research it further; she still had a few days before her new deadline.

Her thoughts turned to Pasquale and then to her paying guests. She had put the two younger ones, Darina and Renate, American and German respectively, in the same room and hoped they would get on. Jill, the English publishing editor, was gentle, polite to the point of self-annihilation. But Paola knew the English well enough not to take this at face value. Tonight the fourth guest would arrive, the Irishman Colm Nugent. She was satisfied that he couldn't be the student she had met in the amphitheatre.

No. Life had swallowed everything except duty and responsibility. And why not? Paola thought. It was, after all, the common human lot.

She went to the ladies' room. In the corridor she met Silvestro. He squeezed her hand. He was a port of sorts in a storm, but a haven which might just as quickly become a maelstrom. He did not know that she had discussed him, albeit obliquely, with a woman friend.

'Be careful, Paola. Admittedly there is something wrong with his marriage, something is missing. Perhaps he fantasises about living with you; you give him back his childhood and his roots. But it is one thing to fantasise and another to act. It is always the Other Woman who is trampled on.'

Paola knew all this was true. But sometimes she dreamed of his warm bulk beside her, shared understanding, shared intimacy, warmth, so on offer, so available. She dreamed of trusting him. And then her mind, analytical, cautious, would conjure up the consequences. She would become involved on a level she would have difficulty in disciplining; would he become the opportunist? And what would happen then? Whether he knew it or not he was rooted in Erica, his earthy wife, the peasant girl he had married and who now bored him. He was rooted in her because he was rooted in his pride. And if their clandestine relationship were to lead nowhere, would Paola lose him too? It took a very powerful friendship to survive sex.

No. Famine might stare her in the face, but things were better left as they were.

She regarded her reflection, added some shadow to her upper lids. Her sombre black eyes looked back at her. She was aware of her beauty and half disdainful of it; what had it really done for her?

She brushed her tinted gold hair and coiled it on the back

of her head. Once her tresses had been brown, but she had changed the colour for fun in her early twenties, had left them that way to please Giovanni who liked the contrast between black eyes and gold hair. If Colm Nugent turned out to be the same boy as the one she remembered, he wouldn't recognise her in a million years.

Her thoughts reverted to what she would serve for supper. Chicken would be all right. Spaghetti for starters. She went into Silvestro's office as she was leaving, to say goodnight.

He kissed her hand. '*Che gelida manina!*' he commented. Once, long ago, they had seen *La Bohème* together.

'My hands are always cold, Silvestro. It is part of my English inheritance!'

He put his head on one side, in mock supplication. 'I'll warm them, *cara*. Feet too. I'll warm everything. You only have to say.'

She made a playful shooing gesture with her hand.

God, she enquired silently as she left the building, will You leave me with nothing but games for ever?

Part Two

Chapter Eight

This return to Florence after twenty-eight years Colm experienced as surreal: the Inter City sliding into the station of Santa Maria Novella, the light of evening on the platforms, yet another male voice, strident above the station hubbub, announcing departures.

He alighted, found his way through the crowds of backpackers, located the taxi rank, handed the driver the address in the Via de' Tornabuoni. He glanced at the slip of paper in his hand which gave his hostess's name, 'Signora Nosterini', and her address.

He was there as soon as the rush-hour traffic would permit, paid off the taxi, tipping generously to compensate for the short journey, stood by the huge black portal and examined the list of names behind the small plastic covers, rang the bell. A young male voice came through the intercom. '*Si?*'

'Colm Nugent.'

'Pleeze push the door.'

The buzzer sounded. He pushed the small, person-sized door, contained within the greater one, itself so high and so wide that he could imagine a coach and four entering with room to spare. Inside he was in a dim, cobbled courtyard; it led to a further outdoor one, on the far side of which the sun brightened the upper part of old ochre walls. There was a great stone staircase, and a lift shaft enclosed only by a tough wire mesh. The lift descended with a whirring sound, its working steel cables visible, clunked as it connected with the floor and the door opened.

A youth of about sixteen stood in the open door, looking at Colm. He was tall and slim, and had the proud features found in old Florentine paintings.

'*Signore Nugent?*' he asked with a courteous inclination of his head.

'*Si.*'

He stepped out, gestured for Colm to precede him into the lift. Colm's mind was in overdrive, polishing the few phrases he had brushed up through Linguaphone. He remembered he must use the formal address, the third person which was the correct form for addressing strangers.

'*Lei è il figilio di Signora Nosterini?*'

The boy nodded, indicating that he was indeed Signora Nosterini's son. '*Si. Mi chiamo Pasquale.*' Then he said in English, 'Our apartment is on the third floor.'

'Ah,' Colm said weakly, finding that further conversation had deserted him. Pasquale! An Easter Bunny! Alan had been born at Easter too, a long hard labour, and a day of wonder.

The lift deposited them on a mosaic landing. A heavy panelled door was open almost opposite. Pasquale guided him there; Colm put his case down in a red-tiled hallway where a slim, shapely woman, with the same patrician cast to her features as her son, came forward to greet him. She held her classical head as though it were something to be proud of. He registered that she was beautiful.

'*Buona sera. Signora Nosterini?*'

She inclined her head; but something moved in her eyes, a startled instant, a small smile. '*Paola,*' she said gravely. '*Mi chiamo Paola!*' They shook hands.

'*Mi chiamo Colm,*' he returned, adding in English, 'do you speak English?'

'A little,' she replied with a twinkle. 'But you are here to learn Italian . . . No?'

Colm, feeling himself observed, looked around. Pasquale was regarding him, his face inscrutable. The boy moved away, disappeared down the corridor.

The hall of the apartment was square. One wall was taken up with a life-sized oil portrait of his hostess. In a corner was a table, piled high with magazines; on top of these perched a red telephone. Colm turned back to his hostess, noted that she was studying him, her mouth still curved in a smile.

'*Lei è* . . .' Colm began, but she forestalled him.

'We use "*tu*", the familiar form here,' she said in English. '"*Lei*" is too formal for us.'

'Good! Makes life easier,' Colm said.

She showed him to his room. He followed her along a corridor, where a few items of statuary occupied wall niches; her hips swayed as she walked. Her hair was a mass of assisted gold, neatly coiffed, and when she turned to look at him two intelligent black eyes stared out of her lively, sculpted face. Forty-something, Colm thought, and wearing it like a trouper. What a country this was for women!

She showed him his room, indicated the bathroom across the corridor. 'We have three other students staying,' she said. 'I'm a widow. My husband died last year.' Then she added, glancing at him, 'Dinner is at eight.'

Colm closed the door. He examined his room. White walls, mosaic floor. There was a small crucifix hanging above the bed. The louvred shutters were ajar, held by the latch. He threw them wide and looked down upon the street, filled his ears with the traffic roar. To his right the granite Roman pillar with the statue of Justice, scales in hand, occupied the centre of the little Piazza di Santa Trinita. Once, long ago, he had walked this street with a girl called Robin McKay. He searched the pedestrians for sight of a small figure with sun-bleached hair on whom he could pin an almost palpable memory, but was unsuccessful. He saw the faceless traffic, heard the screaming mopeds, smelt the fumes of the rush-hour bustle. He tried to see the river, which he knew was near, but it was hidden by the curve of the street. He also looked for sight of the tower belonging to the Palazzo Vecchio, but again was unsuccessful, although he knew it was only a few streets away.

Down below him horns were tooted in the clammy evening. For a moment, looking down, he felt quite dizzy. I must be more tired than I know, came the thought. The sense of exhaustion did not ease as he willed utter immobility on his body; instead, it intensified until he thought he would faint. He held on to the window frame and closed his eyes. In his ears the city buzzed like the song of far-off bees, a droning sound, the world distancing itself. He opened his eyes in sudden fear that he was receding down some corridor of oblivion, his mind suddenly full of the doctor's warnings. Baroom, baroom, his heart said.

As he forced his eyes to focus once more on the figures on the footpaths below he saw, emerging from a strangely surrealist scene of flitting forms, a young girl on the other side of the street, white cotton top, blue jeans. It was the body language which arrested his gaze first, but even the hair, colour and style was more or less the same, the movement of the body, the small feet in white trainers, and above all the glimpse of her profile. God, it was Robin to the life, young Robin, unchanged, slim, with the same unconscious grace. A van moved along the street, coughing exhaust, cut off his view of her. He waited, excited, confused. The sounds from below lost their far-off resonance, resumed their immediacy. The van moved, but she was gone.

He stood where he was for a moment, then stumbled back into the room, sat ruefully on the bed, aware of the beating of his heart. He took his shoes off and lay down.

His bed was somehow virginal, single, with polished mahogany headboard, a white bedspread. He reached to the small crucifix on the wall above the bed, took it down, put it in a drawer. Two thick white towels, folded neatly, were on the chair. There was a bedside table, a bookcase, a desk and a chair by the window, a walnut wardrobe and chest of drawers. A threadbare oriental rug in faded browns and reds was on the floor.

The only other furniture was a painting of the Tuscan

countryside in a wooden frame. The room was foreign, unpretentious, possessing an effortless elegance. It had a faint scent, unidentifiable but reminiscent of sandalwood. As he lay there, staring at the ceiling, the normal rhythm of his heart resumed and as it did so, he felt strength return to him. He was on holiday! Pondering this he suddenly felt possessed of freedom. No laden desk awaited him tomorrow; no phones would shrill for him; no secretaries would beaver away to fulfil his schedules. It's like being a student, he thought, like being a youngster again: as though everything were still ahead, and only childhood lay behind.

He became aware that his clothes were sticking to his body and decided to have a bath. But then it occurred to him that staying as he was, *en famille*, it would be better not simply to take it for granted; they might have rules. He went in search of his hostess.

'*Posso prendere un bagno?*' He asked this with diffidence, feeling absurd.

'*Si, certo . . .*'

She was standing by the gas stove in the small kitchen, tending a huge pot and turned with a slight inclination of her head. Laughter played on her lips.

Is there something funny about me? Colm wondered.

He went to the bathroom, got into an almost cold bath with relief, splashed around in it until he felt human again. Then he returned to his room, changed his clothes, donned a white Ralph Lauren shirt, lay back on the bed once more. A mosquito which had arrived while he was bathing was now hanging upside down on the ceiling with the immobile patience of a vulture. 'You have to surprise them with their pants down,' Robin had once said. But he knew he was unlikely to be troubled; mosquitoes never bothered him now; his arms and the backs of his hands were too hairy, his skin too tough.

He thought of his hostess. Yes, there was something funny about him. He was incongruous in this world he had invaded.

Enjoy it, you bloody fool, he said to himself. Try it for a

153

few days at least; you can always decamp to a hotel. Who knows . . . you may even find it interesting!

Supper was served in the dining room, a room with two glass-panelled bookcases, a sideboard and an oval, antique table. The French window opened to a geranium-filled balcony which overlooked the courtyard; net curtains shimmied in the small breeze created by leaving the door of the room ajar. But despite this, the suffocating humidity permeated everything, dulled the conversation, so that after the initial introductions and exchange of pleasantries, the talk became desultory.

His fellow guests were three young women. They came to table separately. The youngest, Darina, about twenty-four he guessed, was American. The second to arrive was called Jill. English, pretty, thirtyish, dressed to kill in a pale pink sheath with a bolero. She wore gold jewellery. The third was mid twenties, a German girl called Renate. She had blue eyes, fair hair. Her expression said that life was no joking matter, that it was a serious and complicated obstacle course where only the fittest survived. It also said that she would be numbered among the survivors. Of the three only Renate seemed to be fluent in Italian. All three eyed Colm, covertly. Jill greeted him in a high-pitched, rarefied accent which did not become the language she was speaking; but she laughed at her own mistakes. Renate responded to questions with precise replies, perfect grammar and syntax. The American temporarily reminded him of Robin, but only because of her twang. She mentioned a night club called '*Il Cane*' where she had been the evening before and spoke of some group which had evidently captivated her. Pasquale sat quietly, passing plates and Paola presided over her table, keeping an eye on her son who said little, but who offered the wine with grave courtesy, and helped carry things to and from the kitchen.

Suddenly Colm felt astonishingly old, a dinosaur; the earlier sense of having recaptured the insouciance of his student days evaporated. A titular student he might be, but he was older even than the cicerone at the top of the table.

Renate addressed Colm in Italian, asked him if he were tired after his journey. '*Sei stanco dopo il viaggio?*' Colm understood, acknowledged that he was, a little. He summoned every syllable he knew of the language, but when he tried to explain that he had travelled overland he lapsed into English.

'You must be very tired!' his hostess said, and he conceded that he was.

The meal was good; it began with spaghetti with tomato sauce and fresh basil, followed by roast chicken of a dimension Colm had never seen before, a giant chicken, served with salad.

'Have you visited Florence before?' his hostess asked him in Italian as she served him, and he said he had when he was young.

When Signora Nosterini left the table to take a phone call Colm spoke in English. 'How long have you girls been here?'

'We've just come,' Jill said, giving him a big smile. She showed lots of teeth; she radiated the desire to be kind.

'But we're not *girls*!' Darina put in sweetly.

Colm was taken aback, but he countered with jocularity. 'Sorry. I thought you were!' This last with what he thought was a boyish grin. 'So what are you if you're not girls? You don't look like boys!'

'Women.'

Colm let it go, raising his eyebrows in what he hoped was sardonic comment. 'What part of the States are you from?' he asked, as though this might explain things.

'Philly,' Darina replied in a tone which brooked no further patronage.

He said mildly, reaching for safe ground, 'I've never been to Philadelphia,' foolishly reluctant to let the American amazon have the last word. But this was a mistake.

She grinned. 'It's still there notwithstanding!'

Colm looked out of the window, through the balcony at

the old red roofs on the other side of the courtyard. The comment reminded him so forcibly of someone else, that he could think of nothing that would suit the parameters of the present. But he was tired and wanted no skirmish with the American.

'It's terribly hot!' he said. It was a statement. He knew he sounded foolish, but it moved the subject away.

'You should have been here last week,' Jill interposed diplomatically. 'I've seen the temperature charts and it was like the Sahara.' She turned to Pasquale for endorsement. 'Wasn't it?'

'Yes,' he said politely, in heavily accented English. 'It was very warm!'

Renate said nothing, but looked censorious. Her demeanour reminded everyone that she was not there to learn English. She would make a good dragon, Colm thought, if she were a hundred years older, breathed methane; if, instead of soft, blooming skin, she were covered with scales.

Paola Nosterini returned from the phone, looked at the young women disapprovingly.

'She doesn't like us talking English. She takes her duties seriously,' Jill said *sotto voce*, as though she would draw him into some familial circle, initiate him kindly into the new status quo. For a moment Colm was reminded of another status quo into which he had once sought admittance; the parallel was striking and absurd, the new boy at school trying to find the ropes.

Pasquale, with an inclination of his head towards the phone, said to his mother, *'Chi ha telefonato?'*

'Silvestro.'

He nodded, became quiet again, listened patiently to the halting Italian conversation and replied when spoken to. He dislikes his mother's guests, Colm thought, watching him, catching the spark of impatience in his body language. He feels we're an imposition. He thought of Alan who would have been about the same age now. But Alan had been strong,

156

always had a good appetite, laughing as Sherry had measured him against the kitchen wall. 'Another inch! We'll have to put a stone on your head, young man.'

They had. The stone said 'Alan Nugent, 1981–1994'.

Watching Pasquale he felt the sudden hunger. To have a living child, to watch him grow, your son, to know he carried your life into the future beyond your reach. To have someone call you 'Dad'. To be needed. Even to be loved.

He wondered why the boy ate so little. He picked at his dinner and his mother's eyes were never far from him. Is it because she watches him so anxiously that he does not eat? Colm wondered on a surge of irritation. Why is she so overprotective? Is he playing to her anxiety, looking for attention?

When Darina essayed some further comment in English Paola raised her gold head, stared at her and said in Italian: 'Darina, if you are talking English you are wasting your time here and everyone else's!'

Renate nodded. '*E vero!*' she said, with an aggrieved sniff, and then engaged her hostess in rapid Italian, correct to the last syllable.

Colm applied himself to his meal. I'm too old for this, he thought. I've come here like a moth to a flame, unreasoning, drawn like a creature without a brain, for reasons I can only feel but cannot fathom. Should I take myself off to the four-star hotel in the Piazza Santa Maria Novella which I passed in the taxi? It was not far, he reasoned, a few minutes' walk and he would have complete peace, regain his autonomy, lose the idiotic feeling of being a schoolboy again.

Renate, now centre stage, eyed the polo-playing logo on his shirt, spoke to him suddenly in precise Italian, but there was a twinkle in her eye as though she had divined his irritation and found it amusing. He tried to answer. But while he could understand the question, which had to do with Ireland and its climate, he could not find the words to reply. He was too tired.

'*Mi dispiace*,' he said, to let her know he was trying, but unequal to the task. Then a few appropriate words surfaced. '*Fa freddo in Irlanda . . . piove . . .*' telling her that it was relatively cold in Ireland, raining, making it sound worse than it was to fill out the conversation.

His hostess fanned herself with her napkin and complimented the Irish climate with each flap. Colm could not eat the amount of food pressed on him. The pasta had been very good, the tomato sauce with fresh basil delicious, but he ate only part of it and played with his chicken.

'*Non ti piace?*' Paola asked softly as she took up the plates. Her eyes lingered on him, brightly, curiously. He found her interest unsettling, felt again that he amused her in some indefinable way.

Colm indicated that he did like it, but had had enough. He caught, from the corner of his eye, the small movement Pasquale made as he watched the exchange between his mother and her latest guest.

There was fruit for dessert and then the younger people excused themselves, leaving only Paola and Colm at the table. Paola touched her son's hand as he passed from the room, shot him an anxious look. The boy looked suddenly irritated, sighed.

'I will help you with the English later,' she said to him in English.

Pasquale said, glancing swiftly at Colm, his demeanour suddenly embarrassed, 'I only need you to help with the poetry, Mamma . . . I can do the rest myself!'

Paola brought coffee to the table for herself and Colm and poured them each a Strega, sipped the liqueur, and said with a sigh in perfect English, 'This is my relaxing time . . . We can talk English now if you like. How do you feel after your journey?'

Colm started with surprise. Her English was coolly perfect, down to the last Oxford intonation.

'A moment ago I felt like a child at school,' Colm replied,

'but now I am restored to the adult world!'

She gave a small apologetic laugh. 'I'm sorry, but if I don't intervene Darina would always speak English and Renate would always get annoyed about it.' She considered him for a moment, frowned and then asked, 'Why did you decide to come to Florence?'

'I was here for a while in my student days . . . I was with a friend, an American. I felt a bit nostalgic about it. But now I think I must represent a bizarre figure, among all this golden youth?'

'Golden youth disappeared with our generation,' she replied tartly. 'This lot are pragmatists; we were visionaries.'

Her Oxford accent sat strangely with her Florentine looks, her flashing eyes, and foreign body language. She looked magnificent, Colm thought, a combination of pride and serenity, spiced with humour.

'You speak more than "a little" English,' Colm said. 'In fact you speak it perfectly. Where did you learn it?'

'In England. I'm half-English!'

'So you had the benefits of a bi-lingual upbringing?'

'Not really. My mother died when I was a baby. But I had two great-aunts who lived in Cambridgeshire. I stayed with them while I was at a language school there for a year – in 1970. I also learned English at school here of course . . . and sometimes even press-ganged stray tourists to speak to me.' She looked at him carefully as she said this, and her eyes twinkled for a moment with private recollection.

Colm nodded politely. Something rubbed against his legs as a small black cat crept from its basket and jumped into Paola's lap.

'*Mi amore!*' she exclaimed passionately, lifting the cat and kissing it, turning it to Colm for his admiration.

'You see, she has amber eyes.'

As she lifted her arms in this small movement, Colm felt, rather than saw, how her breasts rose under her cotton shirt and, stirred momentarily, he imagined them at once, soft and round and yielding, with a small brown nut on the top of each. For a moment he longed for the feel of a woman in his arms. It was not even a physical hunger, as once it would have been; it had to do with radical contact, escape from himself.

'So you are on a sentimental journey?' she asked suddenly.

Colm was taken aback. He disliked sentiment.

'Not sentimental exactly. I think I had to come, to understand. Something happened here . . . it's a long story, a piece of adolescent foolishness . . .'

She shot him a keen look, but made no further comment.

When he had finished the Strega Colm thanked his hostess for the meal, said he was going out for a while.

'You will need a key.' She rose, went to the drawer in the bookcase, handed him three keys on a small ring.

'That one is for the outer door; the brass one is for the mortice lock of the apartment and the smaller one for opening the apartment door.'

'Thank you, Paola . . .' He looked around at the table and added, uncharacteristically for he hated housework, 'May I help you clear up?' There was something so patrician about this woman that it seemed improper that she should wait on a group of strangers.

'No . . . not at all, thank you.'

He went to his room for his jacket, let himself down in the lift and ventured into the Florentine dusk. A private mentor inside his head enquired if, given his earlier faintness in his room, he would not have been better off retiring, but he blocked its importunity. The same private mentor asked him why he had almost divulged to his hostess something he had never spoken of to anyone. What had happened in Florence in 1968 was woven into the strange fabric that was his life, a secret, fiercely guarded, a foolish episode. But it had had its benefits, he had long ago decided; it had tempered him, finally taught him invulnerability.

He would take it easy, he told himself. No harm in a short

walk. The doctor had said he should exercise. What he had to avoid was stress.

It took him a leisurely ten minutes to find the Via Nazionale. He stood across the street, looked up at the window on the first floor of the Pensione Zellini.

Nothing had changed. Nothing! There was the same balcony on which she had hung her little cotton knickers to dry; there were the tall shutters that had creaked in the opening. Behind them was doubtless the same lofty room with the tarnished brass candelabrum. The winds of time had hardly passed here; he felt that the room should be festooned in cobwebs, unused, untouched, a shrine.

Ah, Robin, would you believe it, here I am! I did come back after all, despite your scoffing. Will you be there to meet me in the Piazza della Signoria on the fifteenth?

Of course she won't, his rational self insisted. And even if she was, what of it? They would be strangers now. She would be caught up in the weft of her own life.

He retraced his steps, stood at the street corner for a moment with his back resting against the wall. He turned to look back at the Pensione Zellini. On the pavement just outside it a girl in jeans and white top was walking away from him down the street. It was almost certainly the same girl he had seen earlier from his window.

'Robin . . .' he whispered, borne up by a visceral sense of recognition. He wanted to follow her, but reason prevailed. As he watched her she quickened her pace, turned left into the Via Faenza and disappeared.

He walked slowly in the warm night back to the apartment in the Via de' Tornabuoni.

He let himself in, came up in the lift. Paola was nowhere to be seen, but as he walked to his room he heard her talking to her son in the latter's bedroom. The door was ajar. He caught a glimpse of them as he passed. Pasquale was lying propped up in bed, a book on his knees. His mother was sitting beside him, reading glasses on, repeating a verse in English with slow precision, explaining a word.

She glanced up as Colm passed in the corridor, stopped reading for a moment, her expression bemused, before resuming the lesson.

Her son's eyes regarded her gravely. She reached over and put her hand on his forehead. 'You are all right, my son?'

Pasquale nodded impatiently. '*Si, Mamma, si!*'

Colm's first night was virtually sleepless. He dozed for a while and dreamt of Catherine Clohessy. Then he woke, her face still in his brain, did not know where he was and studied the dim outline of the wardrobe in utter perplexity. Memory returned in an instant.

But Kattie did not retreat to the land of dreams. He saw her twelve-year-old face which had inspired his first passion; he saw her fourteen-year-old face on the evening when she would not dance with him. 'Ah, no thanks, Colm . . .' He tasted again the rejection and the slow simmering anger, directed at her and at everything.

Then he saw her thirty-two-year-old face when he had met her again in Dublin. He had met her on Saturday morning, having seen her go into Kilkenny Design. He had followed her in and gone upstairs to the restaurant, stood behind her in the queue.

She turned at one point; he caught her eye. 'Colm!' she exclaimed with a start of recognition. There had been no mistaking her delight.

'Well, well,' Colm said. 'Long time and all that. I haven't laid eyes on you for yonks, Kattie! How many years is it?'

'Your father's funeral,' she said. 'Four years ago!' He insisted on paying for her lunch – smoked salmon salad – led her to a table.

'So tell me what you've been doing with yourself!' he said.

Kattie blushed. 'I'm still working in the Bank of Ireland . . . I'm assistant manager . . . in the Kilgarret branch.' She was

162

evidently proud of this. If she was surprised that he knew nothing about her life, she did not evince it. He never went home now, never saw Alice or Liam any more, could hardly bear to travel the main road to Roscommon. He had tried it once or twice, but found that on reaching Kinnegad his stomach churned and he took the road to Athlone instead. He had not set foot in Ballykelly since his father's death. Liam had the farm now; Alice had married a local farmer and had two sons.

Catherine had a pleasing smile, a reticent manner. Her teeth were still slightly crooked, but her figure was lovely and her eyes were shy. He wondered at the warmth in her face, the animation in her eyes. Anyone would think, he thought on a surge of cynicism, that she had just met her long-lost love.

'You never come home now!' she said accusingly. 'I always ask for you when I meet Alice . . .'

Colm gave his head a small rueful shake. 'Very busy, you know . . .'

'I heard you got married.'

'Yes . . . Would have asked you . . . but we got married in Paris. Wanted to avoid all the fuss.'

'How lovely!' She sounded wistful.

'Are you married yourself?' He directed a covert glance at her ring finger.

'No . . . Well, I almost did . . . several years ago, but you know these things don't always work out.'

He was sympathetic. She glanced around.

'I like this place,' she said. 'Sometimes I meet my friend Eileen here when I come to town. She's a friend from my schooldays,' she added inconsequentially.

'Are you often in Dublin?'

'I come up at weekends a lot. I stay with Eileen. She has a flat in Fisherman's Wharf.'

Colm said that was nice. He was watching her, noting all the small features which had once provoked his passionate love, the funny teeth, the sprinkling of freckles, the shy hazel eyes. They did not inspire anything in him now, except a kind of anger. He even resented this; he knew it was unjust. The passion he once felt had been chopped at the roots. The dying remnants of the same passion had been obliterated by her huddling into the bloody rocking chair while the family watched his humiliation. He couldn't stand women going around as though butter wouldn't melt. It was all that innocence, almost certainly affected, that had possessed him. She had made a fool of him!

But what did you do with the energy that had fuelled a frustrated passion? Did it disappear like last night's storm, leaving obvious wreckage in its wake, or did it linger in the crevices of the mind, waiting for some kind of outlet, ready, if it could not build, to destroy?

'Are you doing anything this evening?'

'Not really . . .'

'Why not come out for a bite?'

She looked troubled. 'That's very kind, but I couldn't.'

'Oh, Sherry's away,' Colm said on a note of amused exasperation. 'If that's what's bothering you. And I'm not going to eat you, Kattie. I'd just like a chat . . . for old times' sake?'

'Well . . . if you really think it's all right.'

Oh God, he thought, spare me the earnestness. He sized her body as he helped her with her coat. Very nice, size twelve, good tits.

She smiled at him from under thick brown lashes. 'Thanks very much for the lunch.'

'A pleasure. Now, if you give me your address I'll call for you at seven-thirty this evening.'

She flushed with pleasure, scribbled on the back of the envelope he produced from his pocket.

'A bientôt, Madame!'

She smiled again, reddened. 'Colm, you're so suave.'

Yes, he thought, but I wasn't suave enough for you that night we had dancing in the kitchen when you wouldn't stand up with me, huddling into the old rocker as though I had the plague!

When she was gone he berated himself. Leave her alone; phone and say you can't make it. But even as he enjoined wisdom on himself he knew that he would ignore it. He wanted this woman for all sorts of reasons. And for several years he had made a point of taking what he wanted. He had learned arrogance; it had gained him everything. You had to season it with inscrutability, of course. People were challenged by the arrogant and the inscrutable, tried to penetrate them, created powerful personae for those who proved impenetrable. It was astonishing how well this operated; how he could fascinate and intimidate from a shallow base; how it had ensured him promotion, made him rich and beyond the reach of the ingenuous or the fatuous. Yes, he had succeeded, so why did everything feel as though it echoed, as though there was no place he could lay his head?

The morning soon dawned in Florence. It was time to rise, face the new day. The misgivings of the night dissolved in the daylight. He found that he was curious about his language course, curious about the small family he had temporarily invaded, curious about his hostess. Give it a chance, he admonished himself. You could have sat at home and watched television. Instead you did something; you came here on an overpowering impulse. Stupid perhaps, out of character perhaps, but no one but you need know. So see what happens. Play it by ear. And forget all this nonsense about the past.

165

Chapter Nine

Thick slices of Italian bread and apricot jam; *caffè latte*; Paola at table in a green silk dressing-gown. Light of morning behind her; hint of burgeoning heat. Elegant head raised to greet him. '*Buon giorno, Colm. Hai dormito bene?*'

'*Si.*'

There was no point in telling her that, in fact, he had hardly slept until dawn. But now he was pleasantly aware of the new day, still cool, of the red tiles on the roofs outside, and the throaty song of the pigeons.

Paola poured coffee; her guests smiled at each other sleepily. Paola went to the kitchen; Pasquale appeared, sat silently at table, drank some milky coffee and ate a slice of bread. The intercom rang and he picked it up, said it was his lift to school, kissed his mother goodbye. '*Ciao, Mamma!*'

Again Colm saw how Paola's eyes followed him.

Darina confided that she was dog-tired; she had been out half the night at a disco. Renate said something in Italian which Colm did not understand. As usual she looked deadly serious, her young face set in anticipation of effort. Jill smiled with good-natured bonhomie and spoke in small bursts of Italian with an English accent. She was wearing a pretty white and navy T-shirt over white jeans.

Colm left after a few minutes to find the Piazza di Santo Spirito, feeling a little absurd with his black leather briefcase which contained a thick student note pad, a dictionary and his gold Sheaffer, but pleased that the school was near, within easy walking distance.

He crossed the Arno by the bridge of Santa Trinità. To his left the brick arches of the Ponte Vecchio spanned the river, sturdily bearing the ochre-painted shops so beloved of Robin. He stopped and turned; the distant hills rose up to meet Fiesole. I'm like a boy on his way to school, came the thought. Except, of course, that he had left boyhood behind him long ago. How do you really leave something behind you? he wondered then. What criteria must be met before it merges into the past and forgetfulness?

In a couple of minutes he was in the Piazza di Santo Spirito, the square where he and Robin had once lunched on rolls and mineral water. He stood bemused, glanced at the fountain playing quietly, and at the façade of the fifteenth-century church overlooking the piazza. No change in nearly thirty years. No change in three centuries probably, so what was a few decades?

It was but a matter of a minute or two to find Scuola Linguistica.

The language school was housed in a sixteenth-century palazzo. It was reached by a massive stone staircase. There was also a small lift.

Colm explained to the school secretary that he had arrived too late the day before to attend for the assessment test. She was friendly, asked him to wait, invited him to sit down. A female teacher came along and took him to a small room overlooking the piazza. Here he was given a written examination designed to show his level of competency. Then there was a brief conversation in Italian, in which Colm trotted out the responses learnt mostly through Linguaphone. After this his examiner excused herself. He waited for about ten minutes, stood by the window and looked through the shutters at the square below. It was novel, this sense of being assessed, of being a student once more. Below him in the piazza he saw a girl sitting on a bench by the fountain with a book. Near her, basking in the sun was a black cat. The girl had long dark hair, and was bent over the book with patent absorption, as though she would race the story to its conclusion. Robin and he had sat there once, he thought. And then, as the girl moved to stroke her cat, it came to him again, the memory that had struck him in Paris at the Jeu de Paume. The girl and the book and the cat. Where? He had spoken to the girl . . . It was during that time in Florence; but he had been on his own. The memory was full of shadows, something squeezed flat between the folds of life. He struggled with it, remembered suddenly the madonna-like young woman, about the same age as Robin, who had given him a glass of water. Where had it happened? There were ruins around; some old place. Of course . . . it was the bloody amphitheatre in Fiesole. He was relieved at the reassertion of memory. He remembered the girl's grace, but could not recall her face. The door opened. It was the teacher, come back to tell him he was in the 'Media' – the class just above elementary level, and to present himself at classroom number three.

Classroom number three was small, with twelve people, most of them young. There was only one student older than he, a woman called Anna who said she was Italian by birth but had spent most of her life in the French-speaking canton of Switzerland. Her Italian, she said, was rusty; she had left Italy as a child, was married to a Frenchman and they spoke French at home.

The morning advanced and the heat gradually reached into the classroom. For a while the windows were kept shut to exclude the city noise. The teachers handed around photocopies of text with missing words, sheets of grammar, comical word pictures which required analysis.

After a while Colm began to enjoy himself. The sense of returning to an innocent childhood absolved him from every responsibility except to shine a little, find the missing words in his dictionary, engage in halting conversation. It was like the early days in the old National School with Mr Roche, the Master, patiently and sternly going over the lesson. At any

169

rate it was a million miles from the hurly burly of the Stock Exchange, the ISEQ index of Irish shares, the FTSE, the Dow Jones, the sly momentum of the international market that could turn in an instant and strike you dead. He was far from balance sheets, business lunches, the stress he lived under, had even thrived on, and the scale of which he never realised until he was away from it.

After an hour the classroom became hot; the windows were opened and the throb of Florence, the screaming of the mopeds, the tooting of horns, flooded the sixteenth-century room. When the bell sounded for the lunch break and he stood up he knew he was far from well. Nausea, the need to lie down in some cool place, filled him. Better to go back to the apartment in the Via de' Tornabuoni, lie in his virginal bed in his Florentine room, where the crucifix was carefully tucked away in a drawer and the fierce light was dimmed.

In the Via de' Tornabuoni he made his way up to the apartment in the lift, opened the door with his key. He did not expect Paola to be at home. He knew she had some kind of job, because she had referred to it the preceding evening; as a secretary he had assumed. But now she was in the dining room in front of a computer, with some books spread before her on the table. She was looking groomed, gold hair perfect, plenty of eye make-up, sitting up very straight, a pair of black-rimmed glasses on her nose. She seemed preoccupied, but she glanced up at him, called out a greeting.

'*Ciao, Colm!*' she said. '*Come stai?*'

Colm lied and said in Italian that he was well, adding as a neutral comment on the heat: '*Fa caldo oggi!*'

'*Caldo a morire . . .*' she replied.

Yes, he thought; she had put it better than she knew. It was hot enough to die.

'Christ,' Robin had said, 'is it ever going to get cooler? I mean it's September, for Chrissake!'

He went to his room, lay on his bed, and watched the light through the slats in the shutters until sleep came, imagining for a moment that there was another bed in this room and that in it there lay a small American, a girl with the fragility of a bird and the pride of a Caesar.

Once Robin had wondered aloud: 'Will you stop turning in that bed, for Chrissake. Anyone would think you were at sea!'

He could not tell her and he could not block it. Things he had forgotten crowded him. There was the bath when Father Madden had sponged him down, there were the other times in his room, where the priest violated a self Colm hardly knew he possessed. He withdrew into silence, co-conspirator with his violator, complicit in his own destruction. He did not understand what was happening, what it meant, what it would do to him.

He did not know it would bring such dreams. They had begun at home after his expulsion. The Goat's face, looming close, distorted, the eyes bulging, the mouth huge and wet. Waking, covered in sweat. Sometimes the dreams were in lurid colour, colours he never saw in the waking world. He knew that what had been done to him was beyond his understanding. Action was one thing, had a beginning, middle and end, but the action's meaning spiralled out of reach.

After he had left Clonarty he had thought: If I could understand! If I could understand it all, I could look at it, deal with it, ultimately dismiss it, grow out and away from it. But he did not understand. He felt like a young tree imprisoned by a creeper, tendrils, tough and insidious, wrapping him round, finding every vulnerability, holding him in a death grip.

If I could talk to someone, maybe they could make me understand.

After his mother's death, when he felt himself crushed under his nameless burden, he had tried to talk to his father. He approached him tentatively. But before he could make any overture which would have set the scene for mutuality, his father had turned so closed and angry a face to him that he recoiled and withdrew. He knew then that he was beyond the

171

pale of parental forgiveness and tolerance. His very existence, he felt, was anathema to his father. But he loved his father and because he loved him he had no choice but to identify with his loathing.

'Wake up, Colm . . .' Robin had shouted. 'Wake up, for Chrissake . . .' It was the second time he had disturbed her in one night. It was as though her flight from him in the Piazzale Michelangelo had precipitated something subliminal, churned up the muck of long ago.

Colm jerked into awareness, the light on, the girl beside him in a cotton nightie, frowning, leaning across him, shaking him.

'Wake up . . . it's only a dream!'

Colm surfaced. His heart was pounding; he was covered in sweat. He covered his eyes with his arm and felt the relief. To be here in Florence, to be a thousand miles away from Clonarty Diocesan College, from a man in a black soutane, with huge appetites and absolute power. To be here in Florence with a friend.

'Sorry . . . Robin . . .'

'What were you dreaming about?'

'Oh . . . nothing . . .'

'You were making a lot of noise about nothing!'

Colm looked up at the ceiling. 'School,' he said. 'It was something to do with school.'

'They were beating you?'

'You could say that!'

Robin straightened, sniffed. 'Guys!'

He felt the bedsprings sigh as she moved back to her own bed. There was the sense of her body, her innocence. Hearing her settle down beneath the sheet he was filled with sudden tenderness. He turned towards her, but she switched off the light.

'Robin?'

'Yeah?'

'I really am sorry . . . about earlier . . . I mean in the Piazzale Michelangelo. I was out of order.'

'Yeah. You sure were!' She turned over on her side and added: 'Forget it! Maybe I overreacted.'

'No . . . you were right. Sorry . . .' His voice was very low.

'You see . . . it's not you, Colm . . . It reminded me of something, but it wasn't you.'

When Colm tried to ask the obvious question, she told him to go to sleep.

But he didn't go to sleep. He lay awake. In the darkness Clonarty came close, brushed against him, sound and light and smell. The echo down the polished corridor, the huge religious pictures in heavy frames, the rattle of dishes in the refectory, smell of boiled potatoes and oniony beef stew, the hubbub of three hundred boys' voices, the steam on the picture of the Last Supper so that all you could see was the misted glass.

And the nausea. It was ever present. It sprang from no physical cause. But why should it even matter so much? he had wondered more than once; it was not as though he had been threatened with death or serious injury; it was not as though his physical wellbeing were impaired. He tried telling himself anything that would convince his mind to ease up, to let him relax, to brush it off. But deep within, in reaches that he had no means of accessing, he felt as though he were not the same person living in the same world.

'Hey, Nugent . . . you coming for a game of handball?'

'OK.'

Beat the ball, scrape the knuckles against the wall; they bled but the pain was clean. In the pharmacy he was given some plasters, told by Matron to stay away from handball until his knuckles healed. The pharmacy smelled of cough drops, a subtle dry, antiseptic scent. It was beside the furnace room, and when the furnace was newly fed with coke a sulphurous throat-catching smell spilt into the corridor and made him cough. He gave the racking cough full vent, as though he might cough up his lungs and with them empty some part of his self.

His turn came to serve Mass. Old Father Moriarty, the chaplain, collared him.

'Colm . . . your turn to be put through your paces!' He knew how to serve Mass. He had done it since he was eight, enjoyed it, the sense of being special, of partaking in mystery, the arcane Latin, the music of words and gestures, the sense of being close to God.

But all that had changed, had been smothered in a mantle of guilt.

There was Confession on Saturday; old Father Moriarty behind the grille.

'Bless me, Father, for I have sinned . . .' He trotted them out, banal sins: laziness, cogging homework, stealing a pencil, bad language when Farrelly slagged him.

'Is that all?'

His tongue froze on what he wanted to say.

'. . . Yes, Father.'

'No bad thoughts . . . no, eh . . . self-abuse or anything of that kind?'

'No, Father!'

'What age are you, boy?'

'Thirteen, Father . . .'

The priest muttered something about the child being small for his age, gave him his penance. 'Three Our Fathers, three Hail Marys and three Glory be to the Fathers for the Pope's intentions.'

Colm saw through the grille that his confessor's hand was raised in absolution and his grey head bent; his stole was deep purple in the dim light. '*Ego te absolvo* . . .'

Colm emerged from the Confessional, walked with careful pious demeanour to a pew and knelt, ostensibly to say his penance. But inside him a verse from the Catechism was repeating itself.

'Those who tell a lie in Confession commit a most grievous

sin by telling a lie to the Holy Ghost and instead of obtaining pardon they incur much more the wrath of God . . .'

He had lied in Confession; he was guilty of a sin against the Holy Ghost. Tomorrow he would have to take Communion, and to take Communion in the state of mortal sin was sacrilege. And the penalty for sacrilege was eternal damnation.

I won't take Communion, he thought. I won't.

He hardly slept. He kept seeing himself, holding the gold-plated paten under his own chin, Father Moriarty approaching with the ciborium after the congregation had taken Communion, saw himself turning his head to one side, refusing.

The morning came. The young priest Father Phelim who slept in a cubicle just off the dormitory intoned '*Bendicamus Domino*' in seven loud stentorian syllables.

Colm pulled himself out of bed. It was cold; he shivered as his feet touched the chill, bare boards. There were muted groans, creaking of bedsprings as bodies huddled for a few seconds' more comfort. Father Phelim pulled the bedclothes off the laggards; the boys went to the washroom which heated quickly with the steam from the showers and wash basins. It was not Colm's day for a shower, so he washed at a basin, scrubbed his teeth, shivering all the time, although it was no longer cold.

When he had dressed he went to the sacristy. Father Moriarty had not arrived. The priest's vestments were already laid out, deep violet for the first Sunday of Lent. He found the acolyte's black soutane and white lace-trimmed surplice on the rack in the alcove and donned them, waited for the celebrant. His mind was made up: when offered Communion he would turn his head to one side. Afterwards old Moriarty would ask him why, what had he done that he should refuse Communion. He would say he had forgotten and eaten a sweet earlier, broken his fast.

The narrow door in the mock Gothic arch opened, but instead of Father Moriarty, whom he had expected, it was

Father Madden himself who appeared. He started when he saw Colm, but did not speak, only glared at the boy before him in tense silence. Colm looked away. He felt as though his limbs had liquefied. A guilt of vast proportions settled on him; he was the cause of everything. He forced a blank on his mind, forced himself to think only of the present.

The priest began to prepare himself for Mass, washed his hands and muttered Latin prayers as each vestment was donned, first the amice, then the alb, then the girdle, then the maniple, then the stole and finally the violet chasuble, splendid embroidered vestments which had been painstakingly worked somewhere by anonymous nuns.

At a nod Colm preceded the priest into the chapel, carrying the cruets of wine and water. Father Madden, magnificent in his canonicals, stood at the foot of the altar, bowed down, made the sign of the cross and intoned in a stern no-nonsense voice, which to Colm carried a covert warning, '*Introibo ad altare Dei,*' and Colm responded to the God who gave joy to his youth: '*Ad Deum qui laetificat juventutum meam.*' The Latin responses were at the tip of his tongue; their chant held a mystique, a power of sorts and a kind of homecoming.

The Consecration came and went. Colm waited with dreamlike dread for the Communion. He watched as Father Madden took the Host into his hands, genuflected and said the prayer that he was not worthy, '*Domine non sum dignus . . .*' In a moment he had taken the Host into his mouth, bent his head in meditation and a few moments later sipped from the chalice.

Meanwhile Colm went about his duties, putting out the white cloth for the communicants, murmuring the Confiteor, and in a few minutes Father Madden came down to the communion rails and began to give Communion. Colm held the paten under each chin, lest any morsel of the consecrated bread should fall. Each communicant closed his eyes and stuck out his tongue to receive the Host. Some tongues were pink and some red; some were short and wide; some were long and waved out of their orifices like tentacles.

And then Father Madden turned to Colm, held out the Host to him. Colm felt as though the floor would surely open for him, that God would save him. He wavered. He saw the big person of Father Madden, his riveting stare, his command, and he obediently held the paten underneath his own chin, opened his mouth, put out his tongue. He tasted the dry, papery unleavened Host, the Lamb of God. He knew he was damned.

His work deteriorated. His English essays became minefields of grammar and syntax errors; history and geography, at which he had formerly shone, were a disaster; religious knowledge almost a joke. It was as though his neural pathways had become impassable, clogged. The only subject he still found his way in was maths, but even there was marked deterioration.

'Report to your housemaster, Nugent. This work is an insult. Rubbish like this from a scholarship boy!'

Then the corridor, its shine and smell of polish, the nicely varnished door with the small name card. Tap on the door.

'Come in.'

'You again, Colm . . . ?' Sudden speculative light in the eye; sudden sheen on the iris. Colm handed him the note from Father Andrew.

'There is no excuse for this kind of thing.'

He took out the heavy leather Biff. 'Take down your trousers, boy.' Father Madden used the Biff, then the palm of his hand. Afterwards he used everything, breathing heavily, righteous with sanction. The boy deserved it.

'You see, Nugent . . .' panting '. . . what you deserve for your conduct!'

The priest's pleasure became fiercer. As Colm began to disappear and a servile, sullen personality to emerge, his seducer seemed imbued with a fierce exultation, like a demonic force triumphant in final possession. The suppliant demeanour which had marked the priest's approach at the outset was replaced by contempt; as though he were saying this creature, this catamite, this fallen boy was now where he wanted him, in his thrall. He detested Colm with all his heart for being there, and would punish him terribly for it.

During Lent the time came for the annual junior retreat, the three days set aside for lectures, prayer and meditation. Conversation was forbidden. Father Lawless, a visiting Franciscan, dressed in coarse brown habit with only sandals on his bare feet, conducted the retreat. He was an old priest, had given many school retreats. One of his lectures was on the subject of sex. The boys listened avidly, all fidgeting temporarily in abeyance.

'Now, boys, most of you will be finding yourselves thinking disturbing thoughts about women and girls. At night you will be having dreams . . . what are called wet dreams. All this is perfectly normal. Your bodies are growing and preparing some day to be fathers . . .'

Small rippling sniggers, nudges, scuffle of shoe leather.

'But you should remember that your bodies are the temples of the Holy Spirit and that you must not do or allow anything which would defile that temple!' He thumped his hand against the lectern. The light from the pointed stained-glass windows gave a coloured sheen to his spectacles. 'You will be called upon by God to give an account of your stewardship!' he thundered, his voice suddenly the voice of Savonarola, consigning the wicked to hell.

There was a hush.

Colm listened. He wanted to be sick. He could no longer distance himself from what he had done; he could no longer pretend that accepting Holy Communion, lying in Confession, didn't matter. God would call on him some day to give an account of his stewardship; he could no longer sustain the carapace he had built around his self. But he sat there, ostensibly impassive, and did not return Fiach O'Carroll's dig in the ribs.

'Nugent,' Fiach whispered when the lecture was over, 'did you know you're down for serving Mass tomorrow? Hegarty was down for it, but he's had to go home; his uncle died.'

Colm checked the list in the corridor outside the chapel. His name had been substituted for Hegarty's. He was in a state of mortal sin, even sacrilege, and he was again to serve Mass. The Devil would get him this time; God would strike him dead!

Next morning Colm fell down the stairs on the way from the dormitory. 'What's wrong with you?' Father Phelim demanded, when he had ascertained that the prostrate form on the floor at the bottom of the stairs was still alive. 'You seem to have three feet.'

'I've hurt my elbow, Father,' Colm said, picking himself up and gingerly feeling his right arm. 'I don't think it's broken, but I can't serve Mass – not like this.'

His left ankle was hurting and, when he tried to put his weight on it, he gave a small cry of pain.

Father Phil made him sit on a bench and examined the elbow and then the ankle. Both were a bit swollen; the elbow was skinned; when he touched it Colm winced. 'I'll only be dropping things if I serve Mass.'

He saw the horror in the young priest's eyes, the mental image of cruets smashed, the paten dropped, the possibility of the Host being desecrated.

'All right!' Father Phelim looked around. Other boys were trickling down the stairs in the direction of the chapel.

'Duggan, you can take Nugent's place serving Mass.' He looked at Colm doubtfully. 'Nugent, you'd better see Matron after Mass.'

'Yes, Father.'

Colm limped to the chapel. He remembered to keep his newfound disability apparent, holding his right arm stiffly. He sank into his pew, watched the Franciscan priest begin the Mass, saw that he looked tired and frail in the vestments, his bare, sandalled feet a testament to self-denial. Blue varicose

179

veins were knotted in his lower calf.

Colm did not go to Communion. He sat in the pew with some relief and let the boys around him go up to the altar rails, saw them glance at him as they returned with bowed heads.

He had a perfect alibi; he need not be expected to move; he then saw Father Phelim glance at him, rise from his prieu-dieu, approach the sanctuary and whisper something to the Franciscan celebrant. With horror he saw Father Lawless take up the ciborium again, speak to Duggan who was serving. Then Duggan, looking self-important, holding the paten and followed by the visiting priest, came towards Colm along the nave. Father Lawless held the ciborium in his hands.

'My son . . . you were hurt,' the old priest whispered with a kindly twinkle, 'so Jesus comes to you!' He lifted the Host from the ciborium and Duggan leaned forward with the paten.

Colm bowed his head. He bit into his knuckle. He heard someone screaming, 'No, no, no!' It was a muffled scream. It possessed a kind of echo. But he liked the sound of it. 'No!'

It was only later that he understood it had come from himself.

Colm surfaced when the knock came on the door. He dragged himself from a tortured half-sleep, wondered briefly where he was, remembered that he was in Paola Nosterini's apartment in Florence.

'Yes . . . Come in.'

The door opened a fraction. It was his hostess. 'I am sorry for disturbing you. I thought I heard you call out . . . Are you all right?'

'Yes . . . yes . . . I fell asleep . . . I was dreaming.'

Colm felt the sweat, unpleasantly sticky on his back and chest.

'I was making myself some lunch,' Paola said, 'just an omelette – with mushrooms fresh from Vallambrosa: would you like one?'

She stood there in the doorway, elegant, beautiful, kind. She did not have to give her guests lunch. She represented normality, decency, strength. To talk to her about anything, the weather, the state of the European Union, Italian politics, would restore him to the world he could control.

'Thank you, Paola. That would be most pleasant!'

His hostess glanced around the room. Her gaze rested for a moment on the wall above the bed where the crucifix had hung. Questioning eyes reverted to him.

'I took it down,' he said. 'I don't like sleeping under crucifixes.'

She raised her eyebrows, but made no comment. Instead she said, 'Lunch in five minutes!'

He joined her in the kitchen. It was a small room overlooking the courtyard. From here, every evening, this woman, after a working day, prepared a three-course meal for six people. The little room was pristine – cream tiles, marble floor, old gas stove, small pine table. There was a pleasant smell of hot olive oil and herbs. The louvred shutters were barely ajar and the room was dim.

Paola served up the omelettes, first his, then hers, the pan tipped with an expert flick of the wrist. There was a bowl of green salad on the table.

'This is very kind of you,' Colm said.

'Not at all . . . I thought you were looking a bit pale when you came in. Are you sure you're feeling all right?'

'I'm fine . . . I think the heat got to me.'

He took a mouthful of omelette. Delicious. His hostess filled his glass with a white wine. 'The heat gets to us too, the natives, if it's any consolation.'

Colm took a gulp of the wine – chilled, tasting of fresh green things. 'This wine is wonderful!'

'Yes. It's Vernaccia di San Gimignano . . . That's a place in Tuscany . . . it's not very far.'

He marvelled at her accent. She spoke Italian with all the lyrical passion the language commanded; but the precision of her English still struck him as incongruous.

'I find it interesting to have someone of my own vintage among my guests,' she said after a moment. 'You're an anomaly, if you don't mind my saying so . . .'

'In what way?'

'Well, you obviously don't *need* to learn Italian – you're not facing university exams, you're not studying to be a translator – you are doing it for pleasure. Sometimes women do that . . . but this is the first time a middle-aged man has stayed with me . . .' She laughed almost coyly. 'It is for this reason that I am breaking all the rules and speaking English to you.'

'I did come for the pleasure,' Colm said. 'The pleasure of being a student again, the pleasure of tasting Italy from the inside, from the vantage point of an Italian family. Staying in a hotel one is always an outsider.'

He raised his head and met her eyes. 'And something more if the truth be told . . . nostalgia . . . a search for something, I suppose you could call it mid-life foolishness . . .'

She pursed her lips. 'It is never foolish to do what one must. But you told me yesterday that there was something more, that something happened here which was important and that you had returned because of it . . .'

Colm looked at his plate. 'I met a girl here, twenty-eight years ago . . .'

Paola started. She watched him closely, but his eyes were on his plate. 'We stayed in the Via Nazionale. She was American . . .'

'Ah . . .' She sat back in her seat. '*Un grande amore?*' she said softly, with a rueful smile. 'We always come back to them!'

'I lost her,' Colm continued. 'When I tried to find her again the trail was cold. The address she gave me in New York was a dead end . . .'

'So you searched for her? The American?'

'Yes. When I got my first job . . . as soon as I could afford it. I took off for New York, stayed for a week, but couldn't find her.' He glanced at Paola. 'She had told me a few lies, you see, which made it more difficult. Eventually I put an ad in the *New York Times* . . .'

'Did you get any replies?'

'One . . . it was anonymous.'

'Was it helpful?'

'It said: "The woman you are looking for is dead."'

Paola leaned forward, the professional newsmonger's instinct patent. 'So what did you do?'

'I had searches made in the American and Italian registers. Nothing! No death certificate. I thought I would forget her. I didn't know whether to believe the story of her death. And I did forget her, after a fashion. But recently . . .' and here he thought of the squeezing in the chest, the sudden call of eternity, and her face there among the stack of files, clear as the day '. . . recently I remembered her again. And I was reminded of a promise we made . . . that we would meet in the Piazza della Signoria on my fiftieth birthday . . .'

He glanced at Paola's face and added, 'That's on Sunday week. But she won't be there of course, although I can't help thinking that she's still alive!'

In the ensuing silence he felt monumentally foolish. He added, embarrassed, 'I know it's pure sentiment.'

'You needn't be embarrassed,' Paola said. 'You are talking to an Italian.'

She put a bowl of fruit on the table, toyed with an apple, sliced it. Colm was aware that her glances at him were full of interest, as though she were trying to make up her mind about him. 'I think,' she said, raising her dark eyes to him, 'that we are intensely alive at one point of our lives, and when we get older we try to find it again. It's as though we are locked into a mind-set created during a fierce span of awareness. We revert to it, to the sense of wonder, the sense of being centred and on course, the energy of burgeoning mastery. You are trying to find an important piece for your jig-saw which you lost in the past! Were you very much in love with this girl?'

Colm was stumped by the direct question. 'In love? I don't

183

know; I suppose I was. I just loved her. We were what she called "buddies" . . .'

'So she loved you too?'

'I thought she did.'

'But didn't she try to contact you afterwards? Write to you, or phone you?'

'No. Why should she? When she needed me desperately I failed her.'

Paola narrowed her eyes. 'Why should she have hated you?'

'I wasn't much use to her . . . I shouldn't have left her when I did. Perhaps she died after all, as the anonymous letter said.'

'Perhaps! But she was young. The chances are that she did not.'

'You think she is still alive?'

Paola smiled at his eagerness. 'I think it very likely.'

'Notwithstanding the anonymous letter?'

'Because of it. A stranger would have given a name, signed the letter. Why not? Anonymity indicates a private agenda!'

'So you think she sent it herself?'

'It's possible . . . Perhaps she did not want to renew your friendship and did not want you to find her.'

'So you think she has forgotten?'

'No. One does not forget, but she may have placed all those memories in a drawer carefully lined and labelled, "The Past" or "My Misspent Youth" or something of that kind.'

Colm tried to look inscrutable, but only succeeded in looking glum.

'Come on,' Paola said with a laugh. 'I don't know anything. I'm just given to conjecture. There must have been other girls you knew whom you fell for in your youth.'

'There was one at home. But I made a mess of it.'

'And you didn't meet any of our nice Italian girls while you were here?'

Paola said this slowly, in a very even voice. But Colm did not notice the fractional change in tone. He remembered sun on an amphitheatre, long brown hair.

'I did meet an extraordinary Italian girl . . . I was reminded of her this morning; I helped her with her English . . .'

'Did she ever write to you?' she asked softly, bending down to the cat who came yawning and stretching from her basket.

The phone rang. Paola rose and picked up the receiver.

'*Sì?*' she said, listened for a moment before adding, '*Vengo fra qualche minuti!*'

She put the receiver down. 'I have to go.'

Colm helped her gather up the plates and cutlery, put them in the dishwasher. 'Leave the glasses,' she said. 'I'll wash them later by hand.'

Colm had the feeling that he had been skilfully plumbed and that this woman now knew far more about him than he had told her.

'What do you work at?' he asked, indicating the dining room with an inclination of his head, through the open door of which a ream of paper could be seen among the books on the table, black-rimmed spectacles resting on top.

'I'm a journalist. I work for *La Nazione.*' She laughed when she saw his expression. 'Don't worry. I'm very professional!'

He laughed back. 'I'm not worried. I labour under no delusions that the whole of Italy is longing to hear my particular sentimental journey!'

'May I ask you a question?' Paola said.

'Of course.'

'Are you a Catholic? It is of no importance to me whatsoever,' she added hastily. 'I'm just curious. I always understood that the Irish were.'

'A Catholic. I used to be. Why do you ask?'

'Well . . . I was just wondering . . . because you took down the crucifix in your room. Most Catholics feel safer with one around.'

'So you think I'm an apostate?'

'Of course not! I don't care what you are.'

'I once knew someone who had a crucifix hanging on the

185

wall behind his desk,' Colm said after a moment. 'He was not particularly Christian, although he was a priest.'

'I see,' she said slowly. 'Was this at school?'

When Colm nodded, something like understanding, even compassion, widened in her eyes. 'What happened to him?'

'Nothing. He leads a charmed life,' Colm replied. 'He's had a successful career, narrowly missed being made a bishop! And recently he even emerged unscathed from a road accident!'

Paola secured the fastening on the shutters, removed the wine glasses to the sink. Something in the way she did this aroused in Colm a sense of the familiar.

'You remind me of someone, Paola, but I don't know who . . .'

'Your wife perhaps?' she replied with a flat laugh and an interrogative glance. 'I'm doing wifely things.'

Colm frowned. 'Perhaps . . .' He was trying to remember Sherry tidying up after lunch, but could hardly make the connection. 'My wife and I are divorced,' he added, anxious for some reason that she should know. 'She is happily remarried.'

'And are you happy, Colm?' She said this very softly, as though to deflect the personal nature of the question.

He glanced at her, said airily, 'Oh, I'm always happy . . .' saw her immediate disbelief.

'One more question to satisfy my boundless curiosity . . . the Italian girl you met, whom you said was so fine . . . where did you meet her?'

'In the amphitheatre in Fiesole. At least I think it was there. And to answer your question a moment ago,' he added with a self-deprecating smile, 'she didn't write to me either!'

There was silence for a moment and then Paola said: 'I must go now. Something has come up at the office . . .' She paused at the door, glanced across the room at him. 'Would you like to come out with us – Jill and me – this evening? The others are going to a disco and she's not interested in them. I said I'd take her to the Piazzale Michelangelo . . . from where you can see the whole city!'

'Why not?' Colm said. He smiled at her. 'I was there once before . . . with Robin.' He looked at Paola. 'That was her name.'

In the morning after his troubled night Colm had said to Robin, 'You women have life easy . . . Men do everything for you.'

Robin said: 'What a load of bullshit!'

'Take you for example,' Colm persisted, 'a spoilt girl who runs off to Italy . . . leaving her dad who has done everything for her, sick with worry.'

Robin was uncharacteristically silent. 'He loves you,' Colm went on, testing her, 'and this is how you treat him! He must have umpteen millions, but what are they compared to the love of his daughter?'

Robin turned her head away. 'Nobody loves me, and never will . . .'

'Why not? Ah, come on, Robin . . . What happened to you? Something has.'

Robin shrugged. 'Someone once told me that what happens is not as important as how you react to it.'

'Who told you that?'

'A man called Jack.'

'And who was this savant?'

Robin hesitated, then said gruffly, 'He was my father!'

'The father whom you won't contact and won't ask for money? The father you despise for his wealth and cynicism? The father who has a sense of humour and claims a royal Irish lineage?'

'Ah, leave it, will you? I'm entitled to my opinions.'

'You're crazy, Robin!'

She gave him a weary smile. 'I know.'

Paola returned to her office, sat at her desk. She thought of the luncheon encounter with Colm Nugent. He was certainly the same person, but he was not as she remembered; the years had marked him. He was haunted in some way. As for this Robin . . . he had evidently been living with her when they had met that far-off day in Fiesole! He had not mentioned her at the time, and now he had returned on some romantic quest. This touched her almost to the point of tears. Silly, vulnerable quest. It spoke volumes for his life that he still set store by it. What on earth had he been doing all these intervening years that nothing had filled his cup with love and fulfilment, that he must still be seeking a pebble from a lost shore? It was interesting, she conceded ruefully, with a small pang of pleasure, that she herself had made some impression as a young girl. He didn't recognise her now, of course; it was too long ago and too tenuous an acquaintance. And neither did he recall that an Italian girl had written him a long letter full of her life and hopes.

She thought of Giovanni in his grave. She remembered the day they had brought her the news; the traffic accident in Rome, the car that had swerved to avoid another in the Piazza Barberini and hit a pedestrian, the pedestrian who had been her husband. They had had their good times and their troubled times, she and Giovanni. Before he had left for Rome they had had a row, one of many in recent times. Theirs had been a turbulent relationship. But there had been love between them, camaraderie, and forays into an eroticism that dared the frontiers of communication. Now he was gone. The void yawned around her still; she would never be used to it.

Pasquale was left to her, and he, brought down with rheumatic fever not long after his father's death, had developed the heart condition that must soon be treated or she would lose him too.

You could plan your life. But your plans were but markers in the changes and turmoil of your narrow span. Whether you liked it or not, much of your energy was inevitably channelled into dealing with things you never expected!

Silvestro came to her office, put a cousinly hand on her shoulder. Oh, hold me, comfort me, she wanted to say. Peel back the last twelve months, annul them and let me start again. She smiled at him. '*Sto bene*,' she said in answer to his interrogative look, adding in English: 'I'm fine!'

He asked if she had a copy of *Oggi*, a certain back number. The magazine contained an article on something he was researching. She said she had it. His hand pressed her shoulder, its warmth reassuring. He would call for it, he said as he left. He would call one day soon at lunchtime. Paola watched his departing back. He raised a hand when he was outside her door, smiled through the glass.

How much longer can I hold out; should I hold out? Paola wondered. I am offered something here that is real, rooted, above all warm and loving. I know there are many levels of being. There is the level which says I must shut the door on any experience which is not sanctioned by wisdom and propriety; there is another level, the primal level, where life embraces life, which cares nothing for wisdom or propriety and thrusts towards its own fulfilment at any cost.

Dare I believe in it? What if I actually dared all and said yes?

Chapter Ten

Colm returned to Scuola Linguistica for the afternoon lecture on the history of art. '*La Sala Conferenza*', the conference room, was dim, shuttered against the afternoon sun, the only sound the slides clicking in and out of the projector. The lecturer was talking about Botticelli. He spoke clearly and unhurriedly.

He said that Sandro Filipepi, nicknamed Botticello ('little Barrel'), was the son of the tanner Mariano Filipepi and was born around 1444. He was apprenticed to Filippo Lippi, and soon began getting commissions. In ten years he established his reputation in Florence . . .

Colm watched as the paintings came up on the screen; *Fortitude*, the *Primavera*, the *Adoration of the Magi*, the *Birth of Venus*.

'. . . But it was the Pazzi conspiracy against the Medici in 1478,' the lecturer said, 'which really pushed Botticelli into the public eye. The Pazzi family, with the blessing of the Pope, organised a coup which attacked Lorenzo and Giuliano de' Medici at Mass. Twenty-five-year old Giuliano was killed and Lorenzo was wounded, but he escaped into the Sacristy. The conspirators were summarily hanged that same evening and Botticelli was given the job of painting their effigies over the door of the Bargello, for the edification of the citizenry, including the effigy of the Archbishop of Pisa, who had been involved in the plot and hanged!'

That must have embarrassed the papal power machine, Colm thought sourly; one of His Holiness's boys hanged for murder!

What was it Robin had said when he asked her what she thought of power?

'It's supposed to prevent abuse,' she said primly. 'But what happens when the baddies are the guys with the beef?'

On the day following his troubled night Colm and Robin had risen late and had then gone out to see the Boboli gardens, the gracious expanse behind the Pitti Palace, once the home of the mighty Pitti family who had rivalled the Medici. At lunchtime Robin had produced from her shoulder bag the usual loaf and bottle of water, some fruit and wafer-thin slices of prosciutto.

'Where did you get this ham? It's so good!'

'I stole it.'

Colm looked at her. 'What?'

'I stole it! As in robbed, purloined, filched, swindled, thieved! I don't want any. I got it for you.'

'Why don't you want to eat?'

'Can't bear the thought of food right now.'

Colm wondered if her recurring indisposition were due to stress. She had every right to be anxious, he thought, having run away from home. He found himself touched to the quick that she should have stolen food especially for him, but he was anxious for her. He regarded the pines stretching above their heads.

'Robin,' he said, 'if you're caught stealing you'll end up in an Italian jail. And I hear they're pretty short on life's little comforts!'

She shrugged. 'I've only a few dollars left,' she said. 'I've no choice, I don't want you paying for everything. I'll just have to get a job.'

'Why don't you wire home? Your father would be only too glad to come to your rescue.'

'I'm not going begging to him . . .'

'Well, why not call on those relatives of yours in Fiesole? They might help you get a job.'

192

'I can't,' she said bluntly, opening out her palms. 'They mightn't be my relatives . . . and besides . . . I don't feel like moving around much. I really don't feel so good.'

'You mean they most certainly are not your relatives and you're making excuses!'

'I've got Florentine blood,' Robin said quietly. 'Whether you like it or not won't change it.'

For a moment Colm doubted his own disbelief. 'I think I'll go myself, tell them about your arrival, prepare them for the ring on the door.'

'If you do that I'll kill you!'

Above their heads the midday sun was slanting through the trees. The bench was stone, one of the many bordering the walks. Nearby, a statue of Vulcan, god of fire, raised his hammer. Colm studied his companion who was looking petulantly away from him. She was in a blue shirt today, which made her tan seem darker, her hair fairer. He was aware of her small breasts, of the curve of her cheek and brow. Desire filled him.

'Did anyone ever tell you you were beautiful?'

She looked at him suspiciously. 'Yeah . . .' Her eyes resumed their faraway stare for a moment, then refocused on him with scorn. 'All the time. Guys are always bullshitting.'

'Not all guys . . .'

She glanced at him again. 'Maybe.' After a moment she added, 'Why were you so uptight last night . . . What were you dreaming about? Who beat you up at school?'

'It's not important.'

'Isn't it?'

Colm did not answer for a moment. He tasted the last morsel of bread in his mouth, the smoky prosciutto, the fizz from the mineral water at the back of his throat. He experienced, as he had not for a long time, the sense of being fallen, contaminated in some way beyond redemption.

'I think something awful happened to you in school,' she added softly.

193

'I was expelled from school,' Colm said in a brittle voice. 'If you must know!'

'Why? What did you do wrong?'

'I don't want to get into it!'

'Why not?'

'Maybe you wouldn't love me any more!' he said on a note of attempted levity.

'I don't love you anyway. Anyone would think you were raped or something . . . you're so coy about it.'

Colm dropped the bottle of mineral water; it spilled on the gravel.

Robin bent to pick it up, put it on the bench beside her, glanced at him. Her eyes narrowed in speculation, her expression changed and she reached for his hand. He pulled away. He felt suddenly naked, hemmed in by a wall of memory waiting to crash and pin him down. These bloody women would hold your hand if it led to satisfying their endless curiosity; but if you reached for them . . . you might as well make a pass at the Virgin Mary.

She rose, moved to a nearby bench, took up the newspaper someone had left behind. She opened it, began to read, frowning like a politician, and studiously ignoring him. Suddenly she froze, glanced at Colm, then closed the paper hastily, folding it, consigning it to the nearby rubbish bin.

'What's in the paper?'

'The usual trash!'

Robin returned for the bottle of *aqua minerale*. 'Do you want what's left in this?' He shook his head. She swallowed the last of the water, stood up to wedge the bottle into the nearby bin beside the discarded newspaper, turned back. Then her eyes sought Colm's, but he did not meet them.

'You needn't be so damn uptight,' she said. 'We all have things we don't like to talk about . . . You probably think you're the only one.'

'What things, Robin?' he demanded. 'What things do you not like to talk about?'

194

Robin did not look at him, but she said, 'If you won't confide in me I see no reason why I should confide in you.'

'Oh, spare me the trade-off . . .'

Robin's eyes flashed.

'D'you know the trouble with you . . . you've got an attitude problem.'

'So what are you hanging around for? Why don't you just piss off then!'

'OK.'

She slung her bag over her shoulder and walked away towards the exit. He watched her to see if she would look back. She paused at one point, threw a quick, almost furtive glance over her shoulder, then tossed her head and was gone.

I suppose she thought I'd run after her, Colm thought sourly. Who the hell does she think she is? She's always doing this! But he missed her already, as though she had taken with her some of the air and the light.

He looked around, saw the newspaper earlier discarded by Robin sticking out of the bin. He got up, took the *International Herald Tribune* from the wire basket, sat down and opened it.

It was the usual thing, international news, ads, photographs. Then a headline caught his eye.

UNDERWORLD BOSS SLAIN BY CALLGIRL

He read the short article; a New York callgirl had killed her protector, a well-known playboy, said to have links with the Mafia; the police were looking for her, but she had disappeared.

Was this the article which had made Robin start? Hardly. He scanned the paper for anything else of galvanic interest, found nothing he thought would have elicited any particular response, shrugged and put the paper back in the bin. He walked through the gardens to the Grotto near the exit, an ensemble of artificial caverns decorated with frescos and sculptures, scanned the visitors, but there was no sign of Robin.

He wondered what to do. She had obviously gone off in a sulk. She'd be back in the evening at the pensione, subdued. But what would he do with the rest of the day? He mentally scanned his options. Then it occurred to him that he could go to Fiesole and satisfy his curiosity.

Colm left the gardens, went to the station and took the bus to the hillside town of Fiesole. He was unprepared for the breathtaking view. The route unwound through stunning vistas, rows of cypresses and lovely villas. He took out his notebook, into which he had copied the address of Signore Di Gabiere; he also got out the guide to Florence. As the driver negotiated the hairpin bends, he ascertained that Fiesole had a classical history, Etruscan and Roman remains, an ancient amphitheatre.

The bus reached its terminus in a sunny piazza. Colm got down, stood for a moment at the railing of a pavement café to regard the city in the plain below. Florence seemed beautiful and tranquil, resting there in the haze. He wondered where Robin had got to. She was like the rest of them, good at the moral high ground. 'We all have things we don't want to talk about . . .' he muttered to himself. But would she clarify what she was waffling about? Oh no!

When he became aware that customers in the shady purlieu of the café were regarding him with curiosity he moved away. Well, he told himself, at least tonight he would have some peace; tonight she would be gone. Good. Let her go! Or maybe she'd be there again, full of her particular brand of insecurity.

He asked directions to the Via Ghiberti and walked until he found himself outside a patrician villa in its own grounds, with a small enamel plate on the gate bearing the number 12. The house, cream stucco walls and black shutters, was enclosed in a garden behind high walls and gates. It was a lovely place, with bougainvillaea spilling over the wall. Through the bars of the gate he could see that it had a well-tended shady forecourt, with terracotta urns and statuary, and that it commanded an uninterrupted view of the valley. As Colm admired it he saw, carved into the stone by the gate, the two words: Villa Carmina.

He started. 'What was your grandmother's Christian name . . . ?' he had asked Robin.

'Carmina.'

A private faltering query now intruded, developed into doubt.

Voices could be heard, a man's, then a child's. Colm peered through the gate, squinted to see through shrubs of mimosa and passion flower – and saw a portion of a tennis court. He wondered if he dared ring the bell and tell this family that an American girl, who stole loaves of bread and bottled water to keep body and soul together, a girl whose grandmother was called Carmina and might have borne their name, would like to meet them . . .

Of course he couldn't! But his deliberations were drowned in sudden cacophony: two huge mastiffs rushed from the shrubbery and launched themselves at the gates. Colm started back from the bared fangs, but before he could collect himself a tall man, dressed entirely in black, of autocratic bearing, was suddenly staring at him through the bars. Colm registered that the man's hair was streaked with grey and that his eyes had narrowed.

'*Si?*' he demanded peremptorily, narrowing his eyes.

Colm was at a loss. 'Oh, hello . . .' he said.

The man switched suddenly to English. 'You are looking for someone?'

'Are you Signore Di Gabiere?'

'Yes.'

'I'm sorry for butting in . . . I was just wondering if . . . You see, there's an American girl . . . a friend of mine from New York . . . who thinks she may be related to you. Her grandmother came from Florence and had the same surname as you . . . At least she thinks she had! Her – the grandmother's

197

– name was Carmina . . . She emigrated to America around the turn of the century . . .'

Colm wished he could disappear; he had been taken off guard, intimidated, and his tongue had betrayed him. 'I'm sorry . . . It's just that she's a great girl, and is too shy to look you up!'

Signore Di Gabiere did not change his expression. 'Of course, she may not be related to you at all!' Colm said hurriedly. This Gabiere fellow was pushing forty, Colm estimated, and did not look like the kind of bloke who suffered fools in any shape whatsoever. He stood uncertainly for another moment and then turned away.

'Wait,' the stern voice behind him called. 'What is this girl's name?'

'Robin . . . sorry . . . Roberta McKay,' Colm said, turning to meet the narrowed black eyes. 'She's with me, or at least she was . . . She went off today . . . I don't know when she'll be back!'

Signore Di Gabiere's expression said quite eloquently that whatever sense of humour he possessed had already been sufficiently stretched. 'She is not related to me,' he said sternly, staring at Colm with his fierce, patrician eyes, 'and I do not like to be disturbed!'

Colm went in search of the Roman amphitheatre mentioned in the guide, found it, sat on the top step of its stone seating. He felt foolish and oddly vulnerable after his brush with the mastiffs and their master. 'You're a half eejit!' he informed himself. 'There's an American girl who thinks she may be related to you . . .' he repeated to himself in mockery. 'Christ!'

He looked around at the semi-circular amphitheatre, saw beyond the Tuscan hills, saw the remains of other ancient buildings, and the steps to what might have been a temple. But his gaze lingered on the young Italian girl who was sitting halfway down the amphitheatre, silken brown hair almost to her waist, a black cat on her lap. She was reading a book, and except for her left hand which stroked the cat, she was immobile.

Colm let his gaze wander again, over the expanse of the ancient arena where a few tourists were picking their steps, looked beyond to dark green cypresses standing like spires, heard the resonant, clicking chirp of the cicada. There was timelessness here, peace: the cricket's song, the stones of two thousand years before, the serene girl with her sleeping cat.

He lay back on the stone seat and felt the heat on his face, needles of fire probing his pores. I wish it would immolate me, he thought, burn me completely so that only ashes were left. I wish it would suck me up into the white heart of the sun.

When he raised his head a few minutes later the girl was looking at him. He smiled at her and she looked away quickly, redirecting her gaze to her book. Colm studied her for a moment; about seventeen, he thought, with the striking classical beauty of so many Florentines. He got up, moved towards her and then sat beside her.

'*Buon giorno!*'

She raised her head from her book. He could not see her eyes behind her sunglasses; she seemed shy, but self-possessed. '*Buon giorno,*' she responded with a half-smile in which there was no hint of coquetry. Her body language was observant, still. She radiated serenity.

'*Parla Inglese?*' Colm asked.

'Yes. A bit,' she said with a heavy accent. 'I learn Engleesh at school!'

The cat stirred in her lap, considered Colm through green slit eyes, yawned, stretched out a paw and flexed its claws.

'Thees is Miranda,' the girl said.

'Do you live here, in Fiesole?'

'Yes. My father have a restaurant. Where do you come from?'

'Ireland. I'm a student.'

'Oh,' she said with a knowledgeable air, 'the country with

199

the . . . *come si dice* . . . ditches . . . to stop the sea!'

Colm laughed. 'You're thinking of Holland. Ireland is an island to the west of Britain.'

She laughed, embarrassed. 'Ah, yes. I know . . .'

'What's your name?' he asked.

'I have many names, but they call me Paola. And yours?'

'Colm.'

She closed her book, said she must go home. Colm glanced at the volume, saw the title, *I Promessi Sposi*. It was an old book, black with faded gold lettering. It might almost have been a missal, he thought, if it had been a bit smaller, and without warning the breviary on the Goat's desk was there before him, the Biff beside it, the big man leaning towards him, the crucifix behind him, the lamplight. It was so sudden that it was like a blow, this memory, and with it came the smell of the room, turf smoke, polish, cigarettes, and underlying it the subtle smell of institution and closed, prurient power.

He felt the nausea rise up, gasped and put his hand to his mouth, rose quickly with a gesture of apology.

'You are sick!' the girl exclaimed behind him. 'You should go home. It ees the sun . . . it ees too strong for you!' And then she stood up, picked up her cat and book and moved away.

Colm's annoyance with the female of the species came sour and bitter; they run away from everything, miserable, frightened little creatures. He stumbled to the shelter of some trees on the periphery of the amphitheatre where he was violently sick. When he looked up the girl was back, watching him. She had a glass of water in her hand; book and cat had been left behind her. She handed him the glass without a word.

He took a mouthful, turned his back to her, rinsed his mouth and spat. Then he drank gratefully, ashamed of his earlier thoughts. He turned back to her. 'Thank you. I must have eaten something . . .' He drank the water and she stood

200

watching him. 'You are very kind,' he added, moved by the concern of a perfect stranger.

Then she said, 'You are too fair to take so much sun. You should have sat in the shade. My father's restaurant, Il Zucchino, is over there,' she added, indicating the piazza. 'If you would like you can sit there in the shade.'

It was kindly meant. But he thought immediately that she was touting for business and he handed her back the glass in silence. She shrugged, suddenly haughty, and moved away. Colm was aware that this girl had presence, a dignity honed by an automatic expectation of respect, and by some immeasurable iron of her own.

'Wait,' he called, following her across the piazza. 'I didn't mean to be rude!'

She waited for him, led him to the restaurant Il Zucchino. Here an arrangement of pergolas covered a small courtyard, where dappled light on wooden tables lent a cool, green ambience. There was a smell of hot olive oil and herbs.

The courtyard was bounded on the far side by an iron fence twined with vines. Beyond this fence was the incline to the valley, where Florence nestled in the heat.

The restaurant was filled with lunching tourists, but Paola led him across the courtyard, through the kitchen into a small and private patio, shaded by a riot of greenery, where two stone urns spilt geraniums on to the flags. There was a stone balustrade and a spectacular view. A woman dressed in black and wearing an apron approached them smiling.

'This ees my step-mother, Maria,' Paola said. She turned to Maria: *'Maria, questo è Colm, un amico Irlandese!'*

Maria shook hands, demanded in a volley of words what he wanted to eat, listed the dishes on offer, rounded on Paola for being late for lunch.

The girl put up her hands in mock acceptance, laughed. Colm saw her kindness, her poise, the interrogative smile she turned on him, the fact that she had introduced him as her friend, her acceptance of this stranger who had sicked up his guts a few minutes earlier. He felt the anger and tension fade. Peace subsumed him as he sat in this green world with the sunlit plain before him, an antique city in the haze, and the sense of a fathomless past enveloping him. The cat Miranda reappeared from somewhere and jumped into the girl's lap.

'You have come to Italy for a holiday?' she asked, turning her dark eyes on him.

'Yes. I'm backpacking . . . you know, with a rucksack . . .'

Her brow furrowed in puzzlement. 'Rucksack?'

'A bag on one's back, like so . . .' Colm gestured, flexed his shoulders, pushing out his chest, holding on to imaginary rucksack straps.

The girl put her hand to her mouth, laughed. '*Ah, si* . . . I understand! My English will be better. I am going to study in England! I have aunts . . .'

Colm, seeing himself as suddenly comic, laughed too.

'You feel better now?'

He nodded. 'Much better. Thank you.'

She regarded him, smiling. 'You are looking not so white. You will eat some lunch with me?'

There was a sizzling in the kitchen; the smell of frying meat came through the open door. Colm thought of his meagre resources; he could not impose for lunch and he was suddenly ravenous. His stomach was empty and his nausea was gone. The cat stretched and yawned, looking at him expectantly. He demurred.

'You are my guest,' Paola said firmly. 'You speak Engleesh to me; I give you lunch!'

She giggled and he joined her in laughing. Then she got to her feet, went into the kitchen, came out with a paper tablecloth and some cutlery and in no time Maria had followed with veal cutlets served with wedges of lemon and salad.

'*Grazie, Maria!*'

'*Buon' appetito.*'

Maria disappeared and Colm and Paola lunched together. She poured him a glass of wine, served him salad, asked about

Ireland, turned to the valley below them as they ate, and pointed out various landmarks. He observed her covertly; she sat up very straight; her silken hair had different shades of brown and caught the light. She was utterly different from Robin; she was serene, whereas Robin was like a strung bow.

As soon as the meal was finished she got out what was evidently an English reader. It was full of short pieces of prose. One was about a knight fighting a tournament.

'Will you show me how to pronounce?'

'Sure!'

'How do you say this word?'

'Knight!' Colm said.

'But that is the same as "night"! What do you do with the K?'

'It's silent! What do you do with it in Italian?'

'We do not have this letter in Italian!'

More laughter. There were further problems with words like 'wither', and 'enough', 'joker' and 'yacht', but they ploughed on.

Later he wrote down his name and address for her. Maria came from the kitchen with a camera and took a photograph.

'What does your name mean?' Paola asked, studying the slip of paper. 'Colm . . . ?'

'"Dove", I think!' he replied with a straight face.

Paola frowned, reached for the dictionary. '*Ah, si . . . un colombo* . . . Your name in Italian is Colombo!'

'It sounds like an elephant,' Colm joked weakly.

It was late afternoon before he left. He thanked her. 'I've enjoyed the afternoon.'

'I hope your life is good for you!' she said. 'Do not take so much sun! I will write to you, but you must write back to me.'

Her madonna's face was grave. He said goodbye to her, took her hand, and on an instant's unpremeditated gallantry kissed it. Behind her Florence lay in the evening sunlight. She was like something from a painting, with the medieval world going about its business in the background.

He wanted to say that if he could meet girls like her from sitting in the sun he would worship it assiduously. But he knew her company was the gift of an afternoon, thrown up by Fate to tantalise him, exotic, perfect, pure.

He did not go back to the pensione immediately, but walked around Fiesole for a while, taking a look at the cathedral of Santo Romolo and the Palazzo Vescovile, until the air began to chill. Then he got the bus from the piazza to the centre of Florence.

When he got back to the pensione it was eight o'clock. Antonio was sitting at the desk in the hallway and picking his teeth.

'*Buona sera.*' He looked at Colm with scant curiosity and handed him the key.

Colm returned the greeting. He was disappointed that the key was at the desk; it meant that Robin was still out. His earlier turmoil had long dissipated; he was at peace with the world, able to deal with Robin and her angst. He wanted to talk, tell her about Fiesole and his day; and he wanted to listen. He had forgotten, for the moment at least, how annoyed he was with her, how annoying she was. She was simply his friend.

As soon as he opened the door of their room he felt its emptiness. He flicked the light switch, entered and shut the door. All vestiges of Robin were gone. Her rucksack, which had been propped against the wall, was missing; her toothbrush and toilet things were gone; ditto the few articles she had hung in the wardrobe. He threw back the shutters and went on to the balcony. The street below contained some pedestrians, but although he scanned them for a few moments, she was not of their number and did not turn the corner of the street.

He came back into the room and looked under her pillow. No sign of a cotton nightdress. No sign of Robin anywhere. He was unprepared for the sense of void; it was as though her defection had reduced him to quasi invisibility, even to himself.

The sense of rejection was overwhelming. He felt that the world had stopped. He went into the hallway, asked Antonio, who was lighting up a cigarette, precisely when she had left. The man squeezed up his eyes against the cigarette smoke as he looked at his watch.

'*E andata via alle sette . . .*'

At seven o'clock! Colm echoed. She'd been gone for a whole bloody hour! So where would she go? Had she found another pensione; she would hardly hitch-hike at night. Or she might be at the station, taking a train. At least that was something he could check.

'*Grazie.*'

He rushed to the marble staircase, clattered down, ran down the Via Nazionale to the Piazza Santa Maria Novella and into the station.

The strident lilt of the public address system filled the air. There were people milling, talking, waiting and making phone calls. He saw a girl with fair hair squatting beside an old rucksack, but when he approached he saw she was not Robin.

He walked along the nearest platform, past the restaurant and waiting room, down towards the railway bridge, found to his surprise that it was not a dead end. There was a pedestrian walk-way out of the station here, a kind of concrete ramp which led down towards a car park. On one side of this ramp towered the ramparts of the railway. The railway line itself was carried by a bridge over the thoroughfare of the Viale Fillipo Strozzi some distance ahead of him. On the other side of this walk-way, to Colm's right, was the almost empty car park. Although a few street lamps burned, the place was deserted, full of shadows.

He scanned the place, was about to turn back, saw the man approaching from the shadows without paying much attention. But as he drew nearer, something in his gait, something in his posture, made Colm freeze. He was of medium height, thick set, powerfully built, and his face, when he came close enough, had a slack-mouthed twist to it of driven self-indulgence.

'*Are we better now?*' the Goat had asked with a leer. '*Fainting like a girl; behaving like a looney! Such a pity to be so weak in body and soul!*'

The man brushed against Colm as he passed.

'*Scusi . . .*'

And then he stopped and smiled into Colm's face. Colm saw the Goat's teeth, tobacco-stained, saw the hot glaze on the eyes, felt the incipient trespass, felt the old powerlessness; and then he was borne up by the crescendo of something that had possessed him only once before, the need to kill. He grabbed the man by the throat, held him against the railway wall. He was banging his head when he heard Robin's voice, 'Colm . . . Colm . . . for Chrissake!' And then he felt her pulling him away. The man slumped. He followed her, heard the cry from behind, the feet stumbling and then ran, down into the Viale Fillipo Strozzi.

The patch of ground where they spent most of the night had trees and desiccated grass. Near them the impersonal roar of the nighttime traffic went on, but they lay together, intertwined. Colm shivered for a while; the terror of himself and of what he would have done had she not appeared immobilised him; his limbs felt as though they had turned to ice. But her warmth permeated him.

'I would have killed him! I thought he was the fucking Goat!'

He smelt her breath, like the scent of hay, saw that her eyes had tiny incipient lines all around them. Suddenly it occurred to him that some day those lines would be etched.

'The what . . . ?'

'I remembered, you see. It came back!'

'What, for Chrissake?'

'This priest at school . . . I tried to kill him!'

'Yeah?' Robin said coolly enough, evidently unfazed. 'Did you succeed?'

* * *

Colm did not remember how he had got to the infirmary. Through the open window he could hear the birds chirping; the blinds were half down, but there was sunlight on the windowsill. He looked around; the room with its six beds was empty. He felt at peace.

But then, with sinking horror, the events in the chapel came back; he could not hide from them, the public shame, his destruction before the school, screaming as the Host was brought to him. His mind began to devise excuses; how could he be mad and be respected? If he pretended to be really mad . . . it would be better than to appear a wimp. He might lose his few friends, but better to be a dangerous madman than be universally despised.

He did not hear the door of the infirmary open, but he did hear the small rattle of beads. It was the visiting retreat priest, the Franciscan, Father Lawless, his rosary moving at his waist, his hands raised in friendly fashion, his brown habit making a small dry rustle.

'Ah, we're awake. How are we feeling?'

'All right, Father.'

'Good. Are you hungry?'

'No, Father.'

The old priest took a deep breath, released it slowly, letting his lips expand with the exhalation. He looked at the recumbent boy and he looked around the room and then he looked back at Colm.

'What happened?' he asked very gently. 'Why did you refuse the Host?'

Colm stiffened and did not reply. He closed his eyes and turned away.

The priest took something from his pocket, put it around his neck. When Colm opened his eyes he saw that Father Lawless had donned his purple stole, the symbol of the Confessional.

'Tell me now, boy,' he said gently. 'It will make things better

207

. . . get them off your mind! Nothing is so terrible that God will not forgive it!' He raised his right hand to commence the sacrament, '*In nomine Patris et Filii et Spiritus Sancti.*'

For a while Colm did not respond at all. 'It's all right,' the priest said. 'You needn't move, or sit up, just tell me anyway you like . . .'

'Sacrilege,' Colm whispered after a few seconds. 'I committed sacrilege!'

'Is that so, my poor boy! And how did you do that?'

Colm looked into his confessor's eyes, saw the patience, the acceptance of human foibles. 'I told a lie in Confession; and I took Communion the next morning! And I've done it since . . .'

'Ah!'

The shouts of the boys could be heard from the playing fields; the door opened to admit Matron, but at a signal from the Franciscan she withdrew. The old priest kept his head bowed; he asked the question so softly that Colm, longing for expiation, almost welcomed it. 'And what was the lie you told in Confession, my son?'

Colm did not look at the priest. He stared straight up at the ceiling. But his eyes filled as he said, 'I did not tell about certain things.'

'Things of the body?'

'Yes!' Colm said fiercely.

Father Lawless seemed unperturbed. 'They are mostly small matters, the things of the body,' he said. 'The body has its own strong will. Eventually we learn mastery, but it takes time!'

He looked at the penitent in the bed. 'If you are talking about things you did alone, God is understanding.' There was silence. 'Were these things you did alone, my son?'

Colm turned his face to the wall. 'No!'

There was silence. The Franciscan waited, nodded encouragingly at Colm when he looked directly at him. But Colm looked away again and was silent.

'Were they things you did with someone else?' the priest persisted in an unperturbed voice.

'They happened with a man, a priest if you want to know! But I took a vow, I swore on the Bible that I would never tell anyone!'

The Franciscan started. Colm turned to look at his confessor, but the latter's gaze did not waver, although there was a new rigidity about the eyes and mouth. 'Some oaths are not binding . . . Tell me . . .'

After a moment Colm, weeping, said, 'OK, I'll tell you . . . I'll tell you what happened, but I cannot tell you his name! OK?'

'OK.'

When Colm was done he glanced into the priest's face.

'Am I damned, Father?'

'No, my son.'

The priest gave Colm absolution. '*Ego te absolvo in nomine Patris et Filii et Spiritus Sancti.*' His face had a closed, concentrated expression. He removed his purple stole from his neck, folded it neatly, replaced it in the pocket of his habit and sat for a moment in silence.

'Colm.'

'Yes, Father?'

'There is something I want you to do.'

Colm waited in mounting dread.

'Tomorrow, when you are feeling better, I want you to ask for me and to tell me again what you have just told me now.'

Colm glanced at him angrily. 'Why? I told you the truth!'

'I know. But you told me under the seal of the Confessional. I want you to tell me again outside of the Confessional. I will be able to help you then! Will you do that?'

Colm felt the panic. If he told the Franciscan outside of Confession the priest would kick up a stink. And God knew what would happen then . . .

But he moved his head as though indicative of agreement, closed his eyes. He wanted to be alone. The old priest left.

Colm spent the following day in the infirmary. He told Father Phelim, who came to see him, that he had banged his head during his fall on the stairs; that he had hallucinated in the chapel – he thought the Host was a toadstool, poisoned. That was why he had screamed.

Father Phil looked doubtful. For someone to scream at the approach of the Host smacked of things he didn't even want to consider. To think that it had turned into a toadstool sounded like the prompting of hell.

Matron examined Colm's ankle and elbow and said he was well enough to get up the next day, providing he rested his ankle as much as possible. He knew she didn't buy the story of the hallucination. She was very gentle with him, whispered to Father Phelim as he left the infirmary that the boy was under some kind of stress; was he being bullied?

Father Lawless came to see him before he left. Colm pretended to be asleep. The priest tried to wake him.

'Colm, is there something you want to tell me?'

Colm shook his head and turned away.

'I'm leaving today, Colm. But I'll give you a phone number where you can contact me.' Father Lawless wrote something on a slip of paper and put it on the bedside locker. 'Please phone me. It is important that something is done, but I am powerless unless you help me!'

He waited for a few minutes and when Colm made no response he left.

As soon as he was gone Colm sat up in bed, seized the slip of paper and tore it up.

Next day Colm was allowed to skip Mass and stay in bed till second call. He had his breakfast in the infirmary and then went straight to class. His ankle was much better; it was bandaged. His elbow was still sore.

But something in him had changed. All day long he felt the rage. Confession had removed the guilt; rage had replaced it. It burned in him, a force. His classmates gave him a wide berth. 'Nutty Nugent' they called him among themselves. He felt in himself new reaches of cynicism. When the priests began class with a prayer he wanted to laugh; when they stood there in their black soutanes and white dog collars, he thought of sepulchres, whitened and blackened. He performed brilliantly in maths, the first time for ages. His rage lent him power. They did not have English, so he did not see Father Madden until the evening. But he decided he would not wait for a summons. Colm would seek him out himself.

He dodged prep after supper, made his way to the priests' corridor as quickly as his ankle would allow him. He liked the pain. He felt like a man, ready to confront his enemy, did not knock at the varnished door, but opened and closed it behind him peremptorily, so that it banged.

Father Madden was behind his desk. He looked up, sat back; his lip curled.

'How dare you burst in here!' he exclaimed, radiating outrage and the power of command. Colm felt some of his resolution desert him.

'What a foolish boy you are, Colm!' the priest said, dropping his voice. 'Behaving like a looney in the chapel . . . Do you know what they are saying about you? That you are mental. Some think you might even be possessed! Pull yourself together, boy, for God's sake!'

Colm breathed deeply through his nostrils, opened his mouth on an angry inhalation, but the priest forestalled him.

'Stop these histrionics . . . you're behaving like a girl.'

Whenever Father Madden mentioned girls or women his lips curled.

Colm said, 'I told Father Lawless about you!'

The priest started, said carefully, 'Did you indeed? In the Confessional?'

'Yes . . . he wants me to tell him about it outside of the Confessional. He gave me his phone number to contact him!'

Father Madden gave a short laugh. 'And do you think

211

anyone will believe your nonsense? A boy who goes around screaming and fainting? You'll be the laughing stock of everyone who hears your foolish story! And besides,' he added, 'you swore an oath on the Bible!'

'Some oaths are not binding!'

'All oaths are binding on men. But if you're not a man . . .'

It was the first time Colm could remember acting without any input from his brain. He saw on the desk the paperknife shaped like a sword, the slender blade, the handsome engraved pommel. He took this knife from the desk almost casually, and launched himself at the priest. Father Madden roared, brought his arm up to deflect the blow. The Toledo steel met bone; the blood stained the black cloth and dripped to the desk.

The door opened. An anxious face appeared. 'I was passing . . .' Father Phil said: 'I heard . . . Is everything . . . ?' He stared at the tableau before him, the boy cowering back, knife in hand, the big priest gripping his left arm with his right, while blood seeped through his fingers.

'This boy is a raving imbecile,' Father Madden roared. 'He has just attacked me with a knife!'

Colm was surprised that Robin did not seem shocked by his revelations. 'You're a cool one,' he told her. 'Listening to all that slop without turning a hair!'

She grimaced. 'Well, it's hardly that unusual, is it? Little kid at school; bent priest. For some guys a bit of power is the ticket to open season. But you were great to knife him, even if they expelled you for it! I hit someone once too, you know . . . only not with a knife! I mean I wanted to do the same thing as you . . . I wanted to kill him!'

Colm wondered if she was bullshitting again. But he could feel the tension in her. He raised his head to look at her. 'Did you? Really?'

When she didn't answer immediately he said, 'Tell me about it?'

212

'Not now. Don't you think we should go back to the pensione, get some sleep? It will soon be dawn!'

'The police are probably looking for me!' Colm said, suddenly aware of the possibilities he had precipitated.

'Unlikely. After all, you could say you were the one assaulted first! How well did that guy at the station see your face?'

'Dunno.'

'Tell you what,' she said after a moment, 'I'll go back . . . suss out the lie of the land . . . You can wait around the corner, or something.'

'No. I'll come with you. I'm not skulking around corners.'

But there was no problem, no sign of anything untoward, no Black Maria waiting in the Via Nazionale to haul him away. Antonio appeared briefly in the hallway, eyes gluey, looked at them wearily as though lovers' tiffs were an everyday affair with him and he had seen enough to last him a lifetime.

When they found their room, Colm took off his shoes and threw himself down on his bed. He felt as though a weight had left him. He was not about to be arrested. He had told someone for the first time; she had not fled him, nor thought less of him. He also realised that he had remembered it all; the memory gap which had so taunted him was gone. It was a small enough gap, a half-minute. He could clearly remember now the bloodied steel and the ornamental pommel. He could remember the immediate aftermath too, Father Phelim's rush to pinion his arms, although by this time the letter opener was already fallen to the floor and the parquet was smeared with crimson.

'Have you lost your mind, boy? You are behaving like someone possessed by the devil!' Father Phil said, panting, eyes full of zeal. Father Madden wrapped a handkerchief around his injury, but his narrowed eyes held Colm's still. Colm said nothing. He said nothing when they sent for his parents, when they expelled him, when his mother wept as they drove down the school avenue, past the playing fields, leaving behind the lordly mansion and his scholastic hopes.

213

He said nothing when his father thrashed him with a horse-whip, when his siblings jeered at him, when his mother became ill.

'You've killed her!' his father told him when she died a year later from breast cancer. 'You've killed your mother. I hope you're satisfied!'

His siblings glared at him with white, tear-stained faces.

'It's called matricide!' Alice said.

Colm had kissed his mother's marble lips that last morning before they screwed down the coffin lid and took it to the church. Then he returned to his work on the farm. He attended her funeral, was present at her wake. Deep inside him a resolution was forming.

Kattie Clohessy came to speak to him after the funeral, almost the only person who made any real attempt to do so. But although he talked, he was merely polite. He would show her too.

'What did you do after you were expelled? Did you go to another school?' Robin asked him.

'No. I just made up my mind to do it all myself. I got a correspondence course and educated myself. You can do anything you want if you put your mind to it!'

He did not tell her how he had withdrawn into himself, wasted little energy on any kind of communication. That he worked on the farm all day and in the evenings studied in his room until the small hours. It was this application which eventually steered him through a brilliant Leaving Certificate, and the second scholarship of his life, the one that got him a place in University College Dublin.

'I hope you didn't hurt that guy . . .' Robin said suddenly.

'Which guy?'

'The one you hammered this evening, for Chrissake!'

'He was still able to howl when I let him go.'

'True,' Robin said, adding drily, 'but I wouldn't make a habit of it!'

'From where did you materialise anyway, Robin? I thought you had gone.'

'I was just fooling . . . I was having some spaghetti in the station restaurant and saw you through the window. I expected you would look in, but when you didn't I followed you.'

'Where's your rucksack?'

'In the station left-luggage. I'll collect it tomorrow.'

'You really were leaving then?'

'No . . . I thought I should . . . that it wasn't fair on you. But I kinda missed you!'

Colm remembered that she hadn't been feeling well that morning. 'Are you OK now?' he asked. 'Feeling better?'

'Yeah!'

'Tomorrow is our birthday,' he said. 'We'll celebrate!'

She laughed softly. 'I've news for you, Colm. Tomorrow has come! I'm eighteen and you're twenty-two!'

She turned out the light, undressed. There was a glimmer of dawn through the slats of the shutters, and lying there, Colm could see her in the shadows. It was the first time she had undressed in his presence; she took off her shoes first, then her jeans, then her shirt. She stood for a moment uncertainly, shyly, before her panties and bra were thrown on to the chair. It was the first time he had seen a woman naked in the flesh. It was different from the dirty pictures; it was human, somehow vulnerable. It was not at all like anything projected by the priests; it was life and mystery and home. And then she came towards him across the room, pale except for her sun-tanned face and arms, pink-nippled, thin, strangely childlike. He opened his arms.

'Is it all right if we just lie together?'

'Sure. I love you, Robin!'

'Ssh,' Robin whispered. 'You don't have to.'

'I've never done this before,' he murmured hoarsely. 'Been in bed with a girl!'

'I've never been in bed with a girl before either . . .'

He laughed, reached for her lips.

215

'Don't move,' she said. 'Please don't do anything! Please let's just be together.'

Soon, lulled by the warmth, exhausted by the night behind them, they fell asleep.

Much later, waking fitfully, Colm looked down at her in his arms, thought how slight and small she was, and how wonderful he felt, like a king, like God. He moved his hands over her breasts, down her taut belly, felt her pubic hair under his fingers. She half opened her eyes but did not pull away. He kissed her, felt her lips answer his, felt her arms around him.

'I've never done this before,' he whispered hoarsely. 'I don't know if I can. I don't think I can! Will you . . . is it all right . . . Robin?'

'It's not a goddam competition,' she whispered shakily. 'And I've never done it before either . . .'

'Honestly?'

'No,' she whispered after a moment. 'Never this.'

'What about . . . you might get pregnant . . . ?'

'No,' she said. 'I don't menstruate . . .'

Colm wondered what she was talking about and then the penny dropped. It was that women's business, the period thing.

She stroked him, yielded to him eventually. As he lost control he cried on a rising note of panic and ecstasy, 'Oh, Robin . . . oh, Robin . . .'

Flopped out on top of her, he touched her face. Her eyes were closed.

'You are wonderful,' he whispered. 'I have never met anyone like you!' When she did not answer he said, 'I do love you. Do you hear me, Robin?'

Robin did not reply, but against his hand he felt her sudden tears. He felt his own begin to flow. At first they came silently, sliding down his face into Robin's hair. But then something broke inside him and he cried convulsively, covering his head with the sheet.

The girl, her body curved against him, held him in her arms.

'It's all right . . . I know . . . Poor Colm . . . It's all right . . .'

They slept and when they woke the day was advanced.

'Happy twenty-second!' Robin said.

'Happy eighteenth!'

She smiled up at him. Colm, remembering that he had wept in her arms, searched her for signs of contempt. But there were none. Suddenly he thought of his encounter the previous day with the annoyed Signore in Fiesole. Should he tell her? It was on the tip of his tongue, but he decided against it. She would only be angry.

'Robin,' he whispered, 'will you do something for me?'

'Sure.'

'Will you tell me about yourself? I don't mean the bullshit! I mean the real story?'

Colm abruptly switched his mind away from 1968. It was like looking back on the dark ages; it had the resonance of fairytale: two lost babes in a foreign land. Two babes with intolerable stories!

It was now 1996, he told himself; only four years remained to the turn of the millennium. He looked around the room at the faces lit by the reflected light from the screen. He saw Anna; she seemed to be asleep, her head was sunk on her breast, her hair silver in the dim light. The lecturer was talking about the hidden inferences in Botticelli's painting, *Primavera*. The female dancing forms with braided hair were virgins, he said; they were as yet untouched. The females with loose hair, such as the figure of Spring, were full-blown women; '*aperta*' was the word he used to indicate that they were 'open'.

When the lecture ended and the shutters were thrown wide to the late-afternoon light Colm caught Anna's eye. She winked at him, making him laugh. She had been fully awake after all.

217

He went to help her from her seat, asked her what she thought of the lecture.

She said mildly that the analogies used were crude and inaccurate. 'But it was interesting otherwise!'

Suddenly Colm found himself wondering what Paola would have made of it, imagined himself sitting beside her and watching her face. Paola was real! She was no memory newly excavated, no shadow with a fearful story, no unsolved riddle from another time. She would be there this evening, talking, breathing, laughing.

He walked with Anna to the lift and came down with her to the piazza. She was lodging nearby, said goodnight, and he walked at a smart pace back to the Via de' Tornabuoni.

Chapter Eleven

Paola was dazzling that evening. She was wearing red and sat at the head of her table, smiling at her guests. Colm wondered if something had happened to produce the glow, wondered at her beauty.

Perhaps something's gone well for her at work, he thought, remembering her rush back to the office after their lunch together.

Despite the humidity of the evening her radiance gave a lift to the conversation, as though her spirit were contagious. She asked Jill and Colm if they were still interested in a trip to the Piazzale Michelangelo. They said they were.

Colm asked a question in Italian, asked Jill what she worked at. She worked in publishing, she said; she was an editor of children's books. She also was looking particularly pretty this evening, in yet another lovely outfit. She said it would be super to go to the Piazzale Michelangelo. Darina and Renate compared notes on discos. Darina's Italian had improved; she was making a genuine effort. Pasquale quietly picked at his food, raising dark eyes to the company.

Renate questioned Colm as to his motives for visiting Florence and Colm responded with platitudes, although when he met Paola's eye on one occasion she answered him with a conspiratorial smile. Why does this woman give me the feeling that she knows who I am? he wondered. It's almost as though we met in a previous incarnation.

A mosquito, wafting in from the open window, alighted on Renate's arm. She was unaware of it. Colm said sharply in

English, 'Renate, you've a visitor!' But by the time she had come down from her high horse because he had spoken to her in English, it was too late. The insect had feasted and avoided its death with a fluent motion, ascending blithely towards the ceiling. Renate swore softly in German, '*Scheisse!*' rubbed her arm, shook her head angrily, and rose, saying she was going to find her anti-histamine cream. Darina said she always smeared Autan on exposed skin as soon as it became dark: 'Otherwise how do you expect to keep the little buggers away?' As Renate left the room she confided, 'Poor Renate is allergic to mosquitoes. Every bite becomes a balloon!'

Paola frowned and shook her head. '*La poverina* . . .'

'Mamma sprays the place every day,' Pasquale said defensively in Italian. 'But they're like Sicilians, you can't keep them out!'

Jill smiled at Colm. Her eyes held his for an instant, albeit a bit absently. Paola leaned towards Pasquale and asked him to eat some more. He made a gesture of impatience. Why does she fuss so much over him? Colm wondered. The boy is almost grown and patently hates the attention. But Pasquale was very pale, and held himself as though it were an effort even to sit at table. Paola, regarding him, became quiet, lost her joie de vivre, continued chatting after an automatic fashion but kept her eyes on her son.

Dessert was fruit. Jill chose an apple, peeled with practised speed, offered with a laugh to peel one for Colm. He shook his head.

When the meal was almost over Pasquale excused himself, and went to his room. Darina then stood up, thanked her hostess, and left to prepare herself for yet another disco. Renate followed her. She would not be going to the disco, she said; she was going to spend the next few hours studying.

Jill looked at Paola expectantly. 'Well, Paola,' she said in English, 'shall we clear up and get going?'

'Will you two forgive me,' Paola said, looking from Jill to Colm, 'if I cry off our little excursion . . . I have work to do tonight, and I don't think Pasquale is too well this evening.'

Colm felt the disappointment. For some reason he had been looking forward to accompanying Paola on this nighttime excursion, but he turned politely to Jill.

'What do you think?' he said. 'Are you game? We can get a taxi.'

'Have you ever been there?' Jill asked. 'The Piazzale Michelangelo?'

'Once, many years ago. You'd better bring a sweater; it can be quite chilly up there at night!'

He turned to Paola. 'Are you sure you won't come too? We needn't stay too long . . .'

'No. I'm sorry . . . I would like to, but . . .' She rose, began to collect dishes from the table, waved away their attempts to help her.

Colm went to his room to get a jacket and when he came back he saw Paola going into her son's room. She was frowning, her anxiety patent. As he passed the open door Colm saw that Pasquale was lying on his bed. If he was my son, Colm thought with irritation, I'd soon shift him – lying on his bed at this hour of the evening when he should be doing his homework or helping his mother! And then he thought of Alan, his own son, lying on the grass beside his new bicycle, almost as though he were asleep, the blood, like an ordinary nosebleed, a small puddle of crimson on his upper lip. Too late to hold him, to tell him how he loved him; too late now to unbend.

Jill was waiting for him in the hall. She was carrying a woollen stole and looked very pretty.

'All set then?' she said brightly. He followed her to the lift, was aware of her perfume as they descended. He was familiar with some perfumes, those Kattie had worn and Sherry's favourites; others were a mystery. But he knew this perfume; it was almost certainly Miss Dior. Kattie had worn it. It had been there on her skin when he kissed her in the early mornings; it was on her clothes, faint and lingering; it was on a silk scarf

221

he had found in his pocket after their rupture and returned to her in the post.

They found a taxi, and as the driver manoeuvred the Fiat into the mainstream traffic Colm, with a start, saw the girl again, the dead ringer for Robin. He even caught a glimpse of her profile. It had to be the same one, he thought. She was ahead of them and turned into the Via delle Terme. The sight of her made him jerk upright, crane his head to look back. But she was lost to view.

'Have you seen someone you know?' Jill asked him.

'Just the spitting image of someone I knew long ago!'

'I know what you mean,' Jill said, 'reminders like that can be startling.'

Colm thought with some irritation that she hadn't a clue what he meant. 'In this case it's a bit uncanny,' he added. 'I could almost believe her to be a ghost . . . She looks just like a girl I knew here twenty-eight years ago, even the same stride . . . the same body language!'

When Jill did not reply, but raised her eyebrows, he felt a bit foolish and added to change the subject, 'It's a pity Paola didn't come with us. I'm sure she could do with the break.'

'Yes. She works very hard and then she keeps students as well, so she has little time.'

'She spoils that son of hers,' Colm said.

Jill turned grave eyes on him. 'Perhaps you didn't know that Pasquale is not very well?'

'What's wrong with him?'

'He needs an operation. She wants to send him to a famous cardiologist and is trying to raise the money.'

'What kind of operation?'

'There's something wrong with his heart; he has a defective valve. It will have to be replaced.'

Colm looked out of the taxi window at night-time Florence. The traffic swirled, horns tooted, floodlights played on ancient buildings. Why do I think other people are immune to life's vicissitudes? he wondered. Is it a form of narcissism?

'How did you learn this?'

'She told me. I was talking to her late recently . . . when I couldn't sleep and found her still up working.'

The taxi left them at the piazzale and they strolled to a café with tables by the balustraded parapet overlooking the city. Colm asked Jill what she would have to drink, ordered two glasses of white wine, sat beside her and looked down on the panorama of the city. She pointed out various landmarks, the dome of the Duomo, the tower of the Palazzo Vecchio, the Ponte Vecchio, the spire of Santa Croce. A cool breeze fanned the piazzale and she took her wool stole from the back of her chair and wrapped it around her. She glanced around, saw the monument to Michelangelo in the middle of the piazzale.

'What an incomparable genius he was!' she said, indicating the monument with an inclination of her head. Colm, half bored, followed her eyes. 'Such passionate creativity,' she went on in an intense voice, 'as though life could never give him time enough for what he wanted to accomplish! As though he was hunting the meaning of existence through the veins of the marble . . .'

Colm heard the suppressed passion in her voice, and leaned forward with arrested interest. The young Englishwoman seemed different, stripped suddenly of a veneer, as though she had real fire in her belly. But she fell silent, disappointingly, as though fearing she had disclosed herself.

'Do you like Florence?' she asked.

The banality of the question, the change in tone, restored Colm to his earlier perspective. He said that he did. But his mind had wandered. Here, almost at this very spot, he had sat with Robin nearly thirty years before. Here Robin had also shivered with the chill evening breeze and he had reached for her sweater.

He could remember the way she had moved to inspect the city below. He remembered the lust, the feel of her breasts, the first breasts he had ever touched, the firm softness, the silken skin. But, in retrospect, he saw only her ferocious

223

innocence, her vulnerability, her extreme youth. In retrospect he wondered again, on a wave of loss and longing, why she had never written, why she had just disappeared. And then he felt the terror that he had failed her. She had never written because she could not. Because he had left her behind to die.

'Will your wife be joining you?' Jill asked.

'No. We're divorced.'

Then he asked, 'How about you, Jill? I see you're wearing a wedding ring.'

'I'm a widow,' Jill said.

'Do you have children?'

'None of my own, but I have two step-children.'

'You're a bit young to be a step-mum!'

She smiled. 'Yes. They're in their twenties! And you? You have children too?'

'No . . .'

He could not bear to speak of Alan.

Jill's hand strayed near his on the table. She released her hold on her stole. The tight silken fabric of her top stretched across her breasts. He smelt her perfume again; it was definitely Miss Dior. The night enveloped them, the lights of the café, the glow from the city, the wafting perfume, subtle and powerful with memory. For a moment it was as if there was no such thing as time; as if the woman before him personified the eternal feminine, Robin, Kattie, Sherry, even Paola, every woman he had ever known. He reached for her hand and, when she did not withdraw it, pulled her to him, let his hand brush against the straining fabric, kissed her. She yielded, a body movement of surprise. He felt the moist response of her mouth. Then she pulled abruptly away. He felt astonished with himself, at himself, not at his actions, but that he should have acted without intent, like an adolescent yielding to imperatives he had not yet learned to control.

'I'm sorry. I shouldn't have done that! But you were looking so pretty . . .'

How trite this sounded! It was the first time he had ever

considered the nature of the lines he had offered in casual encounters when he was away from home. Women, he suspected, rushed into believing what they longed to believe. They wanted to believe that men were offering them not just sex, but everything that sex could be and seldom was – recognition, comfort, love. He knew that, in the moment of contact, even Jill herself had forgotten that they were both strangers, sharing only an emotional scavenging in a foreign land. But now her cold, surprised eyes made him feel suddenly cheap. Because she was silent he felt the weight of his words, their patronising insufferability. Why, he asked himself, did you have to say that? You are acting according to some stereotype, but you are not reacting to the truth of the moment. You are using this woman, as you have used many others, for validation and escape. You are using her to vent an old and complex rage.

'I apologise. I am a bit overwhelmed,' he said awkwardly, 'by many things.'

'Please don't apologise.' Her voice was cold. She drew her stole around her again and suggested that perhaps they should be getting back. He glanced at her as they walked away from the piazzale; she was withdrawn and uncommunicative.

He said to her in the taxi, 'Have I offended you?'

She shook her head with a small dismissive sound. 'You are a very attractive man,' she said. 'You also know it!'

'No,' Colm said after a moment, in a tired, flat voice. 'In fact I don't know it at all!'

When they got back to the Via de' Tornabuoni Jill said goodnight and went in immediately, but Colm lingered, looked up and down the street and then walked to the Via delle Terme where he had seen the girl disappear. The thought of her sent a sudden shiver up his spine. Who said the dead didn't walk? There were a myriad stories about how they came back for people they had loved. You did love me, Robin, in your way. No matter what you said! And then he thought with rueful cynicism: if love is predicated on knowledge of the beloved,

225

you must be the only one who ever did! This made him think of Kattie, who thought she knew him, who certainly wanted to, who loved what she believed of him. I never wanted to be loved, he thought defensively. That was entirely Kattie's own doing! I never asked for that.

When Colm came in Paola was still up. The door of the dining room was ajar and he saw her by the light of an angle lamp working at her computer. She called out softly, '*Buona sera, Colm!*' as though she knew, without turning her head, that he was looking at her, and when he put his head in the door she turned and smiled.

He came towards her in the quiet room. The table, now empty of dishes, was glowing with polish and held a number of books, one on top of the other. He read the title of the one on top: *Firenze del Cinquecento.*

The glass doors of the bookcase reflected the room, the man, the seated woman, the computer monitor. The French windows to the balcony were half open. Paola was wearing her spectacles; they gave her an air of authority. Her hair had loosened a little and some of it was spilling from the combs. The glamour of the early evening had deserted her. She looked tired; a small tic busied itself underneath her left eye. She picked up a dictionary, leafed for a word. Colm experienced again the sensation of having known her before. He compared her mentally with Sherry, who was always leafing through brochures, hunting fabrics and colour schemes, and decided he must be confusing them. Or did Kattie have a way of holding her head so when she was reading? He couldn't remember.

'Did you have a nice time?' Paola asked in English.

'Yes. The view was wonderful!'

She waited, expecting further comment. When it didn't materialise she said, 'Did it jog your memory?'

'Of course! I felt as though I were twenty again. In fact I behaved as though I *was* twenty again. I hope I didn't upset Jill.'

'You probably don't know,' Paola said quietly, 'that she's

grieving. Her husband died just two months ago. They had planned a holiday in Florence for when he recovered, so she decided to keep the date herself. She thought it would help her with her grief.'

'Oh, Christ,' Colm said. You're an insensitive bollocks, he told himself, as Paola raised interrogative eyebrows at his outburst.

'I've been very insensitive,' he said aloud. 'I made a pass at her, Paola. It just happened, nothing momentous, an automatic piece of stupidity. Perhaps I thought she expected it. Do you think I've upset her?'

Paola regarded him in silence and then said, 'You couldn't know that she is in mourning. And, of course, she is attractive! She has probably upset herself . . . if she responded, that is.' Her voice was low; he saw sudden introversion in her eyes. 'Her husband's memory is still fresh, you see. She may feel guilt. But on another level, if it's any consolation, it was probably experienced by her as an affirmation, that she's still attractive, that she is not marked by death!'

Colm heard the hairline fracture in Paola's voice. He had a brief glimpse of vulnerability.

'You're looking tired, Paola,' he said, 'if you don't mind my saying so. Why are you working so late?'

'I have a piece I want to finish. In fact,' she added, 'I was just going to make myself some coffee to keep me awake.'

'May I join you?'

'Why not?'

She rose, went to the kitchen. Colm followed her, stood by the door as she put the coffee into the cafetière, poured in the hot water. She found some cups and handed them to him, brought the coffee into the dining room, put it on the table on a cork mat.

'So,' she said with a wry smile as she poured the coffee, 'the Piazzale Michelangelo revived old memories?' Colm watched her pour, intrigued that she had returned to this topic, that she should interest herself in his peccadillo of the evening and in his long-lost romance.

'Yes. Very much so, in fact. I remembered how Robin was full of enthusiasm for the view; she was a girl who was full of enthusiasm for everything, although she disappeared that particular evening and did not return until very late . . .' He started, struck by the thought that perhaps life was only a programme where one is doomed to repeat the same mistakes.

She glanced at him as she handed him his cup, wondered again at his capacity to obsess himself with a dream. It was at odds with his cool persona, this unresolved emotion; it told her more about him than he could have put in words. But was he using it to side-step something more important? It had to be much more than simple nostalgia for a lost time.

'You have pinned a great deal of your emotional life on this girl Robin,' she said. 'Are you sure you are not just projecting, using her as a prop because she is safely out of reach? If she were to walk through the door and claim you as her own, would you be enchanted or dismayed?'

Colm privately acknowledged her perceptiveness. If indeed Robin did come through the door, he was not sure how he would react. With delight, certainly. But beyond that, what? Would they even be the same people, marked as each of them must be by their separate intervening journeys?

'I think you may have turned her into an icon,' Paola continued in a teasing tone, 'at whose mystic feet you can lay the burdens of your life! But like all icons she doesn't really exist. She inhabited an important slot in your existence; perhaps she helped you; she certainly touched you. But it is long ago and the past is a dream!'

She regarded him in silence for a moment before adding, 'It is certainly no substitute for a living, breathing present.'

'Do you mind if I ask you a blunt question?' Colm ventured after a moment, in which he found himself touched by her acuity, her impervious calm.

'Depends on the question!' she said. 'What blunt question would you ask me?'

'What is the secret of your serenity?'

She gazed at him over her coffee cup. 'Are you trying to flatter me?'

'No.'

She studied him for a second. 'I do not know what you mean by serenity. Perhaps I project more than I feel. I try to accept things and to work within them. At the moment, in fact, I must do just that . . . I try to take the overview, to see life not just as present but also as future . . . and to see it with hope!'

'I see.' Colm said softly after a moment, 'Paola, Jill told me about Pasquale . . . I'm sorry that he's not well.' She turned back to stare at the serried regiments of words marching across her monitor screen.

'She shouldn't have bothered you with all of that.' When Colm waited without comment she added, 'There is a narrowing of one of the valves of his heart. It developed after a bout of rheumatic fever . . . contracted not long after his father died. I have to be careful of him. He will have surgery when it can be arranged. He was very tired earlier this evening, and went to bed. That is why I didn't come with you.'

'But surely you have not shut the door on life? An attractive woman, still young!'

'You don't have to say complimentary things!' she said with a tight smile. 'I don't need flattery.'

'I meant it,' Colm said, deflated.

She shot him a swift assessing glance. He finished his coffee, although he knew it would keep him awake.

'Well, I'd better go to bed.'

'Goodnight, Colm.' She touched his arm as she said this in apparent apology. He flinched. Her face registered dismay. 'I'm sorry . . .'

'I'm just a bit tired!' he said hastily. And then, acting on an impulse, he leaned over and with a courtly gesture kissed her hand.

'Goodnight, Paola.'

229

She did not move, but her face, when he looked at her, was vulnerable.

Colm went to his room, passing Paola's en route. The door was open; he could see her double bed and the photographs on the bedside table. In a silver frame was a young male face – her husband? He was struck by a sense of her personal history, so vivid to her, so unknown to him. Suddenly he felt almost jealous of the husband she had loved, slept with, made a child with.

You want too much, he told himself; you want to corral everything you desire, impress it with yourself, possess it. Stop wanting. Let go!

He visited the bathroom, came back, got into bed, reviewed the evening, thought of Jill and felt angry. Why the hell did he have to behave like an ape? What was he trying to prove? He conceded that it had had something to do with night and wine and scent; but it also had to do with the involuntary dropping of his own barriers, behind which lurked the vulnerable self he feared and loathed. I've made a fool of myself long enough . . . would I be better out of this set-up? I'll book into a hotel tomorrow! Why should I have to bother with people waging battles with adversity! And then the stockbroker in him said that if he wanted a woman he should look for someone cut from the same cloth as himself, a successful woman with assets, a woman with a share portfolio and a bank balance.

What the hell do you want assets for now? a small interior voice asked him. When are you going to live? Robin is gone, is in the past. Her ghost walks the streets of Florence, incorporeal, insubstantial, vanishing like a shadow around corners. The world is full of stranger, more powerful, forces than money. Perhaps she knows you have come and is waiting for you. Perhaps, notwithstanding Dr Kelly's hopeful prognosis, you do not have long for this world!

This was a sobering thought. He got out of bed, went to the window, pushed open the shutters, looked down into the street. There was no sign of Robin's fetch, or whatever she was. Groups of young people moved along the pavements; their laughter rose, crystal and strangely innocent on the still night air.

He felt the nostalgia for a time long gone, the student years he had hardly lived. But you are well again, he told himself. In spite of all your recent conjectures you still draw breath. There is still a life to be had if you reach for it. Forget about Robin. Look forward, not back.

Robin had looked at him with a strange mixture of shyness and embarrassment the morning after their first lovemaking. She spent a while in the bathroom, came back as though nothing had changed between them. He hardly knew what to say. Words of endearment escaped him. He responded to her apparent flippancy with as much normality as he could conjure. He ventured at one point to raise the subject of her real story. She would tell him later, she said, no bullshit. He suggested that they visit the church of Santa Croce. 'It's not far. About ten minutes.'

They went to the café at the corner. Robin refused *caffè latte*, drank a little water.

'Why won't you eat?'

'Yuk! It's too early.'

'Are you sure you're all right, Robin? I think you should see a doctor.'

'No . . . I'm fine . . . just a bit of nausea.'

'But this has been going on for ages now . . .'

She shrugged. 'Don't worry. It'll go! It always does!'

She checked the guide and said Santa Croce had been started in 1294 and was the burial place of Michelangelo, Machiavelli, Galileo. Colm took out the postcards he had bought from the urchin on the Ponte Vecchio, wrote one of them to his family. He looked at the other one, an aerial view of the city, thought of Kattie.

'Are you going to send that to Catherine?' she asked suddenly, as though telepathic.

'No!' Colm said.

Robin regarded him for a moment in silence. 'Did you tell her you would send her one?'

'I may have . . . but I won't!'

'When was the last time you saw her?'

Colm wondered if Robin were jealous. He glanced at her face, but could not detect in it any sign of the green-eyed monster.

'I last saw her just before I came on this holiday. She was in her father's shop.'

'And how was she . . . glad to see you?'

'Yes . . . in fact she asked me to send her a card.'

'You see . . .'

'No I don't! I don't see anything.'

'No? Well, don't let decency muck you up, baby,' Robin said. 'Keep your conscience strictly self-serving!'

The Franciscan church of Santa Croce commanded the square of the same name. They walked around the church, through the three naves with their elegant pilasters and sharply pointed arches, examined the chapels and their frescos.

'So you were never in the States?' Robin said suddenly at one point. 'Not even once?'

He had his arm around her and was pretending to examine a fresco showing the burial of St Francis, while all the time he thought only of her head in the hollow of his shoulder, and their passion of the preceding night.

'Nope.'

'You should visit!'

'I will. I will come as soon as I can afford it. Do you think your posh father will like me?'

He blew on her hair and a few strands danced under the localised hurricane.

Robin glanced up at him, smiled, put a hand to her hair, but she did not reply immediately. Then she said, 'Like you? Sure . . . I guess!

'Know something . . .' Robin continued, gesturing at the wall in an obvious attempt to change the subject, 'I love art but I'm kinda tired of this stuff, the dogma, the male centrality, women valued only if desiccated, for the best part having been thrown away . . .' She glanced up at him. 'You know, like white sugar or any other super-refined junk . . .'

He felt irritated. Robin was in one of her provocative moods. He wondered if she was regretting their lovemaking.

He looked at the wall paintings. Wimps in haloes, he thought. He said aloud: 'I don't see much rampant masculinity in any of these frescos myself!'

Robin laughed, and moved away, turning back a second later and putting a hand on his arm. 'Aw, never mind. Come on, I'll buy you an ice cream! I have just about enough lire left.'

They were near the exit. Colm, who was about to study the monuments of Dante and Michelangelo, recoiled. She stopped and stared at him angrily.

'Why did you do that? Jump away from me?'

'I don't know . . . I'm sorry. I didn't mean to. Sometimes when I'm touched unexpectedly . . . I can't bear it!'

'You were able to bear it well enough last night,' she said in a small offended voice.

'It was different then!'

'So you expected it last night? What we did?'

'No,' Colm said flatly. 'Of course I didn't!'

Robin waited as though she expected him to tell her something, say what last night had meant, put it in language of love and reassurance.

But how could he tell her what last night had meant to him? How could he tell her when it evidently meant so little to her that she could refer to it with such brittle jocosity?

'I don't want to discuss it!'

Robin sniffed and moved ahead of him, striding down the steps of Santa Croce, across the square and along the Borgo dei Greci.

He caught up with her and they walked in silence through the cobbled street, among the yellow ochre buildings, to the Piazza della Signoria where the lordly palace sent up its brick watch-tower to overlook the city. Robin counted her change, stopped to buy ice cream from a street vendor, surveyed the flavours on offer and chose a variety – '*Fragola, cioccolata, e cassata, per favore*' – and then they had a medley of ice creams, all jostling for space in two overloaded cones.

She paid for her purchases, handed Colm his cone without looking at him. They entered the square in silence, stood in the shade of the Loggia della Signoria below the sculpture showing the *Rape of the Sabine Women*, licking their ice creams and regarding the old palace, avoiding each other's eyes. Robin looked around slowly. Colm watched her in silence, following her gaze as it moved around the square, from the equestrian statue to the Neptune fountain, and back to the Palazzo, her head a little to one side, like a bird.

'You like that particular building anyway,' Colm ventured. 'I can see that!' This was a safe topic; he could not discuss love with her; he could not tell her what she longed to hear. He might burst to say it, but he dared not even begin to compose the words.

'Sure,' she said, wrapping her pink tongue around her ice cream, rescuing the dribble which threatened the side of the cone. Then she lapsed back into silence. Colm could not bear her silence.

'What do you like about it?'

Robin sighed like a girl who might as well accept patent limitation. 'I love its understated lines.'

'We could meet here sometime in the future!' Colm said suddenly. 'When we're all grown up and successful! What would you say to that?'

He threw this out, because he already knew he wanted to meet her, keep her for ever, marry her if she would have him, but how to say it? How to tell her what last night had been to him? How to tell her he could not live without her? How to convey the catch in his heart when he turned his head and found her there, examining some picture or sculpture with her peculiar passion, as though she would project her very essence into the matrix of the work, live it from the inside, shine out through tempera and marble? How could he inform her that he had become part of her; that if she were lost to him he was cut off at the roots?

And he would have to go home soon; he was due to start work at the beginning of October. It would take him two days to get back, travelling overland to Paris and then to Le Havre for the boat. He had things he wanted to tell her before it was too late.

'Don't be silly! You'll be going home soon . . . You won't remember . . .'

'I will, Robin!'

'OK,' she said. 'I'll meet you when you're old and grey!'

'Seventy?'

'No, not seventy. Fifty . . . on your fiftieth birthday!'

Colm heard the flippancy, knew it was impossible now to broach anything to her of a serious nature. 'Do I have to wait till then?' he asked on a teasing note.

She looked at him and laughed. 'Maybe not! It depends on how well you behave! But no matter where we are in the world we'll meet here – in the Piazza della Signoria – on your fiftieth birthday, my forty-sixth, twenty-eight years from now!' she repeated. 'We'll meet over there – at the Rivoire restaurant where the fat cats are feeding their faces. Is it a deal?'

'Sure, I'll be an old geezer and you'll be . . .'

'I'll never grow old,' she replied hastily. 'I'll still be Robin . . . still me!'

'You'll forget . . .'

'I never forget my promises. Wait and see!'

'OK. But I hope we'll meet before that, Robin. I hope we don't lose touch!'

She glanced at him sharply. 'Eat your ice cream or it'll go cold!' she said.

235

Colm felt the tension drain from him. He had been uptight all morning, preoccupied with the night before, with a mélange of emotions he found difficult to unravel. Watching her now, as she brought her tongue again to the diminished cone in her hand, as she bent forward and lowered her eyes, he was suffused with a rush of proprietary tenderness.

'Thank you for last night,' he whispered, after a moment. It was the best he could do.

Robin looked away from him across the expanse of the square and then back to her hand in his. Various emotions flitted across her face, exasperation, sadness, even a form of outrage.

'Don't thank me, for Chrissake! Don't you know anything about love?'

'What are you talking about, Robin?'

'Aw, nothing . . . Well, I was thinking . . . you loved Catherine . . . so I don't understand how you could just dump her. You won't even send her a card. I hope you didn't change your mind about that because of me.'

'Don't be ridiculous. And I didn't "dump" Kattie. I never had her to dump her!'

'You had her friendship; you loved the very thought of her. You wrote love poetry for her. Yet you just disappeared from her life. Didn't you care if you had hurt her?'

'She has nothing to do with us! I have never had anything like us!'

'Maybe . . . But if you meet her again you will probably want her. But that doesn't mean you won't dump her again. Maybe you need to hurt people.'

'Don't be absurd!'

'Hmnn . . .' Robin said. 'I'd be too scared to love anyone . . .'

'It has nothing whatsoever to do with us, Robin!'

'Maybe not. Maybe nothing has anything to do with us. Maybe we're in a separate category, damaged goods . . . ?'

'Robin . . .'

She shrugged, regarded him with grave, perplexed eyes.

'There's a story I'll tell you sometime,' she whispered. 'Everything you wanted to know about me. And then you won't want me any more either. You won't send *me* a postcard either!'

That night they returned early to the pensione. She had recovered her good humour, undressed shyly, smiled archly at him and slipped into bed beside him. He joined her, started to kiss her feverishly.

'Easy,' Robin whispered. 'Wait a bit!'

He learnt that night the ecstasy of communion, conspirators' whispers in the dark. She shushed him, wanting silence. But as the night deepened she began to kiss him, small tentative kisses like shivers on his chest and belly, down to his groin, caressed his balls and penis in her hand. He experienced her discovery of him as though it were his own discovery, as though his body were new, terra incognita, untouched; and when she pulled him down on her he forced on himself control, longing above all things to give her pleasure, to prolong the magic. But control escaped him, abandoned him to the vortex of eternity.

'I never thought I could feel like this!' Colm whispered when he surfaced a little later. 'I suppose it must exist after all!'

'What?' Robin asked sleepily.

'A four-letter word,' he replied, touching her face. 'Which exists in spite of all your protestations. It begins with L.'

He wanted her to say she loved him. If she said it perhaps he could loosen the floodgates of his own emotions.

'Ah, have sense!' Robin said. Her breathing deepened, her body was limp and still, but he noticed that she surreptitiously wiped her eyes with the sheet. This provoked in him a mixture of tenderness and anger. She was keeping her essential self from him and he could not bear it.

Then he thought, why should he care? At school when women were mentioned the message had been clear; there

237

were the virgin icons and there were the whores. The perception riding on this indoctrination said that he had got her, screwed her, possessed her; that she was worthless, that she had led him into sin. Why would he need the love of such a creature?

He opened his eyes, saw her small head against his shoulder, felt her slight inert form against his, felt the beating of her heart.

Neat theories, Colm thought, comparison between the dogma and the reality vivid; cruel, shallow theorems imposed on the stuff of life.

'No,' he whispered aloud. 'They knew nothing! This does not lead to hell. This is holy; this is all there is of heaven!'

Robin stirred. He thought she was asleep but her voice was awake: 'Heaven is full of goddamn creeps, for Chrissake!'

Colm was silent for a moment and then said softly, 'Well, something better than heaven. You are my homeland, Robin. My home!'

Colm told himself: I hear the voices of today's youth below me on the street. Tomorrow they too will have moved on, will look back and ask – what happened to time?

The nocturnal chatter gradually left the pavement below his window, reinforcing his sense of isolation. He looked up at the white ceiling, considered if he would bother to read. He had bought a couple of thrillers at the airport and they were in the drawer beside him. But he seldom read now. The passion for literature, poetry, which had once won him a scholarship to Clonarty College, was long gone. What he had lived for, instead, was control. Or was it a form of denial? he asked himself. Have I denied something important, become my own slave?

Whatever he had expected of Florence it had not delivered. At least not so far, and the likelihood was that it never would, despite the 'phantom' who eluded him along the city streets. The answers, he suspected, if any existed, were only to be

238

found in himself. And to find them he would have to do the impossible, delve into what he dared not confront, turn over the old well-tamped clay of his certainties and encounter whatever lay beneath. I won't, he thought. I won't get involved in that kind of crap.

He turned off the light and tried to sleep, drifted away eventually into fitful dreams. The nightmare that woke him two hours later was savage in its realism. The sweat was running down his chest and the sheet was sodden.

The image of Catherine came with such force that he woke as though catapulted into a time warp. In the dream he had been kissing her, had put his mouth to her breast, but the nipple had melted away, the flesh putrescent and he realised that she was dead, that his kiss had killed her. Behind her Alan appeared on a bicycle, calling to him, 'Daddy, Daddy . . .' suddenly turning from him and racing away until only his voice was left on the wind. Colm woke, glad to escape the nightmare.

I should never have re-opened the Catherine thing, came the thought. What right did I have to come back into her life, tell her a heap of lies, take and take from her, give so little? It was as though I wanted to empty her. Oh God . . . because if I emptied her I would be free of her. I would have proved something; I would have had some kind of revenge . . . But not against you, Kattie! Revenge against Seamus Madden, bent priest!

He recalled his first dinner date with her, two adults now, safely in their thirties. Why hadn't he just left her alone?

'Where would you like to dine?' he had asked her and she had said anywhere at all. So he had taken her to dinner in the Mirabeau and knew that she was impressed by being invited to one of the most expensive restaurants in the country. She sat across from him, winsome, happy to be with him, anecdotal. 'Do you remember the time poor Timmy Donohoe was chased by the bull in Murray's field?' Her freckles were almost obliterated under her fluid make-up; she showed her funny white teeth when she laughed. He hated her suddenly for her coyness and provincialism, for her prudery, rolling her eyes modestly sideways when he made some slightly risqué joke. He loved her because he had once loved her; this was what he told himself; surely he could enjoy it and distance himself from it at the same time. He knew their shared history, albeit fragmentary, provided a powerful bond between them, and he gradually came to realise that, because of it, unquestionably because of it, she trusted him.

When he left her back at her friend's flat in Fisherman's Wharf he took both her hands and said, 'I have been admiring you all evening!'

She blushed, said predictably, 'You shouldn't say things like that!'

He phoned her the following week in the middle of her working day. 'Will you have supper with me this evening? I'll be down your way.'

'Oh, will you be staying in Ballykelly?'

'No. No need to mention me to the family . . .'

She sighed. 'It's a pity you don't get on any more. I often wondered why, but Alice wouldn't say . . .'

'Of course we get on! It's just that time is so limited nowadays. I don't have enough of it . . .'

The following week she had dinner with him again – in a newly opened country house restaurant with a French menu – and this time he kissed her thoroughly afterwards, thrusting his tongue into her mouth. He held her close and felt her thighs loosen when he caressed her nipples through the thin silk of her blouse. So much, he thought, for all that virgin propriety! He thought with amusement of the silly poetry he had written for this goddess when she had been twelve.

After that she had been easy enough. He painted his marriage in disparaging terms; it was over, he told her; it was dead. He rationalised this falsehood, telling himself it had never been alive. He knew he had resurrected old hopes and he cashed in on them. Nothing simpler than women when you knew how.

When Catherine had been transferred by her bank to Dublin not long after this, he had been delighted. Destiny had played into his hands. He brought her to a concert in the National Concert Hall. Afterwards she said to him, 'I didn't know you were so fond of music.'

'Am I?'

'Oh, yes. I was watching you. You were transported!'

This comment irritated him. It indicated weakness. To like music was one thing; to allow oneself to be transported was another; to have that transportation visible was intolerable. In fact to have one's vulnerabilities visible in any context whatsoever was inconceivable.

'Don't look so annoyed . . . I was observing you; I'm sorry if it was intrusive.'

'I'm not annoyed.'

She looked earnest. He bought her dinner and considered her life. Eldest of three, small town upbringing, convent school, good Leaving Cert., landed a safe job with the bank as soon as she left school, engaged to a fellow bank official, broken engagement, and now living alone, lonely, devoting herself to her work.

'Why did you break your engagement? Did he push his luck too far?'

'We were not compatible.' Primly said; flash of hauteur. She was a private person was Catherine, for all her ostensible mildness.

I bet she wouldn't let him into her knickers, Colm thought. I bet that's what happened.

In fact he eventually knew that had happened, because he would be the first to get into her knickers. He knew virginity when he met it now; he had encountered it with Sherry, and one or two typists he had seduced with relative ease. Men think it's their muscles that attract women, he had often mused; but it is always a combination of humanity and chemistry.

241

He remembered Sherry on their wedding night, gasping, breath drawn in sharply with the pain. After that he was careful with virgins; they had a right, he felt, to pleasure; along with a few weekends it was the only thing they were going to get.

But Catherine was important to him, her conquest a validation. He set out to be very gentle with her, took it slowly, orchestrated it carefully over several weeks. He brought her out to dinner, to plays. He encouraged her to confide in him, assured her that his marriage was an empty sham, hinted at leaving it if he could only find the right woman. Catherine, gently prodded, confided the reasons for her erstwhile virginal state. 'I was always so afraid of letting go . . . I have difficulty in trusting men. Must have been something my upbringing instilled into me. You know, the nuns and the endless lectures . . .'

'But men don't come in packages. There are more differences among men than there are between men and women. Look at me, for example! I just enjoy your company and have no designs on you . . .'

He watched to see if it would pique her that he had no designs on her, and was gratified when he saw that it did. He knew then that the scene was set.

When he finally seduced her his triumph was not unmixed with wonder. But Catherine was in love; he might have known she would be. It was axiomatic that women fell in love with their seducers. Get the body, possess the soul. He felt the surge of triumph at the moment of final penetration, felt as though he had won a coup. At night he lay awake beside Sherry thinking of his old love, who was now his mistress.

'I think you're wonderful,' Catherine said on one occasion, stroking his face, her eyes full of tenderness. 'Isn't it great that we found each other again! I was so fond of you when we were children . . .'

'You wouldn't dance with me once . . .' Colm said lightly. He did not expect her to remember this, but she did.

'Oh, yes . . . I was furious with myself afterwards . . . It was

242

because I wanted to so much that I couldn't!' She glanced at him. 'You'd need to be a young girl to understand that. And you had changed so much . . . after you came back from Clonarty. You had become so hostile that I thought you hated me!'

'Did you?'

'I know you were expelled. But Alice was never very sure about what had caused it, just said that you had lost your temper and hit one of the priests, that you were lucky they hadn't got the police!' She threw him a swift glance. 'It seemed so strange, so unlike you. I kept asking myself: why on earth would Colm, the nicest boy in the world, have hit a priest?'

She waited expectantly. 'It's a long story,' Colm said smoothly. 'I don't want to go into it now.'

But things changed in spite of every safeguard. His relationship with Catherine deepened, as though in response to some prescriptive order; they shared their ambitions, their disappointments; he discussed his 'failed marriage'. They had long conversations. He even told her about a recurring dream. In the dream someone would put a pillow over his face. The pillow was wider than the bed. The person wielding the pillow had a face which must not be looked upon, wore a black mask. In the dream he tore off the mask and woke up with a start at what he saw. But he could never remember the unmasked face.

'What do you make of that?'

'The person with the mask could be yourself . . . Did you ever think of that?' she said. He saw how her attention was transfixed by his introspection, how she felt he had made her privy to his inner self.

'Stifling myself, you mean?' This made him smile.

He told her about Robin, well, just enough to make a story. He told her this when she asked if he had had many other relationships with women.

'Was she pretty?' Catherine asked, then laughed. 'Usual female question!'

243

'Very pretty. But so are you!'

He did not tell her about the typists; there was no point in running the risk that she would regard him as some kind of philanderer, be put off. Women saw these things differently.

He never denied himself anything. 'I will not deny life to Colm Nugent' was his private, justifying maxim. He even said this to Catherine.

'So long as you don't confuse life with licence,' she quipped, secure as to her own position in his affections. She could not know how he detested any hint of criticism. Her conviction that she had detected something in him worthy of devotion annoyed him. 'You're clever, Colm. You have acquired ruthlessness, but your inherent sensitivity will overtake you yet. Behind it all you're a very intense person. And intense people cannot escape from themselves!'

'Behind all what?'

'The calculation!'

This rattled him. 'Calculation? Me?'

She laughed, passed it off.

He even acknowledged to himself that, quite apart from the physical passion which both of them shared, he had become fond of her, not with the rarefied spiritual worship of his early youth, but with the comfortable intimacy of having everything his own way. At the time Sherry, sensing perhaps his sensual absorption elsewhere, tended to spurn his advances, complaining of headaches. He even dreamed for a while of a life with Catherine, spoke to her of it, gained her complicity. 'I want to be entirely devoted to us! You and I are here to stay, Kattie . . .'

This implicit betrothal proved the way to Catherine's explosive sexuality; she longed to trust and was ready for an abiding love. He was touched in some way; the old feelings surfaced briefly, like a mythical country buried beneath the sea and thrown up by tectonic activity; but he submerged them again. He found his way around her body with passionate pleasure, delighting in her inexperience, her gasps, 'Oh, don't

244

. . . please don't . . .' in the dammed-up torrent of her sexuality. 'Oh God . . . oh God . . . !' He sensed that her will had been overcome in some way, making her doubly vulnerable to him.

About this time she sent him a poem:

> 'You brought me to a place
> Above an abyss
> Wild with freedom, where time died
> And my life stood still,
> Knowing and not knowing the
> place.
>
> I am afraid.'

Colm had taken her in his arms. 'You silly girl . . . what is there to be afraid of?' He had laughed. 'You're not afraid of me, are you, Kattie?'

He put the poem in his file of private correspondence. If she but knew how he detested poetry, especially self-indulgent drivel!

He saw the slats of street light through the shutters, heard Paola move in the next room, wanted, in a sudden surge of relief that someone should share his vigil, to go to her door, knock, talk to her. He wanted to pay her homage, for her fortitude and her spirit, for the way she wrapped up her vulnerability in her pride. He wanted to wallow in her beauty.

But he knew the signs; whatever demon possessed him was about to start again on Paola. What was it Robin had once said: '. . . don't let decency muck you up, baby. Keep your conscience strictly self-serving!'

He would have to leave this apartment; he would have to distance himself from Paola, leave her alone. Then he thought cynically: only Robin saw through me. But she won't turn up on Sunday week even if she can.

Chapter Twelve

But things seemed different in the morning. Sunlight, cheerful voices, a smile from Pasquale at the breakfast table, chased away the gremlins of the night.

And as the days passed Colm forgot his resolution; he was too busy relishing the new tenor of his life. He went to classes, enjoyed them, not least for the change in pace of his existence. He maintained a friendly demeanour with Paola, but he drew a mental line in the sand and was careful not to overstep it. His esteem for her grew nonetheless. Touched by the dedication of her life, he brought flowers back occasionally, or a bottle of fine wine, to honour her as his hostess. He stopped trying to fit in, and therefore fitted in very well. He was an urbane male presence in a predominantly female household. He sensed that Pasquale was pleased he was there.

Darina decided to accept him, Renate smiled at him. He presented Jill with an illustrated copy of Dante's *Inferno*. She thanked him; she knew it was an apology, but she had too much grace to hint at it.

But where Paola was concerned the sympathy in him blossomed. Every morning she was there at the breakfast table, cheerful, offering encouragement to Darina who, after the rigours of the night before, was sometimes despondent. '*Buon' coraggio, Darina!*'

Every evening, after her day's work, she presided over the dinner table, dished up a first-class meal, cleared up and then went back to her computer. She seldom went out for the evening.

Sometimes he felt her eyes on him, thoughtful, as though he represented some kind of puzzle. But he sensed that she liked him. He was avuncular towards Pasquale, who was now under doctor's orders to rest as much as possible and who occasionally asked Colm to help with his English homework. Going over the boy's essay with him he would catch Paola looking at him with a strange expression. He wondered if he reminded her of her husband, whom she had so precipitately lost, not in personal attributes but as a mentor for their son. The boy was clever, had a swift and retentive mind. There was an immense and unexpected pleasure in teaching him.

'What would you like to do, Pasquale?'

'I want to be . . . *un avvocato* . . .' he hesitated, searching for the word '. . . a lawyer.'

'Well, don't be a stockbroker anyway!'

They laughed. This banter was almost like having a family. He forgot his guard when with Pasquale.

The boy now frequently stayed in bed for the morning. And sometimes Colm would remain behind to keep an eye on him while Paola went to her office. He did not pause to examine the pleasure he got in talking to Pasquale, in listening to his observations, his innocent acceptance of the human condition. Love, anger, passion, error, were, for Pasquale, the natural, universal baggage of the race. He liked poetry and was fond of stories by Oscar Wilde.

'Eet ees very good in English too!' he conceded of *The Little Prince*.

When he asked Colm to read some of Yeats's poetry Colm obliged.

'You did not read it with . . . feeling!' Pasquale said.

'I'm not too keen on poetry,' Colm admitted.

'Why not?'

'I can't help feeling it's for wimps,' Colm replied with a short embarrassed laugh.

'A wimp? What is a wimp?'

Colm looked into the narrowed brown eyes.

'A man who is weak . . . you know . . .' he searched his Italian vocabulary '. . . *un cretino*!'

This brought a spirited rejoinder.

'A cretin? But poetry is for the soul! It is for who a man is! It is like music; it speaks to the . . .' he clapped his hand on his chest '. . . it speaks to the . . . core!' He raised both hands and suddenly laughed. 'Why are you afraid of poetry?'

'I'm not afraid of it!'

The youth smiled. 'Perhaps it has power over you? If you were an Italian you would not be afraid!'

Paola returned one day at lunchtime to find Colm there. He had done some work with Pasquale and had then taken a long walk, enjoying the morning, the timeless mystery of the narrow streets. He walked the length of the Ponte Vecchio, examining the jewellers' windows, admired a magnificent pearl necklace. Then he thought of it around Paola's neck, imagined her in an evening gown. How she would sparkle, how she would outshine every woman in the room!

He bought some prosciutto, salad, the makings of a lunch, a bottle of Antinori, and went back to the apartment. Paola returned not long after him. Pasquale was asleep. Paola looked in on him, closed his door softly. She seemed tired, Colm thought. He offered to make lunch. 'I'm not much of a cook, Paola. But I'll rustle us up a mean little salad . . . You put your feet up!'

Paola registered surprise, then hesitancy. 'Well,' she said, 'I won't look a gift horse in the mouth. Thank you very much!'

She sat down at her computer. Colm came back from the kitchen with two glasses and the bottle of Antinori he had bought that morning.

'Madame would like an apéritif?'

'Thank you.'

'But,' Colm said, 'this is not allowed. No work is allowed at lunchtime!' He took her by the hand, led her to the sofa in the *salone*.

Paola laughed.

'I'm serious!' Colm said. 'You are to relax. No more work until after lunch.'

Paola tossed her head, but she smiled and reclined on the striped silk cushions. 'OK, OK,' she said. 'I haven't seen you domesticated before, Colm, but I'm always happy to submit to idleness . . .'

'No, you're not,' Colm called back en route to the kitchen. 'You don't know the meaning of the word!'

He glanced back, glimpsed the set of her head against the cushions, saw that she had drawn her legs up. He cut the prosciutto into strips, mixed the salad, humming, privately amused at himself. He prepared a tray and brought it through. '*Il pranzo è pronto, Signora . . .*'

'*Mille grazie!*' she exclaimed. '*Sei molto gentile!*'

Outside the sun was merciless, but it was cool inside, dim with the shutters closed, like a glade in a forest. Colm carried a small table to the sofa. Paola raised her hands as Colm shook out a napkin and put it on her lap. Then he returned to the kitchen for the oil and vinegar, the essential feature of every Italian table.

'Bring water,' she called. 'I have to keep my wits about me.'

'What do you want wits for?' he called back. 'Forget them!'

'I wish I could! But, around here, things tend to depend on them.'

This was said with such a suddenly subdued voice that Colm asked when he returned: 'Is everything all right?'

'Everything's fine. My work is going well. But there is no sign yet of a purchaser for some property I have in Sicily. And I need to sell it quickly so that Pasquale can have his operation . . .' She brightened. 'Never mind. I'll probably have a buyer soon! The plot of land is quite a bargain . . . I'd sell this apartment, buy a smaller one, if there was any point . . . but there wouldn't be much left after repaying the mortgage . . . Poor Giovanni! He had such dreams for us . . .'

You'd think he'd have thought of insurance as well, Colm said to himself, but he probably imagined he was immortal.

Paola let Colm fill her glass. He is really such an attractive man, she thought; oddly vulnerable, so much suppressed intensity. But he is spoilt by that recoil reflex, the occasional sudden retraction of his self. She wondered suddenly if this preparation of lunch was the prelude to some intended seduction. If it was it would be a pity, spoil everything.

But he made no romantic overtures, was simply gentle, and simply kind. He sat facing her, perched on a stool, his legs apart, his eyes searching.

'Tell me about your English roots,' he asked, taking a forkful of salad. 'You're an interesting mixture, Paola. You look so Florentine, yet when you speak English you might have come straight from the Home Counties . . .'

'Well, as I told you, I spent a year in England when I was eighteen, staying with my great-aunts. I went back to Cambridgeshire many times. English is my maternal language, after all, and although I don't remember my mother, there has to be something in the genes!'

'Where did your aunts live in Cambridgeshire?'

'A village by the name of Upper Easton. The aunts' house was called Manor Cottage; it overlooked the small village green.'

Paola's eyes focused on something in the past. 'It was so different from Italy,' she said. 'Such a different tempo, everyone so restrained, polite . . .' She laughed. 'Not a passion in sight! Lawn tennis and afternoon tea! But they were interesting people, the aunts. Both had had fiancés who were killed in the first war. Aunt Dora even showed me the death certificate of Toby, her long-lost love. "Killed in action" it said. He died in October 1918, shot down over northern France.'

'A month before the armistice!' Colm exclaimed. 'Poor bugger!'

'Yes. But Aunt Dora was convinced they would meet again. She used to say, "We will meet again, dear, that much is

251

certain!" It made me cry at night when I thought of it . . . to think of the waste . . . and to think of her lonely yearning all her long life . . .'

Colm was silent. Aunt Dora didn't really interest him. He was aware of the peace. It came to him from the immobile woman on the sofa, from the depths he sensed in her, from the booklined walls, from the shuttered room, from the defeated intensity of the noonday light. Muted street sounds came from below as from another plane, tooting of horns, high-pitched screeching of mopeds.

Paola's voice was very soft when she said after a moment's silence: 'And you, Colm? What do you want from the rest of your life?'

'I have led a strangely solitary existence,' Colm replied without looking at her. 'Even in my marriage, even with my friends. I think I would like to end that solitude . . . if I can . . .'

'You can,' she said. 'Life is always there for the courageous! But change involves risk . . . and a kind of mourning for what you leave behind you.'

'I'm used to certain kinds of risks,' he said. 'But not others!'

He rose, came to her on an overpowering impulse and gently kissed her forehead. Paola felt the resonance of the salute; she allowed its pleasure, made no move.

'You are beautiful!' he said, drawing away and staring into her eyes. 'You are timeless. I wish I had met you before . . . when I was young!'

'Maybe you did!'

Colm smiled at what he thought a small pleasantry. 'Your husband must have loved you very much.'

'I certainly loved him.'

She made a small gesture. 'Giovanni was easy to love. He was not afraid to love, was fun in so many ways. He liked himself, which is the secret of much in life!'

Paola looked away from Colm to the slats of light coming through the shutters.

I remembered *you*, Colm Nugent, she said silently, the moment you came in my door. What do I have to do to make you remember me, remember of your own accord! And why are you so restless, so lost in some way? What is tormenting you . . . ?

She turned her head at a small sound and saw Pasquale standing in the doorway, regarding them, his eyes narrowed and his face expressionless.

'Come and have some lunch, darling,' she said. 'Colm has made a delicious salad!'

When Paola had gone back to her office, Pasquale, with studied indifference, asked Colm if he had ever been to Florence before.

'I was here long ago, you know,' Colm said. 'When I was a student. I was here with an American friend.'

'A girlfriend?'

'Yes!'

'So you have seen all the sights?' Pasquale said with a sly, man-to-man look at him.

'Not all. There is too much here to see on a short visit. But my friend and I tried to see what we could.'

'Did you not meet anyone else when you were here . . . any Italians?'

'Yes . . . But only briefly.'

Pasquale nodded. 'No Italian girls?'

Colm laughed. 'You're too curious, young man! I spent most of the time sightseeing.'

In fact there was hardly a part of the city that Robin and he had not visited, the churches, the museums, Dante's house, Forte Belvedere, the Casa Davanzati. They pooled resources, counted their money daily, set out what they could spend, looked glumly at their dwindling store. As Robin was now obviously broke Colm had put the whole of his resources at their joint disposal, retaining only his fare home.

'We're running out of money. Why don't you wire home for some more, Robin?'

One morning she rooted around in her rucksack and produced a gent's gold Rolex watch, handed it to Colm. 'We could sell this.'

Colm looked at her suspiciously. 'Where did you get it?'

'It's my father's,' she said. 'But he has dozens of them, so he won't miss it.'

'What would he want with dozens of them?'

Robin shrugged. 'He's very eccentric.'

Colm looked at her doubtfully. 'You didn't swipe it, did you?'

Robin was all indignation. 'What do you take me for?'

They found a small jeweller's on the Lungarno, hovered around outside, looked in the window. Robin seemed nervous.

'Are you sure this is your dad's?' Colm asked again.

'Of course I'm sure!'

She was wearing the brazen expression she sometimes assumed when he questioned her too closely.

'Look,' she said on a sudden note of irritation, 'you needn't look so shit scared! I'll go in on my own. You wait here!'

She tossed her head, assumed a jaunty hauteur, and entered the shop like a confident American.

Colm moved away from the window, crossed the street and looked over the wall at the Arno, studied the blue hills in the distance. When he turned back she was crossing the street, grinning like an imp.

'Mission accomplished!'

'How much did you get?'

She waved a fistful of notes at him. 'Thirty thousand lire!'

Colm did some rapid calculations; about sixteen pounds.

'I told him the watch was my husband's; that although we were recently married he had deserted me for a beautiful Corsican he met in the hotel and left me destitute!' She laughed. 'The poor man was almost in tears; he said Corsicans

254

were all *banditi*. He was ready to give me the shop!'

Colm laughed until his sides hurt. 'Robin, you should be an actress or a politician!'

He was relieved she seemed so well this morning. It's all stress, he reassured himself. As soon as she has a bit of money she relaxes. But she can't go on like this . . . She'll have to wire home . . .

They celebrated with lunch in the station restaurant – spaghetti Bolognese with lots of sauce and a bottle of wine. Because they were hungry they ate too much and when they came out were torpid with food. It was early afternoon and very hot; they returned to the pensione, paid Antonio for another week, lay down together on Colm's bed and fell asleep.

'Are you asleep?' Robin asked later in a hoarse whisper.

Colm surfaced. 'Wha . . . What?'

The shutters were closed and the room was dim. She was standing by the side of his bed. 'Come back to bed . . .' He took her hand, pulled her towards him.

'No. I've got awful stomach cramp. It's either something I've eaten or my period is about to start! Are you feeling all right?'

'Never better. Come back and I'll show you!'

She pulled away, lay down on her own bed. Colm was disappointed; he wanted to make love; he was embarrassed that she had mentioned her period. Such things were unmentionable where he came from, some kind of pains women got.

'It's crazy trying to live like this . . .' Robin said with a sigh. 'From hand to mouth. I'll have to get a job. I don't want to go back to the States just yet. Do you think anyone would employ me?'

'Course they would! But why don't you want to go back to the States? You'll have to face up to things, Robin. You can't run for ever!'

She sighed again, said, 'The cops are after me!' looked at him and added scornfully, 'I'm joking, I'm joking!'

'Maybe you could get a job teaching English. There must be loads of jobs of that kind.'

'Yeah, but they like bits of paper called diplomas. Unless I get an au pair job or something . . . I'll look around tomorrow. Maybe I could get a job in a restaurant for the time being . . .'

Colm listened to her quiet breathing for a while. She seemed disinclined to talk any more.

'Robin, tell me the story you promised me, the one you mentioned in the Piazza della Signoria last week . . . when you said you would tell me everything . . . about yourself?'

'Ah, my life is really too boring . . . You've no idea how tedious it is being able to have everything you want.'

'Tell me anyway. I told you about me!'

'I'm kinda tired,' she said in a spent voice, as though she were examining the parameters of her life and found little there to please her. 'But I'll tell you a story about someone else . . .' she said in a whisper. 'It's more interesting . . .'

Colm sighed. 'Go on!'

Robin took an audible breath, allowed a few seconds of silence.

'There is a place in New York,' she said, 'called the North Bronx. A girl lived there with her father. Her mother was dead, and her father was a salesman; he drank heavily. But he tried to be a good father and gave her an education, paid for her schooling with the Sisters of Mercy. He liked books and because of him she got to love reading and got good grades. She wanted to get a scholarship, go to Art School. She had a great art teacher . . .'

'It wasn't that fellow Mario Vespucci by any chance?' Colm enquired innocently. 'The guy who was going to turn you into a contessa?'

'Don't be dumb! This girl was taught by a nun! Her name was Sister Anna. Anyway, when her father died of liver cancer she was sixteen . . . he left her without a cent; all his money was gone on doctors. She had to give the apartment back to the landlord; she had to drop out of school because there was no money for the fees. She didn't want to be a burden to anyone . . . She sure as hell didn't want Welfare . . .'

'What happened to her?'

Robin took a deep breath. 'She packed some things, clothes, her mother's crucifix . . . she had some crappy idea it would keep her safe . . . library art books so she could keep up her reading, and set off to find herself a job . . .'

Colm had a mental image of a young girl, small bundle on a stick, closing the door behind her.

'Did she get one?'

'Yeah. She saw an advert in the window of a deli in Fordham Road: "Help wanted". She got the job. The place was owned by a big fat guy who said she could have the room at the back until she got herself fixed up. She thought it'd do her until she could get something better . . .'

'And?'

'She was so goddamn pleased to have fifteen bucks a week, and a place to stay! But it was the worst thing she ever did. She couldn't have done a worse thing if she'd tried!'

'Why?'

'The guy who owned the place had only one thing on his mind . . .'

The silence lasted so long Colm thought she had gone to sleep.

'What did he have on his mind?'

Robin sighed; her breath was erratic. 'What do you think? One thing! "Pretty chick like you!" he used to say to her. "Pretty little chick like you needs someone to take care of her!"'

'Did he take care of her?' Colm asked, his voice now full of double entendre, and his interest stimulated.

'Sure. When she'd been there a few days he said he'd give her fifty bucks if she took her clothes off so he could photograph her . . . He had all these cameras and junk in the storeroom and was taking pictures of girls who used to call around in the evening. He'd pay them something, ten bucks maybe. He told her he'd get her picture into *Playboy*, that he'd make her a star! She told him to get stuffed, decided to get the hell out the next day. But that night he came to her room. She always locked the door, but he got in the window from the fire escape. She was asleep. She dreamt she was being smothered, that some kind of goddamn gorilla was squatting on her. She woke up, but this guy put his fat hand over her mouth, pulled down the sheet. Then he was grabbing her and saying, "Easy, baby . . . take it easy now . . ."'

Robin stopped abruptly.

'What happened?'

'Well, what do you think happened? Bend your great brain to it. What do you think a big fat creep does when he has a young girl half his size in bed? Tell her stories, sing her lullabies, tuck her in? Tell her he knows she is alone in the world and he'll behave like a gentleman? Does he say to himself, now is my chance to show I am a human being and not an orang utan? No. "You're my baby now . . ." he keeps saying; "you're my baby now!" Can you imagine how his breath stinks? Can you imagine . . . how her skin felt as though it was crawling, as though she could never bear to live inside it again!'

'Who was the girl, Robin?' Colm asked in a subdued voice, beset by a terrible and overwhelming doubt.

'Aw, she was just someone I heard about!' Robin said, abruptly changing the charged tone of her voice to one of conversational normality.

'How did you get to know her?' he asked after a moment.

'I didn't know her! How would I know her? She was just a friend of a friend. Her story sure makes me mad . . .'

'Life isn't fair, Robin. Not everyone is privileged.' When she didn't answer he let the silence deepen. He heard her move, glanced over at her bed and whispered in a rush of tenderness, 'Robin, you shouldn't let yourself get upset about these things. If you take all the horrors of the world on board you'll die . . .' Then he added, 'You know I have to go home to

Ireland soon. But you will write to me, won't you? You'll come to visit?'

'Sure . . .'

This sounded so non-committal that he added, 'That doesn't sound very enthusiastic!'

'Goddammit,' she replied. 'You're my friend! I'll come when I can. I'll write. I'm gonna miss you, Colm!'

'What are you going to do when I'm gone? Will you go home? You should go home . . . at least contact your parents. You can't go wandering around on your own for ever! Robin, make up with your family . . .'

'It'll be OK!'

'I worry about you, Robin!'

'No need . . .'

Colm heard her small voice, her eighteen years as frail, breakable, the enigma she represented incomprehensible. She was a mystery, a child and a woman, a porcelain warrior. He could not bear the thought of leaving her to weather everything alone. She was his friend, his love. The words he blurted out came without being planned: 'I'd like to marry you, Robin . . . sometime, if you'll have me . . . when I'm a stockbroker I'll have something to offer you!'

The silence was broken only by the rustle she made as she turned to look at him in the gloom.

'You're a really nice guy, Colm. I like you very much. But I need someone who would take care of me . . .'

'I'll take care of you,' Colm said.

'You can't!'

'Why not, for God's sake?'

'Look, leave it . . .'

But when Colm pressed her further she said, 'You can't because . . . well . . . you don't really know who the hell you are! You need someone strong. And I'm not very strong, Colm. I just pretend to be, because I am very proud. But I'm not strong at all. I'm all broken up inside!'

Colm digested this. 'You're a very tense person, Robin.

259

But what do you expect when you run away from home?'

There was silence and then her voice came, tiny and apologetic, 'Never mind. I was just messing. You're a great guy, Colm! There'll never be anybody in my life like you . . .'

Colm sniffed. Damned with faint praise, he told himself. He felt deflated; it was claustrophobic in the darkened room.

'Would you like to go out for a while?' he said.

'I'm tired. I'd rather stay put . . .'

The light through the shutters spoke of a golden Florentine evening. He thought of the market at San Lorenzo where he might pick up some presents cheaply, a tie for his father, a belt for Liam, a scarf for Alice, small offerings to placate their relentless ire. He thought of a walk along the Lungarno. But she didn't want to go out and he didn't like to leave her when she wasn't feeling well.

'Do you know what happened in the end to that girl?'

'What girl?'

'Oh, for Christ's sake, Robin, the one you were talking about a minute ago!'

Robin sighed. 'Well, the creep tried to sell her!'

Colm gasped. '*Sell* her?' He looked over at her bed. 'That's impossible!'

'Is it?'

'Of course it is! You can't go around selling people!' When she made no response he asked softly, 'How did he do it?'

'He had a stake in a peep show!' Robin said, her voice suddenly brittle. 'He figured he'd broken her . . . and he had this friend, who had a peep show . . .'

'What's that?'

'Oh God . . . Which planet do you come from? There's a place in New York called Times Square. It's full of signs saying "Sex Show, Peep Show, Live Girls!"' Robin's voice had risen with each of these descriptions. Suddenly it fractured and she shouted in bitter passion, '"Live Girls! . . . Live GIRLS" . . . you know, like those boxes of live chicks with their plaintive cheeping, putting their little beaks through the holes, asking,

"Please, sir, can I live?" . . . But no, put them in a battery, destroy them . . . consume them . . . wank while you do it! Be the great fucking users of the entire fucking universe . . . !'

Colm thought the whole building must hear her raised, furious chant, and he wondered for a moment if she had gone mad.

'Keep your voice down, Robin, for God's sake!'

She dropped her voice. 'The women are naked and the men watch through these openings in the wall, and they pay another dollar or something if they want to feel them, and the women have to let the hands of strange men grope them, feel their sweaty fingers, on everything that is private, and they want to die! They want to fucking die! But they have to pretend . . .'

'Robin!'

But she was crying in broken gulps. Colm got out of bed and went to hers, lay beside her, held her.

When she was still he said, 'Look, Robin, there's no point in getting yourself worked up over a slut!'

Robin stiffened. 'I'll say this for you, Irish . . . you're a real pillar of rectitude. Straight and strong and knowing everything! Why don't you try to imagine what it's like . . . to be dependent on people who are your enemies!'

'I know what it's like, Robin.'

She was silent for a moment. Then she said: 'Yeah . . . But you're still into judgement! Now get the fuck out of my bed!'

Colm obeyed. He listened to her continued sobbing, but when he tried to comfort her she said, 'Just go out and leave me alone!'

It couldn't possibly have anything to do with her, he told his resurrected doubts. Robin would never get herself into that kind of mess. She was too streetwise for that!

'I can't go out now. I can't leave you like this. Anyway, Robin, that story could be bullshit for all you know! You could be getting yourself worked up over nothing!'

'Look, I even know the guy's name, the one with the store

in Fordham Road – Lemming – Dave Lemming!'

'Lemmings are rodents,' Colm said. 'They're arctic rodents who self-destruct! How did you come to know his name?'

'My friend told me!'

'What happened to that girl in the end?'

Robin's voice resumed some control, dropped to a lower register. 'She got out! One night she broke the guy's head with one of his cameras, stole some money and stuff and ran away!'

Colm waited. 'And . . . ?' he said eventually.

'And nothing! She disappeared.'

'Maybe she left the country,' Colm said. 'But to do that she'd need to have a passport.'

'Oh, she had that already,' Robin said. 'Some school trip she never got to take . . .'

'How come you know so much about her?'

'My friend told me. She said she was too damn smart for the lot of them!'

'What was the girl's name?'

Robin was silent for a moment. Then she said, 'Some dumb name . . . I forget!'

She turned in the bed. 'The point was – she got out and away and if she's any goddamn use she'll find another life . . .'

When he was silent she said softly and almost sadly, 'You should do the same, Colm. Do you know that?'

Colm heard her; he suspected she was being provocative. 'How do you mean, another life?'

'Ah, nothing. Look, I need to sleep!'

He got up, said he was going out to the San Lorenzo market to buy some souvenirs.

'What happened to your friend?' Pasquale asked. 'Did she go back to America? I have a schoolfriend whose mother is American.'

'I don't know what happened to her,' Colm said. 'I wish I did!'

Robin, the morning after her stormy outburst of the evening before, looked glumly at her sheets. 'Christ, I'm bleeding like a stuck pig!'

Colm propped himself up, looked at the other bed, saw the crimson tide soaking the sheet.

'Robin . . . what is it? What is it?'

'What do you think? Paint spray?'

'Oh God . . . you need a doctor!'

'No, I don't! You guys know nothing!'

Colm sat rigidly. 'Oh God, this is terrible. What can I do?'

'Nothing! Women bleed; didn't you know that? Jesus, where have you been hiding?'

'Is this normal?'

She was doubled over in sudden spasm. 'You do need a doctor,' Colm said, pulling on his trousers, and making for the door.

'Wait! It's all right. But we'll have to wash out the sheet.' She moved crablike in her bloodied nightdress to her rucksack, searched in it. 'Turn your back, for Chrissake!'

He did. When he turned around again she was wearing clean underwear and was evidently fixed up, but she moved slowly to the one chair in the room and sat down, holding her stomach.

He took the sheets from her bed, ran cold water into the wash basin and steeped the cotton. The water ran red. He changed the water several times, scrubbed the blood stains with soap and a nail brush until the sheet was clean. Then he wrung it out, folded it and placed it on the backs of the two plastic chairs on the balcony.

'My sister never has periods like this,' he said.

'What the hell would you know about it?'

'Not much,' he admitted. 'I thought periods were pains . . . headaches, I mean!'

She laughed – a sudden peal of mirth which filled the room; then she drew her breath in sharply, groaned. He picked the bloodied nightdress from the floor, wiped the red stain from the mosaic, brought the nightie to the basin and washed it out.

'You do have husband potential!' Robin laughed huskily, then doubled up again. 'Oh Christ, I'm too much of a smartass for my own good.'

'Are you sure you don't need a doctor?'

'We haven't got money to throw around on doctors.' She glanced at him, lowered her voice. 'I'm fine, for God's sake: just women's trouble . . . Throw me the towel over there.'

He obeyed and she placed it folded on her bed, lay down with a groan.

He stood looking down at her.

'Go away and play with yourself or something. You're giving me the creeps!'

He went on to the balcony. He was assailed by the scents of fresh bread and coffee from the café at the corner, watched the world below for a while, fingered the wet sheet and reckoned it would be dry in no time. He thought of breakfast; he was hungry, had had nothing but fruit to eat since lunch the day before; he could go down to the café at the corner and get some rolls.

'Would you like some breakfast? I'll go down and get something . . .'

'Yeah. Good idea . . .' She spoke slowly, as though it were an effort. 'Take your time!'

Colm went downstairs and out into the Florentine morning. He decided that, to give Robin time to rest, he would take a walk, and so he directed his steps to the nearby Piazza di Santa Maria Novella, examined after a desultory fashion the church of the same name, its naves and pilasters, its chapels, its frescos of the Last Judgement and Heaven and Hell.

But his mind was milling, with Robin, with her present condition, with alarm despite all her assurances. How could it be normal? If it was, women were seriously hamstrung by these cycles of creation. Then he remembered something she had said when they first made love: '. . . I don't menstruate.' He hadn't understood exactly at the time, but he knew now that she had been lying.

Oh, Robin, he wondered in exasperation, do you ever tell the truth?

But, leaving the church, he forgot these considerations in the enjoyment of the morning. Well, she should know, he told himself. She should know what's normal.

Usually he loved this time of the day, before the searing heat could do its worst. But today he noticed that the air hung heavy and still, and that the sky had a deepening haze. He decided to make the most of it; except for the day in Fiesole he had not had much time to himself since Robin's advent, so he directed his steps towards the river and took a leisurely walk along the miles of the Lungarno.

On the way back he bought some rolls with prosciutto in the café at the corner and two large milky coffees in polystyrene cups. When he came out the thunder was growling overhead and he entered the pensione as the first drops of the downpour spattered the streets.

The rain was coming through the shutters and spitting off the floor. He put the food down on the small table in the corner, ran to shut the window. Then he turned to the bed.

'Brunch is served, Madame!'

Robin was lying very still and did not respond. Her eyes were closed. He thought she was asleep, but on closer inspection he saw that her face was deathly pale and her lips were blue. On the bed beneath her the folded towel was stained crimson. Beneath the noise of the rain he thought he heard another small noise, like a faulty tap. He wondered at it for a moment, located its source when he looked under the bed. Blood, which had soaked through towel and mattress, was dripping on to the floor.

'Robin!'

She moaned, but she did not open her eyes. Colm raced from the room, found Antonio who knew no English.

'My girlfriend . . . *la mia fidanzata è malata* . . . get a doctor . . . *medico* . . . *molto presto* . . . emergency!'

Antonio came to the door of the room, looked in, rushed to the phone on his desk. Then he went off calling his wife. She emerged from the deepest recesses of the pensione, a small woman with a managing aura, normally only sighted with a mop. Now she pulled herself up short when she saw the girl in the bed and the thick crimson seeping to the floor.

'*O Dio!*' she exclaimed. '*O Dio . . .*'

She stared at Colm, her mouth open, whooshed her husband out of the room.

The ambulance came a little later. The doctor who accompanied it was small and avuncular, regarded the recumbent Robin with patent alarm, spoke English – 'She must go to hospital immediately!' He issued abrupt commands to the two ambulance orderlies who had brought a stretcher up the stairs.

'What's wrong with her?' Colm demanded.

The doctor narrowed his eyes, gesticulated again at the obvious. 'Your wife is having a miscarriage!' he said sorrowfully. He shook his head and placed a commiserating hand on Colm's shoulder.

'She's not my wife; she's my girlfriend!'

The doctor sighed. 'Where does she come from?'

'America!'

The orderlies gently lifted Robin from the bed and put her on the stretcher, covered her with a sheet, lifted the stretcher and carried it downstairs. Colm followed, got into the ambulance behind the doctor. The doors were closed, Robin lay inert; a saline drip was fixed into her vein. The vehicle took off into the wet traffic mainstream, sirens screaming.

'Has she any family in Italy?' the doctor demanded in a

266

whisper as he pumped the blood pressure gauge and released it, studying the mercury with a professional frown which made Colm's blood run cold.

'No . . .' he said, adding with a start of recollection '. . . unless, of course, the Di Gabiere family are related to her . . .'

The doctor stared at him as though he were either mad or low enough to joke at such a time. 'The Di Gabiere family?' he intoned severely, with a small, scornful laugh.

'Yes. She had some notion that she had relations in Fiesole . . . She thought Di Gabiere was their name. I even enquired, but the man I spoke to didn't seem to think so . . . Have you heard of them?'

The doctor looked from Colm to his patient as though vetting them both for the madhouse.

'There is no one in Florence who does not know of the Di Gabieres,' he said. 'They are one of the foremost families here! They are immensely rich, have an apartment in the city, a villa in Fiesole; other houses elsewhere . . . Rome, Paris . . . London . . .'

He seemed to ponder the absurdity of the claim and added, 'I never heard that they had any American relatives. They are an old Italian family . . . bankers . . . modern Medici . . .'

Colm felt as though he was expected to apologise. Christ, he thought, you'd think he had shares in the bloody Di Gabieres!

The doctor added in a low voice, 'Signore Di Gabiere would not take kindly to imposture. He is very eccentric . . . When his wife died – she was killed last year in a skiing accident – he was so possessive of her body that he delayed burial . . . he told the priest, the undertakers, to go away! There was concern for a while that the business would become unpleasant . . .' He raised his hands in silent comment on the vagaries of Di Gabiere, modern Medici, wealthy widower, spoilt, heartbroken man.

To hell with him, Colm thought, recalling the man he had spoken to through the bars of his gate in Fiesole. He can afford eccentricity; but he can't hold a candle to the courageous girl in front of us who is bleeding to death! His throat tightened. He watched Robin's white face as the ambulance screamed through the city and asked the doctor in a hoarse whisper as her pallor deepened: 'Will she make it? Will she live?'

The doctor gestured, raised his hands: '. . . But she will certainly lose your child!'

Colm's heart swelled. Tears started in his eyes. My child! He looked at the fragile form before him, bent and whispered in her ear: 'You are a wonderful girl, the bravest, the very best, and now and for ever . . . I love you!'

But Robin did not seem to hear him.

What happened to you, Robin? Why did you never answer my letters? Did you die?

Colm was awake when Paola rose. He heard her alarm clock go off, and the small sounds in her room and then the clatter in the bathroom. He had not slept well, dammed with the overflow of memory. He could hardly bear the thought of breakfast, of trying to make urbane conversation, of Pasquale's pale face, his incipient crisis – successful surgery or mortal decline, of Paola's anxiety and fatigue, Jill's determined cheerfulness in the face of her bereavement, Renate's tenacious drive towards whatever she and the world regarded as success.

He was definitely losing the control he had cultivated over nearly thirty years; he'd known nothing like it since Robin was whisked away to hospital in the downpour. With Kattie he had been in control; he had broken the relationship when it suited him, hurt her, devastated her. Why?

I'm a dangerous lunatic, a control freak, he told himself. I should never have come on this absurd journey. How this coronary, this brush with death, has softened me, acted like a spiritual expectorant, has me coughing up the foolish sentiment of the years! Well, he conceded, it was easy to remedy

268

the situation. Paola would be better off without him, Pasquale too.

He looked at his watch. Quarter to eight. He sat up abruptly in bed and reached for his Michelin, took out his mobile phone and booked himself a room in the Hotel dei Angeli, got his suitcase from the wardrobe and began to pack his things. He put the thrillers he had bought at the bottom of the case, packed his Ralph Lauren shirts, the light Armani suit he should not have brought, and the rest of his things. Then he went to the dining room. The balcony beyond the French windows was in shadow, but the sun was already probing the east-facing stones of the courtyard.

Paola was putting out the breakfast things. Her long hair was in a plait over her shoulder. Watching her, he wanted to undo her hair, to let the waves of it ripple down her back. Why was he moved by this woman? He did not want to be moved by her, to be moved by anything ever again. I'm getting sucked in, he thought; I'm getting involved with this family. Perhaps Paola thinks I nurture romantic intentions. What they don't know is that I'm a Jonah of the spirit. What they do not know is that every human relationship I touch turns to ashes!

'*Buon giorno*, Colm!' Paola said, bending her dark eyes on him. He felt the punch of her presence, the movement of her body in the kimono. She seemed pleased to see him; she smiled.

He sat at the table, accepted *caffè latte* in a big cup, helped himself to a roll.

'Paola,' he said, 'I will be leaving today.'

She turned, stared. Her eyes had narrowed and two parallel lines scored her forehead. She had the alertness of a thoroughbred. '*Perché*? Has something happened at home?'

'No . . . there's nothing at home. It's just that I think it's the best thing. But I will be staying on in Florence and will finish the course . . .'

'You are uncomfortable here!' She said this with definitive

certainty, as though vetting recent events. 'I understand – you are bored. We are a small little unit, too domestic.'

'No . . . But I'm out of place,' Colm said, reaching for the first excuse that came to mind. 'Your other guests are all much younger and I feel absurd!'

'You shouldn't.' She gestured with her hands. 'I often have students older than you. People come from all over the world to attend courses in Florence.' When he didn't respond she added, 'Which hotel will you be at?'

'The Hotel dei Angeli.'

She raised her eyebrows, her face pale. 'Four stars!' she said with a reproachful smile. 'You should be very comfortable there. I'm afraid I can't compete with that!'

'Paola,' he said, 'I don't expect you to compete. Thank you for looking after me so well.'

She put down her cup, looked at him with suddenly narrowed eyes. 'Will you be all right?'

'Why shouldn't I be all right?'

She shrugged, ran a hand along the thick plait of her hair. 'I don't know. Sometimes you look so fatigued . . .'

Darina came in and said, '*Buon giorno.*'

'*Colm va via oggi!*' Paola said in a dead-pan voice.

'Why are you leaving?' Darina demanded.

'I must go,' Colm said, meeting her speculative eyes. 'I have business to attend to.'

Colm went back to his room to get his suitcase. When he came out he met Renate in the corridor. She beckoned to him.

'If you are leaving you should look for a refund!' she said earnestly in English, dropping, for the moment, the obedient propriety of speaking in the vernacular.

'There's no question of that! I don't want a refund.'

'But you won't be here . . . You will have paid for something – your food, lodging – you will not have received.' Her voice rose a fraction; she sounded personally upset at the prospect of money squandered, value not received.

Colm put a hand on her arm, looked in her prematurely stern face, saw the two lines already etched between her brows. Why did this girl, pretty, brilliant, already perfectly trilingual, take everything in life so seriously? It was as though something rode on her narrow shoulders, some imperative to push herself to her limits, to master existence. From where did she receive this work ethic which was impeding her spontaneity, weighing down her life?

'It's all right,' he said, adding: 'Ease up a bit on life, Renate. Don't wait for it to ease up on you!'

He went back to the dining room, shook hands with Darina and Jill, taking Paola's hand last, feeling suddenly treacherous as their fingers touched, and his closed over her hand. He distrusted the electricity. Nothing in life was simple, particularly relationships between men and women.

'Thank you, Paola, for everything!'

'Goodbye,' she said. Her voice was polite and very cold.

He went to Pasquale's room to say goodbye. The boy was in bed, propped up, surrounded by books. He seemed deflated at the news.

'I am sorry you are going . . . My mother tries to make our apartment comfortable for her guests,' he said in a voice of contained reproach. Colm saw the dark eyes, the pallor, the sudden haughty cast to the face. He wanted to hug this boy, wish him well. He wished, in a rush of compassion, that there was something he could do for him. He could not bear that Paola should face what he had faced, the loss of her son.

'It's very comfortable here,' Colm assured him, 'but I have other reasons for moving . . .'

'*Certo!*' Pasquale said, raising one sardonic eyebrow. 'You need to go away from us. You need to be alone!'

'I do,' Colm said simply. 'And not for any reasons which your sixteen years could conjecture . . .'

Pasquale turned his face away.

Colm walked to the front door, glanced once at the dining room where Paola was still sitting at table. She raised her eyes, regarded him expressionlessly. He gestured silently that he was leaving the keys on the hall table. Then he left the apartment, closing the door behind him.

When Colm was gone Paola went to her son's room, sat on the edge of his bed.

'How do you feel?'

He raised a hand dismissively. 'He is gone?'

'Yes.'

'Had you met him, Mamma?' he asked quietly in English. 'Before he came here?'

Paola seemed to weigh her reply. 'Yes,' she replied candidly after a moment's pause, frowning at her son. 'Why do you ask?'

'Sometimes I thought you had . . . the way you looked at him as though you knew him . . . The feeling I had when I saw you together . . .'

'I met him many years ago, while he was visiting Italy and I was still at school . . . a Saturday. He came home for lunch. Maria even took a photograph . . . but he clearly does not remember!'

'Are you sure it is he?' the boy demanded with a small derisive laugh. 'It is too much of a coincidence . . .'

She shrugged. 'But life is full of coincidences, my son, because everything that happens is eternal and is thrown up again, sooner or later . . . like the small stones in the sea. You cannot go through life without coincidence!'

'Where is the photograph?'

'I don't know. I tried to find it . . .'

'Is it the black and white one I used to ask you about when I was small and you always said, "*Un bello straniero . . .*"'

'Yes!'

'*Una storia molto romantica!*' her son said, looking at her quizzically. 'And he is even handsome, rich!'

Paola said, 'You see how romantic he is! He is gone.'

When his mother left Pasquale wondered where he had put the old tattered album with the black and white snaps.

Chapter Thirteen

Colm brought his suitcase to the Hotel dei Angeli. When he had signed the register he decided Scuola Linguistica could do without him for another day and he strolled to the bus terminal in the Piazza della Stazione and took the bus to Fiesole, sat by the window and watched the twisting roadway, the land falling away into the breathtaking views of the valley. He took the snap of Robin on the Ponte Vecchio out of his wallet and examined it, the young girl, the laughter, then put it away.

In Fiesole he sought the restaurant Il Zucchino. It was there, but under another name. 'Bella Vista' had been painted dull pink; but otherwise it was more or less unchanged. He walked to the edge of the balustraded terrace to look down on Florence and as he did so he had a glimpse into the restaurant's small, private courtyard, a space overflowing with geraniums in terracotta pots, with a round white table in its middle. He had a sudden *déjà-vu*-like recollection: sunlight and shade, the smell of *vitello alla limone*, a girl and a book, laughter. It was the girl he had met in the amphitheatre . . . They had lunched together here! They had pored over her English textbook here.

Where was she now? Married with six children, a fat matron? He could not recall her face. The only thing he remembered with clarity about her was her long brown hair and her grace.

He sat in the shade and drank coffee, watching the relentless light on the valley, wondering about the girl. He tried unsuccessfully to remember her name. But the fact that the restaurant was here still gave him a sense of continuity – that he should have known the girl of the long brown hair, albeit briefly, that he should have touched her life.

He finished his coffee, wandered into the piazza, turned in the direction of the Via Ghiberti, intending to walk past the massive patrician villa where he had once confronted the irate proprietor through the gate.

He approached the cream villa slowly, his mind conjuring up the dark man and the two mastiffs which had heralded his presence with so much enthusiasm. Looking through the gate he saw that the house seemed untouched by the intervening twenty-eight years; the black louvred shutters were closed; the spacious enclosed garden seemed prolific as ever. The front door was open and a maid in a black dress with a white apron was wiping the panelling down. He had a quick glimpse of a mosaic hall, an onyx and gilt table beside a mirror, a parlour palm, and two white marble statues bearing the unmistakable stamp of antiquity.

He walked slowly on, heard some youthful voices and the whack of tennis balls from the other side of the wall.

'*Stai zitta*,' a girl's voice said on a note of laughter, in response to some teasing remark from a male companion. It was the kind of thing Robin would say, laughing; 'Ah, shut up, for Chrissake and just do what you're told!'

Why had she never replied to his letters?

He wrote to her, first to Florence, and then to the address she had given him in New York.

'Robin, why don't you come to Ireland? It'll be ages before I can afford to go to the States; I have another three years to put down before I am qualified. I miss you.'

He gave the Ballykelly address; at the time he was moving between lodgings in Dublin. But he never received a reply.

He'd had to accept that Robin had disappeared from his life. He wondered if she had gone home to America. Or maybe she was wandering the world with her tatty rucksack, stealing a loaf of bread here, a tomato there. He imagined her in Paris and London, Moscow and Madrid, living from hand to mouth, a wanderer. Or had there been truth in her story? Had she gone home to inherit a fortune?

Time passed. He met other girls; they were pretty; they scanned the marriage market, regarded him as eligible. But, after Robin, they were one-dimensional. The quality of contact, the life and death nature of their short time together, made other relationships seem trite.

When he had completed his apprenticeship, he heard that Kattie was engaged. It caught him unawares, a casual comment by Alice on one of his few visits home: 'Kattie's engaged!' Such simple words. Too late, too late, they whispered. He realised that he had classed Catherine as an immutable feature of his life, fixed, known, available when and if he deigned to lift the phone. When he later heard that this engagement was broken off, he experienced an unbidden pleasure; but by then he was himself engaged to Sherry and the date had been set.

He withdrew behind a carapace of tough and ruthless competence. He began to make serious money, became a partner in his firm.

Sherry, whom he met at a party, was pretty and bright. She knew how to cook, how to decorate, how to convince him that they would make a team. She was looking for a husband. She looked good on his arm; he was envied by his peers. But before he proposed to her he wanted to be certain that Robin was lost to him. He contacted a firm of private investigators, and they in turn set about making enquiries in the United States.

They confirmed that Robin's father had certainly not been a captain of industry. Not one single shipping magnate in the United States answered to the name Jack McKay, or apparently ever had. Eventually the private eye had turned up a birth certificate of a Roberta McKay, father John Anthony, mother Maria, maiden name Carella, with an address in the North Bronx. The date was Robin's birthday, 15 September 1950.

Further searches disclosed that John Anthony McKay had

worked as a salesman, had died in July 1966, and that his daughter had dropped out of her school – the Sisters of Mercy – and disappeared.

Nice one, Robin! he thought. So this was the daughter of the wealthy American with the mansion in New England, the Park Avenue apartment, the yacht in Long Island Sound, the private jet painted shocking pink to match his wife's nails! She was something infinitely more interesting. She was a survivor, an alley cat, an inventive masquerader! He laughed. He had suspected as much anyway; in retrospect it was obvious. But her memory was still vivid; her fair head turned to him when he made some cutting comment before a work of art: 'Aw, don't be such a shit, for Chrissake. When you know nothing about nothing you should just keep your big mouth shut!'

He never forgot the story she had told him that late afternoon in Florence, while the sunlight patterned the floor through the shutters; the story of the young girl who had thought she had got herself a job and had walked into hell. He tried to recall the name of the man – something reminiscent of rodents. It hit him one day on the Stock Exchange Floor while he watched the fervour of buying for some hyped, high-risk shares. The bidders were all bloody lemmings, he had thought smugly. In two months they'll be trying to unload them. And then, suddenly, the name Lemming surfaced, the scent of Florence, the voice of a fiery waif called Robin! He remembered her passionate outburst, and the morning's tide of blood on the mattress.

He put an advertisement in the *New York Times*:

Will Robin (Roberta) McKay, born 15 September 1950, formerly of Channing Road in the North Bronx, please contact Colm at Box No. 4421.

He waited. The days passed. Eventually an airmail letter came bearing an American stamp. The printed note inside was short. It said: 'The woman you are looking for is dead.' The postmark said New York; the date was 11 August 1973.

Before he closed the book on her, Colm needed one thing. He needed to walk through the North Bronx. He also needed to know if there was or had been a storekeeper by the name of Lemming in Fordham Road.

'I can't go back to New York . . .' Robin had said almost casually. 'The cops are looking for me!'

The private eye eventually informed him that no such trader now existed in Fordham Road, but that a David Theodore Lemming, white Caucasian, had run a store there during the sixties.

'Where is he now?'

'Feeding the worms. He was found in the East River, generously ventilated with what the Yanks call "lead injections"! Seems the guy was a small-time pornographer, drug trafficker . . . Must have got up somebody's nose and not for the first time. The autopsy reported a five-inch scar from an old scalp wound!'

'Would it be possible to find out if he ever abused a girl called Robin McKay?'

'Not unless she made a complaint.'

Colm went to New York. He stood outside a brownstone house in Channing Road in the North Bronx. He visited the Sisters of Mercy Catholic School for girls. He walked down Fordham Road, lingered at the premises formerly owned by David Theodore Lemming. He navigated Times Square. He wanted to weep.

A memory surfaced. He and Robin in the station restaurant eating the cheapest pasta in Florence.

'I'll get fat on this stuff!' she had said.

'The way you are at the moment,' he said mildly, 'it'll take you about ninety years!'

'I don't have ninety years! There is only today and tomorrow.'

What happened to you, Robin? Did you really die?

Colm went to the Roman amphitheatre and sat for a while on the top step. There was no girl there today with a book and a cat.

There was no Robin anywhere.

There was no chance now of going back to Kattie, telling her about Florence. There was no point now in sending her a card.

The parameters of life are like patterns of light, Colm thought: here in an instant; gone in a trice. It was what you loved that really mattered in the end.

He left Fiesole and returned to his hotel in Florence in the hot afternoon. His room looked out over a courtyard. It was luxurious and anonymous. There was a romanesque-style bathroom, a television, a mahogany wardrobe in an alcove, an antique '*matrimoniale*', with carved cherubs on the bed head. On a table was the hotel brochure, a slip for ordering breakfast, and a copy of the Gideon Bible. The shutters were closed and the air-conditioned room was cool. He removed his shoes and socks, padded to the bathroom for a shower. Afterwards he lay down. He felt very tired, and was soon asleep.

It was early evening when he awoke; the sun was no longer beating at the shutters. He listened for a while to the distant hotel sounds, to the muted traffic noise, the sound of the mopeds, busy wasps in the rush hour. He was glad that the room did not overlook the street; he could sleep here. And he needed sleep. It was something he had not done for years, it seemed to him, slept like a child. His mind would normally not permit that kind of surrender; business matters tended to occupy him half the night. He normally used the hours of darkness to vet the next day's agendas, catching up on lost sleep with cat-naps when he had a spare moment. It was how he kept exhaustion at bay, kept ahead of whatever posse he felt was on his tail.

Why had Kattie loved him so passionately, seen him quite

differently from the way he saw himself? At first he had found this exciting and then intrusive. He felt the old sense of guilt about her, and an old useless longing that he had done things differently.

Well, that was life! There was no point in fruitless regrets. He put her from his mind, blocked the impertinent sense of loneliness suddenly gnawing at him, thought of taking a stroll, of finding a small restaurant, a light meal in his own company. But, all the same, he found himself wondering how they were this evening in the Via de' Tornabuoni; he wondered how Paola was, and how Pasquale would finish that English essay he had begun two days before. He acknowledged that he missed the boy and that he missed his mother even more.

He put away these thoughts. Had he not the prospect of having Florence to himself for the evening?

Florence by night! Floodlights on the Palazzo Vecchio, narrow streets of medieval secrets! He found his way to a trattoria, ordered *Cotoletta alla Milanese* with a green salad and a half-bottle of red Antinori, sat back and watched the passersby.

When he had finished his meal he walked down to the river, around by the south aspect of the Uffizi Gallery. This led him to the Ponte Vecchio.

There it was, the old bridge so beloved of Robin, solid on its arches. Lights were on in its shops, the jewellers who monopolised by tradition one of the oldest shopping precincts in Europe. Only goldsmiths had been permitted to trade there, he remembered, in the august days of Lorenzo the Magnificent, and the tradition continued. Tomorrow, he thought, I will visit the Uffizi and see the *Birth of Venus* again. Robin had some bee in her bonnet about that painting that I could never understand.

He walked back around the Uffizi until he was looking into the square of the Signoria and at the Rivoire restaurant where Robin had once told him she would meet him again. He glanced down the Piazzale degli Uffizi, the passageway through the colonnades and arches flanking the gallery, with its rows of statues. He saw the girl in the jeans and shirt walking away from him towards the Lungarno Medici, where he had just been walking himself a moment before.

It was the elusive 'ghost'! But this time, he turned and followed her, hurrying, his feet raising an echo in the colonnade. But the girl did not look back; she proceeded at a smart pace, passed underneath the arches, turned right and was lost to view. He ran after her, called 'Robin!' but when he reached the Lungarno there was a group of young people in his way and he could not see her.

Winded, he leaned against the wall of the gallery. I'm losing it; I'm crazy. Oh Christ, I'd better get out of this city. I'd better go home!

Robin, he thought, when he recovered his breath, if by some stretch of the imagination you have come back for me, you will find me on Sunday in the Piazza della Signoria as arranged. And what then? Are you a spectre come to claim me? Is my number up?

He went back to his hotel. But the thought of Robin would not recede. The girl was her veritable image. Who the hell was she? Robin's fetch come to fetch him? This made him smile, but the mystery played on his mind, and, as the night advanced, danced in his brain in small reluctant frissons of nostalgia and dread.

He turned on the television. There was a Western on, dubbed and incongruous; he turned it off. For some reason he was suddenly subsumed by desire, but the desire he felt was more of the spirit than the body. He wanted to talk to Robin, put her head against his shoulder. He wanted her to tell him it was all right, that he had not failed her; he wanted her to give him absolution; he wanted, horribly, incongruously, to be loved!

Robin's dead! he thought then.

He thought of reading, but his books were still packed at

the bottom of his case and it was too much like work to look for them right now. He picked up the Bible on the bedside table. It fell open at the Song of Solomon.

'You have ravished my heart, my sister, my bride,
You have ravished my heart with a glance of your eyes . . .'

Oh God, he thought. There has to be something else in this tome . . . distractions like war and pestilence and death. But leafing through it he came upon:

'There is a time for every season under heaven
A time to be born and a time to die
A time to win and a time to lose . . .'

He knew all this. But what was the time for him now? Not to win or lose, surely; he had already done enough of that! It occurred to him that all his adult life he had taken, venting an anger he could not rationalise. Perhaps the biblical verse could be improved on! It made no mention whatever of the most important time of them all . . . a time to give!

His mind reverted to Paola. He remembered her that morning, her face suddenly cold. He thought of her bringing up her son on her own, slaving for the money for his operation. He thought of the boy, Pasquale, who might never live to be a lawyer. He thought, with a surge of self-loathing, that he had never thought to offer her what she needed for Pasquale's operation. She was selling some potentially valuable land for a song, waiting for a purchaser. His idiotic fixation with another time, with something that was dead and gone, had prevented him from seeing what was under his nose.

Yes, he said to himself, now is the time for general clearance. The past may have been the era for many things, but the past is over. I do not want to think of it again! Pasquale shall have his operation as soon as money can pay for it. I will go to see Paola tomorrow.

He undressed, turned off the light, went to sleep easily. When he awoke it was late, how late he did not know. He was unable to move a muscle; he heard the sounds from the street as though they were far away, found himself caught in a darkness which did not belong to any dimension he had ever known. He felt the presence of something alien.

'Who are you?' he whispered silently, letting the terror wash through him.

There was no answer from the impenetrable gloom. Am I really awake? he wondered. He tried again to move. Anguish flooded and overpowered him – grief for his loss, the theft of his innocence, the man in black with his erect penis, the useless longing for love and mercy, the denial of recognition, his own curiosity-impelled complicity. He suddenly knew what the presence was in the darkness. It was his life.

But I had a choice, he told himself. I could have let it go! It need not have destroyed me!

He found his strength, launched himself into the shadows, crawled across the marble floor. In the bathroom there was a razor. A hot bath and a razor. He needed nothing more.

The silence of the night was rent by the scream of a fire alarm in the corridor. It was loud enough to wake the dead. Feet came hurrying; voices were heard. There was a knock on his door. Reality intruded. Colm dropped the razor, grabbed a towel, opened the door, noted with curious detachment that his hands trembled. The hotel official said apologetically: 'We are very sorry, sir, the alarm has been set off by accident!'

Are there any accidents in creation? Colm wondered. Or are we impelled by circumstances to some predestined end?

Chapter Fourteen

Paola got up early after a sleepless night. She threw on her silk wrap, opened the shutters to a Florence which was already a hive of activity. She heard the eternal resonance of the traffic, the horns, the high-pitched sound of the Vespas. Usually these noises never bothered her; she was used to them, filtered them out of consciousness, and was always surprised when visitors said: 'How on earth do you stand that racket?'

But she heard the noise today. It made her feel hemmed in. The world was crowded and in ferment. There was no space left in it for individual striving, little space for hope. She looked for a moment at the shuttered windows across the street, the roof tiles, baked red and old grey, the small chimneys only used in winter, the muted walls flooded with light.

She sat at her dressing table and regarded herself in the mirror, ran a finger along the line of her cheek, let it glide under her eyes and over her lips. Her skin was still very smooth, although in recent times a few lines had come to live around her eyes. Today those eyes looked hollow and had dark circles. She was filled with fatigue, not just of the body after a night without sleep, but of the spirit. Her usual optimism had deserted her, and the void yawned at her feet. Would Pasquale get well? All night she had lain in a fever of anxiety. She felt Colm's departure like a bad omen. He was, of course, perfectly entitled to make whatever arrangements for his comfort he thought proper, but she couldn't help feeling that she had been, in some way, found wanting.

She picked up Giovanni's photograph, gazed into his laughing face. She had taken it in Capri on the second day of their honeymoon. Behind him was the blue shimmer of the Mediterranean, the sails of a few yachts, the distant summit of Vesuvius. At night she had felt the rasp of his beard, his hands, his lips. 'I love you, Paola Anna Maria, princess of my heart . . .'

Breathtaking lovemaking in that huge bed, the bridal suite of the little hotel, with the sea sighing through the open window and the picture of the Pope hanging discreetly in the corner. Lying in her new husband's arms while he slept, afraid that she would cut off his circulation. 'What is love?' she had asked him in the morning, languorously watching him place her long hair across his chest. 'Can you define it?'

'It can only be defined by the objective,' he said, indicating the picture of the Pope on the wall. 'Those not loved or loving! Only they presume to see it. And they are always wrong!'

Later he had said with some annoyance, leaping out of bed and removing the pious countenance from the wall, 'I'm taking that thing down, Paola. I don't want anyone's blessing on how I choose to love my wife, or anyone staring at how she chooses to love me!'

Laughter. The Pope ended up in the corner.

Giovanni's body had been warm, hairy, the coarse black hair slick with sweat after hours of lovemaking. But now their bed was empty, silent.

She regarded her face in the mirror, fingered the tiny lines around her eyes. If she had been younger perhaps Colm would have remembered her. There was no point in kidding herself that time had worked no depredations, that she was in any way immune. But the coincidence of his arrival at this juncture of her life, apparently free, had caused her to wonder if Fate still had a few tricks up its sleeve. She was aware of his attractiveness; she was intrigued by the vulnerability, the torment, she sensed in him sometimes, for all his studied urbanity. She liked men who were macho enough to know that they were men and sensitive enough to know that they were mortal.

Perhaps she had been too informal with him. It was hard not to be so, when she knew who he was, when she remembered him as the boy in the amphitheatre all those years ago. Perhaps she should not have allowed him to help Pasquale; she should have kept him firmly at arm's length. After all, he was really a stranger.

But there was an empathy there, she told the reflection of her morning face. Or was it just that I had known and liked him when we were young? She thought of his tentative kiss just two days before, wondered in a sudden angry surge of confusion why he had kissed her, paid subliminal court to her, prepared lunch for her, helped with Pasquale. Why had he done all that and disappeared? Some men were just into playing games!

But there had been something lost about him at the same time. He was like someone who had committed or witnessed a crime and was trying to find some way to edit the story. She sighed, wondering what had really happened in Florence when he was young.

She thought of Silvestro, who was due to call at lunchtime today, ostensibly to collect an article on corporate corruption. She thought of his assiduous courtship. At least she knew where she was with him; he made no secret that he wanted her, body and soul.

She slipped her negligée from her shoulders and studied her still lovely body. Is all that, she wondered, to go to waste? Or should I say yes to Silvestro and let things take their course? The future, after all, is more than just conjecture! His feelings may be strong enough to weather upheaval, strong enough for things to work out. Then she wondered: but are *my* feelings strong enough? There is a shared bond, chemistry. But is that enough? In some fundamental way I do not really trust Silvestro! Her thoughts reverted to pragmatic matters, Giovanni's investment, the stony land in Sicily, overlooking

Taormina Bay and Mount Etna. To sell it now would be to lose the potential bonus of a lifetime. But there could be no vacillation when Pasquale's condition was worsening. Suddenly overwhelmed, she prayed for him, her son, dropping to her knees and putting her face in her hands.

En route to class that morning Colm passed by his erstwhile lodgings in the Via de' Tornabuoni, registered that he intended to call on Paola that lunchtime and hoped that she would not misinterpret what he would offer.

He crossed the Arno by his usual route along the bridge of Santa Trinità. His mind dwelt on the events of the night before. He did not try to block it, as he had so many nightmares. He should listen to it, he told himself, learn whatever it was trying to teach him! He realised that, in some reaches of his unconscious, something was clearly very wrong. He forced himself to acknowledge that during the darkest night of his life he had crawled to the bathroom in search of oblivion. If the fire alarm had not gone off, where would he have been this morning? In the city morgue, red weals across his dead wrists? He felt foolish, even frightened; but above all he felt relief that his insane purpose had failed. If he was going to commit suicide it would be by ostensibly accidental means; no one would ever know the truth.

It's like being an ex-junkie, he mused, paying for an old mistake, liable to be ambushed by trips conjured in an evil hour which cannot now be evaded. He wondered if it would happen again; he wondered if he should seek professional help, and gave the thought serious consideration for the first time.

We'll see, he told himself. When he winced at the shame of what he would have to disclose to any counsellor, he thought: I'm not the first and I won't be the last. I was a child; it was not my doing!

He looked at the Ponte Vecchio as he always did, but today Robin's image was less powerful. He knew that he would have to let her go, accept that she had died. There would be one last remembrance: he would wait for her in the Piazza della Signoria on Sunday. After that he would pick up the pieces of his life and move on.

He caught his reflection in various shop windows, a man in the prime of life, 'well preserved' as they used to say in Ballykelly, as though you automatically contracted gangrene when you hit forty. The term was oddly apposite, he thought; there is more than one kind of gangrene. This caused him to laugh inwardly and the unbidden gust of humour did something to redress the balance, restore him to himself.

He wondered, as he walked through the portals of the Scuola Linguistica, why they did not tell him to get lost. He attended class so infrequently that it must be frustrating to the teachers. And then he reminded himself that there was no reason why they should give a damn. It disrupted nothing; no exam or anything of that order hinged on it. His was a holiday course, advertised as such. They might as well take his money and let him please himself.

Class, in fact, was entertaining that morning; there was a fair amount of laughter. He felt compassion for the effervescent young people. Life would catch up with them also, draw them away into the labyrinths of effort. He essayed a few jokes in class. Favourite books and authors were being discussed. Some of the students spoke with considerable fluency, having improved immensely, but Colm, who only came to class when it suited him, spoke with difficulty. He was not widely read, had no favourite authors. When asked why the Irish were so heavily into writing he said it was to escape their sense of loneliness – sought for the words, '*per scappare il senso del isolamente*'. He surprised even himself by this comment. Until recently he had known nothing of loneliness, had even scorned it.

There was a newcomer in the class. She had been promoted from the elementary level. Her name was Kathryn. She was Welsh, dark-haired and about thirty. When asked to introduce herself she said she needed Italian as a second language for her job. She was a high-powered secretary, attractive after a famished fashion, with large grey eyes. She reminded him suddenly and forcibly of another Catherine, and this involuntary association deflated his attempted serenity. He heard the voice of the teacher, but his mind was elsewhere.

Not that there was any one reason why Catherine Clohessy should return to him so vividly nowadays. It was as though all the most powerful elements of his life had returned to plague him, now that he was not preoccupied with work. What was happening to him that they should present themselves together and demand analysis? You do not really know who the hell you are, Robin had told him. If only Kattie had realised this too.

As Colm's affair with Kattie had progressed they had travelled, here and there, London, Paris, once to Peruges in southern France, taking the TGV to Lyon and then hiring a car.

It was in Peruges that things had started to fracture. The medieval town was intact to the last cobble, full of half-timbered houses with mullioned windows. Some of them were part of the hotel, had dark medieval interiors, and king-size beds.

The first thing he and Kattie always did when they signed in anywhere was go to bed. Before bags were unpacked, or refreshment taken, their clothes came off and then they were under the covers, making love until ambushed by sleep. That evening in Peruges was no different. They got there at four, went to bed, got up for supper, dined in the hotel restaurant. This restaurant had oak-beamed ceilings, a plain wooden floor, a trestle table burdened with desserts – crème caramel, fresh fruit salad, meringue chantilly. The meal eaten, coffee drunk, they walked hand in hand through the darkening cobbled streets, stopped at the end of the ancient village to look out over the fields. A couple of bats came winging from somewhere; cicadas chirped rhythmically in the warm darkness; a motorway whispered in the distance.

Kattie was happy. He felt her happiness. He was happy too; if the moment could last for ever he would be always happy. But he did not believe in for ever. The trick was to live for the now, and bugger tomorrow. He had often preached this to Kattie when he felt her restlessness, her desire that he should put their relationship on a footing that did not play games with her self-esteem.

'Darling, you should live in the present. It's all we have!'

'I know. And tomorrow's present will be the outcome of today's,' she said lightly. 'So if we make a muck of today's what price tomorrow?'

'Well, we're not making a muck of today, are we?' he said reasonably.

In fact he often spoke of their future together; he alluded to it as a destination, a certainty. Privately he did not think it was a certainty; the inertia represented by Sherry and his professional life prevented that, but he said what Kattie wanted to hear in order to keep her. Whenever she articulated any query as to when this destination might be reached, he backed off. In those moments she reverted to legitimate prey who must not be allowed to impinge on his marriage. His marriage in those moments was sacrosanct, not because it fulfilled him, but because he had formally undertaken it, because it was safe and demanded nothing of who he really was. He did not pause to consider the gulf between what he promised and what he performed, or that Kattie was entitled to something better than cynical and self-serving manipulation. He was not even sure why he backed off; it was instinctive, the insistence on not being railroaded into anything by anyone. It was not so much for Sherry's sake that he felt this; it had to do with his own pride. He loved women for what they gave him. But, when the chips were down, he could not love enough to give anything back, or, at least, anything that mattered.

'It's easy to love!' Kattie once said to him. 'It is the courage to be loved that is so difficult.'

Kattie was often analytical. He feared her perceptiveness and his need of her; he feared her for what she would take and what she might discover.

That night in Peruges he and Kattie came back from their walk, got into bed, lay companionably naked in the dark. It was still early, eleven o'clock. Hours of love still lay ahead. The windows were open to the warm night air, and they were in conversational mood, torpid and intertwined. Kattie idly traced her fingers down his arm, wandered to his belly, caressed it with the palm of her hand. He felt her love; it was like balm, or scent. It was real, elemental, powerful and pleasurable. But it was also threatening the ramparts he had built, his defence system.

'Do you ever talk to Sherry like this?' she asked shyly.

'No. We don't really talk; the lines of communication are not there in the same way. Although,' he added musingly, 'she came to bed the other night quite randy; must have been something she saw on television.' He paused, remembering Sherry reaching for him. 'It was quite sweet,' he added reassuringly. 'Nothing cataclysmic, but quite nice!'

Catherine did not reply. She got out of bed, grabbed her negligée and went to the bathroom, locked the door. He waited. She did not come out. 'Are you all right?' he called out eventually, approaching the door and speaking against the jamb.

'Fine,' her muffled voice responded. 'I just need to be alone!'

Her pain flowed out under the door; the anger and despair were almost tangible. Her voice betrayed her, the effort to keep it flat, the strain, the muffled timbre.

Half an hour went by. He waited in bed, aggrieved that she should treat him like this, that she should ruin their night together. He wondered what she could be doing in the cold bathroom in the middle of the night; he heard no water run.

When she did come out she was very quiet and cold, and lay beside him like a stone.

It's almost as though she had epilepsy or something, he thought, that she should act so convulsively. Why has she behaved like this? But when she apologised in the morning he smiled forgiveness.

'You shouldn't get so intense about things, darling,' he reasoned. 'You know I cannot live without you!'

She smiled, but the shadows lingered in her eyes. Later she muttered something he wondered at: 'When one is snared by an impossible love, not even God will give one mercy!'

'What did you say?'

'Oh, nothing. Just something I read somewhere.'

The high-pitched revving of a motor scooter just below the classroom window jerked him back to the voice of Professore Delanno and the scrape of the felt pen on the white board. He looked around at the young faces in the class, the Swiss girl who seemed to have a crush on the dashing young German, Anna with her white hair and her long, good life behind her.

The classroom seemed airless. He excused himself, left the room, went into the empty conference room and sat down. He would have liked to take out his mobile phone and call Kattie. Tell her anything; that he was sorry; that he had always loved her; that his life was pointless after she had gone; that he was a screwed-up bastard. Or even call Sherry for the normalcy of hearing her voice. Sherry, he conceded, had been right to go.

When Sherry found out about Colm's relationship with Catherine she had confronted him, calling Kattie a variety of unpleasant names. He suspected that she already knew about the affair, and that she was reacting more to the stereotype of the betrayed wife than to her innermost feelings. He also suspected that her reaction was predicated on fear of losing the trappings of this marriage, the house, the social standing around which she had built her life. But her ultimatum had been real enough, spurred by an uncharacteristic flash-flood of outrage from a wife who had hitherto kept her own counsel and had used patience as a force.

'You can take your pick. Her or me! That whore or me!'

Suddenly, faced with the prospect of upheaval, listening to the wounded voice of his wife, he felt like a child about to be set adrift and was filled with a desperate need to hold on to the known. He had never really intended this to happen; momentarily he saw his avowal to Catherine as lines thrown from the opportunist to the starving. He decided that he would sever their relationship, at least temporarily. He could always resume it when Sherry was appeased.

'I'm sorry I made such a mess of things, darling,' he said to Catherine with just the right degree of ruefulness, the one calculated to elicit forgiveness. 'I'll always love you, you know!' He thought this set the right tone. Kattie had turned expressionless eyes on him. She did not weep, but he suddenly felt like a sub-species being examined under a microscope.

'It's only for the time being . . . We'll never let go of each other, of course . . . We love each other . . . Let's hold on to that!' Colm continued in the tone of one placating a child.

Kattie was silent. She was pale. 'What are you saying, Colm? That our relationship is some chattel of your own that you can turn on and off like a light switch? That you can be as mercurial and treacherous as self-interest demands, without any regard for *my* feelings, or how you might compromise me?' She asked this quietly, but there was contempt in her eyes.

'Of course not . . . The whole mess is my fault entirely. It doesn't mean that my feelings have changed . . . It's just that there are certain realities . . .'

'Yes. Some of those realities belong to me! Why are you doing this, Colm?'

When he didn't answer she said coldly: 'There's something wrong with you, Colm! I don't know what you've done to yourself, or why you've done it. But you are into more than just presumption; you are into abuse. You should see a therapist!'

Why can't women just take their pleasure and get on with it the way men do? he wondered. That would spare everyone all this angst!

But when he saw her drive away in the taxi, without looking back, he felt like someone poised above a precipice, a man who had sold out on his birthright. But, even then, he was sure she would return to him. Give her some time, a week or so, to simmer down. She loved him too much to go away for ever.

In this he had been wrong.

Kattie never willingly spoke to Colm again. A few years after their split-up she married a widowed banker. Colm bumped into her socially from time to time, but she always behaved as though he were invisible. He had found the first such meeting difficult, but had schooled his face and body to deal with it. He heard his own voice, urbane, stiff, as she allowed herself to be introduced to him as though she'd never met him before. When she did not extend her hand he was glad he had waited for her to make the first move. Catherine was now a force to be reckoned with. She had acquired a formidable presence; her old diffidence had disappeared, been subsumed into poise and remoteness. She had become beautiful. Her marriage had given her considerable status; her husband was a banking power in the land. This forced on Colm reluctant introspection, unsettling thoughts intruded that his received parameters, the ground-plan for life, were nothing but lies which had betrayed him. Is there something the matter with me? he wondered. Of course there isn't! his rational self insisted. She knew what she was getting into. She knew I was a married man!

Why am I plagued with all this recollection? he silently asked the sky above the open Florentine window. And then, unbidden, as though memory were not done with him and would rub his nose in what he detested, came Clonarty.

He felt his body shiver with recall. What had taken place in Father Seamus Madden's room had always brought distress beyond his adult endurance. He reached for the old cynicism which had protected him. If he had to think of the past it was better to stay with his own peccadilloes, the acts of his own commission, however insensitive. At least they were done in dominant mode, by someone fully intent on them. They were done by him as perpetrator and not as victim. When he asked himself if it was better to be a perpetrator than a victim he said of course it was better to be a perpetrator. But on reflection this seemed the very dialectic of despair.

'Who needs people anyway!' he had said to his mother after his expulsion, when he felt the eyes of the curious upon him.

'Ah, Colm, my son, whether you like it or not, people are the source of all your joy and all your sorrow!' Then she had asked him, in a voice too low for anyone listening to hear, 'Did anything happen to you at school . . . to make you . . . do what you did?'

For a moment he had longed to tell her. But looking into her sick eyes he knew he must be silent.

'My son to attack a priest!' she had said then. 'My son to attack a priest!'

I am a vessel full of secrets, Colm thought, but they are so heavy that the vessel may break. What if I simply complete this progression and go mad? This made him think of Savonarola, the intriguing icon of his childhood, crazed with rage. Perhaps some secret to which history was not privy had divided him also against himself?

He returned to class, but he could not concentrate on the lesson and was rescued by the mid-morning bell. He invited Kathryn to join him for coffee. She complied, was pleasant, but uninterested. It was patent that she found no hidden vistas in him, no excitement. He knew his peers had aged; he knew the world around him had moved on, but had felt himself untouched by time. Now, aware of the deliberately pleasant young woman before him, he saw himself as someone who could no longer impress by the promise once inherent in youth. He had reached the stage of life where he was either someone or no one, where his stature could no longer be predicated merely on money.

He did not return to class after the break and went instead to the Uffizi Gallery.

He stood before Botticelli's *Birth of Venus*. There she was in her beauty, Robin's obsession, winsome face, classic pose, blown shoreward by the intertwined 'Winds', the attendant with billowing cloak waiting on the shore. Robin had stood and stared at the canvas for a long time all those years ago. What had she seen in it?

Then as he gazed again at the painting he suddenly saw, as though the picture had come alive, that it was saying something about the dynamic inherent in life, the possibility of joy. He saw the mastery over form and colour, the eternal summer. Above all he saw simplicity, innocence and grace. The gold hair reminded him of Paola's long tresses, plaited for the morning.

He left the Uffizi and went to the Via de' Tornabuoni. It was lunchtime and chances were Paola would be at home. He would invite her for dinner, he thought; it would be the most delicate way of asking if he could help fund Pasquale's operation.

She buzzed the door for him readily enough, was waiting in the open entrance of the apartment when the lift disgorged him. Her eyes flickered, whether with pleasure or anger he did not know, and then she assumed a mien of polite enquiry.

'I came to ask you, Paola, if you will dine with me this evening?'

Her demeanour was cold. 'I'm sorry, I have to work.'

'Well, some night . . . name a night?'

She thanked him politely, but shook her head.

'Why not?'

'I really must work!' she repeated. Then she added, 'I hope you are comfortable in your new lodgings?'

'My leaving was not a comment on your hospitality, Paola.'

She smiled without warmth. 'I do understand that certain liberties were taken of you, helping Pasquale for instance . . . I should not have allowed it . . . You were bothered unnecessarily. I apologise! In the circumstances I'm sure you have done the right thing. I will arrange for a refund for you.'

Her hair was beautifully coiffed as always, but the eyes in the Florentine face regarded him with cynicism.

'For heaven's sake, Paola . . . it had nothing to do with my being "bothered", as you put it. I want no refund. My lodgings are fine . . . luxurious and sterile. The reason for my leaving was not to do with your standards, but rather with myself. I need to be alone right now! There are things . . . to do with my personal life, that I have to think about. This is the first time in my adult life that I have really had time to think!'

When she merely nodded coldly, he said gently, 'Paola, will you give me an indication of how much money you need for Pasquale's operation?'

She started. 'That is none of your concern!'

'But I would like to help . . . if you would permit it . . .'

'No, thank you . . . certainly not!'

'Why not?'

She gave a dry laugh. 'It should be obvious!'

'You mean because you hardly know me, because you're a proud and stubborn woman who'll die before you'll be beholden to anyone. But Pasquale is young. And I have no children . . . It would be a privilege!'

Her eyes were hard. 'No, thank you,' she repeated sternly. 'Now if you will excuse me . . . I'm expecting someone.'

Colm regarded the white walls of the hall, the portrait of a much younger Paola, without being able to think of anything galvanic to say. He had only to step out of her apartment and out of her life.

'You do not understand,' she continued coolly, seeing his

hesitation. 'I must go now . . .'

'I understand this . . .' he interjected bitterly. 'That if anything or anyone could give me back my son, my only child, I would bend my knee, my neck, my soul. I would not let my pride kill him! But he is dead and I do not have that option. He died three years ago on his thirteenth birthday. Unlike you, Paola, I was not given a say in his recovery!'

He heard her intake of breath, walked away from her, turned into the stairwell, heard her voice behind him, 'Colm . . .' heard her step on the stairs.

He turned to face her.

'I'm sorry . . . I didn't know . . .' Paola said. 'I knew something was troubling you. But you should talk about it! What tortures us must be spoken!' Her eyes were full of tears. 'You are trying to hold everything inside you, and human beings are not designed for that.'

There was the rattle of the lift in the shaft, and then the sound as it connected.

Paola looked uncertain. 'I would ask you in, but I am expecting someone . . .'

The lift had arrived. Paola went back to her door. Colm leaned against the banister in the stairwell. He was curious and strained to catch sight of the new arrival. He glimpsed a pair of men's shoes on the corridor floor, and then their owner, with confident stride, was heading in the direction of Paola's door. Was this the person she was expecting. Had she a lover?

He heard Paola's voice, 'Silvestro . . . *come stai?*' Heard the masculine response. '*Sei bellissima, come sempre!*'

'You are beautiful, as always!' Colm muttered to himself. Hmph, it had to be a lover! He was surprised by the pang of jealousy or something very close to it. He waited for her door to shut. But Paola's door evidently remained open and she continued to converse with her visitor in the hall. It was as though she deliberately didn't want to be alone in the apartment with him.

Colm heard the male voice assume a disappointed register,

saying something he could not catch.

There was a rustle of paper. 'I have it for you here,' Paola said.

Colm continued on down the stairs. He heard the door of the apartment shut and footsteps proceed to the lift which clanked past him on the first floor. Through the mesh he saw the male figure and, in a small, surprised moment of elation, realised that Paola's visitor had gone.

In a minute or two he stood in the shade of the courtyard, took out his mobile and phoned his bank in Dublin. Later, he went to the Banca di Toscana, walked back by Paola's apartment, dropped an envelope in her letter box, before turning his steps north-west in search of the church of San Marco and Savonarola.

It was hot. He walked slowly, past the Battistero and the Duomo and the milling tourists, along the Via Cavour to the Piazza San Marco. A street sign pointed to: 'Chiesa e Museo di San Marco'. He entered the portals of the church. It was almost empty. A couple sat near the altar and talked together in whispers. He found the sculpture of the mad monk that had once been stroked by Robin's fingers.

Savonarola was unchanged. Colm sat in the pew in front of him for a while.

'Look,' he told the fierce bronze face, 'I'm here again! I have repented of my life. Do you want me to bundle my assets together and burn them in the Piazza della Signoria? Isn't it better to use them for someone's benefit? There is a boy, splendid, his innocence intact, who needs a chance of life. I need peace. If I do not find it I will go mad or die. What would you have me do to find it? I will do anything you want!'

He moved back in the pew, considered the statue, the figure leaning forward, eyes full of fury. He felt this fury. It was in himself, a storm, barely containable. It was eating away at him, destroying blood vessels, capillaries, haunting him in the night, refusing to be tamped down any more, refusing consignment to oblivion. It had to be dealt with, faced and acknowledged, even honoured, before it killed him.

He looked around the ornate church, at the wooden pulpit, felt the centrality emanating from the stones, the sense of ecclesiastical power.

Very well then, he told the mad monk in a half-whisper, the truth is that I was hurt and wronged; my own complicity I acknowledge. What can I do about it? It's in the past, in my childhood, out of my reach. The trouble is – I cannot bear myself!

This man had once challenged even the Papacy, screamed fury at ecclesiastical corruption, been excommunicated, hanged and burned. What lesson did he have for Colm, this unbending one?

He would fight to the end, Colm thought. He did not flee. He was taken from the cloisters of this place to his barbaric death. He had not raised his hand against himself; he had stayed for the finale.

'We are both of us damaged . . .' Robin had said with a shrug, as though damage was one of life's ordinary hazards. It was as though she didn't identify with the hurts life might offer. Why couldn't he do the same? The thing had happened; but it wasn't him. He could work on that. He was about to rise when words his mother had once whispered returned to him.

'You must forgive,' she had said. 'Forgive so that you can be free! What you hate will possess you for ever!'

Colm put his head between his hands. All right, he whispered. All right, he told himself, looking back on the years, staring all that complex suffering in the face.

I forgive! If I can be forgiven, I forgive!

Chapter Fifteen

Robin sipped her espresso in the Piazzale Michelangelo and looked down on Florence. It was the hot middle of the afternoon, a time when she might normally rest, or read, or dictate instructions to her secretary. For many years the art world had sustained her passion for the beautiful; she had poured her energies into it, becoming a well-known patron and something of a connoisseur. Great wealth, which might have been a burden and a force of possession, had given her the means to indulge her passion. She funded restoration work, was committed to Italy's artistic heritage, and was presently involved in exposing the illegal export of art treasures vandalised from Etruscan graves and then sold for huge sums in London. Since she had been widowed, the role she had made for herself in the international world of fine arts, in art itself – young artists and sculptors whom she sponsored – absorbed more and more of her time. She needed another secretary, she realised, would have to delegate more.

But today she needed some solitude. She had come here to the Piazzale to be away from everyone, to think. She was unlikely to meet any of her friends or acquaintances here at this hour. She had taken the Ferrari, parked it, sought out the spot where she had drunk wine with Colm on that long-ago evening. They'd had some sort of row after he'd tried to grope her. It made her smile to think of those two children, here on the Piazzale long ago.

She gazed at the panorama before her, the city, the river, the hills, the living history. The tides of time, the Etruscans and Romans who had populated this valley and those hills; their culture and languages, their artifacts and works of art, informed the fabric of her life. She did not know how anyone could live without art. Frederico had indulged her in this, just as he cocooned her emotionally and in every other way, just as he had forced her to talk about her nightmares after she had woken crying in the night, just as he had insisted on the truth and then dismissed it, eventually writing it all down on a sheet of paper which he had ceremoniously burned. 'Now!' he had said. 'There is only the future!'

He had been an extraordinary man, ruthless, passionate, possessive. But she had thrived with him, been happy. He had taken her back to New York, made her walk with him down Fordham Road, made her point out the shop where Dave Lemming had conducted his undercover operation. She knew that Dave was still there; she stood outside the shop and saw him through the window, knew at last that the blow she had dealt him that night had not killed him. She turned to Frederico in panic, but he did not ask her to go in. His face was closed, and his eyes narrowed.

'You are sure it is he, *amore*?' he had asked softly.

Robin thought she would faint. But she nodded and Frederico had immediately hailed a cab and taken her back to the hotel.

'You won't . . . go near him, Frederico?'

'A hyena like that!' he said with a curt laugh. 'Certainly not.'

But, later, she had heard him on the phone, speaking in low urgent tones, heard the name Lemming pass his lips, and an inexplicable shiver had passed through her. But when she essayed a question, he just smiled at her and said: 'Nothing you need concern yourself about, *mi' amore*. I was just passing the word to appropriate quarters!'

'The police? But, Frederico . . . I cannot bear to talk to the police!'

He had patted her hair. 'Who said anything about the

304

police?' Then he had added, 'Think no more of it, Roberta. Just know that you are avenged!'

It was a command.

Being possessed by Frederico was like being held in the arms of God. No harm could ever come to you; you were free within a privileged, protected space. This suited Robin. She knew that outside that space the world was cold and uncertain, and initially she had had no wish to step outside it. But as the years had passed and she had tentatively ventured into, and then become known in, the world of fine arts, her confidence had blossomed. Imperceptibly she had changed, become grounded, shrewd, mature, found the iron axis of her own being. Sometimes she reminded herself that so much of her happiness was due to the boy she had known here long ago who had, literally and figuratively, saved her life. She thought with compassion of the two lost children they had been, she and Colm, there in the city below. It also saddened her to remember that she had written to him twice and that he had never responded. He had sent her some money after his precipitate return to Ireland, when he had left without saying goodbye. After his departure, when he hadn't come to see her again in hospital, she had assumed that, having twigged the truth, he had had no further interest in a girl like her. But she had long since lost the sense of being damaged. Frederico had once said: 'It is true that hyenas prey on gazelles, Roberta. But a hyena remains a hyena and a gazelle,' he kissed her hand, 'is always sublime!'

Once, she had tried to question him about Dave Lemming and what had become of him, but his face had turned to stone and there had been no reply.

It was only after Frederico's death a year ago that she had found out about the ad in the *New York Times*, realised that her husband had hidden it from her. In going through some private papers in his desk, she had chanced upon a yellowed newspaper cutting, was about simply to discard it when her own name caught her eye.

Will Robin (Roberta) McKay, born 15 September 1950, formerly of Channing Road in the North Bronx, please contact Colm at Box No. 4421.

She had read it several times in astonishment and then she had wept. Had Frederico done anything about this ad? Had he answered it?

She cornered his private secretary, who had been with Frederico for years. He widened his eyes as he read the small notice, shook his head, said he knew nothing. Why hadn't she been informed? Robin kept demanding silently. Knowing Frederico, it wouldn't surprise her if there were more to the story. Had Colm, for example, written to her again, after his return to Ireland, and had Frederico intercepted the letters?

But although Frederico would have assumed that he had to protect her, what right did he have to keep something like that from her? She conceded then that Frederico would have kept everything of her former life from her. Had he not burnt it on a slip of paper that evening in New York after his mysterious phone call, embracing her then as though she were reborn?

This is my life! Robin thought, looking down on Florence. This is how it has turned out. I have riches and even power of a kind; I have a family; I am content!

What would Colm have said? She thought of the string of lies she had told him. But the truth was that in September 1968 she had really been a piece of flotsam on the tide of life. And though Frederico had symbolically burnt the past, he had not erased her memories.

She thought of her father, as she often did these days, wondering what he would have thought of the way her life had worked out. Jack McKay had been no shipping magnate but an erratically employed salesman and they had lived in the North Bronx in New York.

She remembered how Jack drank and was often garrulous, how he would speak of the past and his home in Ireland, airing a bit of fantasy about being descended from the last High King.

'The world has much to tell us, Robbie . . . You should see as much of it as you can!'

She thought of him now with sadness and affection. She remembered the proposed school trip to Europe. He told her she could go, and she got a passport. She had been fired by a piece of paper she had picked from the sidewalk, a torn page from a travel brochure containing the picture of a strange yellow bridge with windows. The caption underneath said 'The Ponte Vecchio, Florence'. She had spent part of an evening copying it, drawing it and then painting in the colours. Her father had come to see what she was doing.

'There's staying-power for you, baby,' Jack had said expansively, studying the bridge. 'Did you know your granny's people came from somewhere around there – Florence?'

Robin wondered if Jack were bullshitting again. But she knew her grandmother had been Italian; it was often mentioned whenever Jack wondered where his daughter got her good looks.

'It's from your mother's side. I'm no oil painting, and the bunch back home all looked like a ram's backside!'

'Can you remember what the name was, the family name?'

'No . . . It was her mother's name . . . you remember your granny Carmina?'

'She died when I was two, Dad! Have I cousins over there . . . in Italy?'

'I don't know. Your mom never mentioned any!'

She had got a book on Florentine Art from the public library. The section on Botticelli pleased her, particularly the painting called *The Birth of Venus*. The picture portrayed an innocent place far from hot sidewalks, stressed cops, elevators grinding along on their cast-iron prop, skyscrapers, tornadoes, or freezing winters.

'She looks a bit like you, Robbie,' her father said, referring to the winsome Venus. 'Her hair is longer, of course . . . and she needs a vest!'

Robin laughed privately, remembering. She had done a charcoal sketch of her father around this time, pinned it on the wall for him to find when he came home.

'Hey . . . that's not bad, Robbie!'

'I'm going to study art, Dad, when I finish school. Sister Anna says I have talent.'

'What good will all that stuff do you?' he had demanded later, in a tone of gentle remonstrance. 'What you really need, Robbie, is something that keeps the bread on the table. This art stuff is all right for people with money!'

Jack had tried to be a good father. Sometimes he took her to the Zoo or the Botanical Gardens, or Edgar Allen Poe's cottage, where he recited a poem to her about a raven which kept saying 'Nevermore'. In the stifling heat of summer he sometimes took her on day trips to Coney Island. There, dreaming in the sand, she would watch the planes leaving and approaching Idlewild, wondering where they came from and where they were headed. Italy, she thought, ascribing a destination to one of them, watching it until it disappeared. Could it be headed for Florence?

'How long would it take to fly to Florence?' she asked Jack.

'Florence? Let me see . . . ten to twelve hours, I suppose . . .' He turned to her and said, 'Unless, of course, you flew by jet. But you'd have to be a member of the Jet-Set! Ha . . . ha . . .' Then he added, 'Tell you what . . . if I win the lottery, I'll take you!'

It was then she had said: 'There's a school trip to Europe. Can I go?'

'Sure . . .'

He hadn't had the money, but she got the passport anyway, just in case.

Robin glanced at the ruby-studded bracelet on her wrist, at

her thin manicured hands and their rings. The sunlight flashed on a diamond. Once those hands had done all the housework, loosened Jack's tie when he fell asleep in the armchair after a session at the bar.

The apartment in Channing Road had not been far from the Cross Bronx Expressway, a brownstone house converted into walk-up apartments many years before. The wallpaper was a kind of muddy yellow.

'We could paint this, Dad . . . paint it white?'

'Yeah . . . spend a fortune . . . the landlord would laugh all the way to the bank!'

But she had painted it white, and put up some prints, made cushions for the couch, They had plenty of cockroaches and the man came to spray the place on Saturdays.

There were Jews and Irish and Poles in their neighbourhood, each clinging to their own tight-knit, ethnic group. There was a lot of humour. Jack would drink at Von O'Brien's in Orchard Avenue, come home in the early hours boasting of how he had won the stool-lifting competition. (The stool had to be lifted over one's head with an outstretched arm – no bending allowed.) She would lie awake waiting for him, listening to the traffic sounds and the noise of the elevator at 145th Street. On Sundays he went to Mass, hangover or not. She remembered the inevitable political content of the sermons, the words of support for the boys in Vietnam. There were two flags; stars and stripes at one side of the altar and, on the other side, the papal flag, yellow and white with the Keys of the Kingdom. Afterwards, on Sunday afternoons, there was a poker school which Jack seldom missed.

She felt about her father that he treated life like a pair of dice – something to be rattled for ever in the hope that eventually he would turn up a pair of sixes. And if and when he did he would shake the dice again, and lose.

When she was sixteen, Jack discovered he had liver cancer.

'I've a little problem, Robbie . . . but sure, they'll fix me up . . .'

The disease whisked him into the grave with indifferent speed. Almost to the end he assured her that he would be better soon; but three days before he died his eyes became glazed and hardly focused. It was as though all his being was turned inwards, that he was looking at something no one else could see. He did not say goodbye or evince any knowledge of his impending death, but he whispered something when she said she loved him. 'Take care of yourself, my darling . . .'

'You can come and live with us,' Mrs Cassidy from the apartment overhead offered. 'At least until you've got yourself organised. You need someone to look after you . . . a foster home.'

'No way! I'm grown up . . . I'm going to get a job.'

'What about school?' Mrs Cassidy asked. 'You have to go back, get your scholarship.'

'I'm sixteen and I don't!' Robin said, suddenly aware that a kind of freedom was staring her in the face. If she got a job she could save and go to Italy! And she could get some sort of job there, surely, and see those paintings and that bridge! She did not advert to the loss of her education; her thought process was a maelstrom of grief and panic. She couldn't bear the possibility of Welfare poking its nose into her life; I'd better move fast, get a job, get a room. Gotta move quickly, girl . . .

She cut her hair into a ragged bob, stuffed her clothes into Jack's big old rucksack, the one he used for fishing trips, found his sleeping bag, and put the library art books into her canvas shoulder bag along with her sketch pad and some pencils. She packed her mother's crucifix, which her father had held while he was dying, and left Channing Road for ever.

Even now, Robin said to herself, I cannot understand how I just walked into it! There were other shops, bona fide places where a job meant a miserable goddamn job!

She had seen the notice in the shop window in Fordham Road: 'Help wanted: no experience necessary.' It was a small store, owned by one Dave Lemming, a sideline, as she later discovered, to certain other activities for which he needed a legitimate front.

He had studied her with a smile.

'The job,' she said. 'The one in the window. I could do it!'

'What's your name? Where d'ya live?'

'Robin McKay. I have to get a job and a room. I've left home.'

'What age are you, Robin?'

'Sixteen.'

'Yeah?'

'I've got my birth certificate.'

She extracted it, a crumpled square.

'How do I know this is yours?'

'Because I have it, mister, and I don't go around stealing birth certificates!' She dug into her bag and produced her passport. 'This convince you?'

He glanced at it, compared her face with the photo. 'Experience?'

'I worked in a drug store weekends.'

'Where do your parents live?'

'Dead. My dad died ten days ago.'

She remembered how his eyes had gleamed. Rolls of fat were flopping over his waistband.

'When can you start, Robin?'

'Right away! But I have to get a room.'

'You can stay here for a while. There's a spare room back of the store. If you give me a minute I'll show it to you.'

He had shown her to a room with a window opening on to the fire escape. The room had lots of photographic equipment.

'I do a bit of photography in my spare time . . . my hobby,' he had added when she commented on the cameras and tripods.

'Are you any good?'

'Sure . . .'

Robin grimaced, remembering. That smile alone, she

thought, gritting her teeth on the memory, should have been enough!

She had made chicken and ham sandwiches in Dave Lemming's deli, and salad rolls, and had prepared pizzas. Dave showed her where everything was stored, how to make the different salads.

It's a start, she had told herself. OK it's not much, but it's a start.

She had worked late that first day, putting things in the storeroom in order. Then she went to her room, put on the light which shone from a bare bulb. She sat on the mattress, taking from her rucksack the things she had brought from home.

The night was falling; the window looking out on the yard reflected her, the bulb hanging from the ceiling, the cameras and the cardboard boxes.

There was a knock on the door.

'Yeah?'

'It's only me, Dave . . .' He was whispering.

'Yeah?'

'Just wondering if you're OK . . . if you need any-thing . . .' She heard a sound as though the doorknob was being softly turned, but she had already shot the bolt. 'I'm fine, Mister Lemming. Thanks. Just going to sleep . . .'

There was silence for a moment. Then he said, 'OK. But call me Dave . . . willya?'

'OK.'

'I'll give ya a wake-up call in the morning!'

'OK.'

She heard the sound of his footsteps move away.

The nightmare had started a week later. He had come through the window from the fire escape while she was asleep. She had woken, half suffocated, to the violation of her will, her body, her understanding of and trust in the world. There are some things you cannot imagine when you are sixteen and believe in God.

How weird memory was that some events were like yesterday, while others could not be accessed at all! But at least I had the guts to hit him with that camera, Robin thought. I believed I had killed him! I was so knotted up about that. I thought it was why I was getting sick in the mornings! Christ!

Thank God I stole his money and that goddamn watch he was so proud of, and ran. What if I had stayed, demoralised, paralysed like a rabbit before a predator? Where would I be now? She shuddered. I thought that God had deserted me, but He was only waiting for me to act; any action perhaps would have done. Any decisive, assertive action! You always have to meet God half way!

She remembered the airport, the effort to look relaxed, the fear that someone would see the mark of Cain upon her. She had told the Alitalia clerk that she was flying out to meet her mother. And then there had been a few days in Rome, going around in circles like a headless chicken, trying to thumb to Florence, losing most of her money after a scuffle with another predator who had given her a useless lift, and then the Irish student had been there, at that small beach near Civitavecchia, when she thought she might as well just swim out to sea and be done with it.

God had sent her Colm Nugent. She had known instinctively that as long as she was with him she would be safe. She remembered their mutual promise of meeting in the Piazza della Signorina, found it frightening that the date – 15 September 1996 – was already upon her, her forty-sixth birthday.

She looked down at the jewels on her hands, at the shining bracelet. I am wearing a king's ransom in broad daylight, she thought ruefully; is this a badge of insecurity or a careless gesture by a rich woman with more money than sense?

Perhaps I think my worth is in these things? Or perhaps it is a contemptuous signal that these things are worthless. Or perhaps I wear them in memory of Frederico who wrapped me up in love until I found my life!

The sun was moving around to reach for her beneath the umbrella. She shifted her chair. Nowadays she was very careful with her skin, wore a total sun block.

But it's absurd to imagine for one moment that Colm will be there on Sunday, she thought. He must have forgotten me long ago.

I wonder what he did with his life; is he successful, happy, married with children? Did everything work out for him? Did he forget what had happened to him in that school from hell and finally find himself, find peace?

She glanced at her watch. I'd better get back . . . There's a meeting at five with the Uffizi people; and I have to talk to Luigi about the house in the Bois de Boulogne. As far as I'm concerned he can sell it. It's a waste keeping it up when it's used so seldom.

And there's Graziella to worry about. She wants a goddamn motor bike! At her age! But she's sure as hell not getting one!

She sighed, anticipating the battle to come. 'I've enough on my plate,' she whispered aloud. 'It's idiotic to be maudlin over something which happened twenty-eight years ago! If Graziella knew, how she would use it to beat me!'

She looked across the red roofs of Florence to the hills.

But why doesn't time make you forget? Why does it seem like yesterday when it's been so long?

As she walked away something surfaced, a whisper in a far-off night. 'You are my homeland, Robin. My home!'

Well, we'll see, she told herself, blinking at the sudden tears. It depends on how foolish and sentimental I feel on Sunday.

In the Via de' Tornabuoni Pasquale handed his mother the letter he had earlier found in the post box.

It was evening. Paola was just home with two full shopping bags. She had donned an apron and was in the process of preparing the evening meal. A new student was arriving this evening, replacing Jill who had gone home. He was an

American boy who was studying the History of Art. His parents would also be coming for dinner.

She was very tired; the small nervous tic that bothered her whenever she was exhausted had returned to its site beneath her left eye, and shivered to its own small beat. But she was pleased that a purchaser had been found for the land in Sicily. The estate agent had phoned to inform her. Cinzia was preparing the contract.

Colm's visit at lunchtime was also preying on her mind. She knew she had been rude, knew he had meant everything he said. She had reacted badly, because his leaving had upset her and she did not want to show him that it had. To think that he had lost a child, his only child! It was her own nightmare!

Her heart reached out to him. She wanted to see him, apologise. He had meant the offer of the money kindly. She acknowledged the terrible temptation in the thought of it, a surcease of effort. Pasquale's white face was like an accusation.

She took the envelope from her son, glanced at the writing, saw her own name. She finished what she was doing, then reached for a kitchen knife, slit the envelope open, pulled out the contents.

Dear Paola,
You can line a cake tin with this draft if you want. But ask Pasquale before you do, because it's for him!
  Colm
  P.S. There are no hidden agendas.

A bank draft for fifty million lire fell out on the table. She re-read the short missive, folded it with the bank draft and sat down.

'What's in that letter?' Pasquale asked her as he came back through the kitchen and saw that his mother was sitting down, staring at the paper on the table. She picked up the letter and handed it to him.

Pasquale examined the contents in silence, read the short note. His eyes flared with excitement.

'What do you say, my son?' Paola said. 'The decision is yours.'

He turned to his mother, said quietly, 'What do I say, Mamma? There is nothing to say except that I choose to live!'

Next day Colm entered the Scuola Linguistica with a lighter tread than he had known in years, greeted the receptionist, smiled at Anna who approached him from the lift, leaning on her silver-handled cane.

'*Buon giorno, Signora!*'

'*Buon giorno, Colm,*' Anna said, looking at him quizzically over her glasses. '*Hai l'aria molto contenta!*' Colm understood her comment on his apparently happy demeanour, but did not answer, searching for words.

'Perhaps you are so happy because the day is lovely!' Anna said in English, glancing over her shoulder like a naughty schoolgirl who is afraid of being caught. He heard the secretary's voice call him.

'Signor Nugent . . . *una lettera!*' She was holding aloft an envelope.

Colm went to the desk, examined the missive with his name on it. It had an Irish stamp; it took him a moment to recognise the handwriting. Once he had known Alice's writing well, but he had not seen it for years. It brought a curious sense of foreboding to receive correspondence from her here. He tore it open.

Dear Colm,
Your neighbour Sue Donnelly tells me that you have been ill and that you have gone to Florence to recuperate. I hope you are feeling better now. You are on my mind lately, because I've been thinking back on things and am sorry about what a rotten bloody time you had after the business in Clonarty. I blame myself and I blame

Liam but most of all I blame Dad. After Mam's death he was never the same.

You can remember it yourself, the silence, the solitary drinking. It was he who ordered me to burn those letters that came for you from Italy. He opened one of them and when he saw it was from a girl he made me put all of them behind the fire. I never told you about them and it's been on my conscience for years. I meant to tell you on the day of his funeral, but somehow the moment never seemed right. I hope they were not important, but I had to tell you now. I have been diagnosed with a breast lump and will be having a biopsy soon. I'm optimistic, but you never know with these things; it has made me determined to tell you the truth, just in case!

Colm went on to the terrace overlooking the courtyard and sat down heavily. He turned to the next page.

It's weird how everything changes! The boys are getting ready to return to college and it will be lonely here in a few weeks. I saw Kattie Clohessy recently, the first time for years. She asked after you, and when I told her you had been ill she said to give you her best. I was glad to see her because it's horrible to see old friends drift away. But at least families are a source of strength if they remember to stay together.

There's been more of those paedophile scandals. A priest from Clonarty College – none other than the former headmaster – is the latest person to have been charged. He has pleaded guilty to fifteen counts of buggery and indecent assault! These crimes were committed years ago, but several former pupils have come forward in recent times with complaints. I saw the priest on TV, a shaky old fellow who kept trying to avoid the camera. His name is Father Madden. The name rang a bell and I couldn't help wondering if he was the priest involved in your expulsion. Oh, Colm, I hope I'm wrong! It doesn't bear thinking about . . . and the awful time you had at home afterwards . . . I'm so sorry! I wasn't much of a sister!

What would poor Mam have thought if she had known you had been sent into the clutches of such a fiend? He was recently in a motor accident where he had a lucky escape. But he won't escape this rap; he will be sentenced next week; the Law is mercifully unfazed by dog collars.

Liam knows I am writing. He sends his best and hopes you will come to visit when you return. He said to tell you that he never saw so many trout rising in the Sureen!

Your fond sister, Alice

P.S. Poor old Johnny Munroe died last week. He was in a home for the past few years.

Colm read the letter slowly. So! he thought, when he came to the end of it. The wheels of God do indeed grind slowly. I knew I couldn't have been the only one! Fifteen counts! And he has pleaded guilty!

He leaned back against the wall, closed his eyes, heard the ordinary sounds of the city, the normalcy of life. Years of his turmoil were laid to rest by the piece of paper in his hand, a simple thing, a letter from his sister.

He read it a second time. 'He made me put all of them behind the fire,' he echoed silently. So she *had* written. Robin had written, but her letters had been consigned to the flames!

He read it a third time. Kattie had sent her best! The power of words!

And old Johnny had died, the man who had said to him all those years ago: 'Go on this journey. You will find something on it which will matter greatly to you in the end!'

Well, it isn't the end yet! Colm thought. But I think it just possible that it is the end of the beginning!

After a few minutes he sat down and wrote to Alice, thanking her for her letter and wishing her well.

'I will come and see you when I get back,' he wrote. 'And Liam too. It is a long time since I spent an afternoon by the Sureen!'

Another missive was waiting for him when he returned to the hotel that evening. A stiff, white envelope, unstamped, was put into his hands. He brought it to his room, opened it. There was a sheet of paper, and appended to it a photograph.

Dear Signor Nugent,
Mamma showed me your letter and its contents. I wanted to tell you my gratitude. My operation will be quite soon, I think. The doctor is arranging it.
　　I am excited and I am afraid. Soon I will be able to play football again.
　　We will repay you when we can, but I will never forget what you have done for me. Thank you.
　　I am sending a photograph you might find interesting.
　　It was taken many years ago in Fiesole.
　　Pasquale.

Colm detached the small black and white snap from the paper clip. It showed a girl and a boy sitting at a table in a sunny geranium-filled patio, with Florence behind them in a light-flooded valley.

'Christ!' Colm exclaimed aloud after a moment as he examined the two young people smiling at the camera, saw a very young Paola and his own young face.

Chapter Sixteen

On Sunday, 15 September Paola slept until she was woken by the bells. Emerging from the first truly refreshing sleep she had had for a long time, she found herself surprised by bliss. For an instant she was not Paola Nosterini; she just was, a being without gender, needs, past or future. The moment passed; the parameters of her world returned: Pasquale's health, Colm's largesse, the sounds in the room across the corridor, Darina's voice raised in sudden laughter.

Her heart lifted in hope, remembering her phone conversation with the family doctor the day before. He was arranging Pasquale's private operation, said he would get back to her on Monday with an appointment with the specialist in Rome. The operation would probably take place, he thought, within a matter of weeks. He saw no reason why it should not be completely successful. Pasquale's heart would have a new valve. Paola dwelt on the vista: her son would be restored to health, to his future.

She dwelt on Colm with a mixture of gratitude and unease. She hadn't even thanked him yet. It was something she would have to do in person, go to him, apologise for her peremptory rudeness, interpret the real reasons for his extraordinary gesture. It could not be predicated merely upon whim or lust. Silvestro had had a typically male perspective on Colm's offer, but she had felt the sadness in Colm, his own tragedy, the dammed-up grief. She felt humbled by it. She would thank him today, seek him out at his hotel, invite him for supper.

She rose, threw the shutters wide. They clattered against

the catches on the outside wall. The morning air already promised heat. She heard the doorbell, went in her dressing-gown to open it. It was Silvestro, come to take Pasquale to Vallambrosa for the day. She saw the desire in his eyes, turned from him to summon her son.

Pasquale's voice came from the kitchen where he was breakfasting: '*Ciao, Silvestro . . . Sono pronto . . .*' adding in English to please his mother, 'I'm ready!'

She watched as they moved down the hall to the lift. Pasquale waved goodbye. Silvestro turned, his eyes taking her in from top to toe.

Oh God, Paola thought, I am walled up, stifled, behind these ramparts of discretion. If there were only someone I could really love and trust!

In the Hotel dei Angeli Colm phoned room service, ordered breakfast: orange juice, coffee, rolls. It arrived in ten minutes on a small tray, white coffee pot, white damask napkin, a small floral spray.

He tipped the waiter, sat down to eat, drank black coffee abstractedly, although he was thoroughly awake. In fact, he had hardly slept. It had been a sleeplessness of reflection and revision, even re-birth. He reached for the small photograph which Pasquale had sent him, propped it in front of him, against the porcelain vase.

They were laughing, the young pair in the photograph, looking up from the table and the book, surprised in their moment of concentration.

Why hadn't he made the connection? Why had he forgotten her, the girl in the amphitheatre? He could remember her clearly now, grave one minute, laughing the next, studious, ambitious. She wanted to be a journalist, she had said. Or a writer.

He wondered if Pasquale had sent him the snap with his mother's knowledge or even at her behest? If so, it opened interesting possibilities. Had she known who he was all the time, known they had met before, said nothing? He would call on her again, perhaps this evening, and thinking of this a warmth spread through him and he began to hum.

When he had breakfasted he bathed and got dressed. He continued humming in the bath, old Beatles numbers, one from Elvis, studied his body in the mirror. He was reasonably lean, muscular, had lost a bit more weight. He flexed his biceps and his chest, tightened his stomach. He was not haunted by the fact that just a few nights earlier he had come to this same bathroom in search of surcease. He had let go of the past; or at least he had let go of its power. Whatever was left of it to haunt him he would face and deal with, seek out help if necessary. But right now his concern was for the future. He was no longer beset by guilt that he was not working. Today, for a mélange of reasons he didn't try to untangle, he expected joy. The world seemed precious, as though he were seeing it for the first time. He donned a white shirt, sallied into the Florentine morning, directed his steps to the church of Santa Maria Novella, where he had been that long ago morning when he had left a dangerously ill Robin behind in the pensione.

Mass was being said. Groups of tourists moved quietly around the portion of the church permitted them. The rows of pews fronting the altar were reserved for the congregation and were roped off from the profane. The sacrifice itself was well under way; he heard the sonorous voice of the celebrant intone in Italian the words he had once known so well in Latin. In his mind he heard the echo of the past, '*Sanctus Sanctus Sanctus Dominus . . .*' The bell was rung, once, twice, three times. The smell of incense came powerfully, so that he hardly knew how much of it was real and how much was memory.

He stood at the back of the church. The evaluation process which had kept him awake all night had not abated. He thought of Sherry, the wife he had never truly loved. Love, unlike the groceries, did not come to order. It demanded too much chemistry and esteem, did not automatically follow on promises or good intentions.

Now she had love with her new husband, but had lost Glendale. He, Colm, had given her nothing, not a penny. She had taken from a marriage of twenty-two years only her clothes, her jewellery, bits and pieces from the house and whatever was in her bank account. But he could no longer access his vindictive pleasure in this. He felt a new compassion towards her, as though she were not his ex-wife but his child.

What if he were to give the house to her? He was a very rich man, to whom a house was just a house. But she loved it! Let her have it and an income too. Let her have something worth a damn from having been Colm Nugent's wife. If he had not brought her fulfilment let it be said he had dealt by her generously! She had made his work possible; she had borne his one and only child; she had organised his life for years, made sure his shirts were laundered, his clothes dry cleaned, waited, if not for his love, at least for his recognition. The thought of work triggered the image of his office and his laden desk, the certainty that all of his tomorrows would be the same as his yesterdays, competitive, time consuming. How much more time could he afford to have consumed?

But he could retire at any time, he reminded himself, if life held something worth retiring for . . . if there was a prospect of stimulus, mutuality, or – something he had spurned for so long – love . . .

He moved forward to join the worshippers near the altar. He saw the sunlight from the stained glass strike the floor and nearby pillar, emerald, ruby and sapphire light. He saw the crucifix above the altar. He heard the responses from the small congregation. He saw the priest in long alb and chasuble bow low and kiss the altar, then make above the host and chalice the three signs of the cross. He saw himself as though he were someone else, a child, strike with a knife for the heart of a big man in a black soutane. He waited. But all he heard was the

324

priest's voice; all he saw was the light from the windows. The memory of the soutaned man who had once seemed so omnipotent had shrunk; he was the creature depicted in Alice's letter, an old pariah. For the first time a shadow of sorrow for this creature crossed Colm's soul. And then he realised that the pain was gone.

He hadn't been to Mass for years, but now he wanted to attend the ceremony. He walked through the nave to where the sacrifice was in progress, sat in the left-hand side chapel below the frescos of the Last Judgement, Hell and Paradise. He remembered he had stood and looked at them that morning long ago.

Like so much in his life, Colm had always shied away from recalling the remainder of that fateful day: the screaming ambulance rushing Robin to the hospital, the white veils of the nuns, the trolley bearing her away to theatre, the questions, his inability to be more than marginally helpful, the wait for her return from surgery, the plastic tube dripping blood into her vein. She had surfaced, opened her eyes, registered that he was there, whispered: 'Sorry about the mess!'

'Oh, Robin . . . It's my fault . . . I should have been more careful!'

'It's not your fault . . .' She reached out her hand for his. 'But I'm sure glad I met you, Colm Nugent . . . Otherwise . . .'

'I should not have left you alone this morning. If only I had come back sooner . . .'

'It wasn't your fault, for Chrissake!'

'Shh . . . You shouldn't talk; you should save your strength.'

'Sure.' Her voice was tired. 'I'll be fine tomorrow!' Then she added tonelessly, 'I told you some lies, you know.'

'Who would have guessed?' he said with a smile, adding, 'What lies were those, Robin?'

She gestured, hesitated, said confidingly, 'There was no Mario Vespucci, for instance . . . I made him up!'

Colm regarded her uncertainly. 'I know you did. But, Robin,

325

there are some other things I would like to know, if you're not too tired . . .'

But she shook her head. 'Tomorrow,' she said, adding in a whisper: 'I feel as though I don't really exist. I feel like a goddamn shadow!'

A nursing sister in a wimple approached, told Colm he should leave, '*Ha bisogno di dormire* . . .' She changed to English. 'She must sleep.' Her skin was sallow against the white wimple, but her face was kind.

As he moved away from the bed, Colm drew the nun to one side. 'Sister . . . may I ask you a question?'

'*Si?*'

She waited, frowning, while Colm formed his query. He knew little about women. But he had done a simple calculation. It bugged him, and he needed an answer.

'Can a woman have a miscarriage after being just ten days pregnant?'

The nun looked into his face, as though trying to locate his intelligence. '*Certo!* Many pregnancies are lost early and the woman never even knows.'

'Ah,' Colm said, indicating the bed where Robin slept. 'But in that case . . .'

'Eet ees quite different in this case . . .'

'Why?'

The nun raised alabaster hands at the obvious. 'Because she was nearly three months pregnant,' she said. 'Not two weeks!'

Colm started. 'Are you sure?'

She looked at him quizzically, as though suspecting his bonafides. 'Of course I am sure!'

Colm went back to look at the sleeping Robin. 'I told you a few lies . . .' He thought of what the doctor had said: 'Your child!' But it wasn't his child, was it?

He walked out of the hospital and made his way back to the Pensione Zellini. It was still raining. Florence looked muddy grey. He kept hearing her voice when they had first made love: 'No, never this!'

'Never this!' She was a past master of prevarication! She had already had it off with some randy oaf, was even bloody pregnant! And he had confided in her, made love with her, trusted her!

As he went up the stairs to the pensione he promised himself: This is the last time I will make myself vulnerable . . . The last time! All one needed to get through life was money and awareness. People were all the same, racked with deceit and secret vices. He would never trust anyone again!

He went to the station, bought his ticket to Paris for the following day. He had better things to do than bother with a tart.

But by the morning his anger had cooled. As he packed his rucksack, the sight of her things in the corner provoked an unwelcome rush of emotion. Her rucksack was open and on its side. When he picked it up some of her stuff fell out, jeans, underwear, socks, and a thick book bearing the title, *Florentine Art*. Inside on the fly leaf was the inscription 'New York City Library'. As he was about to put them back, something caught in the folds of the T-shirt, clattered to the floor. It was the small crucifix.

He jumped, but restored the things back to the rucksack, was about to fasten it when he saw her sketch pad on the bedside table and remembered her work: the streetscape and the crazy, talking roofs of Florence.

He picked up the sketch pad. It was still open, but not at the streetscape drawing. Instead there was a kind of scrawl. There was a central blob, a spider with a man's head and, radiating from it, a web in which a small female figure was caught. Woven through the web spaces were letters and when he deciphered them he saw that they spelled one word: L E M M I N G.

The story Robin had told him two nights before suddenly assumed frightening proportions. A girl trying to come to terms with rape, lying to distance herself from the intolerable!

He felt as though it was his own history waiting to ambush him in another guise, and as he examined the gloating spider and the web, he gagged on the nausea urging him to flee. He wanted to put miles between him and the pathetic waif in the white hospital bed. He did not pause to consider what exactly he fled, rationalising it on the basis that he had to go home.

He tore a strip from the map of Florence and on the back of it wrote a note to the man he had recently disturbed in Fiesole, posted it en route to the station.

Dear Signor Di Gabiere,
I am the student who disturbed you last Saturday. The girl I spoke of, Robin McKay, is in hospital. She has no one to look after her. She may or may not be your relation, but she could do with some luck. She hasn't had much and I have to go home.

You may say this is none of your business. That's true. So it's up to you!
    Yours sincerely,
    Colm Nugent

He sent a note to Robin.

Dear Robin,
I have to go home. Antonio will take you back when you are released from hospital; I have squared things with him for another fortnight at half price. It's low season now anyway. I'll send you some money as soon as I get home.

He wanted to leave it there, but he could not.

I've sent a note about you to Signor Di Gabiere. If I've acted out of order I'm sorry! And I'm sorry I have to go. You should go home too, Robin.
    Colm

He stood in the doorway, looked back at the empty room and her solitary rucksack. 'Goodbye, Robin,' he said silently.

He hitched to Milan and from there took the train to Paris. He stayed a night in the youth hostel at Rueil-Malmaison; from there made his way back to Le Havre. The crossing was choppy. He had no money for a meal, but hunger did not bother him much; he was numb, cocooned in a space where he could not be touched.

It was raining when the ferry put in at Rosslare. He found a few pence in the lining of his jacket and bought a bar of chocolate, walked to the main road and thumbed a lift. He took several lifts, was eventually dropped off a mile from Ballykelly and he walked the remaining distance in a downpour. He stumped along the wet roads, hardly aware of his dripping rucksack, the small rivulets streaming from his hair, his wet jeans which clung to his legs. Florence, Italy, the hot sun were behind him. Before him was normality – the chill of approaching winter, the family farm, his apprenticeship, the pristine future.

Packy Flynn was coming down the path from the Bridge Field and gave him a welcome: 'Ah, the young wanderer is back from forrin places!'

He looked over his shoulder, lowered his voice and added eagerly, 'Did ye see any o' thim statues of naked wimmin?'

Colm shook his head, but Packy followed him. '. . . Sure thim forrin places does be full of o' thim . . . I once saw somethin' in the paper about it . . .'

'No!' Colm said. He went through the open kitchen door.

Moll was by the range. She smiled, said, 'Ah, hello, Colm. Welcome home! Sure you're half drowned!' She pulled a towel from the line above the range and gave it to him. 'Take off those things this minute before you catch your death.'

He looked down at the small pool forming on the floor, took off his dripping jacket. The smell of turf smoke, the warmth of the kitchen, were like an embrace.

His father came in, clumping in wellingtons; Alice and Liam followed, also in wellies. He felt an unbidden surge of joy at the sight of them.

'So you're back,' his father said, sitting down on the chair inside the door and removing his wellies. He seemed pleased, and for a moment Colm thought it was because of his return, until Alice said as she shook off her own wellingtons, 'The big Friesian has just had her calf. Grand little heifer calf!' She went to wash her hands in the sink. The scent of Palmolive soap filled the air.

'Did you get my card?' he asked. They said they had, that morning. Alice, drying her hands, added with a sniff that it was well for some, being able to gallivant around the Continent. Liam muttered something pointed about the rest of them having to slave, not having any inheritance from *their* mother to fall back on. Colm went to the sink and silently washed his own hands.

'You must be famished!' Moll said. 'I'll have a cup of tea for you in a minute.'

'Let me change out of these wet jeans first,' Colm said, picking up his rucksack and heading for the stairs.

His room was unchanged, which was a relief. It was marginally bigger than either of his siblings' bedrooms and he had half expected someone would commandeer it. He checked that the secreted twenty pounds was still where he had left it among the pages of a text book. Then he changed out of his saturated jeans, took out the small gifts from his rucksack, and went back downstairs, handed them around.

'Thanks very much, Colm,' Alice said in a tone of surprise, holding up the pink silk scarf to the light. Liam thanked him too for the leather belt. Moll exclaimed in delight over the plaster replica of the Duomo. His father looked at the tie and said nothing, folded it and put it in a kitchen drawer.

When Colm had had his tea and several hunks of brown bread and jam, his father said he could hose down the milking parlour. He obeyed, slipping on his old wellingtons and anorak, crossing the wet yard. He went to the cowshed and looked in on the big Friesian and her new calf. The calf was suckling. She would be left with her mother for a week; after that they would be separated and would drive everyone mad as they roared for each other. In the manure heap outside was the bloodied straw and the afterbirth.

He went to the milking parlour, attached the hose, hosed the place down, brushed Jeyes Fluid over the floor and the old railway sleepers which were used to separate the stalls.

Liam joined him later, stood in the doorway, his size blocking the last of the light. 'Did you meet any nice birds in Italy?' he asked conspiratorially, man to man.

'No.'

'Ah, go on! You must have met some!'

'No.'

'Did you enjoy it anyway?'

'It was grand!'

'You're a mine of information!' When Colm just grunted he said, 'Thanks again for the belt.'

'That's OK.'

'Incidentally,' Liam added, as he was about to leave, 'there was a thing in last week's *Sunday Independent* which might interest you.'

'Oh?'

Liam took a folded newspaper page from his pocket, handed it over and walked away. Colm brought it to the door for some light, found the X which Liam had marked with ink. There was a head and shoulders photograph of a priest, a face well known to him. Underneath the caption read: 'Father Seamus Madden, B.A., who has been appointed the new headmaster of Clonarty College, County Roscommon. Father Madden is a distinguished historian with special interest in early Irish history.'

Colm thought of the letter he had written to the Bishop

before his departure. For a moment he saw the smug, bloated face of Robin's spider. He felt his stomach heave. He went to the manure heap and retched.

Next day the rain had stopped. The air was full of autumn, a chill edge to the wind. The chestnuts were already turning, leaves gold and russet. Before he left for Dublin, Colm walked along the Sureen and then to his old retreat in the pasture. Liam had told him their father intended to bring in a bulldozer to clear the old rocks which made up the 'castle', so he knew it might be the last time he could visit this haven of his childhood. He saw Johnny Munroe in the distance, stood for a moment to watch the old man, whose sight was poor and who did not see him, turn into the path which led to his cottage. Colm, remembering his encouragement to go to Italy, felt as though Johnny had betrayed him.

You're a strange bugger, Colm thought sourly. What I found will always matter to me, but what you didn't tell me was that it would never give me peace!

He lay on his back among the doomed rocks and looked up at the grey Irish sky. 'Did you have a place where you liked to be alone?' Robin had asked him once. How was she now? He counted the days on his fingers. Four days since he had seen her! She was probably sitting up in bed. She would have received his letter. Antonio and his wife would have been to see her. They were kindly people. But he knew he should not have left her like that, before he knew she would definitely recover. What would she do when she was discharged from hospital? Would she phone her folks, go home? And then a terrible thought struck him: what if she was not sitting up in bed? What if she had started to haemorrhage again? What if she were discharged from hospital, ill and penniless in a foreign land, this girl who had listened to him, comforted him, saved him from himself, hidden her own problems? His friend!

But she has a rich father, he told himself. All she has to do . . .

You know perfectly well she hasn't a rich anything, a quiet

perceptive part of his mind interrupted. She's got nothing and you've abandoned her!

He took his twenty pounds from its hiding place, caught the Dublin train from Roscommon, wrote to Robin as it sped towards the capital, addressing the letter care of the pensione. Antonio would see that she got it.

Dear Robin,
I'm enclosing £18.00. I'd send you more if I could. Please write and tell me that you are well again.
    Love, Colm

Had she replied? He would never know for certain. But it must have been her letters that Alice had consigned to the fire.

Colm had his head in his hands, and jumped when someone touched his shoulder. It was the collection. He searched for some money, put a few thousand lire on the plate.

'Signore . . . are you all right?' the man said, regarding him uncertainly.

'Yes . . .'

'It's the heat!' someone, a middle-aged American tourist, confided. 'I can't wait to go home, to tell you the truth. Maine will never have looked so good!' Her laugh was conspiratorial. 'Where do you come from?'

'Ireland.'

'You need to get acclimatised,' she advised. 'Are you staying long?'

'A month.'

Colm listened to his body. He felt fine. It was just the heat, he assured himself, and his sleepless nights.

When the priest and the acolyte had left the altar Colm walked out into the noonday heat and back to his hotel. He wanted to be fresh for his rendezvous – if there was one. If I lie down, for an hour say . . . The agreement was for three o'clock, but I'd like to be there around one. I wonder . . . will she come . . . ?

'I always keep my promises,' she had said. If she came, would he even recognise her? He reached for his wallet, extracted her photograph, the eighteen year old laughing at him on the Ponte Vecchio. He realised that he was desperate to see her, not because he nurtured any dreams of resurrected romance, but because he needed to know that he had not left her behind to die.

Lying down he watched the light through the shutters, but despite all his intentions, he fell asleep.

Paola went to Mass in Orsanmichele. She liked this small Gothic church, its windows as light as lace. Her heart was high. She met some people she knew and chatted to them after the ceremony, took a coffee with them in the Piazza della Repubblica.

Shortly after midday she presented herself at the Hotel dei Angeli and asked for Signor Colm Nugent, but the receptionist said Signor Nugent was out. Was there a message? Paola said no, she would return later.

'No, grazie. Ritornerò più tardi . . .'

Paola glanced at her watch. It was just gone twelve. Where was he likely to be? Well, she would try again this evening. And then, as she walked back towards the Via de' Tornabuoni, she remembered. Of course, this was September the fifteenth! He was due to keep his romantic tryst with the American in the Piazza della Signoria. She felt certain that this person would not show up. It would take an eccentric to remember an assignation made so long ago, in early youth, and on a holiday romance to boot. There would have to be some extraordinary circumstance for a person not only to remember a promise made in the flush of adolescent fervour, but to act on it!

Being Sunday, the centre of Florence was quiet, free from the screaming weekday traffic. As Paola walked to the Piazza della Signoria she saw a mother and daughter she recognised browsing among leather goods in the Straw Market. The girl was at school with Pasquale, having suddenly left the Imperiale, the exclusive academy for children of the rich. Her father had died a year earlier and the girl had reacted badly, becoming, almost overnight, an intransigent teenage rebel. Pasquale said that her mother was overprotective and that that was the reason.

Children! Paola thought. If we are childless we feel we have missed the boat. But, when we have children, our lives are utterly ransomed to the vagaries of their existence!

When Paola reached the Piazza della Signoria she paused at the entrance to the Rivoire terrace restaurant and scanned the tables. Then she looked around the square. No sign of Colm. She wondered, momentarily, if she should stay; was she intruding on his privacy? But she felt certain the American would not show up, and she chose a table, sat back and looked around her, at the brick tower of the Palazzo Vecchio. She took in the Sunday peace of the ancient square. The head waiter, who knew her well, came to greet her. '*Buon giorno, Signora Nosterini!*'

'*Buon giorno, Andreo . . .*'

She ordered a Greek salad and mineral water. As she ate she kept a look-out for Colm.

There were plenty of tourists, but all of them were in couples. It pleased her that Colm's old girlfriend had not come. He represented a possibility that she only now dared examine for its potential. He was, despite all her misgivings, a complex, generous and interesting man. She looked forward to knowing him better, as she must know him now, joined as they were by his generosity and her own determination to repay it as soon as she could. Thanks to him she need not now sell the land in Sicily until the time was right; she had cancelled her instructions to her lawyer.

She saw the mother and daughter she had observed a few minutes earlier approach and enter the restaurant by the potted shrubs at the restaurant's entrance. The head waiter rushed to greet them:

'*Buon giorno, Signora Di Gabiere . . . Signorina . . .*' He led them towards the one remaining table.

Paola observed them from behind her sunglasses, aware that every head in the restaurant had turned to look at the striking newcomers. Both of them were slim and fair; they bore a startling resemblance to each other. She knew the Di Gabieres had an apartment nearby – their parked Ferrari was a standard local feature during the winter months; they also had a villa in Fiesole where they spent much of the summer. She knew the romantic story about how the wealthy and eccentric Frederico Di Gabiere had met his second wife. A widower with a young son, Luigi, who was now a banker, he had found her in hospital where she was recovering from some accident or other, given her a job as au pair to his child, married her a year later. She was the daughter of an American shipping magnate, and had run away from an unhappy home to study art in Florence. She had been living like a hippy at the time.

But some said her accident had been no ordinary one and that a young man had been involved. Some hinted that Signora Di Gabiere had been wild. Some said that her father had been no shipping magnate.

Well, it doesn't matter now, Paola thought, regarding the table at the restaurant's wrought-iron perimeter, and the slim matron who was talking in low, reproving tones to her daughter. The latter was lounging back in her chair, fiddling with a piece of bread and listening to her mother with an air of laconic defiance. Paola saw the jewels flash fire on the mother's hand. She had scooped the most eligible man in Florence. But no wonder! She was beautiful, aristocratic, with the bearing and the unconscious hauteur of privilege. She was a well-known patron of the arts, a powerful, rather reclusive woman. Roberta, she was called; she was said to have Italian ancestry.

But her prize had not come untrammelled. Her husband,

famed for his eccentricity, had hardly let her out of his sight, although when they were seen together they gave the impression of being so allied against the world that they were a byword for marital harmony. Had this been genuine or deliberately projected? If genuine, Paola mused, Frederico's death must have been a triple bereavement; his wife had lost not only husband, but mentor and friend. And her daughter, Paola thought, watching the girl as she finally broke the tormented piece of bread into fragments, was the living image of her.

Roberta Di Gabiere suddenly turned her fair head and looked first around the square and then around the restaurant, scrutinising each table swiftly. Her eyes rested for a moment on Paola's table and then moved on.

Paola remembered meeting this woman at a function, and also at parent-teacher meetings at the Liceo, and was momentarily piqued that she did not acknowledge her. But then she observed her preoccupied expression, and knew her mind was elsewhere.

Paola lost interest in the Di Gabieres, finished her meal, lingered over an espresso. She watched the people coming and going in the square. She loved this place, this heart of Florence, soul of the Renaissance, her home. Her eyes wandered from the equestrian statue of Cosimo de' Medici to the fountain with the gigantic Neptune, to the sun-washed façade of the palace and the replica of Michelangelo's *David* and the Hercules guarding the entrance. She looked at her watch. It was nearly three. The torpid hour came and went. Colm must have changed his mind about turning up.

Well, he hadn't missed anything.

She saw that Roberta Di Gabiere had given up the argument with her daughter, that she drank white wine, glanced at her watch, scanned the restaurant and the piazza once more. Her expression was wistful and resigned.

As Paola was about to signal for her bill she saw the male figure hurrying, and realised immediately that Colm had made it after all. She was about to wave at him but some instinct stayed her hand. She shrank back into the shade of her sun umbrella, observed him approach and examine the piazza, then turn towards the terrace restaurant and tentatively scan the tables. She saw him start as his eyes fell on Graziella Di Gabiere. The girl had turned her head away from her mother; she had one arm draped over the back of her chair and was throwing crumbs to the pigeons bobbing outside the wrought-iron fence. Colm stopped, almost in mid stride, staring in abrupt fascination, frowning. Then, as though knowing what he must find, he turned his head very slowly to look at Graziella's mother.

When Colm had woken in the Hotel dei Angeli he knew at once that he was late. A glance at his watch confirmed his fears. He had jumped off the bed, put on his shoes and headed immediately for the Piazza della Signoria.

He scanned the square carefully as he approached, making a visual grid search, and then he had turned his eyes to the terrace restaurant.

He saw the girl immediately, the 'ghost'. But she was no phantom. She was large as life in the sunlight, a teenager lounging in a chair. As soon as he saw her face he knew, without a shadow of doubt, who she must be. The resemblance was patent, but the eyes and mouth were different. He turned with a sense of arrival to regard the woman with her.

She was both the same and different. He saw that she was elegant, stamped with a life story that had completely overtaken anything she had been at eighteen. She was not a girl now; judging by her bearing and demeanour she was a woman accustomed to wealth and position, and well able to use the power of both. She was no longer little defiant Robin McKay. Instead she was a formidable presence, rooted in the child he had known, but long grown out and away from that small waif, branched into her own history of which he knew nothing.

338

She turned and met his eyes.

We rarely find salvation in this life, Paola thought in sudden, bittersweet certainty as she saw the expression of both these people as their eyes met.

Even before Roberta Di Gabiere held out her hand to Colm, Paola was sure she should leave. But she stayed and saw the sudden tears in the woman's eyes, saw Colm Nugent sit down beside her. Neither of the two exchanged a word, but as they leaned towards each other in silence Paola saw that he held her thin, bejewelled hands in both of his.

Paola paid her bill, rose. She left the restaurant, walked rapidly away. But as she turned the corner into Via Vaccheria she heard her name being called: 'Paola . . . Paola!' She stopped, turned. Colm was hurrying after her.

'Wait, Paola,' he said. 'I didn't see you . . . You move like a Harrier jet. Come back and meet someone I knew long ago and never really expected to see again!'

'No,' Paola said. 'I'm intruding. I just came to thank you . . .'

He regarded her quizzically. 'Intruding? Don't be ridiculous!' He dropped his voice. 'I'm sorry I didn't recognise you, Paola . . . realise that we'd met long ago! . . . Pasquale sent me a photograph . . .'

When Paola stood uncertainly and directed a glance towards the shrub-lined terrace where two women waited beneath a sun umbrella, he continued: 'You surely didn't think . . . Oh, Paola, you don't understand! It's not romance I find here today! It is something called reprieve; absolution! Or even freedom!' He touched her hand. 'Please . . .'

Paola allowed herself to be conducted back to the terrace.

'This,' Colm said to Paola, indicating the woman seated there with her daughter, 'is Robin, an old friend of mine!' He turned to Robin. 'This is Paola Nosterini.'

Paola took her proffered hand. 'Signora Di Gabiere,' she said politely, 'I think we may have met at school functions.'

'Please call me Roberta! Or Robin if you like,' Robin said, 'although no one has called me by that name for a long time. This is my daughter, Graziella,' she added, and then gestured to a chair. 'Won't you sit down?'

Graziella looked curiously at Paola. 'I know Pasquale!' she said in Italian, as Paola shook her hand and the girl shifted her chair to make some room. 'He's in my class at the Liceo. He's very popular; everyone is hoping he'll be better soon.'

'He has to have an operation,' Paola said. 'Then he'll be fine.'

Paola sat down and Colm followed suit. 'Di Gabiere?' he intoned softly, looking sideways at Robin with a smile and raised eyebrows. 'Didn't I hear that name somewhere before?'

'Long ago,' Robin replied *sotto voce*, her eyes focusing on him with a lot of humour, 'in a previous incarnation! You saw it in a phone book tied by a string to a café wall. You contacted the owner of the name. Because you took that chance, you precipitated a life beyond my dreams. Frederico came to see me in hospital. He was curious at first and then . . . He died last year . . . He was very patriarchal. But his strength and love made me very happy! I often wondered what you would say,' she added, 'if you had known the sequel to our time here. I did write . . .'

'They burned your letters!' Colm said. 'I never got them.'
'Why?'
'It doesn't matter now. But I did try to find you.'

Robin's voice became so low he had to strain to hear her. 'I know! I found out last year after Frederico's death. He kept things from me. Did he ever reply to that advertisement?'

'After a fashion,' Colm said. 'I received an anonymous note to say you had died!' He smiled at her, asked in a very soft voice: 'Were you actually related to him?' Robin smiled ruefully and shook her head.

Graziella, who had been discussing Pasquale and school with Paola, suddenly leaned forward, and fixed Colm with curious eyes.

'Where did you actually meet my mother, Mr Nugent?' she demanded in English. 'Did you know her here? She's never told me very much about what brought her to Florence or how she met my father.'

Colm looked at Robin, saw the almost imperceptible, warning shake of her head.

'Oh, I met her when we were students . . . on a beach, in fact! She helped me with a problem I had at the time . . .'

'When was this?'

'It was in the year nineteen hundred and sixty-eight.'

'God, that was in the dark ages!' Graziella said with a laugh. 'I don't know how you can remember things that far back!'

'You'd be surprised what you can remember,' Colm said, studying this pristine Robin look-alike, with her shining future ahead of her and the past only a story told by middle-aged people on Sundays.

'I bet Mamma cannot remember things so well!' Graziella said provocatively. 'Her energies are taken up with the burden of a teenage daughter . . .'

She directed a smouldering glance at her mother, who said mildly, keeping her voice level: 'It is precisely because I remember a time before you that I hold you so precious!'

There was silence for a moment. Then the girl said, addressing herself hurriedly to Colm, as though shrugging off maternal sentiment: 'Autumn is a good time to visit Tuscany. Are you on holiday here . . .'

Colm knew that she was deliberately making conversation. Here was a young person with shining agendas trapped at Sunday lunchtime among the tedious and trying to make the best of it.

'. . . or are you here on business?' Graziella added.

'In fact I'm about to retire,' he said, knowing the certainty of this for the first time.

'And what will you do then?'

'Oh, I don't know,' Colm responded, briefly meeting Paola's eye. 'But I think the time is ripe for a new beginning!'

Kitty Rainbow

Wendy Robertson

When the soft-hearted bare-knuckle fighter Ishmael
Slaughter rescues an abandoned baby from the swirling
River Wear, he knows that if he takes her home his
employer will give her short shrift – or worse. So it is to
Janine Druce, a draper woman with a dubious reputation
but a child of her own, that he takes tiny Kitty Rainbow.

Kitty grows up wild, coping with Janine's bouts of
drunkenness and her son's silent strangeness. And she is as
fierce in her affections as she is in her hatreds, saving her
greatest love for Ishmael, the ageing boxer who provides
the only link with her parentage, a scrap of cloth she was
wrapped in when he found her. Kitty realises that she
cannot live her life wondering who her mother was, and in
Ishmael she has father enough. And, when she finds herself
pregnant, deprived of the livelihood on which she and the
old man depended, she must worry about the future, not
the past. But the past has a way of catching the present
unawares . . .

'An intense and moving story set against the bitter squalor
of the hunger-ridden thirties' *Today*

'A rich fruit cake of well-drawn characters . . .' *Northern
Echo*

'Fans of big family stories must read Wendy Robertson'
Peterborough Evening Telegraph

'A lovely book' *Woman's Realm*

0 7472 5183 5

HEADLINE

The Quick and The Dead

Alison Joseph

Working in a hostel for the homeless, Sister Agnes had, for a while, felt an unaccustomed contentment with her faith. But when Sam, a sixteen-year-old runaway, is forced to return to her family and then goes missing, Agnes's hard-won equilibrium vanishes.

Sam's friends recall her saying she planned to join anti-road protesters in their tree-top encampment at the edge of Epping Forest. Sure enough Agnes finds Sam there, amidst the beggars, travellers and anarchists, revelling in their fireside talk of apocalypse, though contemplating returning to live with the father who deserted her sixteen years earlier and who, suspiciously to Agnes's mind, has suddenly reappeared. For the moment however Sam seems secure at the camp, though its tents and tree houses can only provide a temporary bulwark against destruction.

But even that safety is illusory. Only hours after Agnes's arrival a body is found. Of a brutally murdered young girl . . .

'Enjoyable . . . with a satisfyingly believable conclusion' *Glasgow Herald*

'Nice one that doesn't start with a bang and end with a whimper' *Newcastle-upon-Tyne Journal*

'A refreshingly different character' *Bolton Evening News*

'One helluva nun' *Hampstead and Highgate Express*

0 7472 5263 7

HEADLINE